THE TAMING OF LORD ASTOR

THE TAMING OF LORD ASTOR

MOLLY MADIGAN

FIVE STAR

An imprint of Thomson Gale, a part of The Thomson Corporation

THOMSON

GALE

Detroit • New York • San Francisco • New Haven, Conn. • Waterville, Maine • London

LIBRARY OF CONGRESS CATALOGING-IN-PUBLICATION DATA

Madigan, Molly.
   The taming of Lord Astor / Molly Madigan.—1st ed.
    p. cm.
   ISBN-13: 978-1-59414-572-8 (alk. paper)
   ISBN-10: 1-59414-572-5 (alk. paper)
   1. Great Britain—History—Victoria, 1837–1901—Fiction. 2. London (England)—Fiction. I. Title.
PS3613.A28438T36 2007
813'.54—dc22
                                    2006029973

First Edition. First Printing: January 2007.

Published in 2007 in conjunction with Tekno Books.

Printed in the United States of America on permanent paper
10 9 8 7 6 5 4 3 2 1

For Judy and Blase

ACKNOWLEDGMENTS

To Tricia, Laura, Mandy and Ash, thanks for the years of ear time, and, of course, thanks to my brilliant editor, Alice Duncan. This book would have never seen the light of day had it not been for my agent, Mary Sue Seymour, whose dedication has earned my deep and sincere gratitude. Also, I must thank Professor Leigh Bienen and her wonderful web site at http://homicide.northwestern.edu for much useful historical information.

CHAPTER ONE

England 1874

Tilly Leighton knew men. She read them plainer than English. Within five minutes of an introduction, Tilly could deduce every material aspect of a man's personality. Good thing, too, since her occupation depended on just this talent.

It was for her occupation that Tilly lifted her lantern to study the bookshelves lining the wall. A creak sounded behind her, and she whirled around. Nothing. Just the London townhouse making noises.

Tilly shook her head in relief. Maybe this housebreaking business didn't agree with her. Really though, the mistress had invited her into the house. She had only committed study-breaking.

Tilly blamed Lord Astor for this new foray into crime. How could she train the man—as his sister was paying Tilly a fortune to do—if he refused to turn up? She'd had no choice but to pick the lock on his study door and try to glean something about his personality from his possessions.

Lifting the lantern higher, Tilly tilted her head to one side. Her auburn curls fell over one shoulder as she read the book spines—all sturdy tomes bearing titles such as *The Wealth of Nations* or *On the Principles of Political Economy and Taxation.*

Quite serious. No poetry or plays whatsoever. Not a romantic man, clearly.

Tilly set the lantern on the large, recently ransacked,

mahogany desk before taking a step back to study the shelves as a whole. Ah-ha! What was this? Tilly picked up a newspaper clipping folded on the shelf in front of the books. Hmm . . . Lord Astor was following the so-called "missing wives" cases.

"May I help you?"

Tilly twisted toward the voice. Her heart lodged in her throat. *Bloody hell!* The man would choose now to turn up!

Then Tilly caught sight of him and her heart, so recently transported to her windpipe, plummeted to her stomach.

Even lounging against the doorframe, he towered over her. Immaculately tailored black evening trousers and a waist jacket showed his manly form to every advantage. Neither slim nor bulky, one could only describe him as large . . . and appealing.

Her eyes drank in his loosened cravat and the golden tan neck beneath it. Yes, large and very, very appealing. What would his skin feel like under her fingertips? Under her lips?

Tilly didn't like strong men, a voice in her head reminded. She preferred them weak and ineffectual and—should it prove necessary—easy to outrun. The voice went unheeded.

And then she met his expression.

Tilly stepped back. Her hand flew to her chest. His eyes! She attempted to adjust to their piercing blue. They glowed the color of heated sapphires. The startling shade exactly matched his sister's eyes, but Adelaide had the decorum to temper hers with forgettable reddish-brown tresses, while Lord Astor's hair shone midnight black. Had she not known better, Tilly would have sworn he had a double row of eyelashes. Only a man could possess such a deplorable sense of decency that he would inflict all who gazed upon him with such a striking visage.

His nose, too, lacked all notions of humility. It jutted proudly forth in a manner admitting no shame—though, in truth, it at least matched the rest of his uncompromising appearance. But then his mouth had to go and ruin the whole effect. It positively invited pretty girls in studies late at night to test his lips' firm lushness with their mouths. Maybe even with their teeth!

Oh, dear. Tilly had signed on for a more difficult case than she had anticipated. Adelaide had hired Tilly to make her brother more pliable. Apparently, he frightened his intended, the unfortunate Miss Haversham. Adelaide wanted Jaiden more gentle with the chit, but this man looked about as pliable as steel.

A jet-black brow quirked in amusement. "Who are you?" he asked, a hint of amazement tinting his voice.

Who was she? Oh, right. She'd broken into his private office. Hadn't planned on getting caught, of course. Well, in such awkward situations, a woman had but one course of action left to her. Invariably, the duty fell to her to dissipate all excess awkwardness by . . .

Tilly threw out her hand, catching the edge of the bookshelf. "I . . . I . . ." She swayed from foot to foot and executed the ever-popular eyelash flutter. She could just imagine what a pretty picture she made, as she forced her body to go limp and crashed toward the floor.

Strong arms caught her before she landed. *Bloody hell! How'd he get there so quickly?* Her eyes flew open in shock, but indeed, he clutched her against his hard body. Luckily, she regained her senses quickly and closed her eyes before he noticed, occupied as he was with maneuvering her body to get a proper hold on it. It wouldn't do to ruin the effect by having him witness her studying him.

Tilly whimpered softly for good measure. All men appreciated a delicate whimper. She debated sending a shudder down her spine but decided against it. She didn't want to overplay her hand.

He lifted her. One arm supported her knees, the other her back. Her legs dangled freely in the air, a sensation Tilly would have enjoyed but for her head lolling about.

Didn't men learn somewhere along the way that a woman's head should always rest against a man's chest when he carried her in the "Damsel in Distress" position? Truly, what did they teach boys in those so-called higher-educational schools?

As if reading her thoughts, Lord Astor shifted her diagonally so her head rolled against his shoulder—with very little help from Tilly. Much better. Hmmm . . . delightful, really. She breathed in the scent of him and was surprised to find him lacking the usual late-night male stench, too often reminding one of rancid meat or stale ale. Indeed, he brought flashes of soap and woods and mmm . . . something else that eluded her.

Tilly curled pleasantly against him. Only her one remaining shred of willpower restrained her grin of contentment.

But the walk ended much too quickly. Already Jaiden was lowering her to the couch. She should have faked the fall over by the windows.

Ah, well, she'd remember that tidbit for next time.

Lord Astor laid her full length on the couch. The leather chilled her cheek, leaving her longing for the warmth of his torso once more. His heat, however, still wafted around her, alerting her to his continued proximity.

She flung the back of her knuckles to her forehead, taking care to keep the movement close to her body. She didn't want to strike his arrogant nose. Not yet. Maybe when she got to know him better.

A carefully timed moan. A restless twist, and Tilly peeled open her eyes, again with much fluttering, which no doubt was well appreciated.

"Lord . . . I . . . ," she began, her gaze landing on his lovely throat before sliding to his face.

Jaiden knelt beside the couch, hovering over her in concern. Indeed, his brow furrowed, and a muscle twitched in his jaw. All the blatant indications of anxiety presented themselves.

Even his voice emanated soft and low. "Don't try to speak. I'll send for a doctor presently."

His tone was so comforting. It reminded her of . . . "A *doctor*? What? Why?" she bellowed, sitting up. Thankfully, her holler stopped him before he reached the door.

Returning to the couch, he slowly spoke. "You must calm yourself. You're overexcited." He bent so their eyes met on the same level. "You've had a spell. Don't worry. We will send for the doctor."

Honest concern radiated from his every move. It slapped Tilly across the face. Hadn't the man spent any time around females? One would think he'd never seen a well-feigned swoon before. Of course, Tilly did pride herself on her *faux* faints, but this was too much.

Letting out a sigh, she refrained from shaking her head at his ignorance. He'd taken all the fun out of the game. Imagine getting so worked up over a little collapse. And what would happen the next time a female employed one? Maybe even a woman not as well-intentioned as Tilly? Why, he'd be at the chit's mercy!

Never mind that these little weaknesses were exactly the thing Tilly should pass on to Miss Haversham. Adelaide had hired Tilly specifically to make certain Miss Haversham could handle Jaiden, a task Tilly could easily accomplish . . . except, well, curse it! A man who couldn't hold his own at the sight of a collapse—why that just wasn't fair. Someone needed to explain the rules to him, and she looked like the only volunteer.

Tilly gave him a quick nod, coming to her decision, then winced when she saw the worry etched on his features. "Have a seat," she said, in her no-nonsense voice. She patted the sofa next to her.

Jaiden's eyebrow arched at her tone, but he moved to the edge of the couch and sat nonetheless. Mostly to keep her calm,

Tilly suspected. No doubt he feared she might up and faint again.

"Now, Lord Astor," she began, "there's something you must understand. Women never *actually* faint. Indeed, in all my years, I've only known one silly chit to swoon legitimately, and that was entirely her own fault. Imagine, lacing up a corset more taut than an acrobat's rope and then participating in a rousing game of lawn tennis. Simply ludicrous! Of course, she ended up in the grass. But still, you see? Very different altogether from a healthy woman in her loose night rail and wrapper merely browsing through bookshelves."

Jaiden's mouth twitched at her explanation. Most likely it did so in concentration, though it looked a bit like suppressed humor. He swallowed and stated, "I thought perhaps I'd given you a fright, catching you unawares like that."

"And so you did," she said, praising him and patting his hand where it rested on his thigh. She didn't want to discourage him. Who would have thought someone with such dark hair could prove so sensitive? "But you see, it takes more than a tiny start to bring most women to their knees, I assure you."

He bit his bottom lip, then nodded. "Ah, I see. Thank you for clearing that up."

She smiled at him. "Happy to oblige."

"So then, when you pretended to succumb to nerves just now . . ."

"Yes! I was merely trying to distract you from the fact that I was lurking about your private office." She gave his hand one more tap to show her satisfaction.

"And you were lurking about my private office because . . ."

Oh, pooh! She'd forgotten about that. Again. A small sound of dismay escaped before she could shush it.

". . . you were looking for a book to help you fall asleep?"

Tilly nearly let out a whoop of relief. Yes, reading to help her fall asleep! Certainly the dull stuff in this room supported that excuse.

"Of course, the door was locked . . . ," he drawled, raising a hand to his chin to stroke the day's growth of beard in confusion.

"It was not!" she burst out, sitting straighter.

He frowned. "That's odd. I've never forgotten to lock it before."

Tilly plopped her hands on her hips and glared at him. "And I suppose you couldn't possibly have made a mistake this time. No. After all, you are a man. How preposterous. A man who forgot to lock a door. Much easier to believe I sprouted wings and flew in through a closed window—"

"Obviously, I stand corrected," he said, cutting her off with a wave of his hand. "I was wrong. I apologize."

Tilly nearly fell off the sofa. She caught her balance at the last moment, but she could do nothing to close her gaping mouth. He'd apologized! And he was a male! She wouldn't have believed it possible had she not heard it herself. Usually, you couldn't get a man to apologize with a gun aimed at his heart. Hell, he'd even admitted he was wrong. Surely, he'd just set a new first in history.

"No, no, I'm sure you knew the right of it," he continued. "I probably left the door wide open, too, now that I think about it. How could you help but come in and look over my collection?"

Just a drop of guilt latched onto Tilly's chest. "Well, I admit the door wasn't *wide* open," she muttered.

"Oh, no, you needn't worry about sparing my feelings," he continued. "I've been doing things wrong all week." He shook his head, not daring to look at her.

Tilly clasped his hand between her own. "Now, Lord Astor, you mustn't be so hard on yourself. I swear to you, I found the door firmly closed. Indeed, I had to jiggle the knob quite forcefully to get it unstuck," she told him. She'd had no idea he'd take this so hard. "And who doesn't make mistakes now and again? You're only human, after all."

"Yes, that's true," he said, lifting his melancholy gaze to hers. "All too human sometimes."

"As are we all," she reasoned. Interesting, indeed. She'd never encountered a man such as he. So huge and yet so humble. Suddenly, she felt rather protective. Very singular feeling for her, too. She'd always gone out of her way to trim the excess confidence of men, and here she found herself praising one.

Tilly considered him again, correcting her first impressions. Yes, his eye and hair colors tended to shock upon first notice, but now that she'd grown accustomed to them, she thought the combination rather becoming.

And the way he'd followed her explanation of fainting! Usually, men took much longer to understand what fools women made of them.

Tilly came to another decision. She'd never attempted such a forthright approach with one of her clients, but no one else had shown Lord Astor's capacity for education. She would tell him the truth. Well, part of it at least.

Mustering her resolve, she plunged in. "I wasn't *entirely* looking for a book to read," she admitted.

"You don't say! But it made so much sense. Why if I were a woman in a strange house, the owner's study would be the first place I'd look for some light reading. Well, you know, after the library, naturally."

"Naturally," she allowed.

A suspicious twitch shook the corner of his mouth. "And then there's the drawing room with its bookcases filled with my aunt's novels, of course."

"Of course," Tilly agreed, wondering if she'd lost control of the conversation.

"And we mustn't forget the bookshelves in the guest room stocked specifically with the kind of light reading a guest might search for during the night."

Narrowing her eyes, Tilly began to wonder if he wasn't perhaps poking fun at her after all. If, perhaps, he'd been teasing since the moment he walked through the door.

His eyes sparkled suspiciously. "And then, there's my sister's—"

"Enough," Tilly said, raising her hand. Her first opinion of him had definitely been the correct one. Black double lashes around blue eyes, indeed! How could she have doubted herself? She should have hit him on the nose, after all.

He widened those foul blue eyes in an obvious pretense of dismay.

Feeling churlish, Tilly folded her arms over her chest and grumbled, "I already said I wasn't looking for a book."

He crossed one long leg over the other, linked his fingers over his knees and leaned back. "Ah, so you did. Which brings us back to my original question. Who are you?"

Folding her hands in her lap, Tilly raised her chin a notch, attempting to regain a speck of dignity. "Allow me to introduce myself, Lord Astor." She couldn't resist throwing in his name to show her slight advantage over him . . . if only for the moment. "My name is Mrs. Charles Leighton. Your delightful sister asked me to visit for an extended period this season."

Lord Astor tilted his head. "That's odd. My sister hasn't mentioned you."

"Well, I doubt she's had time to tell you much of anything lately."

His legs abruptly uncrossed. "What the devil does that mean?" he demanded.

Tilly delicately rearranged her skirts. "I, your lordship, have been staying here an entire week, and this is the first time I've so much as learned what you look like. Since I'm more in the habit of late-night tours than Adelaide, and as it is now well past one in the morning, *and* as you've obviously just returned home, I must assume quite some period has passed since your sister had your attention long enough to mention new friends or, for that matter, to discuss any of her concerns," she said, glancing up at him.

Jaiden's large shoulders hunched slightly. His nostrils flared, reminding Tilly of a huge overgrown rabbit cornered in a hunt.

"And so, you see," Tilly proclaimed, "I'd begun to believe you were merely a figment of your sister's imagination. Honestly, I was so concerned tonight when she insisted you not only existed but lived here, I felt that I was left with no choice but to come down and investigate, to see if I could unearth any evidence of your existence. Which, Lord Astor, is why you found me in your private study this evening." She let the words ring in the room for three seconds before rising to her feet. "Now, if you will excuse me. I've accomplished my mission. Your sister's sanity is no longer in question, though I cannot say the same for the rest of the family. It grows late and is time for me to retire. Good night," she finished, striding out of the room, head held high.

Only after five steps down the wide hall did she allow herself a well-deserved smile. Silly man. Whatever had he been thinking playing games with the man-tamer!

She'd surprised him. He hadn't known such a thing was possible. But she had. First, for breaking into his study and then, even more, when he'd caught her. Instead of the shrieks of fright he expected, she leisurely perused his entire form. Nothing had astonished him more than the desire written on her face then. Her tongue had flashed out and licked her bottom lip.

Then she deigned to look him in the face. And all her longing disappeared. He couldn't say the same of his. Not even as her scowl grew darker. She was magnificent—petite, but very curvy. He'd always thought he preferred his women . . . actually, he'd never thought he had a preference, but he did now, and she was it.

And her face! Large green eyes. Small lush mouth. Every emotion in her head had showed on that heart-breaking face— her surprise, her guilt, her defensiveness—forcing him to imagine what thoughts lurked in her mind.

When she swayed on her feet, his concern amazed him. She'd fooled him all right. His heart still beat out of time.

But it was her confession that intrigued him the most. The girl had picked the lock on his door, and yet she could not stand to see him succumb to the ploy she had cast for him.

As curious as he was to know why she had broken into his office, Jaiden had been more eager to find out what she would do next. Even when he thought he had her backed into a corner, she bested him in the end.

Well, if Mrs. Leighton wanted him home more often, he would just have to oblige her. No doubt her residing there would prove entertaining . . . and convenient, since his mistress cut his strings earlier that night. Their "uncomplicated" affair had taken a nasty turn when she'd confessed her love. Too bad he couldn't love her back. Bev was a fine woman, prone to gossip, but all in all, the best Society had to offer.

Unfortunately, she bored him. All people did. Give him a problem, a task, a goal, anything he could do, and he was fine. Well, women definitely had *that use,* but what was a fellow supposed to do with them the other twenty-two hours a day.

Jaiden scratched his eyebrow, remembering Bev's accusation—that she would never be more to him than a sleeping draft. The charge was more accurate than Jaiden cared to admit.

Lately, the only time he could sleep was after an evening of sexual fulfillment. Even then, slumber wasn't a certainty.

Alas, no sleep for him now . . . not until he could convince Mrs. Leighton of the mutually beneficial relationship they might establish.

Picturing the swing of Mrs. Leighton's full bottom as she walked away from him, Jaiden's grin widened.

And here he'd thought the night would be dull.

CHAPTER TWO

Tilly couldn't decide what to wear.

Every one of her outfits had been designed specifically to portray one illusion or another. Her dark gray silk screamed aggressive intellectual. Her red satin seduced all who dared to touch it. She'd designed the lavender so no one would take her seriously. And in the rose muslin, men couldn't refrain from declaring their love.

The yellow put them on their guard, while the pink disarmed them. The mauve turned her near invisible, and the peach inspired protection. She owned a purple garment which, when worn with white gloves, motivated all to feed her. She did enjoy that outfit, she thought with a smile.

She even changed her hairstyle depending on what she wanted a man to feel that particular day—but that was her problem. She hadn't the faintest idea how to proceed with Lord Astor.

When Adelaide's maid asked how she wanted her hair designed, Tilly simply opted for the most flattering style. When instructing a gentleman, it never hurt to look one's best . . . except it often did. But never mind that.

With a nod, Tilly decided on her green muslin. She did not know if it made her pretty, but it certainly made her *feel* pretty, which, on the whole, was more important. Men were lazy creatures. If one acted as if one were attractive, men would take the action as truth without bothering to judge for themselves.

Ah, well, if they were more complex creatures, they would not be so easily manipulated, and Tilly would need a new profession.

Once dressed, Tilly glanced at her reflection in the mirror above the dresser in her room. Several curly tendrils had escaped their bindings. No matter. She doubted she would play Miss Proper with Lord Astor anyway. A little late for that charade.

Tilly made her way downstairs. She and Adelaide had begun taking a stroll every morning after breakfast, and Tilly expected Adelaide to be waiting for her already.

Just as she reached the first floor, however, Tilly realized Adelaide wasn't the only one awake so early. Adelaide's great-aunt Henrietta came prancing out of the dining room.

"Why, good morning, Lady Durth," Tilly greeted.

Great-aunt Henrietta was an ancient. She'd once stood three inches above Tilly, Adelaide claimed, but no longer. Hen now stood at eye level with Tilly. As always, she'd swathed herself in pale mint green, which made her look older than Egypt.

She amused Tilly no end. Adelaide, however, found Hen overpowering. Adelaide's eyebrow twitched whenever Aunt Hen spent more than a few minutes with her.

Aunt Hen waved her hand. "Tilly, I've told you to call me Aunt Hen. There's no call for 'Lady Durth' so early in the morning."

"Excuse me, Aunt Hen. Can't seem to reconcile such a spry figure with the title aunt," Tilly countered with a straight face.

Aunt Henrietta laughed. "Yes, not everyone can be as sharp as I. It's true."

"Visiting with Mrs. Beesley and Lady Wexham at this early hour?" Tilly asked. Mrs. Beesley had moved in with Lady Wexham after both their husbands died. Great-aunt Henrietta spent every waking hour with them. She planned to move into Lady Wexham's house, too, just as soon as she married off Adelaide.

Aunt Henrietta had mostly given up hope of the blessed day occurring in her lifetime . . . or Adelaide's either, for that matter.

"Oh, yes! I'm spending the day with them," Aunt Henrietta said, clapping her hands as if this were a rare occurrence. "I'd tell you what we have planned, but it's best you don't know. Just in case Adelaide asks, you understand." Aunt Henrietta shook her white head. "You know how that child worries."

"That child" was four years Tilly's senior. Tilly nodded. "Better I don't know anything when the constable calls."

Great Aunt Henrietta winked. "Don't worry. We have the constable under control." She flounced out the front door, a puff of mint green. Tilly smiled at the sight.

When she got on in years, Tilly hoped to have two best friends she enjoyed as much. Having no living relatives, Tilly knew she'd have to create a family out of her friends if she wanted to grow old in company.

Well, that shouldn't prove difficult. Most of Tilly's friends had had enough of marriage and wanted only to live out their lives in peace and friendship. Tilly had always looked forward to joining them eventually.

So, she didn't know why this morning the prospect sounded just a bit . . . well, dull.

Then, Tilly heard a deep voice through the dining room doorway and knew at once why she was out of sorts.

God's truth, Tilly looked forward to sparring with Jaiden again, and by the sound of it, the sparring was about to begin.

Jaiden had taken her advice and deigned to breakfast with his sister. A quick learner indeed. She'd have him the consistency of bread pudding in no time.

His mouth opened but no words emerged as he stared at her, stunned. His gaze lighted on her unbound curls, and Tilly felt a moment's pleasure . . . all because she'd disconcerted him yet again. Certainly, it had nothing to do with the fact that he might find her hair appealing.

"Good morning, Adelaide," Tilly said, floating into the room. "And to you also, of course, Lord Astor," she said, turning to the man who'd stood as she entered.

"Good morning, Mrs. Leighton. I trust you slept well?"

"Delightfully," she replied. She took the opportunity to inspect Jaiden's standing form leisurely. Yes, still all big and appealing. She widened her eyes in mock innocence. "I'm delighted to see you suffered no permanent injuries from your fall last night," she commented, moving to the side bar to help herself to eggs and various baked goods.

"You fell?" Adelaide questioned, glancing at her brother in concern.

His eyes didn't wander from Tilly's face. "I believe Mrs. Leighton is mistaken. 'Twasn't I that fell so much as my pride, which, I assure you, will not get over the wound in this lifetime, well, at least not until after breakfast."

So he could admit he'd come out the loser in last night's confrontation. Tilly did admire a male who had some grasp on his ineptitude. Too often, they lost hold of it somewhere in the fog of their overpowering conceit.

Pausing with her dish, Tilly couldn't stop herself from bestowing a smile on Jaiden, but the moment her eyes met his, she knew it'd been a mistake. Their gazes caught. The good-natured smile slipped from his lips as tension built between them.

Out of the corner of her eye, Tilly saw Adelaide blink and then shake her head. "You two met? When? Last night?"

Tilly tore her gaze away. She looked down at her plate to compose herself. She must speak before Jaiden did if she wanted to avoid listening to his version of the night's events. Adelaide might want her brother instructed, but she'd never advocated the breaking into his private domain. "Why, when your brother mistook me for a spy, of course. I dare say, had I not explained myself so speedily he would have bludgeoned me to death with his ledger."

"Oh, Jaiden, no!"

"I'm afraid Mrs. Leighton and I have different ideas of what makes haste," was all he said.

A flash of gratitude hit Tilly. He hadn't revealed the location of their introduction. She deigned to take a seat at the long table so that Jaiden could regain his chair without breaking social dictate.

Time to change the subject under discussion, Tilly surmised. Nodding to Jaiden's copy of *The London Daily*, Tilly asked, "Anything of import this morning?" She bit happily into the buttery muffin.

"We were just discussing the missing wives investigation," Adelaide answered.

Really, Tilly could never be bothered to pay attention to conversation when baked goods so delicious filled her . . . *the missing wives!* The muffin turned to clay in Tilly's mouth. Swallowing, she tried to appear unconcerned. "Oh, any new developments?"

"Not according to T. L. Edwards," Jaiden said ruefully.

Ugh! T. L. Edwards had been slandering Tilly for the past five months—granted, he didn't know of Tilly's involvement, so it wasn't slander *per se*. But his stories heavily implied a common kidnapper was responsible for spiriting away four prominent women who had vanished this past year.

Complete rubbish! Anyone who had met their husbands knew that those women had left of their own volition. Just because Tilly had provided the escape route didn't make her a kidnapper.

"Perhaps you would prefer to read the piece yourself, rather than just scowl at it from across the table," Jaiden offered, tossing the paper next to her plate of eggs.

So much for appearing nonchalant! Tilly smiled and waved dismissively. "One does need to keep up with the goings-on." Then, turning the paper over, she began to read voraciously. Thank God! Nothing new! Tilly took a bite of her eggs.

"You must know more than what's being reported," Adelaide was saying to her brother as Tilly finished the story.

Jaiden shrugged.

"I wager you wish this were your investigation," Adelaide pressed.

Tilly's head swung up from the paper. "Your investigation?" she repeated. Adelaide had told her Jaiden was some sort of industrialist. "What do you mean 'your investigation?' " she demanded.

"Just that Scotland Yard has employed no better investigator than my brother," Adelaide announced proudly.

Investigator. Scotland Yard. Oh, God, she had taken up residence with the enemy. Dear Lord, the danger her friends would be in if he learned anything!

Tilly stood, but her legs hit the underside of the table with such a force that it bounced her back into her chair. She shook her head. "Investigator," she whispered, even as a voice in her head screamed for her to flee the house at once.

"Chief Inspector for the Metropolitan Police," Adelaide corrected.

"Former Chief," Jaiden clarified off-handedly. "Are you feeling quite all right, Mrs. Leighton? All color has drained from your face."

"Former?" Tilly whispered.

"Haven't worked for the government in the last seven years. Maybe you'd like a brandy? Or a rest, perhaps?"

Praise the heavens! Seven years! She would be quite safe! Tilly let out a breath and smiled. Time to change the subject yet again. "Thank you for your concern, Lord Astor, but truly, I'm fine. Indeed, Adelaide, I am very much looking forward to our walk this morning," Tilly announced, scooping egg on her fork.

A crash filled the room. Pausing with the bite halfway to her mouth, Tilly glanced down at the source of the ruckus. Adelaide's spoon lay haphazardly on her plate under her down-turned head and closed eyes. Her chest heaved with deep breaths.

"Dear, are you all right?" Tilly asked with a semblance of concern. She proceeded with her bite of breakfast. She could spot a fake headache across a room. Adelaide couldn't compete with a professional—though Tilly did wonder what the girl was about.

Adelaide pressed her fingertips to her forehead. "Suddenly, I've the most horrid pain." She raised her napkin from her lap and discarded it on the table with an unnecessary moan.

"Oh, you poor thing," Tilly sympathized, shoveling in more egg casserole. The Astors' cook did make every meal a treat. Tilly would have to buy a whole new wardrobe if she kept eating like this.

Jaiden's brow furrowed as he studied his sister with concern.

Really, falling for this farce after the lecture she'd given him only last evening! Clearly, the boy wasn't as quick a learner as she'd thought. Tilly barely refrained from tut-tutting in disapproval.

"Let me help you to your room," he said, standing. "You can lie down while I ask Mary to send up some tea."

Adelaide stood and gazed at her brother. "You are too kind, Jaiden, but truly, I can manage the stairs on my own. No really. You needn't concern yourself further. Except . . . oh dear." Adelaide bit her lower lip as though she dared not continue.

Tilly knew the gesture. It was always employed when someone planned to impose but didn't want to look too eager about it.

Jaiden nudged his sister. "Addie." He smiled. "Anything," he swore.

The vow finally stilled Tilly's fork. Tilly felt an unfamiliar ache. She didn't have any siblings. She couldn't imagine someone offering her *carte blanche* so sincerely. It made her almost wish she'd had a brother. She had always assumed siblings hated each other as much as husbands and wives did. Apparently, blood proved kinder than vows.

But where was the ruthless man Adelaide had warned her of?

Adelaide raised her shoulders, then dropped them in relief. A trembling smile appeared on her lips, a touch even Tilly judged to be pure genius. "I just feel terrible for canceling my walk with Tilly after she'd so wanted to go—"

"Think nothing of it," Tilly said, waving a hand in dismissal. In truth, she could use the rest. Eight inches shorter than Adelaide, Tilly sometimes found herself gasping for air just to keep up.

Adelaide shook her head at Tilly. "I couldn't rest knowing I had kept you indoors on such a lovely day."

"Adelaide, stop worrying," Jaiden commanded. "I will be happy to escort Mrs. Leighton anywhere she might wish to go," he promised at the same moment Tilly realized what Adelaide was about. That sly girl.

"Truly, that's not necessary—" Tilly began.

"Oh, Jaiden, thank you! Are you certain it won't interfere with your work schedule?"

"Not at all." Jaiden turned his startling sapphire eyes on Tilly. A slow grin spread across his face. "It will be my pleasure."

Tilly's stomach flip-flopped. She had to look down to break the gaze. For the first time in her life the gesture wasn't an affectation.

CHAPTER THREE

A half-hour later, Tilly strolled through a deserted Hyde Park, trying unsuccessfully to stop admiring Jaiden's saunter out of the corner of her eye. He'd slowed his stride by half to keep pace with her shorter legs. Somehow the more leisurely amble transformed him into the ultimate unhurried gentleman. She loved that illusion—no pressing concerns, nothing more important than appreciating sculpted nature around them.

Jaiden would never complain, Tilly judged. If something bothered him, he'd simply reach out and change it, no talking involved—a trait Tilly admired much in her unsuspecting pupil.

Tilly had never understood the purpose of whining. Then again, she had never had anyone to whine to. Self-sufficiency was at least one benefit of being orphaned at a young age. Probably Jaiden hadn't had anyone to listen to his grievances, either.

So far, she'd gleaned little of Jaiden's personality. She had expected him to pounce on this opportunity to interrogate her about her reason for breaking into his study. They both knew she'd lied through her teeth the previous night.

He hadn't so much as mentioned it since the veiled reference at breakfast though. Tilly could only imagine his silence came from one of two motives. Either he wisely did not trust her to admit the truth, or his sense of fair play granted her privacy for outwitting him. In either case, she suspected he meant to trick the story out of her eventually. Tilly turned positively giddy at the prospect. He was no match for her, of course, but he did keep her awake.

Now, all she had to do was find his weaknesses and turn them to her advantage.

Since she couldn't think of a particular starting point, she decided to bring up his childhood. Men talking about their parents invariably revealed a great deal about themselves. All Tilly had to do was discreetly introduce a conversation she could turn to his childhood. Maybe when he first learned to ride a horse or his first memory of Hyde Park.

"Yes, Mrs. Leighton?"

"Have you ever hit a woman?"

Tilly came to an abrupt halt. She hadn't just asked that. Certainly she hadn't. She must have said something else, something that went with her plans and her reason for being there and . . .

"No." He stated it simply, looking her directly in the eyes. Yet, his expression held no amusement at her discomfort or the *faux pas* she'd committed.

"Not even a prostitute? Or your sister?" Tilly asked. *When had her mouth taken leave of her mind?*

His eyebrows lifted only a fraction of an inch. "I do consider prostitutes to be women . . . by and large."

She nodded slowly, unable to move her gaze from his.

"Then again, I've never employed a prostitute, which would undoubtedly make striking one more uncouth, if not anymore reprehensible."

Again, she nodded. She couldn't open her mouth. She had no idea what might pop out of it.

Transfixed, she could not miss the two fingers he brought to the top of her forehead. She flinched at the contact nonetheless. The breath caught in her lungs. Slowly, he traced the outline of her face, sliding a loose tendril behind her ear. He then twined his fingers with that curl and brought it near to his face to study it. His head dropped closer to her. His voice came out a whisper. "Has any man hit you?"

"No," she breathed. Then, realizing she hadn't spoken the word, she swallowed and tried again. "No."

Tension melted from his face. A smile tugged at his lips. "I suppose the more likely question is, have you ever battered a man?"

It took her a full minute to realize his impertinence. When she did, she threw back her head and laughed, dislodging his fingers from her hair. If he only knew what she'd done to men, he wouldn't be blithely grinning down at her now.

How had she let the conversation run so far afield? She couldn't deny the rush of relief his answer inspired, though.

The sound of whistling surprised her as much as anything, for she was the one making it. Somehow her lips couldn't confine the joy exploding in her belly.

Without thinking about it, she linked her arm through his and twirled him back on the path.

What a lovely morning it was turning out to be!

What an intriguing woman! More mercurial than Hermes, himself! Jaiden couldn't get enough of her surprises—and surprise him again she had! He'd not expected her to reveal any vulnerability. She'd proven herself well practiced in the art of evasion, and instead she'd come right out and asked him what bothered her most. Of course, she'd obviously been more surprised than he.

And he still hadn't a clue why she broke into his study or where she had learned how to pick locks. Not the easiest of skills—he knew well from his Scotland Yard days.

He was used to employing very persuasive means when extracting information from suspects, but with Mrs. Leighton, all he had to do was listen. She would eventually reveal everything, if this walk were any indication.

No wonder Jaiden allowed the walk to go on longer than he should have. Daniel must be waiting for him. He'd sent a note to his friend asking him to meet at his townhouse instead of his offices. The least he could do was be there to greet him, and yet, Jaiden had found it impossible to lead Mrs. Leighton back a moment before he had to.

Tilly whistled a merry tune next to him, practically skipping despite their linked arms. Every step made her fascinating curls bounce. Her green dress matched her eyes and seemed to reflect her soul's giddiness.

Loathe to disturb such perfect happiness, Jaiden nonetheless felt the need to converse with her once more before depriving himself of her company.

When his white stone townhouse came into view, he spoke, "You have twice now hinted that my sister lacks spine. I don't know where you acquired that notion, but let me dissuade you of its truth."

She looked up at him, surprised, the song dead on her lips. "I didn't intend to call your sister a coward, only I fear you rather intimidate her."

Jaiden let out a bark of laughter. Him? Intimidate Adelaide? Impossible. The girl had spent most of her life testing how far she could push before she outright killed someone. She had more daring than all of Wolseley's armies combined.

"I promise you, Mrs. Leighton, had I ever raised a hand to Adelaide, she would have chopped it off." He shook his head. How had these two women become friends? Mrs. Leighton appeared not to know his sister in the least.

"And the late Mr. Leighton? What did he think of your penchant for wandering into locked rooms? No, my apologies. Unlocked rooms."

Tilly slid him a glance. "How do you know he's dead?"

"Adelaide."

"So, you made time to talk to her . . . finally," she said under her breath.

Mrs. Leighton had appointed herself Adelaide's protector, Jaiden realized. Rather like the hare protecting the fox. Adelaide would never have asked such a direct question as whether or not a man had hit a woman. Instead, she would have organized a bevy of spies to investigate for her. How Mrs. Leighton had cast his sister in the role of victim he would never know.

Then there was the way she treated him: as though he were some untried innocent. He remembered her last night, ignorant of the abundance of curves her silky wrapper revealed as she sat on his sofa and explained women's wiles. Did she not realize how close he was to ravishing her?

They walked up the front steps in silence. Ross, his butler, swung the door open just as Jaiden reached it.

"Sir Sheldon said you expected him. I put him in the drawing room."

"Thank you, Ross," Jaiden said. He turned to Tilly. "Thank you for the walk. It was . . . educational." He bowed formally, not for manners' sake but to see how she'd react.

She dropped into a curtsy, though her eyes remained sparkling up at him.

"Miss Astor is also in the drawing room," Ross announced.

Tilly raised amused eyebrows. "Imagine that. Must be over her headache."

"Let's find out," he said, leading her across the foyer to the second door on the left.

Opening the door, they discovered Adelaide and Daniel sipping tea, surrounded by a painful silence. Daniel stood at their entrance.

"Sorry I'm late," Jaiden offered. "I haven't any excuse other than the gorgeous view in Hyde Park this morning. Speaking of which, please allow me to present Mrs. Leighton. Mrs. Leighton, Mr. Sheldon."

Daniel bowed stiffly as Tilly sank into a flirtatious curtsy. "In truth, sir," she said, "blame me for Lord Astor's tardiness. I insisted on taking the long route."

"Think nothing of it, Mrs. Leighton. I commend anyone capable of distracting Lord Astor from his business. I enjoyed catching up with Miss Astor."

Miss Astor? Jaiden's eyebrows jumped. Adelaide and Daniel had known each other for an age.

"Well, let's to it, then," Jaiden said. "If you'll excuse us, ladies."

The door closed behind them. Daniel let loose a wide grin. "The view of the park, indeed."

Jaiden shook his head. "Mrs. Leighton's stunning physique is the least of her fascinating aspects." Jaiden let out a breath and laid a hand on his friend's shoulder. "You've no idea."

CHAPTER FOUR

"Made any progress with your missing wives?" Jaiden asked Daniel once they were ensconced in his study. Daniel possessed the unhappy duty of trying to solve the controversial case, which seemed to lack all evidence of criminal activity. Jaiden did not envy him the job.

"Very little," Daniel admitted, sitting in the chair in front of Jaiden's desk. "Interested in signing back on?"

Jaiden was tempted. He missed the *esprit de corps*, the life-or-death drama, but it was time he grew up. Time his friend did, too. "I'm having enough difficulty finding my missing employee." He gestured to the brandy decanter, but Daniel shook his head. Jaiden sat behind the desk.

"It's been over four years now. Maybe it's time you gave up."

Jaiden smiled. "Can't. It's too strange. Debtors disappear, never creditors. It's an immutable law of nature, and this anomaly must be studied." But Daniel had not set up the appointment to speak about Mrs. Elizabeth Underplumb. "Tell me what you've learned."

Daniel leaned back in his chair and shrugged. "Just another sighting of the green-eyed lady." He laughed ruefully. "The witnesses can't even agree on her hair color."

Jaiden picked up a pen and began rolling it around each knuckle of his right hand. "Maybe it's not the same woman," he suggested.

Daniel's lips tensed. "It is."

Jaiden gave a mental sigh over his friend's stubbornness. "Look, Daniel, you've now met each one of these abandoned husbands, and you yourself have cataloged their shortcomings. Don't you think it's likely that most of these women left of their own volition? That each is in fact an individual case, and it is only the newspaper editors who connect them? Lady Maltrose is probably drinking wine with her lover on a boat in the Mediterranean at the moment."

"Jaiden, women who leave their husbands don't disappear without leaving a trail. You taught me that."

Jaiden considered the man he'd trained ten years earlier, three years before his business ventures had paid off well enough for him to quit the investigation post and enter into business full-time. His finances had prospered better than anyone could have predicted since then—well, anyone but Jaiden. He'd paid off the last of his father's debts over five years ago, but he hadn't lost touch with his old underling. Indeed, his last action as chief inspector had been to promote Daniel to take his place. The man had proven himself more than equal to the post over the last three years, but this missing wives case had plagued him from the beginning. "Not unless they don't want to be found."

Daniel mulled over the idea, but then shook his head. "These are ordinary women we're talking about, not agents of the Special Branch. They wouldn't know how to disappear. Not unless they had help." He scowled. "If you're correct, if they all left of their own volition, how do you explain their jewelry, their assets? Everything is accounted for," Daniel reminded him. "When a man runs, he liquidates first."

"Ah, but we are not talking about men." An image of Tilly flashed through Jaiden's mind. "We are speaking of women, and they are a breed apart."

Daniel did not smile. "It's precisely because they are women that their leaving behind their personal possessions does not make sense. You know how difficult it is for a single female to support herself."

"Well," Jaiden drawled. "You don't think it's kidnapping, so are you thinking homicide?"

Daniel ran a frustrated hand through his dark blond hair. "I've met their husbands. All are complete bastards—bastards who might be capable of murder."

"And yet you still insist the incidents are connected?"

"Maybe it's ritual. Perhaps some club . . ."

Jaiden pictured the possibility and immediately shook his head. "Then their wives would be the last persons they would choose as victims. Besides, you said the husbands are the ones pushing the investigation."

Daniel's head jerked up. His eyes narrowed. "That's just it. I'm afraid the cocky bastards have found a way to get rid of their unwanted wives and are rubbing it in my face."

Jaiden looked at his friend, at his shining hazel eyes and tense mouth. "This case bothers you like I've never seen before."

Humor tugged at Daniel's lips. "But of course. It's the case I can't solve."

"Maybe it's time you quit and retired to your estate, fulfilled some of your responsibilities. Your father would die of shock. Surely that's motivation enough for you."

White teeth flashed behind tan skin. "And leave my mother a delighted widow. I wouldn't dream of it."

A second son, Daniel had inherited a title from his maternal grandfather along with a more than modest estate. His father, however, had made certain Daniel couldn't touch a farthing of his inheritance. He promised to loosen his grip only when Daniel settled down—something Daniel refused to consider— not while in the army, not while leading expeditions into the heart of Africa, and certainly not now when he supported his safari adventures working at Scotland Yard and winning more than he lost at White's tables. At this rate, Jaiden doubted that Daniel could accept a life of ease, one where his estate ran smoothly and his biggest concern was checking on how the steward managed the books.

Jaiden, on the other hand, would have given his right arm for an unencumbered inheritance when his parents died a decade before. At seventeen, he'd had little choice but to take up investigating to support his sister and great aunt while in his free time he pawned his mother's jewelry and invested it in ventures, which, thank God, had paid off handsomely.

He'd been raised to believe he would be a gentleman of leisure. He had planned to spend his time tinkering with mechanics, but had not thought he would need to support a family with technology. A good thing he didn't have to, either. He'd made one small chemical advancement, useful in a limited number of forensic investigations, but it had been enough for him to make the necessary contacts, and to discover his true gift—projections.

Jaiden would never be a great scientist. The world would never know his name, but it didn't matter, for he knew the world. He knew what people wanted, needed, and what would help them get it. He'd used his talent to build his own business, which bought and sold patents, as well as funded scientists to work on specific advancements.

It wasn't finessing confessions out of criminals, but it kept him entertained. Lately, it was the only thing that kept him entertained.

The image of Mrs. Leighton shimmered in his mind. Maybe business wasn't the only thing worth his time.

Daniel interrupted his thoughts. "Other than retiring, do you have any suggestions for me?"

Jaiden smiled. This might be the first time Daniel had asked for advice. This case did obsess him. "Nothing. Sounds like you're doing all you can."

Daniel sighed and stood. "Unlike you, I need to get to work. I would bid you good day, but since you've your own mysterious green-eyed lady under your roof, I doubt you need my wishes."

CHAPTER FIVE

The moment the door swung shut behind Jaiden, Tilly bounced over to the sofa where Adelaide sat blushing.

"Did you enjoy your walk?" Adelaide asked.

Tilly laughed. "Don't bother trying to distract me. How long have you been in love with that dangerously handsome gentleman, and why haven't you done anything about it?"

Groaning, Adelaide buried her face in her hands. "Is it so obvious?"

Tilly patted her back. "Either that or someone stole your tongue and covered your face in tomato juice."

Adelaide whimpered.

"So how long have you wanted him and why aren't you Mrs. Sheldon yet?"

Adelaide peeked up at Tilly, long enough to shake her head. "Oh, Tilly! It's hopeless. He doesn't even realize I'm here." She waved her hands. "He never thinks of me except as Jaiden's sister. Daniel's always polite and courteous, and he treats me the exact same way he treats Aunt Hen! When we were younger, we were . . . friendly. But lately he's grown distant toward me, and I think I've missed my chance!"

"Cheer up," Tilly commanded. "This is good. He ought to treat you as politely as he does Aunt Henrietta. That is, until you give him the signal you want him to behave differently. Have you given him the signal?"

Adelaide furrowed her brow, then bit her lower lip, and finally shook her head. "I don't think so."

Tilly patted her hand. "Then you haven't. What are you waiting for?"

Throwing her arms in the air, Adelaide stood. "I don't know what to do!" She paced the room. "I don't know how to make him . . ." She covered her forehead with her palm and closed her eyes. She sighed and met Tilly's amused expression. "*See* me."

Tilly lounged in the chair, supporting her head on her fingertips. "Oh, sweet, when we're through with him, he won't be able to see anything but you."

Adelaide crouched in front of her, grasping her hand. "Do you really think so?"

She looked so pretty, all hopeful and flushed at the same time, Tilly thought. The girl hadn't a clue how devastating her charms would be if employed properly on the male sex. Not that it was difficult to catch any male's interest, but tolerably pretty girls had a distinct advantage, and Adelaide could be so much more than merely beautiful.

Covering Adelaide's hands with her own, Tilly smiled. "If you want him, he's yours for the picking."

"And you'll help me?"

Tilly let out an inelegant snort. "Dearest lamb, I spend my life trying to avoid men's attention. It'll be cake to capture one."

Adelaide shook her head. "I'm so embarrassed."

"Oh pooh! You've no idea how delighted I am to see you are more than tea and high collars. Now, have a seat. Let's get down to business."

Adelaide sat on the sofa, her eyes so wide open Tilly feared they might pop out of her head. Tilly forced Adelaide to tell her about Daniel, and it was no easy task. Unlike most women in love who can't shut up about the recipient of their affections,

Adelaide seemed incapable of saying more than monosyllables. She uttered not a word of praise, and, yet, her longing reverberated in her every sigh.

"Ah. Perfect!" Tilly finally exclaimed. "I know exactly what type he is. Your Daniel enjoys a challenge. I should've realized. The wavy, dark blond hair gives it away every time. Now, we just need to present you as the greatest challenge of all."

"And how are we going to do that?"

Tilly waved a dismissive hand. "Easily enough. Next time you see him, you must be just awful to him, as mean and disparaging as you can be. Then, after that, positively exude niceness. On the third time, simply ignore him. On the forth, it's back to sweetness."

"Won't . . . won't he hate me?"

So much the girl had to learn! "A rational creature would. Men, however, are hardly rational. Really, voluntarily putting themselves in the path of bullets? Traveling over half the world to hunt animals, which happily hunt them back. And Daniel's kind is the least rational of all." Tilly looked at the perplexed woman and let out a sigh. She knew it was hard to understand. It'd taken Tilly years to accept the challenge-hungry male for what he was. How was Adelaide supposed to take her word for it when her advice contradicted human reason?

Besides, Tilly supposed she *could* be wrong—she wasn't, but it was theoretically possible. Perhaps she should just let Adelaide handle Daniel however she saw fit.

But that was the problem. Adelaide hadn't a clue how to handle him. She'd not needed to learn how to manipulate men by the age of four to stay alive, as Tilly had.

It was true. Tilly made mistakes—just never where men were concerned. At least not since—oh, but that was a lifetime ago. No sense dredging that up.

"Look here," she said. "If you follow my instructions, Sir

Sheldon will be yours by the end of the month. If you're too uncomfortable with this plan, however, we'll figure something else out. It may take longer, but it will still work."

Adelaide whimpered. "I couldn't be mean to Daniel. I just couldn't."

"Then you shan't. I'll think of something else. In fact . . ." Tilly grinned, hearing a door close across the hall. "Stay here," she commanded, jumping up and running to the door.

"Tilly!" Adelaide called.

"Be right back," Tilly sang, sliding through the doorway and out into the hall just in time to intercept Adelaide's future husband.

Did she really want to encourage a marriage? And for Adelaide? Such a sweet, innocent thing.

Ah, well, this was what her friend wanted. Besides, if women realized how worthless men were and stopped wedding them— the way they should—well, Tilly'd be out of a job, and that was no good, especially given her narrow range of skills.

"Mrs. Leighton," Daniel greeted.

"Oh, Sir Sheldon," she gushed. Too bad she hadn't worn the lavender morning dress. "I know we only just met and you don't know anything about me, but I was hoping . . . that is I thought . . . I might be so wretched as to impose upon you." She peered up at him from under her lashes, then looked at her feet. She ground one toe into the floor and swiveled her foot back and forth. "No, no, it's really too terrible."

"Mrs. Leighton, if there's anything I can do to make your stay with the Astors more comfortable, I would consider it my honor and duty as Lord Astor's friend and former subordinate."

"Yes, well, this hasn't anything to do with business."

"Nonetheless—"

"Adelaide and I were left in a bit of a lurch," she blurted out. "We told Mrs. Grimmway we would attend her ball tomorrow, but our escort—" She sighed deeply but quickly, before Daniel could interrupt. "Well, could you—might you—be so kind as to fill in?" She beamed up at him, her eyebrows raised in what she knew signified desperate hope.

His lips turned down. "To escort you and Miss Astor to Mrs. Grimmway's?" he clarified.

"Yes. Oh, please. I would consider it such a favor—"

"Of course, Mrs. Leighton. It will be my honor."

"Oh, thank you, Sir Sheldon. You are too kind."

"My pleasure, truly," he said.

"Well, we'll see you at eight tomorrow evening then," she instructed. "See you then," she called, moving back to the drawing room.

"Er . . . yes. See you then."

Tilly was dancing in front of Adelaide before Daniel had got out the front door. Adelaide perched on the edge of the sofa. Tilly didn't think she so much as breathed.

"What happened?" Adelaide asked, her eyes bulging again.

Tilly did a little waltz. "Daniel has requested—most desperately—your . . . well, *our* presence tomorrow night. At Mrs. Grimmway's affair."

"And why did he do that?"

Tilly shrugged. "What's it matter? We have more important things to discuss. What shall you wear?"

CHAPTER SIX

At exactly five minutes till eight, Tilly gazed down at the foyer from the top of the stairs. No one cluttered the entrance. She smiled privately, then watched her coral evening gown swish as she descended the steps.

She looked good, but, more important, she didn't look *too* good. She'd made certain Adelaide's ensemble showed her person to every advantage. Tilly had no desire to detract from her friend by wearing anything too showy herself—or her hair down, for that matter. Tonight was all about Adelaide.

"Swish. Swish. Swish," she murmured happily in time to her dress. The evening promised much excitement. Just because Adelaide refused to toy with Sir Sheldon's emotions didn't mean Tilly felt the need to be so kind. No—not at all.

She executed an extra little kick as she stepped onto the dark marble of the foyer floor and then paused, noticing the shiny dress shoes at the edge of her vision.

Any hope some uncouth person had left them there to dry was violently dispelled as her gaze traveled slightly upward and found trouser-swathed legs standing above them.

"Damn," she muttered. Collecting herself, she met the amused sapphire eyes studying her.

"And good evening to you, too, Mrs. Leighton." Jaiden lounged against the side wall, clad in midnight black formal attire. No wonder she hadn't seen him. He disappeared against the dark wallpaper behind him. Why had Adelaide allowed the foyer to be decorated as though only men lived in the house, Tilly wondered grumpily.

"Lord Astor, forgive me. I failed to note your presence. I'm afraid I'm not used to you lurking about so early in the evening. Usually, that pleasure is reserved for after eleven. Now," she continued before he could spit out whatever hid behind his grin, "has Sir Sheldon arrived?"

"Arrived and gone, I'm afraid."

Arrived and gone? Tilly blinked. She must have misunderstood. Surely Sir Sheldon hadn't abandoned Adelaide at the last minute. "Excuse me?" she demanded, plopping her hands on her hips.

"Yes," he said, finally straightening. "Adelaide mentioned a change of plans, something about helping Mrs. Grimmway with party arrangements. Daniel called an hour ago and escorted her there."

"Well how do you like that?" Tilly exclaimed. She shook her head. No wonder Adelaide had asked for help dressing hours ago. Adelaide had meant to abandon Tilly all along—not that Tilly minded being left behind. She just couldn't understand why Adelaide didn't explain her intentions. After all, she had asked for Tilly's help. If she didn't want it, she needed only to say so. The least she could do was keep Tilly informed.

Tilly frowned, not liking this left-out feeling at all.

Well, at least Adelaide had possessed the courage to be alone with Sir Sheldon. That was a step in the right direction. Indeed, if Adelaide could arrange that, she could manage the rest quite easily. Yes, she would fare well.

Really, it was much better this way. Adelaide would forever know she'd enticed Sir Sheldon into proposing all on her own. A wife needed such knowledge. It proved a constant reminder that she could always fall back on her cunning during the long miserable years between the wedding and widowhood.

Jaiden stepped in front of Tilly and bowed. Tilly scrambled a step back. How had she forgotten him yet again?

"If you would allow me to take Daniel's place," he was saying as he straightened.

"Oh, pooh," she said dismissively. "That's not necessary."

"I insist." Tilly didn't remind Jaiden that he hated dances. No sense alerting him to the fact she'd researched his preferences. Still, there was no call for him to escort her. "Go back to your ledgers. I'll be quite happy to amuse myself in my room. I'm told it contains all sorts of delightful novels awaiting a female guest such as myself in need of some light reading," she threw his words back at him. Never hurt to remind a man that he was no match for her wits.

Unfortunately, her wits failed against the strength of his large hands, one of which currently encircled her waist most inappropriately. The other rested on her elbow. It radiated warmth up her side.

Thyme! That's what it was! Jaiden smelled of soap and woods and thyme. How could she have failed to recognize that?

"Now, now, Mrs. Leighton. No reading for you on such a lovely evening. You must enjoy the night. Adelaide insisted. She'd have my head if I didn't show you a pleasant time." He led her toward the front door.

Tilly crushed men's confidence for so much as glancing in her direction, and here Jaiden was positively manhandling her. And she wanted nothing more than to stay in his heated half-embrace. How peculiar. She couldn't gather so much as a thread of indignation at this mauling. Instead, she didn't want the familiarity to end.

Surely, that couldn't be right. She shook her head. Maybe she was falling ill: consumption mayhap, or a mere head cold. Truly, she felt light-headed and altogether wrong. Or was it too right? What if she really did faint? Jaiden would never believe in its validity.

"Now, none of that headshaking, please," Jaiden said. "We'll go. We'll dance. We'll have a drink. Nothing untoward in the whole plan."

But what if she wanted something untoward to happen?

"You wouldn't want to have Adelaide upset with me, would you?"

Right. Adelaide. Maybe Tilly's employer needed her there. Maybe Adelaide wanted to attempt Daniel on her own, but felt it necessary to have reinforcements standing in reserve just in case things got out of hand.

Then again, maybe Mrs. Grimmway had honestly needed Adelaide's help, and for whatever reason, Adelaide had thought it improper to include Tilly. Adelaide hardly qualified as the manipulator Tilly was. In which case, her friend might be near hysterics at being left to her own devices in entertaining Sir Sheldon.

Either way, Tilly was certain she could help. And, if help proved unnecessary, she'd concentrate on her original goal: softening Jaiden.

Yes, she was merely doing her duty as a friend and employee. Her decision to allow Jaiden to escort her had nothing to do with the appealing mixture of soap and thyme. Truly nothing at all. . . .

CHAPTER SEVEN

The butler called out their names, and for once Jaiden did not have to stifle a yawn.

He hated balls—balls, dances, plays, large dinners. They wasted time and were ridiculously contrived. Still, that didn't begin to explain the extent of his loathing.

They bored him—bored him to the depths of his soul. All these people milling around, trying to impress each other. What did he care for their good opinion? What did he care for their opinions on anything? They weren't the people who could help him in his business affairs. Not anymore, at least, and they certainly would never revolutionize the world. They were a dying breed, consumed by a dead age. They added nothing to society, accomplished nothing in their lives.

What did they have to celebrate? Nothing. And still, they always seemed to be celebrating. They actually seemed to take pleasure in frivolity, and Jaiden couldn't understand how.

Maybe he just envied their simple contentment, their delight in each other. How he wished he could find such excitement in another human being, could care about something beyond his latest acquisition, his latest sale.

Never did he feel so alone than when he was surrounded by other people who were immersed in their own gaiety.

And the ladies! They had their uses . . . or at least use, but it was hard to take advantage of that in the midst of this proper ensemble. Besides, Jaiden didn't like an audience, though he knew a few of the room's inhabitants who did.

Jaiden could remember his parents relaxing in front of the fire on winter evenings in the country. Sometimes they'd read or sit companionably silent, but at other times they'd talk—not about politics or the latest hunt necessarily—but about things important to their hearts: their children or the tenants or the price of hay. Jaiden could never understand how they'd gone to those country discussions from the gilded, overcrowded rooms he found himself in now.

Tilly squeezed his arm. It pressed against her soft breast. "Smile, my lord. This is supposed to be amusing."

Her small stature struck him again. The top of her head didn't even reach his shoulder. She might be small, but she hardly appeared delicate, despite her tiny wrists and slender hands. There was an earthly realness about her. She wouldn't break if handled.

And that's why he'd agreed so readily to Adelaide's demand that he escort Tilly. Somehow, that first night when she'd pretended to faint and he'd rushed to her side, she'd enchanted him as no one else ever had. She'd seen that he couldn't tolerate females and their emotions—the fainting, the pouting, the ignoring, and, worst of all, the crying. Tears killed him. Just the eyes welling up bored him to insanity.

Give him death and duty, but keep weeping women out of his sight—weeping women like Miss Clara Haversham.

"Really, Lord Astor, there's no reason to crush my hand. We don't have to stay if it's so bad that you're stooping to physical retaliation."

Jaiden forced his grip to relax. She wiggled her fingers beneath his.

"Much better," she said. "Thank you."

That was yet another thing he appreciated about her. When she wanted him to do something, she told him straight out. He didn't have to waste time guessing what she was angling for.

Or maybe he was so entertained by the way she made him guess, he didn't mind. She thoroughly amused herself, too, a talent he needed to learn for social situations.

He wanted to know what secret fancy she mulled over, but for the moment it was nice simply being with her and not worrying that he might inadvertently crush her tender feelings. She seemed untouchable, as if nothing he could do would have the slightest impact on her unfettered joy.

"My lord," Tilly said, "you look as if you could use a reprieve. Why don't we find the game room?"

He could tolerate winning someone else's money for a while. "Would you like me to help you find Adelaide first?"

"Never mind that." Tilly gave a wave of her hand. She led him out into a long, dim corridor, "I've got these two extraordinary feet which can walk even without a man guiding them. What think you of that?" Her mouth turned up in an impish smile.

"I think watching you walk—your hips swaying from side to side like a pendulum—is a more amusing pastime than any I shall find in the game room," he commented.

"Of course, you appreciate it. That's why women walk this way," she replied, unfazed.

Except other women didn't. Not the way she did, as if it were completely natural and her body had no other way of getting from place to place.

The corners of her lips tugged downward. "You do know not to make such intimate observations, don't you?" she asked, uncertain.

He turned to her then, stopping her mid-stride, so that they stood improperly close. "I was under the impression you found these social dictates as much a waste of time as I did," he murmured near her ear.

She turned her face toward his, and their lips hovered inches apart. "Ahh, but my lord, all these niceties do serve their purposes." She smiled again, that devilish smile that made him want to run his fingertip along her bottom lip. "They're just not purposes that should take precedence most of the time. Truly, it all can be fun if you don't take it seriously," she whispered, running her hand down his forearm.

"Mrs. . . . Mrs. Leighton!" a man stuttered.

Jaiden looked up at the voice and found an older gentleman turning all shades of blue, red, and purple. Jaiden slid a protective, if improper, hand around Tilly's waist.

The woman next to the man let out a gasp and then a tiny smile, repressed quickly by a look of outrage.

"Lady Marcum, Lord Marcum," Tilly said with a nod at each of them.

Lady Marcum shook her head and waved her arm. "Don't even try to play civil! I know it all!" She walked a wide circle around Tilly, as if frightened of contaminating herself with an accidental contact.

Lord Marcum grimaced. He fidgeted from foot to foot. "I . . . I . . ."

"Geoffrey!" his wife snapped.

"Yes, dear," he called, looking relieved to trot after her.

Tilly turned to watch them go. Jaiden followed her look.

He had a wild urge to call Lord Marcum out for such rudeness. Hardly appropriate when not he, but Lady Marcum, had snubbed Tilly. Besides, dawn was better spent on investments than on the dueling field.

He was turning back to Tilly when Lady Marcum's hand caught his eye. It folded behind the woman's corseted waist. The fingers fluttered open and closed in a manner that could only be described as a fond adieu.

Now, what was that about?

Jaiden looked down at Tilly. She studied the couple as they

turned through the last exit. A whimsical smile softened her features.

"You are not upset," he stated. She should be, but she wasn't.

She looked up at him, laughed. "Of course not!" She linked her arm through his once more. "Only that's the price you pay for not playing by the rules." She peeked sideways at him. "Not such a harsh penalty, after all. Better than having to listen to Lord Marcum's diatribe about his latest fishing expedition, I assure you."

She practically skipped with good-humor. Jaiden had no idea what had just transpired, but clearly it hadn't upset Tilly in the least.

"Ah, the game room, as promised," she said, halting in front of a large room filled with men. "And here's where I leave you. I'll find you later," she assured him, turning and swaying down the hall.

He watched her, admiring that walk yet again before turning into the card room. His mind refused to leave the temptress.

CHAPTER EIGHT

Tilly sought Adelaide, anxious to see how things had fared on the Daniel quest.

With that thought in mind, she hurried down the corridor toward the ballroom again. Tilly moved so quickly that she passed the gowned woman by several paces before twirling around.

The woman stood erect against the wall between two unfortunate ceramic busts. When Tilly faced her, her lips remained tense but her eyes couldn't contain her merriment.

"Lady Marcum," Tilly said.

Lady Marcum tilted her nose high in the air, walked passed Tilly, and entered a door on the opposite side of the hallway.

Tilly glanced up and down the passage, but could detect no one. She followed Lady Marcum into the women's retiring room.

Arms grasped her immediately, hauling her against a bony chest. "Tilly, Tilly! It's been an age!"

Tilly returned the embrace good-naturedly. "Sarah, my dear. How do you do?"

"Wonderfully!" Sarah exclaimed. She relinquished Tilly.

Tilly took the opportunity to look around the gaudily decorated room. They appeared to be alone, though only recently. A musty perfume permeated the air. "Shall we?" Tilly said, leading her to the sofa. They only had to worry about Lord Marcum's discovering them, really, and the chances of him resting in the ladies' room were non-existent.

"He's never suspected anything?"

"Never," Sarah swore. "The bloomin' idiot!"

Tilly had first met Sarah two years earlier. A previous client had introduced them, which was how Tilly gained most of her cases. She had liked Sarah immediately and quickly agreed to help her sort through her problems—or, more to the point, her problem: her husband, Lord Marcum. Seems he'd caught her in a most compromising position with one of his hunting cronies and had been making her miserable ever since.

Lady Marcum claimed innocence in the affair. She maintained she'd been tricked into being alone with her husband's friend and had frozen under his avowals of desire—which was, of course, precisely when Lord Marcum had walked in.

Had she been at all interested in passing judgment, which she wasn't, Tilly would have believed Sarah. It didn't matter, though. As far as Tilly could tell, marriage made happiness impossible for women, and good wives had a right to find pleasure anywhere they could, no matter how fleeting that pleasure might be. The notion of fidelity seemed decidedly odd, but then, Tilly found the institution of marriage irrational and unreasonable. Of course, the idea of sexual congress was just plain silly. Too bizarre to fathom.

Then again, never having partaken in a love affair, marriage, sex, or even romance, Tilly had very little personal experience from which to judge—thank God.

What she possessed in abundance, however, were second-hand reports, and as far as she could tell, none of the dealings between women and men seemed to lead to anything bearing any resemblance to contentment.

Still, Tilly found the idea of Sarah having an illicit affair quite impossible. For all her height and haughty airs, Sarah was actually quite biddable. Even after all the ways her husband had mistreated her, she had yet to pummel him in the head with a fire poker as he deserved. Tilly had suggested it immediately upon hearing Sarah's story.

Sarah, however, hadn't taken to the notion nearly as fondly as a married woman ought. So they'd devised a second plan—one that involved Sarah finding Tilly in Lord Marcum's wide lap. She'd placed herself there despite his heated protests. Faithfulness really was overly important to him.

"And still he doesn't realize we set him up?" Tilly asked.

Sarah laughed. "Of course not! The silly, arrogant knob! He thinks you're in love with him." Her smile dimmed. "Though I must say, I don't hate him nearly so much as I once did. Don't misunderstand me, there are still moments when I want to do as you bade me and beat him with a blunt object, but all in all, for the most part I just feel a constant distaste of him." She pressed her lips together, her gaze gone distant. "Until I met you, I thought it was my duty to love him because he was my husband, but how could I? I could not even bring myself to like him. Not only did I hate him, but I began to hate myself for not being a decent wife," she sighed, "for not being a decent human being." She smiled shyly, and Tilly remembered the girl she had first met. "Then, I met you, and you taught me it was okay to judge him for his actions and that intolerable guilt disappeared. And you performed a miracle and made him behave. Now I realize he's truly not so bad most of the time—stupid, yes, and still diffident, but all he wanted was my feigned anger and jealously to show him I cared." She looked Tilly in the eye. "How did you know that would do the trick?"

Tilly patted her friend's hand. "While they might be illogical, men are never complex," she said ruefully. "Still, I'm glad I was able to help."

"You did! And now, I must help you." Sarah tapped her thigh. "Do you need any money?"

"Who doesn't?" Tilly sighed. Sarah didn't know where Tilly's wages went though. Tilly couldn't take charity from her. Besides, with Adelaide's generous payment plan, she was easily staying afloat. She'd worry about the future when it arrived. "But truly, no. I'm fine."

Sarah tilted her head. "Well, if you don't need money, you must be on a job."

Tilly shot her a fierce look. Like most tall, bony, haughty women, Sarah loved to gossip. "You know I cannot discuss that."

"Well, I couldn't help but notice you with Lord Astor, gorgeous man that he is, but everyone knows he's not married. He's considered quite the catch. His reputation for incivility at these affairs only seems to whet the mamas' appetites."

Tilly made a noncommittal "Hmmm. . . ." She filed the information away in her head for future reflection.

Sarah's smile nearly exploded. "Aha! This is personal, not business! Isn't it?"

Tilly burst into laughter. She tried to stop her unladylike cackles, but couldn't. It was too far-fetched—her spending time with a man for pleasure's sake. The absurdity of it!

Sarah wouldn't give up. "You mean to acquire him, don't you?"

"Oh, Sarah! Really! He's not a Persian carpet to be purchased!"

Sarah snorted. "Men are purchased by other means. Hmmm. It would be business and pleasure. For what better way to demonstrate your powers of instruction than by marrying the year's most eligible bachelor."

Tilly rolled her eyes. "My work doesn't mean so much to me that I would willingly chain myself to a male for eternity." Tilly used the word male with the same distaste most people reserved for plagues or famines—but they all amounted to the same thing didn't they? Misery. "There are always other career op-tions, my dear—laundress, tavern wench, selling ones' dead body to the quack school."

Sarah shook her head. "Before you drink hemlock, might I remind you of something you once told me? Yes? Well, you once said, being stuck with a husband isn't so bad if you know how to manage him."

"I stand by that, but compare 'not so bad' with the splendors of spinsterhood and you'll understand why I've vowed to remain forever single."

"Yes, I see your point," Sarah agreed, "but do you really want to spend the rest of your life living hand to mouth? Do you want the risks and insecurities of having to support yourself?"

"Over the insecurities of having a husband gamble away everything I own? Yes, give me independence and work and maidenhood! I'll have none of your lovely baubles when my husband could legally strip me of them at any moment. I prefer the simple gold anklet left me by my mother, for at least that will always be mine. Married women, on the other hand—" Tilly cut herself off. Heat rose off her face. Her chest heaved with rapid breaths, and for what? So that she could preach to a nearly empty lady's resting room?

"Yes," Sarah sighed. "The rules do need some changing."

"So they do."

"Of course, if you married a member of the House of Lords—Lord Astor for example—"

Tilly shook her head. "You are incorrigible!" She stood and brushed the wrinkles from her skirts. "I must bid you adieu. Events unfurl, and I want to set their form."

Sarah rose also. "You know where to reach me should you need anything."

"Yes, if I get desperate, you'll receive a note from 'Luciana,' but honestly, for once, I do not seem to be involved in anything dangerous. I don't expect I'll need your gracious assistance."

"The offer always stands," Sarah said. She held Tilly's shoulder for a moment too long, then sighed. "Now, if I can only keep my mouth shut about your upcoming nuptials—"

"Please see that you do," Tilly said sternly. She didn't even want to joke about such a distressing rumor. She couldn't afford that much attention. "Anonymity is vital to my work."

"I know," Sarah breathed.

The women said their goodbyes and Tilly continued her search for Adelaide.

CHAPTER NINE

Mr. Bryant Duggles threw down the five of clubs, reached for another card and studied Jaiden over his hand.

"Saw you step into the ballroom earlier, Astor. Can't say I recognized the goddess on your arm."

Jaiden played his hand slowly, in no hurry to answer the speculative gleam in Duggles's eye. "That would be Mrs. Mathilda Leighton, my sister's dear friend."

"Mrs. Leighton? Here?" Sir Pumbermeyer shot straight up in his chair. These were the first words he'd spoken all evening that didn't pertain to the game. His ruddy complexion had gone stone white.

"Are you all right, man?"

"I . . . I must . . . collect my wife and leave at once," Pumbermeyer stuttered to himself. He threw his cards on the table. "Excuse me, gentlemen. Excuse me." And with that he rushed from the room.

"I'd say he folds," Duggles announced with one raised eyebrow.

"Can't say that I disagree," Jaiden said. What had transpired between Tilly and Pumbermeyer? Tilly would leave an impression on any man, but one that made him fear for the safety of his wife?

Quite the mystery, Mrs. Leighton, and one he could keep himself from no longer.

"I'm afraid I must also be going," he said, dropping his cards and standing.

"What—but, the game!" Duggles exclaimed, gesturing at the pile of coins in the middle of the table—a small fortune for some.

But not for Jaiden. "Congratulations on the win," he said, turning away.

He had a mystery to solve.

CHAPTER TEN

"But, of course, she's terribly sought after," Tilly continued. "How could she not be? Such a lovely, kind, beautiful woman!" Tilly wanted to add intelligent and entertaining, but she thought that might be overdoing it. "I've only agreed to stay at the Astors' because I'm on tenterhooks wondering what lucky man will finally win her!"

Tilly would have thought that she'd gone too far, but the muscle in Sir Daniel's jaw twitched. These challenge-seekers really were the easiest men to manipulate. A total waste of her talents.

Tilly looked out into the dance floor where at least thirty couples moved to the waltz. She easily located Adelaide with her latest partner. Adelaide looked magnificent. Her hair glowed under the chandelier, with the drop of oil Tilly had rubbed through it. And Adelaide's teeth sparkled up at her suitor. Of course, she smiled from joy of having Sir Sheldon's escort, but he wouldn't know that. He would think she beamed up at the tall, blond fellow swinging her in circles.

Tilly regretted not being there when Daniel first laid eyes on Adelaide that evening. She knew he would approve of the changes in Adelaide's appearance—any unrelated male would—that was the purpose of a plunging neckline with well-placed ruffles.

Still, Tilly doubted the dress did nearly as much to win Daniel's heart as the reaction of the other men at the party.

From the looks of it, every eligible bachelor in England had bent over backwards to secure a dance with her.

Tilly praised herself silently on the little she'd done to move this suit along. Why, she wouldn't be surprised if they were engaged by morning. Adelaide didn't need her here, after all.

Tilly excused herself from Daniel, not that he noticed, with his eyes and his frown glued to Adelaide. Without a definite destination, Tilly wandered into a hallway off the ballroom. Oil paintings of old men lined one wall, while the other disappeared in a series of windowed alcoves.

With the sound of couples laughing in the background and strains of music drifting through the air, Tilly couldn't have said exactly what made her steps slow to a halt. All her life this sensation had plagued her. It was the first thing she remembered, this feeling—nay, this knowledge that something was wrong . . . that someone had been wronged.

Every time, the hair on the back of her neck stood on end and her whole body tensed as if ready to flee. As a child, she had run in the face of the knowledge—the knowledge that nearby was a woman in pain.

Closing her eyes, Tilly strained to block out the noise of the music and conversations and concentrate entirely on her curse. She took a step forward and felt the awareness increase.

She opened her eyes and slowly walked toward the darkness of the last alcove. It wasn't until she was two yards away that she finally made out the huddled shape of a woman bearing more than any god had the right to demand of her.

The woman's legs curled on the window seat in front of her. Her arms clung to them, pulling them protectively toward her torso as if in that way she could keep herself safe, as if she could make herself so small she might disappear. Yet, despite the near-fetal position, the woman's head leaned back on her hunched shoulders. She stared without expression into the darkness beyond.

The moonlight lit her face while casting the rest of her in shadow, or maybe that was the way the woman wanted it. Maybe she needed to forget her body and all the abuse it suffered and think only of the garden outside the window.

The garden that led to a street.

A street that tied into a city.

A city with ships leading anywhere in the world.

A world where she could discover escape.

If only she had the courage to step into the garden.

"Tilly," the woman sighed, not turning to face her.

"Nora," Tilly whispered, sitting on the window seat beside her. Tilly wasn't the only one who'd developed a sixth sense. Years of listening with impending dread for the sound of a man's footsteps had honed all sorts of talents in Nora—how to take a beating without fighting back, how to hide the marks afterwards, how to bury herself so deep she got lost.

"So, here I am," Nora announced through tense lips. "Still lacking the courage to run." She turned her face to Tilly's. "The weakest woman in all of Christendom."

"You're not weak, Nora. You have survived things no man in England could survive. That is how strong you are. And you sit here, now, alive—that alone takes away anyone's right to judge you. Especially mine." Tilly's heart broke in frustration. She hated this! Hated it. These were the only moments in her life when she would give anything to be able to manipulate people, to be able to persuade a woman to walk out of a bad, unfair situation, and she couldn't do it. She didn't know how. The right words got drowned in her desperation. It was so easy when she didn't care, but now . . .

In Tilly's experience, a woman who left an abusive husband either had spirit still alive within her or she had discovered the freedom of having no pride at all. It had little to do with Tilly. And yet, Tilly could not accept her own helplessness.

She wanted to drag these victims away from danger. She wanted to bully them until they could regain some semblance of self-respect. But it was impossible. No matter what Tilly wanted, these women had heard too many threats, seen too much violence, had their wills overpowered too many times for Tilly to subject them to any more abuse.

Nora shook her head. "I'm not alive. I'm a shell."

"The shell's the important part, Nora. It protects the rest. Everything you've ever been, it's still there, waiting for you to rediscover it."

"I hope so," Nora whispered.

"I know it," Tilly promised.

"I wish . . . I wish I were as brave as you."

"You are a million times braver than I." Tilly clasped Nora's hand with hers. "I'm asking you to do something I've never done. It's difficult. I'm sure I don't even know the half of how difficult it is. But it's not impossible. That I do know. In the end, you put one foot in front of the other and walk out of his home and everything you know—the good along with the bad. But I swear to you, that's the only part you'll have to do on your own. I'll help you the rest of the way."

Nora nodded, but it was a nod with no conviction behind it. "He hits me, and I swear I'll leave." She shook her head. "Then he says he needs me, and I'm trapped."

"It doesn't matter if he needs you. You don't need him."

"I might." Nora's lower lip trembled.

"Come," Tilly commanded, pushing an arm behind Nora's shaking shoulders to help her stand.

Nora stumbled repeatedly as Tilly dragged her to a door down the hallway. Opening it, she pulled Nora outside and around the corner of the house where no one would see them.

The night was cold enough to keep even the most ardent of young lovers inside the warm mansion.

"I'm sorry," Nora said, shaking. "I never cry," she announced as tears overflowed her eyes and streamed onto her cheeks. "What's the point?" she asked, bending her face as sobs wracked her.

Tilly wrapped her arms around Nora's shaking form, trying to give her comfort as well as warmth. She held Nora's fragile body as tightly as she could.

"The point is to make you feel better, and how you feel is the only thing that matters," she murmured, though Nora couldn't hear her over the sounds of her own agony.

Tilly rubbed Nora's back and shoulders. She knew this drill well: comforting a woman's soul after a man had battered her body. She'd done it all her life.

Compared to this pain and danger, everything else was a joke. What was meddling in a marriage or two? Or misleading a man about the whereabouts of his family heirlooms? They were nothing compared to the danger and pain that had become Nora's life.

Oh, certainly, Tilly provided battered wives with a place to go, a safe haven from men and their cruelty, but so few could bring themselves to take advantage of it. And the rest? There was nothing she could do for them.

Even now, she'd only made Nora's life worse. Nora hadn't exactly been dancing for joy when Tilly'd come across her, but at least she hadn't been sobbing as if she'd never stop. She had Tilly to blame for that.

Maybe if Tilly brought her to Muirfield? If she let her see the beauty and peace of the place? If she introduced her to the women there who'd survived escape?

But Tilly had never taken anyone there who wasn't committed to starting a new life. Her first priority was keeping those women safe, and that meant keeping their whereabouts secret.

The entire mess was giving her a headache.

Tilly remembered the first time she'd comforted Nora. It was the first time they met. Tilly had been helping a friend of hers, a sawbones named Noah Gomes. He had trained her in midwifery so that she could help deliver Kyla. In return, Tilly organized the madhouse clinic until he finally found full-time help.

Nora had come in at the end of a long day. Tilly's head jerked up as though a gun had sounded in the room. Nora's misery throbbed through the entire suite. She knew instantly who was responsible for the pain—despite Nora's story of falling down the stairs.

Dr. Gomes, however, believed Nora's lie. The good doctor did not understand the cruelty of his own gender, or the lengths women would go to deny it, even to themselves.

After Nora's arm was set, Tilly coerced her into taking tea in the hotel around the corner. After much prodding, Nora told her the story of her horrid marriage.

Tilly's stomach still had knots from that conversation.

After forty minutes, Tilly made an offer to help Nora leave her husband. She prayed Nora would agree instantly— sometimes they did—but not Nora. She still held out hope her husband might change. Tilly had hoped Nora was right, but she had not believed it possible. Once a man got into the habit of beating his wife, it took a miracle to get him to stop.

Now, as Tilly rubbed Nora's shaking limbs, she knew she'd been right. Nora's husband wasn't going to stop hitting her, not unless Nora took the chance away.

"Leave with me," Tilly pleaded desperately. "Right now, before it's too late, before he murders you or you have children to consider. Let's go tonight, this minute. I'll be there every step of the way, and you needn't ever come back here."

Nora stepped away, shaking her head. "I can't. Thank you,

but—no. Not yet."

Tears welled in Tilly's eyes, too, now. "Not yet," she repeated, "but some time. Please promise me some time soon."

Nora nodded. "I'll think about it."

Tilly swallowed. She'd have to be content with that.

Nora managed a smile though tears caught at the corners of her lips. "Shall we rejoin the party?"

Tilly shook her head. "You go. I'm going to stay here a few moments."

Nora nodded, then pressed her cheek against Tilly's. Their tears mingled and spread across Tilly's skin. Nora left without looking at Tilly again.

Tilly wiped at the moisture drying stickily on her face and then, pressing her palms against her eyes, took two long, deep breaths. Finally, she felt able to fake a smile.

Tilly turned to go back into the house but stopped short. She found herself gazing into deep blue eyes with double rows of black lashes.

CHAPTER ELEVEN

Jaiden caught a flash of coral through a window and knew Tilly had just escaped outside. He also realized she'd most likely not gone alone.

Evidence of her trysts shouldn't concern him. He forced himself to stare at badly painted family poses for all of ten minutes before stalking outside. Her love affairs might not be any of his business, but ten minutes! Damn, he was making this one his concern.

He had prepared to find her in the midst of an embrace.

But not with another woman.

He shouldn't have cared . . . but he did.

He should have been relieved.

But he wasn't.

The way the two women clung together revealed a depth of heartache that belied Tilly's usual carefree manner. Jaiden's chest tightened. He wanted Tilly's life to be as perfect and happy as she pretended it was.

And yet, as always, her deepening mystery enchanted him. He would solve her. He would know the source of her pain.

And he would destroy that source.

Then, Tilly's friend returned to the house, too preoccupied to notice him standing next to a tall oak in the shadows of the garden.

He knew he should retreat or make his presence known, but the two women looked as if their privacy meant their very lives.

The door closed behind the unknown woman, and Jaiden took a step toward Tilly. The better view of her made him freeze once more.

She buried her face in her hands. Her entire body shook with her gasps.

A crying female. Jaiden froze. Memories of his mother and her episodes came to him, and he recalled his father's puffed chest as he comforted her.

These were not his mother's tears. They were not put on for display, for another's benefit. Tilly cried from the soul. She wouldn't want anyone to witness her behaving this way. He should leave.

He couldn't.

Tilly deserved to have someone take away her pain. He wanted to be the man who helped her.

Tilly looked up then. Her eyes widened in surprise; then, suddenly, they narrowed.

The hate caught him by surprise.

"It's cold," she announced. She lifted her chin and tried to pass him.

Jaiden caught her elbow.

Tilly tore her arm from his grasp and spun on him. "Don't touch me!" she hissed. "Don't ever touch me."

Jaiden's mouth went dry. He had not caused her pain, and he'd be damned if he'd let her push him away because of it. "Tilly," he appealed, using her Christian name for the first time. He held out his arms in appeal, to show he was unarmed. "Have I done something to offend you?"

"Yes!" she spat, then shook her head. "No, not you. I don't know." She scratched her forehead and closed her eyes. "I'm weary of this . . . this impotence and frustration!" She laughed, a desperate, bitter sound, a cry he never expected to hear from her.

"You've no idea what I'm speaking of, do you?" she continued. "You've probably never experienced a moment of doubt in your entire existence, have you?"

His parents' love affair—the inability of one to live without the other. He would never experience that need, and thus, could never experience complete satisfaction, but Tilly was right. He hadn't doubted he would never find love. He'd known it. Always.

Until he met her, and then for the first time, he had doubts.

The doubt kindled a hope he'd forever lived without. The hope, the uncertainty, made the game worth playing. His entire body exalted when she was near. Only she could make the restless indifference retreat. It might not last forever—probably wouldn't—but for now, at least, he wallowed in it, this . . . this . . .

Infatuation.

"Yes, I've had doubts," he said simply.

The hatred vanished from her face, replaced by guilt, then even that disappeared as an all-consuming dejection overtook her. She hung her head. Her shoulders slumped in defeat. "I just wish I knew what to do," she whispered.

Jaiden folded her in his arms. She stiffened, then relaxed. Holding her felt like home.

Tilly hid her face against his chest and clasped an arm around his waist. Her breasts pressed against the bottom of his rib cage. Her skirts barely separated her thighs from his.

How many women had he held, and still he had never felt anything like this. He understood flesh and bone, but couldn't understand why his every fiber vibrated around her. Could one of his engineers discover the chemistry that caused it? Could they bottle it, and make another fortune?

Jaiden didn't think so. For he finally realized what it was he felt. It was interest, and that was something that couldn't be purchased. He knew. He'd tried.

He tightened his hold. Tilly looked up at him, the despair gone but her usual capriciousness absent as well. "I'm all right, my lord," she said, staring into his eyes. "Thank you," she finished simply.

Jaiden lifted his hand to her face and brushed his thumb against her voluptuous lips to make sure they'd ceased their trembling.

She went utterly still.

And what if he lowered his face and replaced his fingers with his mouth? Would she allow that, too?

Her eyes drifted shut. Once again she'd read his mind, and she acquiesced.

His gaze fixed on her lips. He brought his mouth to hers until he could feel her slow breath against his face.

Then suddenly, she was gone.

He found her four steps away, patting her coiffure and straightening her skirts. "I understand you're to be congratulated, my lord," she breathed.

Not at the bloody moment, apparently.

Her eyebrows rose at him. "Your forthcoming nuptials?" she reminded him. "To Miss Clara Haversham? Congratulations."

"Er . . ." Jaiden tilted his head, for once at a loss for words. How had she come to believe he was engaged to Clara? The engagement was far from formalized. It was barely even a possibility. Lord Haversham had made the suggestion, true. The alliance would solidify the men's partnership, but as Jaiden had pointed out, he could hardly wed a child who burst into tears every time she met him.

It probably didn't bode well for the arrangement that Jaiden had no desire to calm her fears. Not even so much as a decent person would have toward a frightened child. Instead, he took a perverse delight in her aversion. It made it all the easier to point out the impossibility of the match to Lord Haversham.

Jaiden supposed he could have been more forceful and simply tell Lord Haversham no, but truly, at the time there seemed little risk of the girl being brought around. There were business reasons for the union. He hadn't entirely hated the possibility.

Until now, when Tilly spoke of it.

What must Tilly think of him? She apparently believed the engagement final. She must think he happily kissed one girl while engaged to another.

He should set her straight at once and get back to the kissing.

Ah, but maybe it was best this way. If she thought him already promised, then she would not get too attached. Remembering Bev's recent display, maybe this was better. No matter how this infatuation currently entertained him, it most likely wouldn't last much longer. Unfortunately.

People just never held his interest for long. Mysteries, puzzles, projects—those kept him fascinated, but not people. Once he solved Tilly's mystery, he'd barely be able to tolerate her presence, just as he despised all the other frivolous acquaintances he'd made over the years. Co-workers were different. They strove with him toward a common goal, rather like his friendship with Daniel.

Tilly would never fall into that category. She clearly hadn't worked a day in her life. He bore her no ill will for it, but it didn't change the fact that he would tire of her. For that reason, it was best he let the misunderstanding stand.

She betrayed no disgust though when she finally met his gaze. "I do wonder, my lord, why you did not see fit to escort Miss Haversham here tonight?"

"Miss Haversham visits cousins in the country at the moment. She won't return for another few days," Jaiden spoke.

"Of course," Tilly said, but Jaiden couldn't help but feel she really wanted to taunt him with a plethora of clichés like "out of sight, out of mind" and "men will be men."

He would have expected to feel a perverse pleasure in misleading her, but he didn't.

"Yes, well, it has turned chilly out here. Shall we rejoin the party?" She didn't wait for a reply but marched toward the house.

Jaiden reached the door barely in time to open it for her, earning a smile as she entered.

"Thank you," she called, not bothering to look at him.

He could not let her go just yet. He had learned his lesson a few moments before though. He would not grab her hand. Instead, he strode in front of her, effectively blocking her path.

Tilly halted, her gaze shot to his face, her eyebrows knitted. Her mouth readied to frown.

Airy strains of music filled the wide hall, incongruous with the stiff, unhappy faces along the wall.

"Dance with me," Jaiden spoke.

Her face registered surprise. Jaiden nearly winced. He should have asked, not demanded. A bow would have been appropriate, and yet his words had been a demand. He meant to leave her no choice.

"What? Here?" She waved an arm to the empty, half-dark corridor.

The *here* mattered not; it was the *now* he needed. "Why not?"

She looked at him as if he'd gone mad. "But you hate to dance," she informed him.

Again, where did she get these ideas? It was true that dancing often was just another waste of time, but it wouldn't be with her. He gestured at the portraits along the wall. "Surely, you wouldn't begrudge these stuffy dead ancestors the only amusement they've had since oppressing their serfs."

He reached for her waist, but she eluded him. He wasn't the only one who needed explanations, apparently. "Whatever gave you the impression I don't care for dancing?" he asked.

Her brows lowered further. "I cannot believe you set out to terrify chits straight out of the classroom because you are malicious. I had hoped you scowled at any ninny stupid enough to angle for a dance with you solely because you disliked the waltz."

"*Au contraire,* my dear, at this moment, the waltz is my best friend." He bowed low to her.

When he straightened, he saw the smile tug at the corners of her mouth. She sighed, shook her head, and then dipped into a curtsy.

Jaiden took her hand in his and placed his other at her waist. They began to step with the music. Within moments he caught the rhythm, and for the first time in his life, he understood the reason for all the fuss about dancing.

CHAPTER TWELVE

She did not like men. She didn't.

Her reminders to herself did no good. Jaiden helped her down from the carriage, looking all big and strong and appealing again.

Tilly blamed the waltz for this unhappy turn of events. He had stumbled his way into her affection. That first minute, before he let himself go, he had bumped against her and stepped on her slipper. Seeing his vulnerability, she'd taken the lead for a half a minute. How lovely it was to meet a man who could admit to possessing imperfections. Then the melody took him. She knew the instant it happened. He stole back the lead, and neither of them bothered to stop when the music ended. Instead, they started right in as the next tune began.

As his confidence grew, he swung her wider and wider until her feet had no choice but to follow his directions. The air whipped through her hair. Tilly closed her eyes and enjoyed the sensations.

Of music.

Of flying.

Of him.

And then he'd laughed. All Tilly's caution with his gender vanished at the delightful sound—throaty and deep. She wanted him to laugh like that again and again.

So, on the carriage ride home, she told him every joke she knew. He told her several, too—some distinctly inappropriate for mixed company. They had her in stitches, even more so when she guessed Jaiden must be blushing as he said them.

No wonder society insisted upon chaperones. A blushing male telling scandalous jokes was too tempting by half.

He was just another case, she told herself once again, but she couldn't believe it. Jaiden's warm hand on her hip as they walked up the front stairs interrupted her thoughts . . . until they came bounding back with a vengeance.

Her case, for the love of God! His sister had hired her to soften him for *his future wife!*

Why did she keep forgetting this essential fact? She'd only remembered at the last second when he had almost kissed her. A second too late, as she'd just realized how much she wanted that kiss.

She couldn't start liking him. Already she was beginning to resent this Little Miss Haversham and her inability to see that Jaiden was worth a thousand other men. Why, he would try to please his wife! That alone made him better than the rest of his ignoble sex.

What would happen if a tailor ran off with a pair of trousers?

It was the same with Tilly. She couldn't kiss Jaiden, no matter how appealing the prospect. She had been hired to alter him for another woman, and by God, that's what she would do. All she would do.

Never mind that he needed no altering. He already fit perfectly.

But not well enough for little Miss Clara Persnickety Skirts.

Tilly had let down her guard some time while dancing with Jaiden, and damned if she could find it again.

"Stupid waltz," she muttered.

"Pardon?" Jaiden asked, glancing down at her.

"Nothing."

She'd learned one thing positive at least. Tilly had realized how to proceed with Jaiden. Most likely, he frightened Little Miss Persnickety Skirts for two reasons. First, his appearance could give anyone a fright. He towered over most civilized beings—and his eyes! Though Tilly had begun to enjoy them, they were far too striking to reassure an innocent lass.

Well, Tilly couldn't do anything about his size or his chiseled features, but she could correct what she predicted to be his other failing in Miss Persnickety's eyes.

It was quite simple, really. Jaiden had never learned the art of doing nothing. This was a true flaw, since the gentry did little else.

All his adult life, Jaiden had a sister and an aunt to provide for and a hundred different business ventures to maintain. It made perfect sense that he had never learned to dance properly or wax poetic about a summer night's chill.

Such usefulness would no doubt intimidate a sheltered, unimaginative chit like Miss Particular Skirts, but the girl needn't worry any longer. If there was one thing Tilly was handy with, it was social polish. All she need do was culture Jaiden a bit—take him to a few plays and museums—that sort of thing.

Adelaide could undertake the endeavor. Tilly would miss the fifty pounds a week, but perhaps it was time to put some distance between herself and this altogether too endearing pupil. Yes, it was time to say goodbye to the Astors. Surely that was the best plan.

The butler opened the door before Jaiden could pull the cord.

"Go to bed, Ross. I'll wait up for Adelaide and Daniel," Jaiden directed.

"Very good, my lord." The man bowed, then turned to Tilly. "This arrived while you were out," he said, holding out a tray with an envelope on it.

"Thank you, Ross." Tilly took the envelope and saw her name

scrawled on the outside. Only a few people knew she was staying with the Astors, and none of them would write unless it was
an emergency.

As always when disaster seemed imminent, Tilly's mind
cleared to a startling focus even as her heart lodged in her
throat. She turned to Jaiden. "Lord Astor, would you mind terribly excusing me while I read this."

"Not at all," he said. "Let me take your cloak, and then I'll
light the parlor for your use."

"Thank you," she murmured. She let him take the cloak from
her shoulders. For once, the brush of his fingertips against her
neck didn't distract her from her thoughts.

He hung her cloak in the front hall closet. "You're not expecting bad tidings I hope," he commented, then his voice grew
more serious. "Tilly, you look pale. Can I get you something to
drink? Brandy, perhaps?"

"No, nothing, thank you." What could have happened?
"Nothing yet, at least."

He turned on several lamps. Tilly immediately sat on a chair
next to one and ripped open the envelope as Jaiden lit a fire in
the fireplace.

With shaking hands, Tilly took out the sheaf of paper. *Please
don't be from Muirfield,* she prayed, though logically she knew it
couldn't be. It hadn't been posted, merely hand-delivered.
Whoever had sent it, sent it from London.

She read the note twice before comprehending its meaning:

*KEEP YOUR DISTANCE FROM MY WIFE OR SUFFER
THE CONSEQUENCES.*

It was a threat! No sooner had the surprise filtered through her
mind than she burst into laughter. Everyone at Muirfield was
safe then. Relief nearly floored her. Her heart slowed to normal.

Jaiden raised an eyebrow.

She shook her head. "Merely a joke," she said, but she must have appeared a sight. Jaiden's brow furrowed. Before she realized what he was about, he plucked the letter from her hands.

Yes, the rude beast needed all the social polish she could give.

Jaiden read the note, his feet separating in a defensive stance. He flipped the paper over, studied its backside, then returned it to her. "And which of your friends possesses such a deplorable sense of humor might I ask?"

Folding the paper absently, Tilly admitted, "Well, I don't know who sent it precisely, but that's what makes it so humorous."

"How?"

She sighed. He did not see the humor. "Well, you see, he didn't sign the note, nor did he refer to his wife by name so I haven't the faintest notion to whom this man refers. If it were a threat not to walk across the West End Bridge, well, that would be different. I know the West End Bridge, but just 'a' wife? What silliness! Do you have any idea the number of wives with whom I'm associated?" Usually, Tilly would know exactly to whom such a note referred. Typically she only plotted with one wife at a time. Jaiden, her current unknowing pupil, was the exception, however, for he hadn't a wife yet, nor had she so much as met Little Miss Particular. "Now, how can I take a threat seriously from a man who's too cowardly to name himself or even the person from whom I'm supposed to stay away. He won't even commit to specific consequences!" She broke into giggles. "Really, it's too much."

Jaiden's gravity seemed all the more extreme compared to her amusement. He picked up the envelope, which had borne the letter and studied it. "Do you often receive threats from unknown quantities?"

"Of course not," she said honestly. Most threats came from men she knew all too well. The thought sent her back into hysterics. She wiped her tearing eyes with a handkerchief, attempting to stem her mirth.

"Mrs. Leighton," Jaiden said, standing over her. "I fear you're suffering from shock. You must go to bed at once."

Tilly took in his grim features. If she protested, no doubt he would escort her forcefully to her bed.

Realizing she enjoyed the prospect too much, Tilly nodded her assent. "Very well, my lord," she said rising. She tried to match his seriousness but didn't think she had much success. "Good night."

"Good night, Mrs. Leighton."

Tilly left the room slowly, wondering if perhaps she wanted to protest after all. Or maybe she could pretend fear? Make him stay with her all night to keep her "safe."

She smiled naughtily, knowing she'd never act so irrationally. She didn't like men, after all.

If only she could convince herself she didn't like this one.

CHAPTER THIRTEEN

Two hours later, Jaiden fingered Tilly's letter. Unfortunately, he could surmise no more now than he had originally.

Maybe in proper light some clue would reveal itself. He could see little in the dim light of the moon that streamed through the bedroom window at an angle, though it illuminated Tilly's sleeping form happily enough.

A murmur escaped her lush mouth. She twisted onto her side, turning her face into her fist. Her lashes twitched against her cheek.

Jaiden pushed the hair out of her face. He marveled at the softness of her skin. His fingertips lingered at her forehead.

Tilly let out a sigh. She turned into his touch.

She must have been the heaviest sleeper he'd ever encountered. She made a racket in her sleep and never woke herself once. She trusted too easily, allowed herself to be vulnerable. She didn't know all the dangers in London just waiting to pounce on her innocence.

Jaiden slid into the chair beside her bed. He couldn't take his eyes from her. Every line of her face mesmerized him—infatuated him. He could watch her for hours and never be satisfied.

Of course, he might have to watch her for days. This threat was real, and she was hiding something from him—threatening letters, breaking into his study, crying in the shrubbery with the aristocracy. How could he protect her when she wouldn't explain the danger she was in?

Protect her he would, however. Nothing, no one, would hurt her.

It wasn't generosity, but self-preservation. He couldn't stand to see her wounded. So he'd make certain she wasn't.

Jaiden leaned back in the chair and relaxed his head against the leather. A precious peace washed over his soul as he watched Tilly's chest rise and fall.

Yes, he would make certain nothing happened to her.

CHAPTER FOURTEEN

Jaiden started awake. His body jerked upright. His eyes flew open. Sunlight stung them.

Squinting, he peered at Tilly in the bed. Her eyes were still closed. Thank God.

He raked a hand through his hair and glanced at the bedside clock. Ten o'clock? That couldn't be right, but the brightness of the room did support the clock.

He must have slept for over six hours. Even the crick in his neck couldn't detract from his feeling of being well rested. He felt good, better than he had in months.

Jaiden stretched, throwing a grateful glance at Tilly, at the room, at the world. Maybe exhaustion had just caught up with him.

He had to get out of there. What could he possibly say if Tilly woke up to find him in her room, wearing the same clothes he'd worn the previous evening. Good thing his staff was used to his odd prowling. They were relatively discreet. Still, best not to bump into anyone on his way out—not looking so disheveled.

CHAPTER FIFTEEN

The door closed, and Tilly's eyes shot open. She'd thought he'd never wake up, and she was beginning to get desperate to visit the water closet.

She jumped out of bed, grabbed her robe, and headed down the hall.

When he'd entered her room the night before, Tilly had believed he merely wanted to peek at her note. She didn't object, and it seemed easier to pretend she was asleep.

But then he didn't leave. Instead, he touched her forehead, and she didn't want him to stop. Once he sat down, she gladly wallowed in his presence, and then sleep had come over her. In her whole life she'd never slept in a room with someone else. She'd never thought she could, but it had felt nice having Jaiden nearby while she slept.

Hell, it felt good having him near when she was awake, too.

Too good.

She had to get away from this Astor household.

CHAPTER SIXTEEN

"But you can't leave yet!" Adelaide wailed, not bothering to employ an ounce of discretion, despite Aunt Henrietta's dozing in an armchair near the parlor window. "You only just got here!"

"Two weeks ago," Tilly reminded her, "and truly, you don't need my services anymore. All your brother lacks is a little culture—plays, museums, books with absolutely no use, you know the sort of thing upon which Miss Persnickety—er, Miss Clara could discourse with him."

Adelaide shook her head violently. Tilly feared for her stylish new coiffure. "Who's going to trick him into reading impractical books and attending *plays?*"

"Why, you will, dear. It can't be that difficult for you—"

"It's not difficult *for you!*" Adelaide accused, swinging her hands dramatically. "It's nigh impossible for me!"

"Now, dear, don't upset yourself. No man's worth that."

Adelaide fell on her knees before Tilly's chair and grabbed her hands. "Please?" she beseeched. "Please stay."

Tilly hadn't the faintest notion Adelaide would take this so hard. After all, the girl could easily handle the problem on her own, and it wasn't as if Tilly's expertise came cheap.

"You've been here such a short time, and already Jaiden is quite changed. He's almost unrecognizable," Adelaide praised.

"He is not!" Tilly bellowed. Immediately, she lifted her hand to cover her mouth, gasping at her own outburst. Luckily, Aunt Henrietta still napped soundly.

Tilly's eyes grew wide as the realization dawned on her. She didn't want Jaiden to change. She liked him just as he was. And certainly, *she* didn't want credit for any alteration. Especially not for one that led him into Miss Persnickety's arms.

Tilly squeezed her eyes shut, knowing where her terrible train of thought had led. Jealousy! She was jealous, but how could that be when she would never allow herself to become involved with a man? Never.

God, she had to get out of this house and as far away from this man who made her forget her lifelong principles as she could get.

Men were not to be trusted.

"He is changed," Adelaide rudely insisted. "He comes home every evening now and stays for breakfast the following morning," she said, gazing at Tilly in awe, as though she thought her a miracle worker. "And just this morning, he said he wanted to escort the two of us to the Hopkins' ball! My brother hates balls!"

Really? Another ball? Hmm . . . another chance to twirl in Jaiden's arms and—

Tilly shook her head. "In that case, perhaps Jaiden has already changed enough to please his intended—"

"No!" Adelaide hollered. She jumped to her feet. "You must stay," she demanded. She paced the room. "You've done so much already. Just think of what you could accomplish in two more weeks."

Tilly sighed. Most likely, she would end up kissing Jaiden, and that would gratify neither Adelaide nor Little Miss Can't-Be-Pleased-By-Anything-Or-Anyone.

"And what about Daniel?" Adelaide demanded, turning on Tilly. "You promised to help! Are you going to break your word now, after shoving me in his direction?"

Where had the shy girl of two days ago gone? "Adelaide,"

Tilly said calmly, hoping to reestablish some reason into the conversation. "You're handling Daniel beautifully on your own—"

"I am not!"

"You are," Tilly insisted. "I'd be surprised if you aren't being fitted for a wedding dress by the end of the month."

Adelaide's lip trembled. She lowered herself onto the large chair next to Tilly, practically sitting in her lap. She tugged on a tendril of Tilly's hair and gazed beseechingly into her eyes. "Please, Tilly, I'll give you any amount of money you like."

"Oh, Adelaide, you're already paying me too much!"

"It's worth it to me!" Adelaide swore. "Just two more weeks. Please promise two more weeks."

Tilly sighed. Surely she could manage to keep her hands off Jaiden for two weeks, although she didn't know how. She watched Adelaide's large eyes, so like Jaiden's. "All right," she agreed. "Two more weeks."

"Oh, thank you! Thank you!"

Tilly feared Adelaide might try to kiss her, she seemed that grateful. Instead, the taller woman jumped to her feet. "Perfect!" she exclaimed. "Now, I must fix my appearance before I go make some social calls. Are you sure you won't accompany me?"

Feeling suspiciously manipulated by Adelaide's quick mood changes, Tilly shook her head. "No, thank you. I've some correspondence to catch up on," she lied.

"Good day, then, Tilly."

"Yes, good day," Tilly agreed.

Adelaide left the room, but Tilly didn't have a moment to let out her pent-up breath. As soon as the door closed, Aunt Henrietta bounded out of her chair.

"Thank God!" she exclaimed. "I thought that girl would never leave!"

CHAPTER SEVENTEEN

Tilly turned surprised eyes on Aunt Henrietta. "Pardon?"

"Adelaide. My God, the way that child carries on," Aunt Henrietta continued. "Worried about this, concerned about that—especially about Jaiden—ever since her parents died. You've no idea how much she's altered from the precocious child who amused me no end, even if you couldn't trust her if your life depended on it. She'd tell you the ocean was pink even as you admired its blue. Still, I do miss the excitement."

"Yes, well, the death of one's parents is never easy," Tilly commented.

"Absolutely, but it's been nearly a decade. Surely it's time she reverted to her old ways." She wagged a finger. "Trust me. Back then she wouldn't have needed your help catching Daniel's eye."

"Yes, I'm certain you're right. However, I'm not sure Adelaide needs my help now," Tilly said. "I'm more of a confidante, really."

Aunt Henrietta snorted. "Adelaide doesn't need a confidante."

Everyone needed a confidante. Aunt Henrietta certainly had hers. "Why aren't you visiting Mrs. Beesley and Lady Wexham today? Usually, you three are wreaking havoc well before tea-time."

The reference to her friends didn't produce its usual happy effect on Aunt Henrietta. Indeed, the older woman scowled.

"I've had a bit of a falling-out with the two of them."

"Oh dear! How unlike you."

"Yes," she grumbled. "Isn't it?"

"Is there anything I can do?"

Aunt Henrietta's sulk disappeared, replaced by a look of contrition. She worried her hands, avoided Tilly's gaze, and pressed the toe of her shoe into the floor as a naughty four-year-old might. "Well . . . er . . . there is *something.*"

"Yes," Tilly prompted.

Suddenly, Aunt Henrietta grasped Tilly's hands and looked at her fervently. A chaos of words flew from her mouth. "They've become lovers. Edna and Polly! Can you believe it? We've been the closest of friends for a thousand years. We came out together the very same season. I'm godmother to both their children, and now, after all these years, they go and become romantically involved, of all things! With no regard to my feelings or how I'll occupy myself while they exchange love words. I'm completely left out. How could they?"

"I can see how that would be quite—"

Aunt Henrietta threw herself into the space between Tilly and the arm of the chair. Did no one in this family recognize that it was a seat for one?

"You must let me kiss you," Aunt Henrietta demanded.

"Excuse me?" Tilly asked, though she feared she'd heard correctly.

"Yes, I must see if I can tolerate heated embraces with women, too. If I can kiss you without betraying my revulsion, then I can join my friends in their new hobby." She leaned within inches of Tilly's face.

Tilly bent away as far as she could, trying to keep her face from wrinkling in disgust. "Lady Durth, I can't kiss you—"

"You can. You must! Who else can I ask? Adelaide?" She scoffed. "That's ludicrous. And repulsive!"

"Why not Mrs. Beesley or Lady Wexham?"

Aunt Henrietta snorted. "They've already been at it for a day. I need practice before I can convince them to accept me on their level!"

"But Lady Durth!" Tilly exclaimed. She tried to stand, but Aunt Henrietta sat on her skirt, jerking her back.

"Just one kiss!" Aunt Henrietta swore, clambering on top of Tilly. "It won't hurt."

Tilly raised a hand to ward her off, only to hear the rip of a seam.

Tilly tumbled to the floor. Aunt Henrietta landed on top of her. The elderly woman took full advantage of the position. She pushed each of her hands against the sides of Tilly's face and kissed her full on the mouth.

Tilly blinked in shock. Lady Durth stuck to her lips, though really, Tilly supposed she should call the woman Aunt Hen now. They had passed the stage of formalities.

A door opened. Out of the corner of her eye, Tilly caught sight of jet-black hair, too dark to belong to anyone but Jaiden.

About time he came and pried his great aunt off her.

But the head of hair didn't move. Unfortunately, that meant the rest of him must have remained equally immobile.

Finally, pulling her hands free, Tilly pushed at the woman's shoulder. The strength in Hen's skinny arms amazed Tilly. Aunt Hen lifted her head at last. She had the nerve to frown down at Tilly. "I guess I could get used to that," she muttered.

Aunt Hen's hands relinquished their hold on Tilly's face, allowing Tilly to turn her head and see below Jaiden's hair.

CHAPTER EIGHTEEN

He appeared more shocked by the unsuitable display than she felt. Not a muscle of his body moved, not even his slightly open mouth, but his eyes traced the two women's entangled bodies again and again, as if trying to make sense of the scene.

Aunt Hen followed Tilly's gaze. "Jaiden! Bloody hell!" She scrambled off Tilly as fast as she could.

To say "It's not what it looks like" was too cliché even for Tilly, especially since it had been exactly what it looked like. She could launch into how the two of them had awkwardly fallen on top of each other, but she knew Jaiden had witnessed too much to believe that.

Had the sight of them turned him into a bloody statue? He had yet to move, to even breathe.

Not one to let such confusion go to waste, Aunt Hen's eyes narrowed. "Don't you bloody knock?"

The accusation woke Jaiden from his stupor. "In my own drawing room?" he asked, incredulous.

"Your drawing room?" Aunt Hen spit back. "Are you certain? I could have sworn you moved out sometime in the last two years."

Having caught her breath, Tilly sat up. No broken bones at least.

Jaiden's face relaxed. His voice came out deceptively soft. "Aunt Hen, would you be so kind as to excuse Mrs. Leighton and myself. I've a matter I'm most anxious to discuss with her."

Aunt Hen crossed her arms. "Perhaps you'd be so kind as to excuse yourself, young man, as I've a matter, myself, I'm most anxious to finish with her."

Great-aunt and nephew glared at each other. Tilly watched from the floor where she sat. She didn't want to stand and risk getting caught in the crossfire.

"Fine," Aunt Hen exclaimed. She threw her hands in the air. "We'll finish what we were doing later."

Tilly sincerely hoped not.

In a huff, Aunt Hen slammed the door behind her, leaving Tilly no one to look at except Jaiden.

When one has no idea what a man is thinking, one should watch him expectantly—raised eyebrows, serene countenance, blinking at regular intervals—until he spoke his mind.

Jaiden's eyes narrowed.

Tilly stood. She would need that added advantage. All for his benefit, she clasped her hands in front of her and waited for him to speak. Curiosity ate her usual patience.

Jaiden's face went red at the sight of her feigned calm . . . or maybe because of his earlier view. He plopped one hand on his hip and with the other pointed to the floor where Aunt Hen had so recently tackled her. "You and my aunt?" he demanded.

Tilting her head to the side, Tilly studied him. Did he think he had asked a complete question?

He let his hands drop. "How long has this been going on?"

He thought his aunt kissed her on a regular basis!

Tilly threw her head back and laughed heartily.

Coupling ever monopolized the male mind. They saw it everywhere. When in doubt about what a man thought at any given moment, coupling was most likely the answer.

Not that Aunt Hen pressing her mouth to Tilly's on the floor would seem innocent to many.

"And may I ask what is so funny?"

She shook her head, laughing still. "Aunt Hen and I . . ." She giggled. He thought she was one of those women who preferred the company of other women to that of men. And so she did, just not . . . that way.

"Yes?"

"Oh, Lord Astor! It's been going on . . ." *ten minutes,* but Tilly didn't say that. Her laughter slowly ended as the solution to all her problems became clear.

First, she found Jaiden attractive. Already she'd nearly let him kiss her. Second, he must find her attractive, too, since he was the one doing the almost-kissing.

All this almost-kissing had to stop, and Tilly had to stop it.

And if Jaiden thought she preferred women to men. . . .

"I'm sorry Lord Astor, this must come as a great shock to you."

He stared at her for a full five seconds, then shook his head. "My God," he muttered, running his fingers through his dark hair.

Tilly wondered what the strands felt like. If they indeed felt as silky as they looked. "I'll understand if you'd like me to vacate your home."

"No," he said without hesitation. "You're my aunt's guest. It's her home, too." He sat heavily on the edge of the piano bench and rubbed both hands over his face.

Hmm . . . she'd have to remind him not to sit while a lady stood in his presence. Perhaps another time might suffice for that little instruction.

"Well," she announced. "In that case, I presume Sir Sheldon informed you of the play he's procured tickets for two nights hence. He would like us to accompany him and Adelaide as chaperones on the understanding that we shan't be vigilant about the task."

"Yes," Jaiden answered, looking back at her. One hand still

propped up his chin.

"I shall see you then, my lord," she said, walking quickly out of the room.

When delivering a shocking blow to a man, a wise woman always disappears from the scene before he has a chance to recover.

CHAPTER NINETEEN

It all made so much bloody sense! How could he not have seen it before? Her fervent embrace with the yellow-clad woman. The note threatening her to leave a wife alone. Even the odd behavior of the woman who snubbed her at the ball and then waved.

She preferred lesbian love.

Jaiden waited for the humor to hit him, for the laughter to well up . . . but it didn't. Amazingly, he didn't find this funny. Not even the part about his aunt.

Because he wanted her to want *him*, damn it.

Jaiden stalked to the secretary where they'd once stored sherry. Apparently they no longer did.

Damn! It was just as Tilly said. He didn't have any idea what went on in his own home. Daniel and Adelaide? When the hell had they begun courting? And why was he acting chaperone to his best friend and his sister?

At a play, too. By God, he hated such wastes of time. Everyone looking at everyone else. Bad acting and a worse plot. How had this come about? She had turned his whole world upside down. Or was his aunt right? Had he been gone too long? Had it all changed while he wasn't paying attention?

He pulled Tilly's threat from his pocket. He had hired a private investigator just that morning to find out who had sent the letter. The runner had asked Jaiden to apprise him of any new development—more threats, light shed on the unknown man's motives—the very kind of thing Jaiden had discovered this morning. Jaiden couldn't tell anyone that. It was illegal, after all. Not that anyone would bother to prosecute her, but . . .

God, how did a woman come to crave intimacies with other women? Had she been born that way?

He remembered her question in the park the morning after they'd met and suddenly stiffened. Was that the answer? Had her husband treated her so abominably that she'd given up men all together?

Jaiden would've killed the cur had he not already been dead. Killed him once for violently touching a woman who should only be cherished. Killed him a second time for ruining all Jaiden's hopes for a real marriage, a true love.

Was there any chance she might change? Could women of that disposition come to accept men again? If he was very tender with her and patient, perhaps he could convince her.

Infatuation didn't cut it. This bordered on obsession. It was her explaining fainting tricks to him. How could he resist that? How could he get her out of his head?

Resolve hardened within Jaiden. Well, he had been an investigator. It was time he started figuring out how to get Tilly out of his heart.

CHAPTER TWENTY

The curtain rose.

Jaiden leaned back in the playhouse seat, shook his head, and let out a chuckle of amused disbelief. Happened every time he contemplated his ridiculous situation.

"My lord," Tilly whispered from the seat next to him, peeking up at him through long, copper-brown lashes. "Nothing funny has happened yet."

Jaiden was competing with his great-aunt for the affection of a woman. He'd say the farce was hysterical.

What if his aunt loved her, though? Even if he could steal Tilly's affection, could he do that to his aunt?

Bloody hell.

"My lord?"

Jaiden turned his head at the faint whisper. On his left, Tilly stared at the stage. A naughty smile tugged at her lips.

Had he dreamed the soft voice?

But Tilly's lips moved slightly, though her eyes stayed frozen forward. "Do try to pay attention for at least the first few minutes," she murmured. "How can you excuse yourself next time on account of distaste if you don't sample tonight's production?"

"I'll plead conflicting plans."

The corners of her mouth strained upward, but she suppressed them quickly. She slanted him a glance. "Behave, sir."

He bowed his head. "Anything for the lady."

"Pretty words," she said dismissively but then beamed at him. She held his gaze for a full minute before returning hers to the stage.

It took him much longer to stop watching her. It was only when an actor announced, "I like to live life the way I play chess," did he bother to listen.

Another actor answered, "You don't play chess."

"Precisely."

Jaiden's interest was piqued. The dialogue flashed, and before he realized it, the story sucked him in.

Jaiden laughed heartily at the witty exchanges. Then the curtain dropped. Lights flickered on for intermission.

"You can leave now, if you desire. I'm certain I can handle this business of chaperoning for the remainder of the night," Tilly teased.

Jaiden grinned, acknowledging that she'd been right. He had enjoyed the play as much as he'd previously dreaded it. "If I didn't know better, I would think you bewitched me," he said. As soon as the words left his mouth, he realized their truth.

Tilly shook her head. "The actors are the only magicians here."

"Somehow I doubt it."

Her eyebrows lifted at his impertinence, but the twinkle in her green eyes revealed her pleasure. She leaned closer to him. He moved toward her. Her breath fondled his neck.

She whispered, "I did choose this production specifically for your pleasure. I knew you'd enjoy it."

He jerked his head around. Their noses nearly collided, but she did not back away. Bits of gold flecked her eyes. He hadn't seen them before.

"My lord?" she prompted.

"I thought Daniel chose the play."

Tilly straightened and rearranged her skirts. "Of course," she said. "That's what I *encouraged* him to think!"

Jaiden threw his head back and let out a bark of laughter.

"How did you get to be the way you are?" he asked in amazement.

Tilly's gaze dropped. Her mouth grew tighter. The afternoon's interlude with his aunt replayed in his mind.

Well, he wanted to understand that, too.

But she didn't look as if she wished to explain.

"I'm sorry," he apologized. "How very rude of me. Please forget I said—"

"Why do any of us become who we end up?" She gave an elaborate shrug.

She didn't want to talk about herself. That much was clear. Jaiden wouldn't press the issue . . . for now. "I've always subscribed to the heredity theory myself."

"The heredity theory?" Her brow furrowed delicately.

"Yes, that we are born with personalities already determined, like our height and our hair color."

"What a bizarre notion."

"Yes. I noticed it first with the dogs my father bred. Some just seemed predisposed to act one way or another, though we treated them all the same."

"Breeding dogs," she repeated, disgustedly, turning her head forward in dismissal. "I'll have to take your word for it."

Jaiden blinked. Tilly wasn't fastidious. What was she up to now? "Pray, pardon my uncouthness, Mrs. Leighton." Jaiden waited, not in vain.

Tilly let out a magical laugh. All stiffness evaporated. She bumped his arm with her shoulder playfully. "I only said it to quiet you. I didn't see how I could win the argument. Seemed better not to play than face certain defeat. I haven't had your advantage of observing animal husbandry, you see." Tilly shook her curls. "My lord, how did you face criminals all day long and never learn when a conversation was being manipulated?"

"I never met a criminal with a dusting of freckles on her cheeks and shiny curls, especially not one wearing a stunning violet evening frock." His glance flickered lower. "Showing off her equally stunning figure," he spoke deliberately. Slowly, he traced her collarbone with his fingertip. He felt her shudder.

"Violet frock? This is a plum masterpiece. And when will you learn? Women are just as practiced in the arts of deceit as any man—probably more so. As the weaker sex physically, we've had to learn other ways to control our environments." She tapped his leg with her opera glasses cheerfully. "We are not to be trusted."

"I trust you," he challenged.

Her levity vanished. "Don't."

"I do."

She swallowed. "My loyalties lie elsewhere," she confessed.

"And where is that?"

"With my friends."

"And isn't that what you and I have become? Friends?"

"I'm afraid as friendly as we might act, Lord Astor, you and I can never be friends." She tilted her head to the side, and once more the little amused smile touched her lips. "I don't make friends with men."

"But my dear Mrs. Leighton. When are you going to learn? Men are just as capable of loyalty as women," he threw back in her face, "maybe even more so."

A flush fanned across her cheeks. Her gaze fell to her lap where her gloved hands fiddled with the glasses. "Yes, I suppose," she allowed.

He had disconcerted her. That was a first. Suddenly, he felt a scoundrel for it. He shrugged nonchalantly. "You shouldn't trust me either."

Tilly's laugh lit up the box. She turned her heartbreaking

face full toward him. "The notion of trusting you never entered my mind." Before Jaiden could delve into that statement, Tilly turned her attention to the other couple in the box. "Sir Sheldon," she called.

Daniel lifted his eyes from Adelaide's face for the first time that night. Adelaide swiveled toward Tilly, too, wearing a becoming flush of her own.

"Tell us about the case you're currently investigating," Tilly invited.

Jaiden watched the candlelight flicker across the back of her neck where her hair swept up atop her head. What would she do if he kissed her there? Would she pretend he hadn't? Would a shiver give her away? Would he tremble, touching his lips to that soft skin? Jaiden leaned closer to find out.

"Actually, Mrs. Leighton," Daniel said, "I'm working on a number of things at the moment."

"Well, what's the most exciting then? Would I have heard of any of them?"

"Have you read about the missing wives investigation in the— Good Lord! Mrs. Leighton!"

CHAPTER TWENTY-ONE

"Tilly!" Adelaide squealed.

Looking up from her sprawl, Tilly caught sight of half the audience. A few fashionable people pointed at her, but her fall had gone mostly unnoticed in the ruckus of the intermission.

Thank God. Not exactly discreet behavior.

Not that she'd planned to fall off her seat. Who tumbled from a chair she was firmly planted in?

Never mind self-flagellation. She had excuses to make.

Strong hands lifted her, then dropped her onto the chair.

"Thank you, Lord Astor," she managed. She refrained from instructing him in the manner in which one should help a lady sit. All in good time.

"Are you ill? Should I call for the carriage?" he demanded, already on his feet.

"No, no. Pray, sit. I just lost my . . . footing," she replied, lamely.

With a raised eyebrow, Jaiden saw her hands gripping the edge of her seat. Following his gaze, Tilly saw her fingers turn white. She forced herself to relax her grasp.

"If you prefer to leave—"

"Nonsense, Adelaide. I'm fine. Sir Sheldon, you were saying?"

Not quite the fool she'd thought, Daniel's eyes narrowed. "The missing wives case. What do you know about it?" he demanded.

"Oh, yes. Of course." Tilly wrinkled her brow in feigned concern, shook her head sadly. "Yes, I knew one of the victims rather well for a short time."

"Which one?" Daniel leaned toward her, crowding Adelaide rudely in his obvious enthusiasm.

"Lady Maltrose," she replied. "Such a sad affair."

Out of the corner of her eye, she saw Jaiden sit. One of his large hands touched her arm in a gesture of comfort.

She liked his touch. Too much. When he'd traced her collarbone earlier, she'd thought she might melt. Now, she found it impossible to concentrate on Daniel.

"Do you have any idea what happened to her?" Daniel asked.

"Daniel," Jaiden warned.

How protective! What a delight.

Not that she needed it. "I don't know," she lied. Daniel frowned. "But I've an idea," she said conspiratorially.

The scowl vanished. "You do?"

"Yes." Tilly leaned toward him.

"What is it?"

"Are you sure you can bear to hear it. It isn't very Christian. I fear for your nerves—"

"Tell me."

"I think . . ." Tilly looked around wildly as though frightened someone might overhear. Her eyes returned to Daniel. "I think," she stage-whispered, "her husband murdered her."

She straightened, nearly hitting Jaiden as he leaned over her. She nodded wisely.

"Why—why do you think that, Mrs. Leighton?" Daniel asked, his torso frozen.

"Why, Sir Sheldon, because Martha always claimed he would, of course."

Music began. The lights dimmed. The curtain rose.

"Oh, good!" Tilly exclaimed. "I'm very excited to see how

things get resolved. Our protagonists are in a terrible mess." Tilly faced the stage.

She pretended not to hear Daniel's promise to talk to her later.

CHAPTER TWENTY-TWO

Tilly could have cut the tension in the carriage with a knife. No one had spoken more than five words since they'd left the playhouse.

Daniel glowered out the window. Every few seconds he'd flick accusing eyes at her, run his fingers through his wavy hair in frustration, and then return to scowling into the night.

Jaiden had delivered a not-so-subtle warning to him. He didn't want Daniel questioning Tilly further. It might upset her.

And so it did. Just the thought of Daniel finding out about her involvement with the missing wives. . . . She couldn't bear to think of it.

She did, however, want to ask him about his investigation, to learn what he knew. Were her friends still safe at Muirfield?

She should have been thinking of a way to manipulate Daniel into revealing what he had uncovered. But her head refused to cooperate. For the life of her, she couldn't seem to tear her mind from Jaiden's earlier declaration.

I trust you.

Her chest ached just thinking about it. And the way his dimples flashed when he called her his friend. It made it impossible to breathe in her corset.

Friendship meant everything to Tilly. Her parents had died years before, and even when they were alive, she'd never trusted them. Only her friends understood her. Hell, only her friends got the chance. She lied to everyone else—so often she had difficulty remembering what had actually happened and what she'd made up.

All in all, she hadn't behaved so terribly to Jaiden. True, she stayed at his house only to train him without his knowing.

But that wasn't so bad, was it? One lie, and for his own good at that. They could still be friends.

She peeked at him. He sat directly across from her, watching Daniel suspiciously.

At her look, his gaze fixed on her. It relaxed immediately. She sent him a soft smile. He grinned back at her. His boot brushed her ankle.

Yes, friends. It would be nice.

But then there was the tiny matter of her involvement with the disappearing women. None of his business, except that now she'd learned his friend's career depended on discovering her secrets.

Jaiden's grin had turned into a frown. What was bothering him?

Then she realized she scowled at him, too. Oh dear, her thoughts were getting the better of her.

She shifted uncomfortably in the chair until she, too, stared vacantly out a window.

So, she'd told Jaiden two little fabrications. Not horrible. She could redeem herself . . . except he also thought her a widow.

Oh, dear. Her fictitious late husband. She'd forgotten. That made three falsehoods.

No, they could not be friends after all. She would never tell a friend three cock-and-bull stories. What kind of a person would that make her?

And he thought she lusted after women. Bloody hell. And she'd encouraged that thought.

Only because it made him easier to train for his fiancée. Yes, exactly. It was *his* fault. Bah! They wouldn't be in this predicament if he hadn't gone out and gotten himself betrothed.

The lie had to stand. It allowed her to do her job. She couldn't reveal the truth to him. Why, such a confession would be tantamount to proclaiming her attraction.

She couldn't do that. She oughtn't muck up things further.

"I'm not a lesbian!"

Her outburst reverberated in the silent carriage. All three pairs of eyes swung toward her. She panted with suppressed emotion.

"I'm not," she repeated, looking at Jaiden. "I'm sorry I gave you that impression. Oh hell! I practically crammed the thought into your head. It's not true. I'm not involved with your aunt that way—or in any other way, really—"

"Involved?" Adelaide repeated blankly. Her eyes widened, and her voice rose to a squeak. "With Great-Aunt Hen?"

Tilly rushed on. "I'm sorry, Jaiden. Can you forgive me?"

He had every right to refuse, to insist upon an explanation or order her from his home or demand pistols at dawn. Instead, he watched her with arched brows.

She should throw herself from the carriage now and save herself further humiliation. If nothing else, that would finally shut her big mouth.

Seconds ticked by, every one bringing a new flush of shame to her face. All the lies she'd told in her life, and she'd never even guessed at the agony of confession. No wonder this was her first declaration of guilt. At this rate it would be her last, too, for surely, she'd expire of embarrassment if he didn't answer her soon.

Then she noticed the amusement in Jaiden's eyes. His lips remained tense around the corners though.

Off ran her mouth. "I only kissed her the once, and it shocked me more than you. I swear it. Adelaide left the room, and she tackled me—"

"Aunt Hen?" Adelaide gasped again.

"—going on about her two best friends becoming romantically involved with each other—"

"Lady Wexham and Mrs. Beesley?" Adelaide exclaimed. She looked ready to faint.

Probably Tilly shouldn't have brought it up in front of the innocent Adelaide. Of course, she shouldn't have mentioned it at all, much less screamed it.

"I apologize. You walked in just as she'd pinned me to the floor, and I couldn't break away, and I couldn't think of anything to say to you—"

"Tilly," Jaiden interrupted, grasping her wrist as she flung her arm out dramatically, nearly knocking Adelaide in the face. "It's all right."

"You forgive me?"

He started laughing. "Completely."

Daniel guffawed, too. "Well, well, Aunt Hen! I always knew she had it in her!"

Tilly giggled then. More from relief than humor. Of course, the thought of Aunt Hen's chapped lips pressed against hers was a little funny. Repulsive, but funny.

Ahhh. But Jaiden really was too good.

Definitely too good for Little Miss Persnickety.

Only Adelaide remained immune to the amusement. "Oh, God!" she exclaimed. She buried her burning face in her hands.

Tilly moved to comfort her, but Daniel got there first.

"Now, now, Addie," he said. "She's your relative, after all. Can't expect her to be too staid, now can you?" He rubbed her neck in a manner that could only be described as familiar.

One eyelash flutter, and she would have him.

Adelaide peeked above her hands. Grinning, Daniel chucked her under the chin.

Then Daniel breathed deeply. Tilly saw the way his eyes fluttered as he took in the scent of Adelaide's hair. Adelaide had won. She'd captured the hunter.

In a low voice, Daniel spoke, "You Astor women do keep a man on his toes."

"Women, too, apparently," Adelaide muttered.

Daniel threw back his head and laughed. Adelaide smiled ruefully, then chuckled, never taking her eyes from Daniel.

Tilly caught Jaiden's gaze. They shared a smile over the other couple's obvious infatuation.

He hadn't lied. He did forgive her.

"I enjoyed tonight," he whispered.

"Enough to let me drag you to a museum this week?" she dared.

His eyes shone. "Well . . ."

"How about a bargain? You come visit the museum, and I'll tour your offices."

An eyebrow rose. "You'd like to see what I do?"

Tilly smiled and nodded.

Their ankles pressed together in the cramped carriage. Neither of them moved apart.

Chapter Twenty-Three

"I can't believe you employ twelve women," Tilly announced as she settled in a chair in Jaiden's office. She'd just finished touring Jaiden's rooms and had found the experience surprisingly interesting.

Jaiden leaned forward on his desk with a small smile. "And forty-seven men."

"Yes, but twelve women."

"These aren't ordinary women, and they appreciate earning a wage typically reserved for men. Gratitude makes them loyal. Loyalty keeps our innovations from our competitors."

Over the course of the day, Jaiden had explained all sorts of technical and business strategies to her. She'd rather taken to it.

Odd that women in society made him uncomfortable, but the ones working for him didn't.

"I'm certain you're right about their gratitude. Such opportunities are rare for women, as I'm sure you know," she said with exaggerated pronunciation—a sure sign that the topic distressed her. Tilly concentrated on keeping the conversation polite. No use spoiling the day with one of her diatribes against the inequities suffered by women.

Jaiden frowned at a paper on his desk, moved it to the side and remarked, "I fear the opportunities will remain rare so long as women's education lags so formidably behind men's."

"Women will always be ill-treated in this world. Education will only make their plight more difficult to accept unless paths of escape are available to them. Until that day, better to keep them—us—ignorant and capable of adjusting to our circumstances."

No papers distracted Jaiden now. An amazed half-smile and wide blue eyes lit up his face. "You are not a proponent of Mary Wollstonecraft's *Vindication of Women's Rights?* I am surprised to learn it."

Er . . . the title sounded vaguely familiar, something her friend Ruth would have mentioned. Tilly never paid attention to Ruth's philosophizing. It did no good. Talk would change nothing. Only helping women one at a time ever did any good.

Still, no use revealing her personal lack of education to a man who clearly valued formal reasoning a good deal more than she. Tilly smiled. "Little use debating the theoretical," she remarked. Time to change the subject. "Now that your camera prototype is perfected, are you going to sell it or manufacture it yourself?"

Shaking his head, Jaiden said, "I still can't believe you knew so much about advances in photography."

Oh, dear. She probably shouldn't have reminded him of her earlier mistake. She'd been enjoying herself so much she'd forgotten to pretend ignorance of the matter. Typical day for her, pretending ignorance on subjects she knew a great deal about while giving the impression that she knew a great deal about things she'd barely heard of. She did love her work. "No, I'm just a quick learner," she tried. "How will you decide what to do with it?"

Jaiden smiled. "I've bored you to tears with all this economic theory, haven't I?"

"Not at all," she answered. "Your enthusiasm is contagious."

He raised his eyebrows, and a dimple flashed. "Sunk costs? Profit margins? Cost versus benefits? You don't have any use for those things."

"You're quite mistaken, Lord Astor. They're universal concepts, ones that apply to my own small life quite nicely."

He looked at her doubtfully.

"It's true. I'm a widow, and how do we widows occupy our time? Why, we matchmake, of course. We encourage men to make fools of themselves over pretty young things solely for our own amusement."

"Is that why you do it?" He leaned back in his chair and linked his fingers behind his head, thrusting forward his too-appealing throat.

Tilly swallowed. What had they been discussing? Oh yes. "Absolutely. Suppose a man proposes to one of my friends, and she doesn't know whether to accept or refuse. Cost versus benefits. He possesses a title . . . benefit . . . but also ill-favored breath . . . cost. He's wealthy . . . benefit . . . but refuses to come to London for the season . . . cost."

Jaiden laughed heartily, revealing a mouth full of perfect white teeth, except that one eyetooth appeared shorter than the other. Tilly rather liked the flaw.

"Next, my young friend has to take into account all the other men who might propose and what they have to offer—a definite cost should she settle on one. An opportunity cost," she clarified.

"I admit I've never thought about it quite in those terms."

" 'Course you haven't. You're a romantic. You just don't know it," she informed him. "Now for my favorite new phrase. Suppose one of my friends has been angling for a certain somebody when he suddenly loses his inheritance in a game of whist. Well, my dear, Lord Astor, there's only one thing a girl can do. Cut her losses and move on to the next project—the next man."

He let out that gorgeous laughter again. Delighted, Tilly smiled. How could any woman resist when confronted with such a jolly sight?

But men's moods changed.

The thought came unbidden and unwelcome . . . and was true. Jaiden's laughter ceased. He gave Tilly a hard stare.

Every muscle in her body tensed, preparing for violence. Her face revealed no fear. She'd trained it a long time ago, but she couldn't stop the tiny trembles that made her legs vibrate under the safety of her skirts. She was so overwhelmed by dread, it took her a full minute to realize anger hadn't caused Jaiden's intensity. Only lust.

She blew out a sigh of relief, feeling excessively silly. Why would he turn on her now, after all? Usually men waited until they had a woman trapped before revealing their true natures.

Lust, however, she could deal with easily enough. What had worked last time? Oh, yes. "So," she announced, much too loudly in the quiet room. "I hear your Miss Haversham returns today. You must be delighted. I am. No, no, you needn't explain. I'm not so ancient that I don't remember young love. And I am so pleased to meet the girl who has stolen your heart. Your sister is taking me to call tomorrow first thing. Must inspect the goods before you say 'I do,' you know. Any *friend* would be so kind."

During the course of her speech, Jaiden had frowned, wrinkled his brow, tried to interrupt, and yet, now that she'd finished, his eyes lit with amusement.

"Friend?" he asked.

Tilly squirmed in her seat, suddenly feeling presumptuous. "Yes, friend. That is what you called me last evening."

"So I did," he said, smiling as she squirmed. "I hadn't realized you liked the notion."

Her conscience pricked her. She picked up a quill on his desk and rolled it between her hands while glancing about the room anywhere but at him. "Well, perhaps I've grown accustomed to it. So long as you might be willing to overlook a falsehood or two."

"Two?"

"Or three," she muttered, flashing him a quick look to gauge his reaction. What was she doing? Her entire career depended on her ability to deceive men, an ability she'd demonstrated artfully until Jaiden. Hell, she usually didn't even think of it as lying so much as helping a man see reason.

"Three. I see. Including the one about you and my aunt."

He would have to remember that. "No," she mumbled.

"Well, I suppose I could forgive three lies told before we became friends—"

"Really?" She peered at him hopefully.

He nodded. "I should think so. So long as you confess them."

That hadn't been part of the deal. She'd have to be mad. She decided to brazen through the rest of the conversation. "Too late for that, I'm afraid," she said with a wave of her hand. "But I'll go ahead and take that offer of friendship. We'll just go on from here."

Jaiden laughed, then nodded. "Well, friends then." He held out his hand.

She took it, shaking it in a man-to-man sort of way. "Yes, friends," she announced.

And as his friend, she'd start work on Little Miss Persnickety tomorrow.

Chapter Twenty-Four

"Mrs. Charles Leighton, allow me to present Miss Clara Haversham," Adelaide introduced formally in the center of Lord Haversham's sitting room "Clara, this is Mrs. Leighton. I've told her of your engagement to my brother. I'm hoping she might help."

Tilly dropped into a token curtsy. A sob cut the gesture short.

Clara trembled in front of her. She shook her head fiercely. "It's not definite. Nothing's been settled. Lord Astor hasn't even asked me. We aren't engaged yet. We're not!"

Her head jerked with a sob. Her hair fell forward, hiding her watery blue eyes. Tears rained down her cheeks and splattered to her grandfather's Persian rug. Her shoulders quaked so violently, Tilly feared she might suffer a seizure.

"Oh, Clara!" Adelaide exclaimed in consternation. "I didn't mean to upset you!" She shot Tilly a stricken look.

Clearly, Miss Persnickety had not come to terms with the marriage during her holiday.

Maneuvering about Adelaide and a delicate sofa, Tilly wrapped an arm around the shaking child. "Adelaide, why don't you visit Mrs. Kensington as planned," she said, thrusting a handkerchief in Clara's hand. "I will just stay here, where Clara and I can get acquainted. Come back to get me in about a half hour."

Adelaide stared at the scene as she nodded and backed out of the room.

116

Without Adelaide's presence, Tilly could finally turn her attention to Miss Picky Skirts. Tall and slender, she would have appeared rather pretty if she hadn't been prey to such a fit of emotions. Really, why Jaiden wanted to shackle himself to such a weak, whiny little creature—

Ah, but he did want to, and it was Tilly's job to make their adjustment to each other as smooth as possible. And Little Miss Choosey was spoiling everything.

With a serene expression that betrayed none of her galling thoughts, Tilly led Clara to a chair and employed only a little more force than necessary when she pushed her into it.

"There, there, child. There's no need to fuss."

Clara shook her head, looking at the soiled handkerchief. Tilly had never seen such a melancholy soul in all her life.

"Come, Clara, there's always hope. Life's unpredictable. Your heart's desire may still come true." She patted the lanky girl's shoulders.

Clara's head popped up. She stared at Tilly warily and with hope.

"That's better now," Tilly continued. "You know, you really shouldn't throw such fits. You don't have the right complexion for it. Why, your face turns the exact color of a ripe tomato. Were a man present, he might mistake you for one, and next thing, you'd have a bite clear out of the side of your head."

Clara's mouth opened in confusion. Then realization struck. She giggled uncomfortably, uncertain whether Tilly joked or not.

"That's better," Tilly praised, pulling a chair in front of Clara's. She sat, facing the girl. "Now," she leaned forward and caught one of Clara's hands between both of hers. "Tell me the problem."

Clara eyed her sadly. "Oh, I couldn't. I mean . . . there isn't any . . . except . . . oh, I can't!"

Apparently, Miss Persnickety needed clearer instructions. Perhaps multiple-choice would do the trick. "Is it marriage in general you loathe or Lord Astor playing the part of the groom?"

"Oh, I want to marry. I mean, I'm not going to be a nun or a spinster or anything."

And Tilly hadn't thought she could like the girl less. Despising marriage as an institution demonstrated a pragmatism and intelligence found in so few girls these days, but disliking Jaiden playing the part of intended? That was plain silly.

"So, Lord Astor frightens you?" Tilly asked, none too gently.

Clara sighed mournfully. "I'm not scared of Lord Astor, really. I mean, he's frightening, but I could get used to that."

How did one grow accustomed to living with a husband she found terrifying? "Then what is it about him?" Tilly prompted.

"He's just . . . he's not . . . He's not my Fred!" she burst out.

Tilly dropped her hand. *Who the bloody hell was Fred?* "Who the bloody hell is Fred?"

"The boy I want to marry," Clara announced. "The boy I will marry," she said with more resolve.

Suddenly, Tilly felt a surge of affection for the girl.

But then Clara ruined it. "At least, I hope to marry him." Her shoulders slumped, and her lip began to tremble again. "But I don't see how I can!"

"Stop that now," Tilly ordered, impatient to get on with a project for which she felt suddenly inspired. "We can't plan if you keep weeping like a cracked teapot."

"Plan?" Clara blinked. "Plan what?"

"How we're—I mean, how you are going to get out of this pickle. Now, you're certain you don't want Lord Astor?"

"Yes." Her eyes grew round. "Yes! But my grandfather. He says Jaiden will make a better husband."

"Then your grandfather can marry him," Tilly announced,

standing. She paced the long room. "Does Fred want to marry you?"

The girl's eyes turned doe-like. "Ever so much. I wanted to tell Adelaide, but I was afraid it might hurt her feelings. Lord Astor being her brother and all."

"Oh, she'll adjust," Tilly dismissed. "So will Lord Astor, for that matter."

"Well, of course, Lord Astor will," Clara said. "He doesn't give two figs whether we marry or not."

Yes, the girl was a delight, after all.

"All right. Then it's your grandfather we need to work on. Is he here?"

Clara worried her hands. "In . . . in his study, I believe, but what will you . . . oh, no! Where are you going? You can't—"

Tilly didn't hear the rest. She'd already left the room in search of Lord Haversham.

Chapter Twenty-Five

The startled housekeeper pointed down a hallway to the second door on the left. Tilly pounded twice and then threw open the door without waiting for an answer.

Smoke erupted from the room, stinging her eyes. Through the burn, Tilly caught sight of a robust gentleman with white hair sitting behind a gigantic mahogany desk. A forgotten shepherd's pie dangled from his fingers, inches from his hanging jaw.

"Lord Haversham, I presume," she began, stalking into the fog and setting her knuckles on his desk. If only she'd worn her grey silk . . . and her eyes weren't so ridiculously sensitive. "You and I have a few things we need to discuss."

His mouth opened and closed several times. When sound finally emerged, it quickly turned into a bellow. "Who are *you?*"

"*I* am looking out for the interests of your granddaughter, which is more than I can say for you."

He slammed his fist on the desk. Peas spilt from the piecrust and rolled across the desk. "What the—"

"Tell me why exactly you would have your granddaughter marry a man she doesn't like?" Tilly demanded.

All outrage vanished from the wrinkled face. A smirk curled in its place. "That's what this is about, hmm?" He nodded, leaning back in his chair. "Want Lord Astor for yourself, eh?"

And Tilly'd thought she disliked him before. How dare he? The very idea!

And didn't he understand the power of suggestion? The rudeness! Putting such a notion in her head.

She wouldn't deign to respond. And she would also do her best to ignore that small twinge in the back of her conscience that nagged for attention.

"She's in love with someone else," Tilly spoke briskly to his face.

Lord Haversham laughed. "Don't I know it! The honorable Fred Glass, man of leisure," he said sardonically.

"Aren't all gentlemen?" Tilly answered with equal glibness.

He shot forward, leaned both forearms on the desk. "I'm not. I worked every day of my life for my title, for the dresses Clara prances around in. I don't care if it's unfashionable, even downright taboo amongst gentlemen like Freddy Glass and his friends. I've kept food on the table for my late son's family and his mother, and Clara will have luxuries aplenty for the rest of her life so long as she marries Lord Astor. Her children will grow up to make something of themselves instead of looking back to a time when their ancestors had meaning." He shook his head in disgust. "Freddy Glass just wants the chit for my money."

Tilly closed her eyes, unable to believe this man. It was true that, normally, she'd agree with him, but at the moment, acknowledging any kinship with the cold-hearted fiend offended her. She opened her eyes despite the smoky haze of the unventilated room. Studying him, Tilly realized his eyebrows stood straight out from his face. A clear trait of the stubborn. "Have you so little regard for your granddaughter's worth, that you truly believe a man could only love her for your money?" she asked.

"My money is what the chit is worth."

Tilly stood up straight. Disgust surged through her. This was Jaiden's vaunted economics taken to an unholy extreme, an extreme that mocked human existence. Lord Haversham no longer made money to fulfill his family's happiness, but used his family to make more money. Marry the girl off to Jaiden, solidify an alliance.

He was just like every other father whose daughters ended up beaten and cowed because no one valued her for herself.

Lord Haversham's mouth twisted. "And if you think I'll watch a dime of that money go to the likes of Freddy Glass, you, my rude wench, are sorely mistaken."

"This is her life," Tilly breathed. Surely, it was only the smoke that made the tears well in her eyes. Anger couldn't have incited them. Tilly didn't get angry. She got what she wanted.

"Exactly," Lord Haversham said. "Her life. Much too precious a commodity to be trusted to a seventeen-year-old chit who knows nothing of the world. With Jaiden, she won't lack for anything—clothes, carriages, sons—"

Sons?

"I know men. He's the kind who will take care of his own. And he knows his business. He'll make a bleedin' fortune with that new camera of his."

Tilly didn't bother to speak. She turned on her heel. This wouldn't work. He wouldn't change his mind. No point arguing further.

She'd botched the whole thing, something she'd never done before. She understood men, knew you couldn't threaten them or employ logic. And she always studied each of their individual natures before attacking. She learned their weaknesses and strengths before plotting her next action.

Not this time, though. She'd barged in without a thought. And now she'd solidified the arrogant curmudgeon's obstinacy.

She could kick herself. She never got emotional about cases. Being emotional ruined her strategizing. And she certainly didn't make mistakes.

At least, she hadn't made them before Jaiden. Now, it seemed she could do no right. What was happening to her?

She came to an abrupt stop in the drawing room. Clara gave her one look and then crumbled. "That bad?" she whispered.

"I'm sorry. I don't think I did you any favors up there," Tilly confessed, feeling like the fairy godmother from hell.

The girl nodded, her face surrounded by red ringlets as she stared at her hands.

Her calm both surprised and relieved Tilly. Then the girl looked up. Silent tears coursed down her face. Her voice shook. "What am I to do?"

"Oh, Clara!" Tilly ran to her side. Curse men and their interfering ways. From the earliest moments of a girl's life they did nothing but make things difficult.

Clara slumped in her embrace, her words a torrent. "I love Fred. And he loves me—so much. I'm frightened what it'll do to him, my marrying Lord Astor. He won't harm himself, or me, I know. He'd never harm me, but I don't think he'd ever recover from it. And I want to be with him. Oh, how I want to be with him!"

Damn the romantic stories, all the rage this decade, filling young people with nonsense about true love and men with pure intentions underneath their brooding exteriors. Might as well believe in fairies and fire-breathing dragons.

"I can't tell you what to do, Clara, but I swear I'll help with whatever decision you reach," she vowed into the girl's red curls.

"But I'm bound to break one of their hearts—Freddy's or Grandfather's, and I can't do it. Grandfather is the only person who has loved me most of my life. And Fred! Oh, Fred. I can't bear this. You must help. Tell me what to do."

Tilly crouched before the girl. She took the handkerchief from her hand and wiped Clara's face. "Love," she said gently, "my experience has taught me that the best of marriages turn awful at times."

"So I should marry Lord Astor?" the girl squeaked, clearly repelled by the idea.

"He is decent, as far as men go. He'd make a better husband than most, and I promise I'll smooth things between you any way you need."

"But he doesn't love me," Clara cried.

Love? Why would anyone make a life decision on such a temporary emotion? "That might make the marriage all the more comfortable."

"That's what you would do? Marry Lord Astor?"

Why did everyone ask her this? She had to block it out of her mind. Marrying Jaiden was not an option. Tilly couldn't marry anyone, not ever.

Very well. This train of thought did not help Clara. The chit had to make this decision on her own, no matter what her grandfather thought. "Clara, your future happiness depends on this decision. I don't know what I would do in your place, but I do know I would make the decision myself. Either way, I could only come to terms with my life if I'd been the one to choose it." She shrugged. "That's all I can tell you."

"But if I marry Fred . . ." She didn't finish. Her expression lit up at the mere thought.

"Your grandfather may cut you off, and you'd better enlighten Fred of that fact before anyone says, 'I do.' Men do not like feeling they've wed under false pretenses," Tilly said stiffly.

"It wouldn't matter to him," Clara maintained.

Tilly stifled a snort. "Still, no use inviting trouble."

"No, I suppose not. I don't know what to do!" she wailed.

"Tell you what," Tilly began, "I'll arrange an outing this week—you, Lord Astor, and me. Lunch or something. That way you can get to know the man. Surely that would help you make your decision."

Clara nodded gravely and then narrowed her eyes in determination. "Yes, I suppose that would be wise," she admitted.

Tilly didn't know if she could agree with the girl. Wisdom flew in the opposite direction every time she approached Jaiden.

CHAPTER TWENTY-SIX

"It's such a lovely day," Tilly breathed. "I'm glad we sent the carriage ahead and decided to walk."

"Me, too," Adelaide agreed, peering into a shop window. "I never realized how much there is to see on Prince Edward Street."

"Of course, you haven't. Much too unfashionable for the future Lady Sheldon," Tilly teased. "But it's quieter than St. James this time of day—which I must say, I appreciate sometimes."

"How did your interview with Clara—*Aahhh!*"

Tilly turned toward Adelaide. Just then, an arm shoved her into the nearest side street—an arm attached to someone smelly, sweaty, and cussing up a storm.

Only when they'd gone ten steps down the road could Tilly break free. She grabbed Adelaide's arm and shoved her behind her back.

The man, a meaty specimen with a big red beard covering most of his face, let them shuffle ten feet away before he reached into his waistband and pulled out a large handgun.

Damn it! Tilly hated firearms. What had happened to good old-fashioned daggers?

"I'm assuming there's something you want from us?" Tilly asked primly. She wanted to start the conversation on the right foot. No messy emotions mucking up what could prove a profitable business affair for both of them. Never mind Adelaide whimpering against the wall of the nearest building.

Staring directly at Tilly, the ruffian announced, "In five minutes, a carriage will come down this street. You and I are getting in it."

Not bloody likely.

Tilly didn't get into carriages with people who threatened her. It was never a good idea. And she *refused* to allow a firearm to divert her from her principles. She'd made the decision years ago. Violence—or the threat of it—would not rule her life—not under any circumstances, including the present one. It was a matter of preferences. She'd rather die than reinforce such caddish behavior. It was that simple.

But she had to know his plans for Adelaide.

"So my friend here . . ."

"Free to go, once you and I have left."

Hmm. She wanted to tell him the impossibility of his plan, but men took the word "no" so hard. It usually made them go all stubborn and difficult.

"You and I have never met," she began. She paced a bit to demonstrate in how civilized a manner she hoped to proceed.

"No, ma'am," he said. His bushy red eyebrows lifted.

"Nor have I done anything to engage your personal feelings, I assume."

His brow wrinkled in confusion. He shifted from foot to foot, the gun heavy in his hands.

"What I mean to say is, *you* don't have any reason to want me dead," she clarified.

He blinked, scratched his head with the gun. "No, can't say as I do."

"Excellent. Then I must deduce this is merely a matter of business for you!"

"Well . . . yes."

"Then . . . ," she drawled, circling him, pretending to study him from all angles. He turned to keep his brown eyes on her, though the gun drooped. "I'd guess you were promised twenty pounds for this morning's labor. Am I right?"

He nodded eagerly. His eyes grew to saucers.

He'd probably been promised closer to five.

"I just so happen to have fifty pounds in my reticule right here." She waved it in front of him.

"Fifty bloomin' pounds!"

She shrugged. "Payday and personal naivety. What can I say?"

"Fifty pounds," he repeated. The gun dropped to his side, endangering nothing but the cobblestones.

"Yes. Much nicer to have fifty pounds than just twenty, isn't it? I tell you what. I'll make a deal with you. I will give you the fifty pounds—though I would like to keep the bag if you don't mind. I think it becomes this dress very well, don't you?"

He nodded enthusiastically, although Tilly doubted the dress elicited nearly as much excitement as how he planned to spend her money.

"Yes, well," she continued, "I'll give you the fifty pounds in exchange for our freedom and the name of the man who hired you."

The brute's shoulders slumped. "I don't know his name. He never gave it."

Damn—though hardly unexpected. "What does he look like then?"

"Red face," the man said quickly. "Fat, bulging eyes, short . . ."

Wonderful. That narrowed it down to ninety percent of Englishmen.

". . . Claimed to be a servant, but I didn't buy the story. Too nice a watch, if you know what I mean."

"Yes, I believe I do. How discerning of you to notice," Tilly praised.

He beamed.

A little flattery never hurt. "So, do you agree to my terms?"

His eyes narrowed, almost disappearing behind all that red hair. "Why shouldn't I take your purse and then stick you in the hackney. I could still collect the money from the fat man too, then."

"Excellent thinking, sir! Very well done. You do have a head for business, I see."

He tried to hide his pleased smile by sucking his lips between his teeth. It didn't result in a pretty sight.

"Unfortunately," Tilly continued, "I know a little something you don't know, which would make double-dealing a trifle difficult. You see, my friend over there. She happens to have just got herself engaged to Sir Daniel Sheldon. You may have read about him in the papers. The famous investigator. Oh, you have heard of him. Excellent. Well, you can understand, he's quite besotted with his soon-to-be bride. How could he help himself?" she asked, although Adelaide's hyperventilating didn't support her argument. "And I'm afraid, if anyone hurt her—or me, for that matter—he would make certain every single British law officer spent the rest of his life hunting the villain down." All friendliness dropped from her voice, as she began to stalk the gunman. He backed away, swallowing. "Sir Sheldon would find you, no matter where you hid, no matter how far you ran. He would bring you down like a rabbit in a foxhunt. He'd feed on your every cry of pain, delight in every mark on your body until you pleaded incoherently for death."

Directly in front of him now, Tilly grasped the handle of the forgotten gun. He stiffened, then let go.

"Hardly worth it for a man who just came into fifty pounds," she commented. "Don't you agree?" She cocked her head to one side.

He nodded, his eyes huge.

"Ridiculous, of course," she said, all amity once again. She pressed her reticule into his empty hand. "But you know how young lovers are." She smiled and shrugged.

He clutched at the bag and stared at her.

"Well, it was pleasant doing business with you. Have fun spending that small fortune, now, won't you?" Tilly called over her shoulder as she slid an arm around Adelaide's waist to maneuver the hysterical woman. She led Adelaide past the man.

The henchman looked down at the purse he held. "Hey," he called, breaking from his stupor. "You said you wanted to keep your bag!" he yelled, jogging up to them.

Tilly debated shooting him in the leg. Not absolutely necessary, but she'd grown tired of him. Of course, knowing her luck with firearms, she'd most likely shoot her own foot.

"Changed my mind. This style won't last the rest of the season as it is."

"Are you sure?"

"Yes," she said, coming to a halt. "Look. You might want to disappear before the carriage arrives. Neither of us knows for sure who will be inside it or what they'll have to say about our private arrangement."

He stared at her dumbly, then nodded. "You're right."

And with that he took off at a trot in the opposite direction.

"Adelaide, you need to help me," Tilly begged, her pretense of levity evaporating. "We have to get into a shop before that carriage arrives." Now that she'd nearly succeeded in keeping them out of trouble, she could feel the anxiety crawling its way up her spine.

Adelaide's body trembled against Tilly's, but she nodded nonetheless. Mustering some courage, Adelaide straightened, walking nearly on her own.

"Good girl," Tilly said. "Not far now."

They straggled into a pastry shop. The owner spotted first

their expensive clothing, then Adelaide's pale face, then the gun hanging at Tilly's side. His face registered four emotions in a matter of seconds before the salesman in him won out.

It didn't take long before the owner's son had gone with a message to Ross, the Astors' butler, to send the carriage round to pick them up.

"Yes, I'd say our walk was quite spoiled for the day," Tilly said, patting Adelaide's shoulder while her friend hunched on a chair. At least she hadn't started crying. "And I'm not exactly in the mood to hail down a hired hack," she muttered. It would probably end up being the same carriage someone had hired to kidnap her.

A shiver ran through Adelaide.

"There, there," Tilly comforted, the smell of sweet butter wafting over to her. "Everything's all right." Cakes of every imaginable color decorated the room. The sight cheered Tilly immediately. How could one be upset when wasting time in a pastry shop?

Tilly wondered how often the owners put out new ones. What a waste. A cake should be eaten, not merely exhibited. Speaking of . . . "Adelaide, why don't you buy us a couple of pieces of cake?"

Adelaide's head twisted to look at Tilly as if she were mad.

"Look at that chocolate one. I bet it's tasty."

"Excellent choice," the baker offered. "It's made with Catalonian chocolate."

Adelaide shook her head. "I couldn't eat anything."

Tilly nudged her. "Buy one for me then."

"Tilly! You were nearly kidnapped!" Adelaide pointed out the window. "Kidnapped! Who knows what could have happened to you—"

"Yes," Tilly agreed. "They might have starved me. I better eat now in case they try again."

"Tilly—"

"Please. Those pastries at Clara's were terrible. And her grandfather didn't exactly inspire my appetite. Oh! This one. White cake layered with raspberry filling. It's so pretty!"

Adelaide shook her head.

Tilly prepared for tears, but Adelaide merely let out a long sigh. Lifting her head, she nodded at the display. "The one with the butterflies is prettier."

"You think so, ma'am?" the baker said.

Adelaide rose from the chair, moved closer. "Yes, but it's too lovely to eat."

Tilly grinned and walked to the counter. "Would you like to place a wager on that?"

The owner smiled and cut her a piece.

CHAPTER TWENTY-SEVEN

Don't worry, but send the carriage as quickly as possible to the pastry shop on Prince Edward Street.

An address followed, and then Tilly's signature.

Jaiden read the note once more as the carriage rattled over the cobblestone streets. Don't worry? How could she write don't worry? Didn't she realize that telling someone not to worry always made one worry?

Not that there were other options with Tilly. Trouble followed that girl everywhere. Or maybe she sought it out. Really! Threatening letters, irate husbands, confessions of deceit. How did she manage it?

Jaiden jumped from the carriage before it had come to a complete stop. A pastry shop stood before him, boasting the name Sugar and Spice. Every muscle in Jaiden's body relaxed as he spotted Tilly and his sister inside. Both women appeared uninjured and having a jolly time sampling sweets while his heart had yet to slow.

He entered the store only to go unnoticed as Tilly and Adelaide watched the baker decorate a cake at the back counter and carried on a conversation so inane that Jaiden shook his head in disbelief.

"I eat scrambled eggs," Tilly was saying, "but I have to make certain the word doesn't pop into my head. Scrambled eggs. Truly, cake is the only food including eggs that doesn't sound absolutely violent. Eggs are whipped, beaten, whisked, fried.

Poor things! But in cake, they are merely invited to mix with sugar and flour and have tea. Much more civilized."

"But then we *eat* them. What's not violent about that?"

"Let's not be silly, Adelaide. Eating cake is the most peaceful activity in the world. If all our rulers would focus on giving people cake instead of gobbling territory, think how much happier and peaceful—"

"Let them eat cake?" Adelaide suggested.

Tilly laughed. "Exactly. Now, Mr. Owen, you've the most delectable wares in town, but you must put on some weight," Tilly continued. "No one trusts a skinny pastry chef. Why, you're practically slandering your own talents."

"Jaiden," Adelaide cried, spying him finally. She ran toward him, then stopped abruptly three feet away. Sheepishly, she looked over her shoulder at Tilly. "Look who's come."

"Care for a slice?" Tilly asked with a jaunty smile. She raised a piece to her mouth and took a bite. Cream stuck to her nose.

Jaiden couldn't believe her. He propped his hands on his hips. "I was under the impression you were in danger."

"Well, we're not," she dismissed, with a cocked head. The bit of cream still stuck to her nose.

Anger heated his face. Didn't she realize what her note had done to him? He'd lost a year of his life. "Then why did you say not to worry?"

Her brows drew together, and her eyes sparkled, begging him to consider his words. Jaiden knew he sounded like a mother hen, but she frightened him with her refusal to pay heed to common sense.

"Oh, but we were in danger," Adelaide jumped in. "A horrible, malodorous man pushed us into an alley, held a gun on Tilly, and ordered her into a carriage!"

Cold rage gripped Jaiden. He turned his gaze on Tilly, demanding she explain Adelaide's tale.

But at his glance, she turned to the baker. "Yes, the raspberry and white cake is wonderful, but I think you should try a raspberry and lemon. I bet it would sell—"

"Tilly," Jaiden spoke in a low voice.

A shudder ran through her, belying the serene expression she turned on him. "Yes, Lord Astor?"

"Who was responsible for this attack?"

She gave a delicate shrug. "I haven't the faintest notion."

"Tilly," he warned. She had to start taking these threats seriously.

Her mouth tightened at his look. She threw her arms in the air. "Don't you think I'd tell you if I knew? Do you think I enjoy having a gun waved in my face? Really, Jaiden! I mean, Lord Astor." She sighed. "Truly, it isn't so bad as all that. Look at us." She motioned to his sister. "We escaped entirely unscathed. Don't upset yourself so."

He couldn't believe she was attempting to calm him. She should be near hysterics, not trying to comfort him. Did the girl have no concept of her own mortality? What was to keep the cur from attacking again? And what the hell would Jaiden do if something happened to her?

Tilly played guiltily with her fork. Once again, she seemed to read his mind.

"Tilly was marvelous though," Adelaide said, coming to Tilly's rescue. "You should have seen her. She gave the ruffian fifty pounds to leave us alone."

Jaiden raised his eyebrows. "You did?"

"Seemed a good buy at the time."

Despite his anger, Jaiden noticed how adorable Tilly looked, icing on her nose, a single slender shoulder shrugging. His frustration ebbed. "Good thinking," he praised.

An ever-ready smile flashed to her lips. "You deserve the credit. All that economic theory you've explained to me. Wage theory and what not. Seemed the obvious thing was to outbid the competition."

Jaiden wanted to laugh. He also wanted to track down the ignoble idiot and make him pay. More than anything, he longed to grasp Tilly by the shoulders and kiss her smiling mouth.

In the end, he sauntered over to her. Ignoring her surprised expression, he wiped the cream from her face.

"Chocolate," he said, gazing into her wide green eyes. "I'll try the chocolate cake."

In response, she let out a huge, happy grin.

It was the sweetest treat of all.

CHAPTER TWENTY-EIGHT

Jaiden wanted to kiss her—was about to kiss her—but the woman's pain grated on Tilly's nerves. She'd waited weeks for this kiss only to have it ruined.

She couldn't even see the lady. She had to find her, though. No one else could offer comfort and stop the eternal weeping. Only then would she enjoy Jaiden's lips as they were meant to be appreciated.

But if she left Jaiden to seek the lady, he would disappear, and she would forever forgo his kiss.

She could ask him to wait for her . . . but then he would know she wanted to touch him, and she made it a rule always to keep men guessing about such delicate matters.

A terrible quandary, indeed.

"Mrs. Leighton, wake up. Mrs. Leighton?"

"No, I haven't kissed him yet," she murmured.

"Mrs. Leighton!"

She bolted upright. "What? I wasn't kissing anyone!" It took her seconds to comprehend that she sat in bed. Candlelight wavered around her. Her gaze swiveled around the dark room.

Right. The Astors' townhouse. Yes, Adelaide employed her. To train her brother.

Oh . . . her brother. Damn it! She'd dreamed of kissing him. Again.

How terrible. She would have to put an end to those scandalous dreams.

Because they always ended before they got any good. Much

137

too frustrating. And where the hell was the man? Half the time, he slept in the chair beside her. It had to be after midnight. What was keeping him?

"And so I puts 'er in the drawing room. Didn't know what else to do," a young chambermaid panted. Her one hand held the candlestick, the other clutched Tilly's shoulder.

Tilly blinked. "Who is in the drawing room? And what time is it?"

"After one, ma'am. And I told you. I don't know who she is. Wouldn't give 'er name. She insisted on speaking to you. Well, not really *insisted*, I suppose, but what with the blood on 'er face—"

Nora!

Tilly felt it then—the intense grip of pain. It came from downstairs.

Flinging off her covers, she jumped from the bed and grabbed a dressing robe. Stabbing her arms in the sleeves, she panted, "Mary, we must be quiet. I don't want to wake the whole house. I don't want anyone to know about this. Can you keep it a secret for now?"

"Aye, Missus," came the immediate response along with a bob of her head. "I weren't supposed to be in the kitchen then. 'ousekeeper 'ave me 'ead if she finds out."

"Good," Tilly exclaimed.

Mary opened her mouth, but Tilly had already left the room to run down the hallway and down the stairs. Her bare feet slapped the marble entrance until she clutched the knob of the drawing room door.

Cracking the door, she slipped inside. Mary had lighted three lanterns before fetching her. They illuminated the silhouette of a woman facing the unlit fireplace.

"Nora," Tilly whispered.

Nora jumped, and then turned around. Blood caked the side of her mouth.

"Oh, God!" Tilly pattered across the floor and embraced the thin woman. Nora stood frozen in the circle of her arms.

"Come. Have a seat. Is there anything I can get you?" Tilly asked, pressing Nora into the sofa.

"No, thank you. I'm fine."

Biggest lie Tilly ever heard.

She settled next to Nora and took her cold hand. It remained limp in her grasp. "Are you ready to leave him then?" she asked, hopefully.

Nora stared into space. Her lips barely moved. "I killed him."

Sweet Lord! "Your husband?"

Nora nodded imperceptibly.

Tilly nearly smacked herself in the forehead. Of course, her husband. Who the bloody hell else would she need to kill? *"Good!"* she bellowed.

Nora started, but finally turned to look at her. "I killed my husband," she repeated. "I'm the worst—"

"Knowing your husband as I do, I can honestly say good riddance." Tilly wasn't helping the situation, but she couldn't seem to stop. "You rid the world of a ruthless idiot. You're a hero by my standard." Hysterical laughter choked out of Nora. She squeezed it off and buried her face in her hands. "God, if only I'd done what you told me. If only I'd had the courage to leave him. He'd still be alive now."

"Oh damn, what a loss," Tilly drawled, oozing sarcasm.

"Tilly!" Nora wailed. "Stop making me laugh. I'll just end up crying," she finished on a sob.

"Cry, then. Wail. Scream, if you want, but don't sit here berating yourself for standing up to that dog! Oh, and don't make any noise. It won't do to—Pardon?"

"I didn't stand up to him. I killed him," Nora repeated.

"Right. How did you get the bloody mouth, then?"

Nora lifted her fingers, touched the corner of her lip and looked at her hand. Blood smeared it. "I don't—oh, yes. He hit me. I'd forgotten. I—Yes, I'd found a letter he wrote. To you."

"A letter? To me?" From Nora's vile husband? Tilly jerked up, scrunching her face.

"A threat."

Why would Nora's . . . oh, dear. The threats, indeed. Nora's husband had sent the threats. She hadn't even guessed. Well, didn't look like he'd be sending any more.

Nora stared ahead, eyes unfocused. "He hit me then. Many times, but I . . . I could just reach the fire poker." Her hand grasped at thin air as Nora relived the moment. "I . . ." Nora's hand dropped. A shudder racked her frame.

Tilly clutched her. "Nora, bloody hell. It's not pretty. I know, but cursed if you didn't do the right thing."

"Murdering one's husband can never be the right thing."

Tilly felt herself go cold at the memory. She forced the words past the lump in her throat. "Right or wrong, I've regretted every day of my life that I can't rewrite the past, to do what you did."

Nora studied her. For once, Tilly had no idea what her face revealed, but after seeing it, Nora nodded. Resolve stiffened her shoulders.

"What do I do now?" she asked, only the slightest quaver marring her words.

Tilly nodded, relieved to find herself standing on firm ground again. Yes, this is what she did. She solved problems.

"Stay here," she ordered. "I'll return presently."

She ran upstairs and shoved on a cloak and shoes. Her gaze circled the room, lighting on anything Nora might need, and then Tilly threw the things into a satchel. She didn't know the details of the law, the nuances of husband-killing as far as the

British legal system went, and one of these days she would learn. However, Tilly did know that Nora had killed a nobleman. Nora had to get out of the country.

Seconds later, she and Nora hailed a hack. Tilly gave him an address as both women scrambled onto the seat. The horses took off at a brisk clip.

"With a little luck, this will all go perfectly. Your sister in Australia, will she still let you stay with her?"

Nora bit her lip, hesitating, then nodded. "Yes, I think so. Yes," she repeated with more conviction.

"Good. Now I want you to take this," she said, handing over the bag, minus one small object. "There's a change of clothing in there and an address written on an envelope. If you ever need me, write to that address. Don't use my name, but the name Luciana. It'll get to me."

Nora nodded. She pulled out a small coin purse from the bag. She frowned and opened it. "Tilly! My God! There must be a hundred pounds in here!"

"One hundred and thirty-eight. It's all I have at the moment. Take it. You'll need it."

Nora shook her head. "I couldn't possibly—"

"You can. Nora, trust me. I can't explain, but this is what that money was intended for."

"Tilly—"

"I swear it. Now, take the money. We don't have time to argue."

Nora sighed. "I'll pay you back. Every pound."

Tilly smiled. "If you ever come into a bit extra, by all means. I won't refuse it, but if not, don't worry. It's only money."

"If only I'd thought to bring some when I left the house. And all his jewels—"

"No sense thinking about it," Tilly said, afraid Nora would suggest stopping by the murder scene for a bit of scavenging.

Nora frowned. "You're right."

Tilly wanted to cheer her. "And just think, Nora! Now that your husband has passed into the hereafter—"

"Shoved, more like it," Nora muttered.

"Details," Tilly said with a dismissive wave. "But now you're free to marry again, should you meet someone—"

"I'll never marry again." The steel in Nora's voice revealed her conviction.

It was Tilly's turn to sigh. "I'm never going to marry either."

"Again, you mean," Nora muttered, staring out the window.

"Pardon?"

"You mean to say you'll never marry again."

Tilly grimaced. "Oh yes, exactly. Again."

Nora inhaled. "You're not a widow at all, are you?"

"Well . . . er, technically, no."

Nora threw her head back and laughed.

Tilly scowled at her. And here, she'd been bantering to make her laugh. "It's not that funny," she grumbled.

"Oh, it is! It is!" Nora squealed. "You, an innocent! No wonder you're so oblivious to men propositioning you!"

"I am not!" Tilly knew everything about men. Her job depended on it.

"You are! You are! That time that man offered you a wild ride, I thought you'd feigned naivety to make him feel like a cad. But you literally meant you had a weak stomach," she howled and wiped tears from her eyes.

It took several minutes for Nora to remember herself. When she did, she beamed at Tilly. "Thank you. I needed that."

"Any time," Tilly grumbled.

Nora's grin disappeared as the carriage came to a halt. Tilly disembarked, saw the giant boat docked in its usual place and breathed a sigh of relief.

"This isn't a safe area for two high-bred women," the driver warned. "You sure you don't want me to take you home?"

Nora studied the dark street nervously. Tilly handed up the fare and a generous tip to ensure his silence. "Just keep an eye on us until we enter that saloon, will you?" she nodded in the direction of The Blushing Wanton.

"Oh, you don't want to go there—"

" 'Fraid we do." She winked at him before leading Nora across the road.

They entered. A single drunk sang at a corner table. He raised his glass high at the sight of them and ceased his racket. "And this one's for the five pretty lasses just walked in." Off he launched into another Irish ballad.

"Well as I live and breathe! If it ain't my soul's owner, Mrs. Mathilda Leighton."

"I do believe Satan holds that particular title, Annie."

The graying blonde plopped her hands on her wide hips. "Well now, what can I do for you? You finally decide to take advantage of me special offer?" she asked with a wink and a grin.

"Special offer?" Nora repeated.

Annie looked at Tilly.

Tilly waved her hand. "You might as well tell her. She knows it all."

"Knows about your late husband?" she asked.

"About his never existing, oh, yes," Tilly answered.

Annie rubbed her hands together in relish. "Well, you see, now, um . . . ," She shot a mischievous glance at Tilly.

Resigned, Tilly turned to Nora. "Fancy any particular name?"

"Excuse me?"

"A new name for yourself," Annie prompted.

"Oh. Oh! I see! Yes, how about Rebecca."

Annie nodded. "Well now, Becca, you understand how the widow here ain't really a widow at all. So, she's never experienced any of the pleasures of the flesh, you see. I, being the generous lass I am—"

Tilly snorted.

"—have offered to rectify that situation."

Nora's brows dipped.

"She wants to sell me to the highest bidder for a night," Tilly explained.

Nora's jaw fell.

"Tut-tut, Tilly. Not the highest bidder. A right fine gentleman. Comes in here quite regular-like."

"A gentleman indeed," Tilly scoffed.

Annie shook her head. "You don't know what you're missing." The grin diminished. "So, if you ladies aren't interested in my services, you must need my brother's. Lord knows, my stew ain't good enough to drag you to this end of London. I'll send someone for him."

No sooner had her large form disappeared though a back door than Nora turned on Tilly. "This is a brothel," she accused in a stage whisper.

Tilly noted Nora's open mouth and wide eyes. "Yes," she agreed.

"But a brothel with . . ." She lowered her voice despite the drunken racket from the corner. ". . . with fancy women," she whispered.

"I think we're about the fanciest women this establishment has seen in the last decade."

"No," Nora exclaimed, "I mean . . ." Her voice dropped once more. ". . . courtesans."

Tilly's eyebrows jumped. "Well, Sally, Bess, and Penelope would be honored to learn that. They think they're just common-variety whores."

"But Tilly, how can you condone a place like this?" Nora squeaked.

Moral indignation? A trifle rich coming from the murderer. "Becca," Tilly said, getting used to the name. "These women are better off here than on the street, and every one of them chose to work here. Annie runs a decent place—as brothels go."

Nora shook her head. "How can you let this go on?"

Lovely, soon she would be responsible for ending prostitution, too.

Nora held out her palms. "I mean, these poor women. Why don't you help them?"

"I did help one. Annie asked me to. Said she had too much intelligence and not enough cynicism to spend her life on her back. She's doing well," Tilly added. Beth lived at Muirfield now. For the first time, she didn't have to worry about men's groping hands . . . and other parts of their anatomy.

"But what about the rest?" Nora demanded frantically. Her chest heaved with quick breaths.

Guilt began seeping into Tilly's consciousness. She tried to block it out, but couldn't quite rid herself of the uncomfortable feeling. She fidgeted, unsure what to say, as Nora grew more upset.

The poor dear had seen too much that night.

She breathed a sigh of relief when Captain Kane walked through the door at that moment. Annie bustled behind the bar to dish up a bowl of stew for her brother.

"Til—" He stopped himself from booming her name just in time. He needn't have bothered after Annie's greeting. Didn't matter. The passed-out drunk wouldn't repeat anything. "My dear," he substituted, "what can I do for you?"

"My friend Becca here needs transport to Sydney," she said, motioning to Nora. "We leave for Australia tomorrow," he promised without hesitation.

Tilly's shoulders slumped in relief.

A half hour later Nora slept fitfully below decks, ready for a new and hopefully kinder world. Tilly had hugged her friend goodbye and now her arms felt bereft without her. Hard to believe she'd never comfort Nora again.

With any justice, Nora wouldn't need any more comfort.

Captain Kane stood next to her on the street, waiting for a hackney to come and take her back to the Astors'.

"I owe you for this, Captain," Tilly said, breaking the silence. "I know it, and I swear I will pay you back every farthing."

"You saved my twin. That scoundral would've killed her if you hadn't convinced her to run. You kept her safe until I returned to England. You delivered her into my very arms." He grunted. "Don't you dare hand me money. I, Annie, Bonny, we are forever in your debt."

Tilly squeezed his arm, and then let go. They waited in silence until a cab came to take Tilly to the Astors'. Climbing into bed only a few hours before she would have to rise, Tilly realized how safe she felt there. And when she awoke, she would prepare for another outing with Jaiden.

CHAPTER TWENTY-NINE

"What about this one, then?" Jaiden asked, stopping in front of yet another oil painting in the neoclassical style. His gaze barely glanced at it before settling on Tilly's face. No man-made art could touch God's beauty shining through her smile.

So where had she been last night? Jaiden had spent most of the prior evening tracking down the man who had ordered Tilly's kidnapping. He hadn't uncovered the cur's identity yet, but he had learned other things about Mrs. Leighton. After making a fair bit of progress, he had returned late and promptly crept into Tilly's bedroom, as he did every night, but she hadn't been there. Jaiden had retired to his room instead. Tilly didn't come home until four in the morning.

"Ah. One of my favorites. Gasquet. It's superb. It perfectly demonstrates one of my hypothesis concerning art."

"And what's that?"

"For a piece of art to be truly gratifying it must be beautiful throughout with one exception. See here, where the appreciators' eyes stray." She pointed at where the swords met. "That's more than beautiful. It's striking!"

"Give me another example," he challenged, quite happy to hear her lecture. She smiled, peeking up at him through her dark lashes.

"You have realized I know nothing about what I'm saying—that I'm purely making this up as we go along, correct?"

"Within five seconds of stepping through the door," he replied.

"Excellent. Then you may have your second example. This way," she exclaimed with such enthusiasm that two other art admirers turned from their rococo study to ogle Tilly instead. She didn't notice them.

Less than a minute later, Jaiden and Tilly sat on a bench in the museum courtyard licking ices.

"I don't see any examples to support your hypothesis out here," Jaiden mentioned.

"Of course not. None have arrived," she answered casually, her attention on her ice.

"So, I'm not supposed to be studying the nuances of sweets then."

"By all means do so if it's your wish, but you needn't on my account. The ices only ease our task."

He looked at her. "How so?"

"Hush for a moment, Jaiden."

She'd used his given name.

Jaiden felt his stomach swish and energy pump through him. He watched her, but she refused to meet his gaze.

Why did his name sound so different from her mouth, so melodious and perfect? How could he get her to say it again?

Two girls with their mother paused on the stairs.

"Oh, Mother, may we have ices?" asked the youngest.

The woman clasped the girl's hand. "After we view the sculptures," her mother answered, pulling the children along.

"Now, which child did you think prettier?" Tilly asked, her gaze fixed on her ice.

Other matters than judging the aesthetic value of small children occupied Jaiden's mind. Still, he thought. A memory of blond curls, blue eyes, and pert little noses came back to him. "The littler one," he answered.

"Exactly. Her every feature appeared flawless," Tilly stated, "but if someone asked you to gaze upon one for a full five minutes, which would you choose?"

"The elder one," he said without hesitation. "The freckles—"

"Exactly! They didn't belong on her pale, perfect face, and at first, you think what a pity for her, but then you realize how interesting those freckles are. How she's much better than merely pretty. Her face contradicts itself. You want to figure it out. And that makes her beautiful. Here, let's look at the man walking this way."

A cadaverously thin gentleman in spectacles with a walking stick and a tense mouth ambled past them.

"His dimples," Tilly stated.

"Of course," Jaiden agreed with a laugh. And that's when he realized he was enjoying himself—enjoying himself and relaxing at the same time, for the first time in his life.

Tilly could have made visiting the doctor entertaining.

They both agreed on a chipped front tooth in the next woman and then on a small birthmark on her companion's cheek. The following lady presented a problem.

"It was her eyes," Jaiden maintained. "They flashed a kindly brown anyone could appreciate."

"But so did her winsome smile," Tilly maintained. "It was her nose that made her interesting."

"Her nose was not her best feature," Jaiden stated because he enjoyed the flush in Tilly's cheeks when she argued.

"Yes. It's large and striking and it makes you appreciate how perfect the rest of her features are. Without it, she'd possess just another ordinary, forgettable face. It's like your eyes."

"My eyes?" He looked at her, cocking an eyebrow.

"They're too dramatic. Such a contrast between the blue of your irises and the black of your lashes. No one would describe them as calming, you must allow, but after their initial shock, a viewer realizes they don't want to look anywhere else," Tilly said. Suddenly, a blush covered her face, and she looked down at her ice. "At least, that's my experience," she muttered. The blush deepened.

No one had described his eyes to him before. Indeed, he'd never thought anything about them. His sister had the same eyes. The whole affair left him feeling . . . odd.

"And what about you, Mrs. Leighton? What makes you the most beautiful woman of my acquaintance?"

She threw her head back and laughed. "My lord! You'll make me blush with such flattery."

"You disprove your own theory, for you are flawless, and according to you, it is our flaws that make us beautiful."

Tilly shook her head. "It is our choices that make us beautiful or horrid."

Her seriousness surprised him. Of course, this entire conversation had left him unnerved. "How?"

She sighed. "I can't tell you. I can never explain the things I truly believe. Only those that mean nothing."

He didn't like the sudden sadness in her voice. "Tilly?"

She straightened, flashed a smile at him. "But because I can't explain it, I won't try to convince you." She stood. "Come. I've a game. We shall go through the entire museum and see who can find the ugliest pretense of art. Extra marks for how expensive it is." She lowered her voice. "The loser has to wear a corset under his clothing when we acquire your future wife."

CHAPTER THIRTY

Tilly and Jaiden climbed the stairs to the opulent Haversham townhouse. A harassed butler opened the door. Bellows blasted their eardrums.

"Oh my!" Tilly exclaimed, though she couldn't suppress the excitement in her bosom. A drama. How exciting.

Jaiden stormed past the butler, Tilly in his wake. They ran up the stairs toward the bellows. Rounding the study entrance, Tilly found herself once more in the smoke-filled den.

"She's eloped!" Lord Haversham yelled upon seeing Jaiden. "Clara. Ran off with that stupid Freddy fellow!"

Jaiden stiffened beside Tilly. "Do we have any reason to fear for her safety?"

"Fear for her safety? The gel's gone. Ruined her whole life. She's dead! Dead to me, I say."

Tilly rolled her eyes. Men. They did blow things out of proportion. Not to worry. As usual, she knew how to civilize the situation.

Then again, it might prove more entertaining to see how far she could rile the old beggar.

"Now, now, Lord Haversham," she began, picturing his enraged face in her mind. Damned smoke. She could only make out a vague outline of him. "It's hardly worth all this melodrama. Freddy sounds like a good chap, and your granddaughter dotes on him. Not a bad beginning if you ask me."

"Ask you? Ask *you?*" His face loomed in front of her suddenly. His finger pointed inches from her chest. "You! This is all your fault! Coming here. Giving the girl ideas. Encouraging mutiny. Why, you—you hussy! I know all about your kind, and I swear, I will make you regret ever speaking to Clara—"

Yes, this was fun!

"You're nothing but a whore dressed as—," but the rest of his tirade choked off. Lord Haversham stared at the hand on her shoulder.

She looked down, too. Only Jaiden's hand could encompass half her arm in a single grip. A hand with no current plans for a wedding band.

Imagine that.

Tilly bit her lip to keep from smiling. She couldn't deny the excitement in her chest. No, no, she was just happy for Clara. These feelings had nothing to do with Jaiden becoming eligible.

After all, why should she care about that? Except that she'd have to start looking for another position.

Even that thought couldn't dampen her delight. Where there was a marriage, there was a woman in need of her services.

Lord Haversham looked back and forth between Jaiden and her. "So that's the way of it, is it?"

"Yes," Jaiden answered, his voice steel.

What? What had she missed? Damn her attention for straying. She now had no idea what they were talking about.

Lord Haversham spoke. "I think the two of you best leave."

"I agree. Good day, Lord Haversham," Jaiden said stiffly.

"Good day," Lord Haversham answered.

"Congratulations on your granddaughter's marr—"

Jaiden pulled her from the room before she could finish. Probably for the best. She didn't know what those last looks had been about, but she had a sneaking suspicion they concerned her. Another emotion had wormed its way into her stomach, too.

Guilt.

Jaiden led her to the waiting carriage and helped her inside.

Tilly fidgeted uncomfortably in her seat. "I don't suppose that went well for your business partnership."

"He'll come 'round soon enough," Jaiden said, lounging in the seat opposite her.

She hated when she couldn't read his thoughts. "And Clara?" she tried. "Do you think he'll forgive Clara?"

"That may take longer."

"Oh." She pushed her hands under her skirts. "Maybe you could say a few words to him, you know, on her behalf—"

"Tilly."

"Yes."

His brows rose. He quirked the corner of his mouth. "I don't get involved in other families' affairs."

"Oh, of course not. No, that wouldn't be right. Yes. Neither do I."

She'd never heard such a blatant lie in her life, not even out of her own mouth. It was so untrue, it restored some of her good humor. Yes, as long as she could still lie, she'd never have to worry about a thing.

Now, how to reunite Clara and her grandfather. . . .

But she wouldn't be able to concentrate on that until she determined Jaiden's mood. She peeked up at him from under her lashes. He, however, stared fixedly out the window. To the casual observer, he looked like a carefree gentleman admiring the changing scenery.

Tilly was no indifferent spectator. She took in everything about him. The plotting behind his dramatic eyes. The suppressed excitement at the corners of his voluptuous mouth. The way his fingertips twirled the top hat in his lap. All of which revealed an impatience that belied his casual posture.

Tilly regarded him warily. Something brewed in that head,

and for once, she didn't have an idea what it was.

Needles of apprehension pricked her. By the time they entered his house, she'd been reduced to a bundle of nerves.

"Well," she boomed. "What an exhausting day. So much excitement. I'm spent." She inched toward the stairs. "I think I'll just mosey upstairs and have a rest—"

"Before you mosey, I'd like a word with you."

"I'd love to, but you understand . . ." She stopped talking as he propelled her into his study. Obviously, the damned man would insist on having his way no matter what excuses she made.

The door closed behind her with a click. It sounded like the last nail hammered into her coffin.

The scent of wood and leather enveloped her, but did nothing to comfort.

Stretching out of his grip, Tilly hurried to the opposite side of the room. She turned to face him, crossing her arms over her chest . . . which was something she never did. With her wide hips and ample bosom, she looked the shape of an apple when she hid her slender waist. At the moment she did not care.

Good God, how he had frowned the last hour. Positively menacing. His indolent pose didn't fool her for a minute.

"So—," he began.

She jumped at the softly spoken word. At least her skirts hid her quaking knees—though his piercing eyes seemed to strip her naked to the soul.

"I understand you convinced my fiancée to elope," he said.

Oh, hell. A thousand arguments jumped to her tongue. She could deny the allegation. Or explain Clara's feelings for Freddy. Or downplay her involvement in the matter.

Truly, she hadn't done much. Just pointed out the obvious and maybe given the girl detailed directions to Gretna Green—only in case Clara decided to visit the quaint town.

Guilt kept her mouth closed. Jaiden had offered his friendship, and she'd repaid him horribly. Oh, he didn't belong with Clara. Clearly, Little Miss Persnickety could never partner such an enigmatic male. Jaiden needed someone livelier, less timid, someone who would love him and only him. Who could understand his successes and wouldn't let his daring eyes intimidate her.

Perhaps someone with curly copper-gold hair and of smaller stature to soften his own dramatic appearance.

But that was beside the point. Jaiden's heart was breaking, and maybe, if viewed in a certain light and by someone with a vile temper, Tilly could possibly be considered to be an itsy bit responsible—perhaps.

She peeked up at him. "I . . ."

"Yes?" he prompted.

His eyes sparkled with amusement.

Oh, praise God! He wasn't upset.

"Well, what have you to say for yourself, my good Mrs. Leighton? Surely, it wasn't proper etiquette to push a friend's intended into the arms of another."

Relief doused her nerves. She wallowed in it. "I suppose it was rather high-handed of me."

"Terribly," he agreed, straightening. "Damned high-handed. Bloody convenient, too." He stepped nearer her.

"Convenient? How so?" She tilted her head back as he slowly made his way closer.

"Saved me the trouble of having to extricate myself from a match I hadn't realized I was part of."

"Oh." She tucked that knowledge in her brain, but it seemed to plummet straight to her heart, for that was the organ that heated. "Hmm. Glad I could be helpful."

"Most helpful," Jaiden drawled. "Were it not for your interference, I could never have done something I've ached to try for days."

Her pulse raced. She sounded breathless even to her ears. "Really, my lord. And what is that?" she asked.

"This." He swooped down and claimed her mouth with an expertise that ran roughshod through both Tilly and all her theories about Jaiden's innocence.

CHAPTER THIRTY-ONE

He'd wanted her from the beginning. The way she had stared at his lips that first night in his study. Their every interaction had been a prelude to this moment when, finally, he held her in his arms and strove to capture her very soul—at least for an instant.

Tilly heard the whimper escape her. She had no desire to fight the embrace. Sensations battered her, wreaking havoc on coherent thought. She wrapped her arms around his neck and tilted her head back, giving him better access to her mouth.

She didn't know how it happened, but his tongue slid between her lips. She arched, wanting to feel him against her everywhere.

Jaiden groaned at her sweet surrender. He shoved a hand into her hair, unable to get enough of this elusive temptress. Without realizing it, he backed her against the desk. At her sudden halt, he swung an arm under her delightful buttocks and sat her on the desk's surface.

Her mouth traveled to his large appealing neck. Her tongue flicked against it. Just as she'd suspected, he tasted divine.

A shudder ran through him. "God, Tilly," he groaned.

She pulled back, aghast. "Did I hurt you?"

"My entire being aches for you. Yes, you hurt me. You ruin me. You break me into rubble and raise my dust to the heavens. Your every look sets me whirling. Your smile intoxicates me. And your kiss . . ." He moaned.

She laid her mouth on his throat. "Yes, Jaiden?" she drawled into his heated skin.

"Your kiss . . . leaves me speechless. . . ."

She smiled against him. "We'll have to investigate that." She trailed kisses along his jaw and traveled up to his ear lobe. Gently, she tugged at it with her teeth. He moved his head toward her, like a cat begging to be petted.

In all her days of manipulating men, she'd never felt such power over one.

It matched only her desire to pleasure him, and she basked in her ability to do so.

Jaiden had never known such a rush of emotion. Her every inch melded to accept him. Her pliant woman's body felt like paradise on earth, all welcoming and bliss. He ran his hands down her silky smooth arms, and laced his finger around her tiny wrists before doing it again. How could someone so small dominate his every sensation? And yet she did. Her body held him in a constant state of excitement. Her mind made him believe in legends.

The calluses on his hands were driving her mad. Tingles spread from every area they touched. All powerful, and yet infinitely gentle. Absolutely perfect. Just like him. She wanted everything . . . and she didn't know what that entailed, only that she would die of frustration if he abandoned her now.

Tilly didn't understand this need—the desperation.

"I'm scared," she whispered.

"You should be."

Of their own accord, her knees spread. She pulled him close in the space between her thighs. His pelvis pressed against her skirts, bringing slight ease to a pain she'd only just discovered.

She wrapped her legs around his hips to pull him closer, but it wasn't enough. Experimentally, she rocked against him.

A riot of pleasure overtook her body.

For Jaiden, it was pure torture. He captured her mouth again and ran his hands over her torso, glorying in her every curve. He moved against her. A moan of ecstasy answered him.

It was his undoing. Reason escaped him. The need to touch her banished his control.

He slid his hands over her abundant breasts and yearned to feel their naked skin. He pulled his mouth from hers so he could draw a shuttering breath.

"I like the way you touch me," she breathed, her eyes closed, savoring their every contact.

The innocent flush on her face made him wonder. "How long has it been?" he asked. Had she been faithful to her late husband, to his memory? The thought of another man touching her burned him with injustice. No other could appreciate her the way he did.

Hell, even if another man could, Jaiden wasn't sharing. He needed her. He couldn't feel anything without her.

The thought made him kiss her again, even before she could answer. It didn't matter. He'd forgotten the question. Only she existed—the feel of her soft, giving mouth. In every aspect, she surpassed his ideal. With every sigh, she transformed it.

"Jaiden, that feels . . . nice," she murmured. Tilly hadn't known she could experience so many burning sensations, had not realized she was capable of such heat and desire.

No wonder women bothered with the marriage bed. Jaiden read her every emotion. He could feel each tremble. They matched the quaking of his soul.

He wanted nothing more than to bury himself inside her. With that intention he pulled away for a moment to rid her of some of that unwanted clothing. Only, then did he see her flushed face, her panting chest, her ravished mouth.

His breath caught in his chest.

This was what he wanted—to see Tilly like this every day for the rest of their lives. To bring her to complete abandonment.

To savor her surrender to his body and hands and lips. He wanted to give her pleasure as she had never known, and afterward he would cradle her limp body against his—forever.

"Jaiden," she murmured, pulling him back. He resisted, cupping her precious face instead. Tilly turned into his hand and pressed a kiss against his palm.

"Marry me, Tilly."

It took a moment for her to digest his words, but he knew the instant she did. Her eyes grew as round as saucers.

"Pardon?" she asked, swallowing.

"Be my wife," he said, picturing her in his bed, and then holding his child, even his grandchild someday. He never knew he had this rot in him, but he was damned grateful she'd inspired it.

"Bloody hell!" she screamed into his ear.

Tilly pushed at his shoulders. He rolled off her and stood on the floor. He offered his hand. She ignored it, and sat up unaided.

"Hell! Hell. Hell. Hell!" She fiddled with her dress, trying to look respectable. All the while, she shook her head violently.

She would be his wife.

"I admit, that wasn't exactly the reaction I'd hoped for," he announced.

"Oh, Jaiden!" She tried to throw her hands into the air, but her fingers got caught in the half-undone laces of her dress. "Damn it."

"Allow me." In a no-nonsense manner, he untangled her hands and arranged the laces of her bodice. Copper curls escaped their pins at every opportunity and cascaded over her shoulders.

"Honestly, Jaiden, you're wonderful, the best man I've ever come across—and trust me—I've come across a lot of men—"

What the hell did that mean?

"— but I can't marry you. I can't marry anyone!" she exclaimed.

His heart froze. "Is this because of your late husband?" he asked quietly. He remembered the conversation in the garden that first day he'd met her, what she'd asked. God. "Did he . . . ," Jaiden trailed off.

She let out a moan and buried her face in her hands.

If only the dog were still alive, Jaiden would have killed him. He kept his rage checked. Tilly needed him even if she didn't know it. Tenderly, he pushed the curls from her face and kissed her forehead. Into her ear, he swore softly, "I would never hurt you, Tilly. I would die before harming you in any way. Surely you know that."

She kept her face covered but groaned into his shirt.

How he wished she would look at him. "Tilly, whatever he did to you—it would be nothing like that between us. I swear it. He's dead. No one will ever hurt you again."

She mumbled something he couldn't make out.

"Tilly?"

She dropped her hands, stared him in the eye. "I said, he's not dead."

Jaiden felt as though a bullet had ripped open his chest. He'd never expected . . . but then he could never predict anything with Tilly. But during his investigation, there'd been no sign of a living husband.

"So you see," she continued, "I could hardly acquire another husband if the first refuses to pass on to greener pastures. Now," she said, scooting off the desk, "I think I'll get on with that nap—if you're quite finished with me, my lord." She headed toward the door.

Oh, he wasn't even close to finished with her. "Tilly, sit down," he ordered. She wasn't telling him something. He would have discovered a living husband. Besides, her chin always lifted an extra notch when she hid something. This time, he meant to ferret out her secret.

She paused, her back to him, clearly debating whether or not to obey his command.

"I'll just haul you back if you take another step."

She muttered something under her breath as she passed. He caught the words "arrogant tyrants" and "innocent beauties" before she primly lowered herself onto the couch. Only then did she look up at him.

"Tell me everything regarding your husband."

"Thank you for inquiring. Your concern is duly noted, but I would rather not discuss him."

"Tilly," he warned.

She shuddered at his tone, and he cursed himself. If his suspicions proved true, she'd suffered enough abuse at men's hands. He wouldn't add to her discomfort.

"Is he really so hard to talk about?"

"Impossible," she breathed, refusing to meet his gaze.

Jaiden began to pace. Maybe he could ease her into this discussion. "Where is he now?"

"Honestly, I couldn't tell you." Her face tensed in discomfort.

"Can't or won't?" he demanded, his frustration palpable. "Are you protecting him? Or does he frighten you so much you won't trust me to take care of you? I will, Tilly. I don't care if he is your husband. If you don't want him to, he'll never touch you again. Can't you believe me?"

"Oh all right!" she exclaimed, standing and flinging her arms wide. "He never died because he never lived! There, are you happy?" She stormed past him and made it as far as the door before he caught her about the waist. She pulled out of his grip and glared at him, even going so far as to stamp a foot.

Jaiden would not give in to her tantrum. She'd confused him past endurance, and he couldn't take it any more. He let go of her when he was certain she wouldn't bolt. Crossing his arms over his chest, he said, "Let me get this right. You've never been married?"

She gave a quick nod.

"And a moment ago, when you said you have a living husband—"

"I was merely trying to stop you from proposing. It's true. I thought if *you* thought I still had a husband, you'd take my rejection better than if I just said I won't marry you. And I won't marry, Jaiden. I mean it. That's not negotiable—"

Hearing her say a phrase he'd taught her made him smile despite her speech.

"But I do care about you. Enough that I wanted to refuse you in the nicest possible way, only I can't seem to lie to you. Not for more than ten minutes. Why is that? It's terribly rude of you to make everything so difficult like this."

He ignored the last remark—her entire speech, really—as something else occurred to him. "So . . . you've never . . ." He motioned to the desk, where they had almost . . .

"*No!* No. I've never done . . . I've never kissed anyone else," she finished, her face red.

She was an innocent! It made such sense!

"And don't you dare smile at me right now. I don't know why everyone takes such active delight in my lack of romantic history, but I'm getting heartily sick of it!"

Her eyes flashed at him, but her riot of untamed curls invited him to give her a *romantic history.*

He could not do that now, though.

Good God. How casually he'd used her already. Why, he'd escorted her all over London without any chaperonage. And what he'd done to her moments ago . . .

He grew hard just thinking of it.

"Well, Tilly . . . if that is your real name—"

"It is . . . well . . . Mathilda Leighton. Actually, Miss Mathilda Leighton," she allowed with a frown.

"So then, Miss Mathilda Leighton, I assume your nonwidowed state is one of the three lies you told me?"

She nodded. "I did warn you."

"So you did," he agreed pleasantly. "Care to reveal the other two?"

She shook her head vehemently, sending her adorable curls bouncing.

"Well, I believe you claimed exhaustion earlier," he said, stepping around his desk away from her. "I won't detain you any longer."

She scowled at him, and then warily trod to the door.

"Oh," he called and watched her start, "don't think our marriage discussion is over yet. One way or another, we will wed."

"Jaiden—"

"No, don't concern yourself now. Tut-tut. Off to bed with you. Go on."

She frowned, then shuffled from the room. Jaiden chuckled.

Yes, Miss Mathilda Leighton would make a fine wife indeed.

In fact, it was time he did a bit of jewelry shopping.

Chapter Thirty-Two

Tilly ran to her room and yanked her trunk from under the bed. She began dumping her clothes inside.

"Tilly, is that you? I've been hoping . . . ," Adelaide trailed off. "Are you packing?"

"Yes. Miss Haversham has eloped with Sir Freddy Someone. So, my services are hardly helpful any longer. It's time I made a move anyway," she said, stuffing her small jewelry box inside her satchel.

Adelaide trod into the room, wringing her hands. "Oh, well, er, when will I see you again?"

Damn! Tilly had completely forgotten about Adelaide and Daniel.

Tilly scratched her forehead. "Fine. Let's plot out the next stage in your plan for Sir Sheldon's proposal. Oh! I've got it! Declare you'll never marry. Not out of the blue, but if you begin a conversation with—"

"I'm going to tell him I love him." Adelaide straightened. She clenched her fists at her side. Every muscle in her body tensed as if preparing for battle.

Tilly's jaw dropped.

Determination and wariness mingled on Adelaide's face. "I am. I'm going to tell him the next time I see him . . . or the time after that . . . if, you know, I can."

"But—er—why?"

"Because!" Adelaide flung out. She threw herself across the

room. She nearly landed on top of Tilly, who sat back on the bed in between her piles of possessions to avoid getting hit. "Because I'm tired of these games!"

Tilly wrinkled her nose. "I had got the impression you enjoyed the games—"

"What I enjoy is being with Daniel! But not like this, with all these lies and pretenses," she spat out in disgust. Her resolve suddenly returned. "So I'm going to declare my love," she said stubbornly. "Whatever he may decide to do with it," she added.

Adelaide watched Tilly with wide eyes, waiting for her response.

Tilly, meanwhile, calculated the probable odds of such a rash maneuver. Surprisingly, they weren't so bad. In fact . . . Tilly finally nodded. "Well, Adelaide, I think—"

"Yes?"

"I think that's a brilliant notion."

"You do?" Adelaide asked, her voice hopeful and timid. "You don't think it'll ruin everything?"

"Not at all," Tilly maintained.

Adelaide slumped onto the bed next to Tilly on top of half Tilly's wardrobe. Relief oozed out of Adelaide's every pore. "I do want him."

"And so, as I've told you a million times, you shall have him."

"Good."

"Yes, this declaration is just the thing to do the trick," Tilly continued. "It's perfect, really. I can't believe I didn't think of it before."

Adelaide's brows lowered in apprehension. "What do you mean?"

Tilly rushed on to relieve her anxiety. "It's so simple. Look at what we know. A man like Daniel craves constant challenge. He likes to be kept eternally on his toes, so to speak."

"So . . ."

"So? Do you think any other woman's ever declared her love to him before, like this, out of the blue and all? No. Of course not. It just isn't done. Until now, when you do it! He won't know what to think. Yes, you've offered yourself to him on a sliver platter, but you've done it in a most aggressive and direct way. He won't know what to do, which is exactly where Daniel likes to be, you see? On his toes. Yes, but there's more. If he marries you—yes, he has succeeded in the first challenge of gaining your hand, but you've now promised him a lifetime of challenges."

"I have?"

"Oh, yes! You don't do the expected thing. You are unpredictable. He'll never know quite where he stands with you," Tilly exclaimed, forgetting her own quandary.

"Oh," Adelaide said.

"Yes, but it gets better. You tell him you love him now, but he's already established that you can't be anticipated. Thus, who knows how long you'll continue to love him? He certainly doesn't. He'll have to spend the rest of his life trying to keep you loving him, and all the while, he'll be terrified that you'll walk up to him just as casually one day and declare you've stopped loving him."

"Oh, Tilly, no!"

"Yes, he'll be so uncomfortable. Which is how your Daniel prefers it. It's perfect. Absolutely perfect." Tilly cackled. Her mind considered the plan, to make sure she wasn't missing anything, but she didn't think she was. "We'll be toasting your nuptials in no time at all."

"No," Adelaide moaned next to her, her eyes shut tight.

"Adelaide, whatever is the matter?" Tilly sat up, for the first time noticing the green tinge in her friend's face.

"No. No. No. No." She looked at Tilly through narrowed eyes and accused, "You're not listening to me."

"I am," Tilly shouted instinctively. She always listened carefully to people. It's what made her such an excellent manipulator.

"Tilly," Adelaide interrupted her ranting, shaking her head sadly. "What's the purpose?"

"The purpose?"

"Yes, the purpose of all this?" Adelaide waved her hand between the two of them.

"Why, Adelaide, to secure a ring for your finger, of course."

"But, Tilly, don't you see? It wouldn't be *my* finger."

Tilly blinked, tilted her head. "Whose finger would it be?"

Adelaide ran a frustrated hand through her hair. "If Daniel decided to propose because of this." She waved her hand between them again. "Then it's not me he wants to marry. It's the girl I've pretended to be."

What did that mean? What was Adelaide getting at? "Adelaide," Tilly explained slowly. "It's all you—just sometimes, it's you on your best behavior. That's what courting is all about."

"No, Tilly, you're wrong. I'm not minding my manners with Daniel. I'm acting like someone I'm not." Her shoulders slumped. "I don't want to spend my whole life pretending."

"Adelaide, once the ring is on your finger—"

"I'll be trapped in a character of your creating forever."

Tilly shook her head, trying to clear it. There was a flaw in Adelaide's reasoning. She just had to find it.

Adelaide whispered, "I'd be duty-bound to give him the wife I promised, and that wouldn't be me."

Aha! "Do you think Daniel worries about this stuff? Do you think he'd forever be whisking you to dances and balls? No, of course not. He's selling himself now, just as are you." Tilly took a deep breath before uttering the truth to her innocent friend. "If you think men behave the same way before marriage as they do after, you are sorely mistaken. In my observations, there is no correlation between the two at all."

"But Tilly. I already know Daniel. I've always known him. I've spent years studying him, years during which he barely noticed me. Don't you see how unfair my advantage is over him? I know who I'm marrying!"

"Adelaide! You're too good! That's not how any of this works—"

"I don't care how it works for other people! I want the man I marry to love *me!*" Her face pale, Adelaide peered at Tilly. Tears sparkled in her eyes. "I want Daniel to love me," she whispered. "How can he do that if he doesn't know me?"

"Adelaide, I . . . ," but Tilly didn't have anything to say.

"No, Tilly, don't try. I—I want to be alone now." With slumped shoulders, Adelaide trudged from the room.

Tilly watched her, her heart sinking, but she couldn't help her friend. As much as she wanted to, Tilly couldn't argue with love.

Damned messy emotion. It had to ruin everything!

Time for her to get as far away from it and this house as possible.

CHAPTER THIRTY-THREE

"Mum, there's a Lord Haversham to see you downstairs."

Tilly thanked the chambermaid and followed her out of the room she had rented for the week—just long enough to figure out where she would secure her next client, although maybe she should stick to gambling. She'd made a packet these last few days. Her exceptional ability to read people came in handy at the gaming tables. She'd supported her friends that way before.

Lord Haversham? Whatever could he want? She hadn't seen Jaiden or Adelaide in the past four days. That's how long it had been since she'd enjoyed a decent night's sleep. There was just no fun in it without Jaiden watching over her.

And how had Lord Haversham found her? No one knew where she had boarded. Lord Haversham must have looked long and hard to track her down.

Better to meet with him than replay her last encounter with Jaiden over and over in her head.

Curious, Tilly met the gruff man in the front parlor. He looked down his nose at the clean but shabbily decorated room. In retaliation, she dropped onto the sofa and regarded him coolly.

"And what can I do for you?" she asked.

He raised an eyebrow. "You can steal the camera prototype from Jaiden for me."

She let loose a laugh. That he would dare betray Jaiden spoke volumes about how vile a man he was, but that he expected her to help! He was a candidate for Bedlam.

But, of course, he hadn't struck her as mad.

"And just why would I do that?"

His grin widened. Malice flashed in his eyes. "Because I know your secret."

Her secret? Which one? She rearranged her skirts, the picture of unconcern. "Yes, it's true. I indulge in a sea-salt bath once a week. Do you think any woman's skin glows like this naturally?"

His grin dropped. Disgust replaced his relish. "I thought you might appreciate my vagueness in deference to prying ears, but now I see I must speak plainly. I know about your involvement with the missing wives."

"The missing wives? I admit I've heard of the investigation," she said, ignoring the chill creeping into her limbs. She had expected him to say something about her lack of a late husband or how society ladies employed her, but how could he have leaned about the missing wives? Even Scotland Yard hadn't made the connection.

Peeking up at his bushy eyebrows, she realized he had ways of investigating to which even police refused to resort.

And this was all her fault. She'd played him wrong from the beginning. Indeed, she'd barely put in the effort to play him at all. She hadn't realized the threat he posed, and now her friends would pay for her mistake.

Her friends . . . or Jaiden.

Bloody hell.

"Don't play the fool with me, Mrs. Leighton, or should I say, Miss Leighton. I know how you spirited them out of London, and it didn't take more than a moment to realize they hide at the estate your father left you in Hendramton. Now, what you should be plotting is how you're going to get me the camera prototype. I expect it in my possession within forty-eight hours."

"Very well, sir." She stood. "Let me see you to the door."

For the first time, he looked uncertain. "You'll do it?"

"Of course. You've made an excellent argument. And, after all, what do I owe Lord Astor? One way or another, he'll land on his feet. He always has, eh?"

Lord Haversham's shoulders slumped, but his mouth remained determined. "Exactly," he muttered.

"So I'll call on you the day after tomorrow," she said, affably, "with a little something for you. Maybe we'll have some tea, get to know each other. That could be nice."

He snorted in response. She practically shoved him through the front door.

"Good day, my lord," she called, forcing herself to wait until he cleared the threshold before closing the door, when really she wanted to slam it into the back of his head.

Repeatedly.

Good God, what was she going to do?

"Was that truly a lord?" Chelsey, the chambermaid asked, blocking Tilly's path after she'd closed the door. "An honest-to-God lord?"

"Aye, Chelsey, and a perfect gentleman, too." Blackmail and all.

"You must be the luckiest girl I know," Chelsey breathed dreamily.

"That's just what I was thinking," Tilly muttered. She had to clear her head. "I'm going for a walk. Don't expect me for dinner."

"But Mrs. Leighton, you're not dressed for—"

The door slamming behind Tilly shut off the remainder of Chelsey's words, thank God.

Tilly rushed into the busy street. Vendors and assorted males called for her attention. A very different atmosphere than in Mayfair with the Astors, but Tilly barely noticed. Her mind was elsewhere.

As always, she sought the positive in her pain. Precious little this time. At least she had forty-eight hours to come up with a plan. She could think of something in two days. Hell, the world could end in two days.

Oh dear, she couldn't betray Jaiden. It would hurt him more than anything, much more than Lord Haversham could ever understand. And Jaiden had worked so hard. He deserved happiness.

But so did her friends at Muirfield. They'd suffered enough, and Tilly had sworn to protect them. In the whole world, it was the only vow she considered sacred. They were her first allegiance, her only loyalty. And Jaiden was a man. That fact alone granted him every advantage. As a mere woman, how much trouble could she cause him?

Plenty, she realized with a sigh.

Tilly walked, her mind tripping along in the same circle. And the thought of helping that scoundrel, Haversham! That alone irked her beyond consideration.

Only when she saw the green shutters did she realize where her feet had led her. Directly to Jaiden's door.

Cursing, she realized what she had to do. It smarted, but she would make the best of it.

She always did.

CHAPTER THIRTY-FOUR

Jaiden looked up from the letter in his hands just in time to see Tilly bang into his office . . . in a dressing gown and slippers.

He stood, but she held out a hand to ward him off when he tried to go to her.

"Don't bother," she said. "I've things to say . . . and . . . and . . ." She closed her eyes and in one breath said, "Lord Haversham threatened to reveal them unless I steal your camera. I don't want to do it. I don't, but I can't tell anyone where those women are. I can't. I'd rather die. They've had such a hard time of it until now—"

"Tilly."

Her eyes opened huge with sincerity. "This is the first time they're somewhere they can feel safe. I won't take that away from them."

"You don't have to."

Finally, she ceased her tirade. Her gaze fixed on his smile.

"Why aren't you shocked?" she demanded, arms akimbo.

Jaiden tapped a short stack of stationery on his desk. "Ten minutes ago, I received a long interesting letter from Lord Haversham." He circled the desk to lean his backside against the front of it. "I just finished it when you walked in. He doesn't mean to harm your friends. Their secrets are safe."

Her lower lip trembled. She looked about the room widely.

Her inability to deal with her emotional turmoil dropped a flutter of warmth into his stomach. "You can read it if you like."

He picked up the pages and offered them to her.

Tilly crossed her hands over her chest, then pushed them down to her hips again, all the while shaking her head.

Tenderness welled inside Jaiden. Damn Lord Haversham for putting her through this. He should have trusted Jaiden's judgment.

But Lord Haversham was advanced in years, and his granddaughter had just hurt him. He'd merely tried to protect a man he'd already come to think of as a son.

No matter what he told himself, seeing the tears well in Tilly's eyes, Jaiden could have happily killed the man.

"They're going to be fine," he said gently. He spread his arms.

Tilly ran into them and promptly burst into tears. He hugged her close.

"Everything's going to be fine," he murmured against her hair. "I think Lord Haversham was angry. He wanted to strike out at you, but the more he learned about your past, the more he respected you. In his letter, he said he wanted to test your loyalties. He needn't have bothered. I never doubted you."

"Oh, but you should have!" she cried, pulling away far enough to look at him through flooded eyes. "I nearly did as he bade me. I thought about it for hours—"

"And in the end, you did the right thing. You came to me," he reminded her. Why couldn't she see what that meant? Why didn't she realize she already trusted him with her life and things she held even dearer.

She shook her head. "But I surprised myself by doing it."

"You didn't surprise me."

Her sobs worsened. "Oh, you mustn't trust me."

They'd had this discussion before. "Face it, Tilly, you count me a friend."

She hiccupped. "I suppose so," she muttered.

He buried his laugh in her hair and rubbed her back. Such a tiny bundle of excitement. How ever had he managed without her?

"I don't know why I'm crying. I never cry, truly, except . . . well at Mrs. Grimmway's party and now, but usually I don't. I think I'm relieved. I didn't realize how much Lord Haversham's threat bothered me."

"You have every right to be upset." He paused and said, "I gather those women's husbands mistreated them."

"Mistreated them?" she squeaked, jumping away from him. "Most beat them black and blue. I could show you photographs that would give you nightmares. Those beasts whittled away at their confidence because of their own vile insecurities. They're worse than beasts. They're monsters. Stupid, ignorant, evil—"

"Men," Jaiden spat. "You shouldn't have anything to do with the entire gender."

Finally, she smiled and looked up at him shyly. "You're a man," she reminded him.

Jaiden was glad she'd noticed. "Yes," he agreed, "but I am the one exception."

Tilly sighed. "I rather fear you might be."

Her words warmed his insides. The tears had dried on her face, leaving behind green eyes, which sparkled for an altogether different reason.

He couldn't stop himself. He leaned forward and touched his lips to hers.

CHAPTER THIRTY-FIVE

A voice came from beyond the doorway. "Excellent. Tilly, you're—oh my!"

Tilly jumped away from Jaiden and whirled to see Aunt Hen's shocked expression. Damn! She glanced back at Jaiden, who appeared unconcerned, even amused.

Recovering her composure, Aunt Hen whisked into the room in her usual mismatched pastels. "I do declare, Tilly. Every time I open a door, you're kissing someone."

Jaiden gave a bark of laughter. Tilly glared at him, and he managed to swallow it, although his grin didn't appear apologetic.

A cup of revenge would brighten the moment. "Dear Aunt Hen," she began, moving to sit in a sofa across from the ancient aunt. "I've been meaning to inquire after your two great friends, Lady Wexham and Mrs. Beesley. How are they faring?"

Aunt Hen burst into radiance. "Wonderfully. They are absolutely divine. Finally, they've ceased all that lesbian nonsense, thank God. Taken up gambling instead. Much more the thing, I must say. And better for outside company, too." She gave Tilly a sly look. "Though you two go ahead and kiss whenever the mood strikes, don't mind me." She turned to Jaiden. "Her lips are amazingly soft, aren't they?"

Tilly felt her cheeks burn once more.

"Deliciously so," Jaiden replied.

Aunt Hen nodded and studied her speculatively. "Yes, I may

have to sneak up on her again sometime."

Dear God!

"Actually, Aunt, I would appreciate it if you didn't assault my future wife."

"Jaiden!" Tilly exclaimed.

"Engaged!" Aunt Hen rushed to Tilly and clamped her in her still surprisingly strong arms. "That's wonderful! Oh hurrah! Welcome to the family, dear."

"Not precisely engaged, Aunt Hen," Jaiden warned. Tilly could just glimpse him past a lock of Aunt Hen's white hair. He didn't look nearly frightened enough, considering the vengeance she plotted. "Tilly has yet to say yes."

Aunt Hen looked at her. "Oh, you must say yes. You simply must. Edna and Polly despise their daughters-in-law. Too high in the instep, all of them. You'll be quite our favorite, and oh, the adventures you get into. The stories I can relate! I'll be the envy of both."

"I . . . er . . . ," Tilly choked, entombed in pastel ruffles.

"Jaiden, be useful for once. Convince her to have you."

"I shall do my best."

"Oh, pooh. If that's all you can do, you might as well go. I've more important things to discuss with Tilly, anyway."

"You do realize, Aunt Hen, that you're attempting to dismiss me from my study?" Jaiden asked, clearly wondering if his aunt's mind had given way completely.

Aunt Hen relinquished her hold on Tilly to wrinkle her nose at Jaiden. "You realize no one here cares a fig what you think, yes?"

Even Tilly winced at that. Maybe Jaiden hadn't behaved like the most attentive nephew, but he'd improved over the last few weeks.

Thankfully, Jaiden appeared unfazed. "I had not realized, Aunt. Thank you for clarifying the matter."

"Jaiden," Aunt Hen interrupted, exasperated. "If you insist on staying, then pray stay silent. I've a very important matter I need to discuss with Mrs. Leighton."

Jaiden half-bowed and swung his arm to convey "by all means."

Satisfied, Aunt Hen nodded, then turned on Tilly. "You must do something about Adelaide. The girl is driving me to Bedlam. She's miserable."

"Is this fuss with Daniel bothering her?" Tilly asked, unsurprised.

"Bothering her? It's killing her. And it's making me homicidal."

"Oh, dear."

"I'm plotting murder, and all you can say is 'oh dear?' I need help. *She* needs help."

"What's this business about Daniel?" Jaiden interrupted. "He called yesterday. Adelaide refused to see him."

"Jaiden!" Aunt Hen reprimanded. "I liked you better when you didn't exist."

"Aunt Hen!" Tilly exclaimed. "It is commendable that Lord Astor cares about the welfare of his sister."

"And it's about time you spoke up. Really, as his future wife, you better be quicker to defend him. Of course, not too quick. You must have something to talk about over tea."

Tilly sent an appealing glance at Jaiden, but he was busy smiling at her—it was an entirely too intimate smile for her comfort. She felt her cheeks warm yet again, and swiveled toward Aunt Hen to hide her blush from Jaiden.

"Duly noted, Aunt Hen," she allowed.

"I should think so. Now, why is Adelaide acting like even more of a ninny than usual?"

Tilly bit her lip. "I think she's having trouble deciding how to behave around Sir Sheldon."

"Can't you teach her? I would have thought you'd be a true proficient at manipula—"

"Yes, yes," Tilly cut her off. "but Adelaide feels any help I give her is tantamount to playing Daniel false."

"Of all the idiotic—"

"Yes, but I'm beginning to think she may have a point," Tilly said. Maybe it was bad manners to manipulate someone you loved. At the very least, it seemed a dangerous business.

Aunt Hen stood in disgust. "Well, it's a good thing you have us adults pressuring you children into marriage. Left to your devices, the human race would die out in three score years."

She sailed from the room, leaving the door open, and Tilly watching Jaiden with too much to say.

What was all that future wife business? And how could she get him to stop?

They both spoke at the same time—

"How have you been—"

"Where are you staying—"

—then smiled self-consciously. Tilly decided she preferred kissing him to making conversation afterward. Everything sounded so mundane with the feel of his lips still lingering on hers.

"I've taken a room in Cheapside for the week while I prepare to make my next move," Tilly explained.

Jaiden's brows drew together. "You're welcome to stay here as long as you like."

"I don't think it would be wise."

"Actually, what with that madman trying to kidnap you, I think it would—"

She shook her head. "That problem has been taken care of."

He studied her face. "And the threats—"

"Yes, one and the same."

Silence reigned for what seemed an eternity. Finally, Jaiden asked the question. "Who was behind it?"

Tilly swallowed, aware she stood on dangerous ground. "Lord Whenceworth."

Jaiden's face registered surprise. "The man discovered dead five days ago?"

"Yes." She smiled ruefully. "As I said, it's taken care of."

He crossed the room and took her hand. His eyes shone with concern. "Would you like to tell me what happened?"

"No!" She winced at the sound of her bellow. "I mean, it's best you don't know."

He opened his mouth, ready to argue with her. The maid stopped him.

"Excuse me, Lord Astor," Mary said, standing at the threshold of the room. "I only just heard that Mrs. Leighton had arrived—how do you do, ma'am?" The girl executed a quick curtsy. Tilly smiled. "I wanted to give her this before she left." She handed Tilly an envelope. "This arrived for you the day after you left. I didn't know where to forward it."

"Thank you, Mary." Tilly turned the post over. Her heart froze.

"What is it?" Jaiden asked, seeing her concern.

She turned her frightened eyes on him. "It's from Muirfield."

CHAPTER THIRTY-SIX

Fear lanced through her.

The women at Muirfield would only write if it was an emergency, and already two days had passed since they sent it. What if it was too late? What if they'd been found?

They would rather die than be forced to live with their husbands again. And after running away, those tyrants would—

A shudder ran through Tilly.

She scratched at the seal, but her hands shook too badly to open it.

"Allow me." Jaiden plucked the correspondence from her hands, ripped it open, pulled out the note and handed it back to her.

Tilly's eyes scanned the single sentence.

We need you. —R

Damn! Of course, Ruth wouldn't go into details. She would fear the letter would be intercepted. Rightly so, but the uncertainty drove Tilly mad.

Concentrate on things she could control, she told herself. That was the chant that had seen her through worse times than this.

How to get to Muirfield as quickly as possible? Ideally, she could hire a hack to take her all the way, but the cost would prove prohibitive.

There was nothing for it. She'd have to take the train to Bruhen, then hope to hire a driver at the station.

Mind decided, she stood. A hand on her arm stayed her. Confused, she found Jaiden standing beside her. How did she keep forgetting him when he stood right next to her? She couldn't get him out of her mind when she was alone.

"Tilly—"

"I'm sorry. I must go. I haven't a moment to spare."

His hand felt strong on her arm, stronger than she felt at the moment. "You're trembling," he stated. "Let me help. Tell me what I can do."

She shook her head, avoiding his gaze. Men had wreaked havoc on those women's lives. She wouldn't allow another one into their midst.

Then Jaiden's hands cupped her chin. He lifted her face until his gaze met hers.

And all reason deserted her.

"You know I would never do anything to harm you or someone you cared about," he said.

And she did know.

"I would kill before I let that happen," he swore.

Tilly knew men. She recognized their deceptions and lack of control. She read them as plainly as she read English.

What she read in Jaiden's eyes made her heart swell with hope.

"Very well, Lord Astor. Take me home."

CHAPTER THIRTY-SEVEN

Tilly barely spoke on the five-hour journey to Muirfield, but she was grateful for Jaiden's presence on the seat next to her—and his obtaining her clothes from the boarding house. His strength flowed around her. Protected in its embrace, Tilly felt hopeful that everything would turn out all right—no matter what emergency drew her home.

The carriage rounded the final turn, and all the usual emotions assaulted Tilly—fear and happiness and hate—though Jaiden kept the thoughts at bay. She didn't know how to thank him for coming. Words could not express how much he'd helped.

An idea occurred to her. Without debating its merits and drawbacks, Tilly threw her arms around Jaiden's neck and tucked her face against his throat. She kissed his neck, breathing in the comforting scent of thyme, woods and soap.

His large hands patted her back. What would it feel like to be him, she wondered. So powerful and large, and yet good. He could strangle her now if the mood struck, but it wouldn't. Jaiden didn't need to harm a woman to feel strong. Strength emanated from him.

Tilly pulled back, just far enough to look into his beautiful eyes—the most lovely pair in the world. She stared into their depths, hoping she could convey her gratitude to him in that way since words failed her.

He smiled and drew one hand to her forehead. He laid his palm against her skin. Her furrowed brow relaxed under his warmth. Her tension eased.

He lowered his hand and gave her torso a satisfied squeeze.

"Thank you for helping me," she finally managed.

His eyes flashed. "Thank you for letting me."

The carriage slowed. Tilly took one last fortifying breath. Whatever ordeal waited for her, she would survive it. With Jaiden's help, she could survive anything.

Wheels squeaked to a halt. Refusing to wait another second, Tilly climbed over Jaiden, revealing immodest portions of her anatomy.

Seconds later she untangled her skirts and dropped to the stone driveway. Above her loomed the home of her childhood, emerging erect between the green hills where she'd found refuge once upon a time.

She could almost see the little curly-haired girl flying from the house as fast as her chubby legs could carry her. If she listened closely, the echoes of screams long silenced would fill her ears.

Instead, the creak of the front door came to her. A tall, handsome woman filled the frame, dragging Tilly into the present.

Ruth ran down the front stairs. "You came!" she exclaimed a moment before grasping Tilly in a huge bear hug, which left the smaller woman's feet dangling two inches above the floor.

She let Tilly go and stepped back, though her hand remained pressed against Tilly's upper arm as though she feared she would vanish any second if not held fast.

"I mean to say," she corrected with uncharacteristic uncertainty, "I knew you would come as soon as you received my letter. I just didn't know how long it would take." She brushed a stray gray hair back into the unfashionable knot at the back of her head.

"Tell me. Please," Tilly breathed. "I've been driving myself mad. Have we been discovered?"

"No, no, nothing like that. It's . . ." Her voice dropped. She stepped closer. "It's Verity. She swallowed rat poison."

Chills thrashed Tilly.

"On purpose," Ruth clarified.

"How did it happen?"

Ruth stared at her.

Tilly took a deep breath.

Ruth closed her brown eyes and nodded once.

"Oh," was all Tilly could get out.

Jaiden's hand rested on her shoulder then. She reached her fingers up and covered his. Ruth shot him a surprised look, then turned her attention back to Tilly.

"I know you're not God," Ruth said. "My head tells me you have no power over life and death, but my heart refuses to believe it. My memory reminds it too often how you saved my life."

"How does she hold up?" Tilly asked.

"Good physically. We gave her ipecacuanha before it was too late," Ruth said. "She's bedridden, but much recovered. Her spirits, however . . ." She shook her head and frowned. Ruth looked down at her hands, as if reprimanding them for her impotence. "I forced her to look at the photograph we took the day she came to Muirfield. With some women that works, but she just blamed herself for the bruises."

Tilly pressed her free hand against Ruth's shoulder for a moment. "It must have been horrible for you," Tilly said, knowing Ruth would never complain.

Ruth shrugged. "She needs you."

Tilly nodded. "I'll go to her at once." She stepped toward the stairs, then turned around, remembering a speck of decorum. "Oh, this is Lord Astor. Please help him situate himself."

"Of course," Ruth said.

Tilly ran up the steps, but slowed as she entered the house. It didn't seem right, entering a sick room at an exuberant trot. Enthusiasm of any sort felt uncomfortable in this home. For too long, it had held nothing but pain and fear.

Those days were over, Tilly reminded herself yet again.

Verity had moved into the room that had once served as a drawing room. Six months before, when she had finally left her husband, the house had overflowed with residents. Several had since left to start other lives for themselves, but Verity had chosen to stay in the former drawing room. She liked the door, which led into the gardens. It made her feel safe. Even here, she always sought an escape route.

Maybe her suicide attempt was just that, the final escape.

Tilly crept up to the drawing room door and knocked softly.

"Come in," a light voice answered.

Pushing open the door, Tilly spotted Beth in the bedside chair. Verity lay in the bed, gazing out the window.

Beth's face lit up. Her chair scratched against the wood floor as she jumped out of it. She threw her arms around Tilly and buried her face in her neck.

"Tilly," she breathed.

Tilly held her, too, for once taller than someone. Beth had only joined their unusual household a few months before, but she looked twenty years younger than when she'd first arrived. Though three years older than Tilly, she appeared no older than a carefree schoolgirl in her loose dress and with her free-flowing wavy blond hair.

Beth had done an amazing job of putting her horrible past behind her.

Unlike Verity.

At Tilly's nudge, Beth shuffled out of the room. Tilly pressed the door closed behind her and wandered over to the chair Beth had vacated.

Verity watched her warily.

"So," Tilly announced. "Get any glimpses of life in the hereafter? Is God a woman?"

Verity's pale lips widened. Her face registered horror a second before she buried her mouth under her hands. Without warning, the girl burst into tears. "I'm so sorry, Tilly," she said, shaking her head ferociously. "I'm terrible, absolutely horrid. You have every right to hate me. After all you've done for me! And I'm still so weak I go and eat that powder—"

"Hush," Tilly commanded, slipping onto the bed. She wrapped her arms around the child. Seventeen, but still a little girl. A girl who'd survived hell. Just like all the others in the house.

Verity's sobs abated after a time. Tilly pulled back and looked at her tear-lined face. A lock of hair stuck to her cheek. Tilly pushed it away.

"Verity, I would never judge you," she swore. "Condemnation has no place in this house. You don't owe me anything, least of all an apology."

Verity squeezed her eyes shut. Tears slipped out and slid across her cheeks.

"I just felt like you, Ruth, Beth, Lizzy, the baby, would all be better off without me. As though the world would be better off without me."

Tilly shook her head. "I need you around. You don't believe it, I know, but without you—and Kyla and Beth and Ruth—my life has no purpose. You give meaning to my breath. You're the reason I get up every morning. How could I be better off without you?"

Verity's mouth trembled, but she didn't speak.

Tilly's mouth tightened. "And as for the world, it isn't your responsibility."

Verity nodded slightly, even as more tears ran down her face. Her voice quivered. "Before my eyes open in the morning, before my mind even wakes, the thoughts are already there. That I failed. That I'm a failure. I couldn't keep my husband happy. If I can't even do that . . ." She trailed off, but the tremor that shook her spoke her pain more eloquently than any words.

"Ruth and Beth, neither of them could placate their husbands. Do you think they're failures?"

"No, of course not," she said instantly. "But their situations were different."

Tilly knew too well the double standard many women employed. They strove for perfection, while demanding nothing of others. Of course, they couldn't live up to their own expectations. Life wasn't designed for ideals.

"Their husbands were true monsters. My Eric could be so kind sometimes." Her voice grew so soft Tilly had to lean forward to hear. "He always apologized afterwards."

Which was how the vile male had convinced her to stay with him long enough to burn half her left arm. Tilly didn't remind Verity of that fact. Her scars wouldn't let her forget, and if she did forget, Tilly could always show her the photographs.

Verity turned her watering eyes once again to the window. "I wake up every morning alone in this bed, and I can't believe this is my life. Where did I go so wrong?"

"You didn't, Verity. As much as we hate it, we can't control the actions of others or how those actions shape our lives."

Verity swallowed. "As a little girl, I never thought my life would turn out like this. I never thought my Eric . . ."

Tilly sighed. "Of course, you didn't. Our mothers wean us on impossible fairy tales of true love and good triumphant. Hell, I planned on marrying Prince Phillip, myself."

Verity's gaze flew back to Tilly. A corner of her mouth turned up. "Prince Phillip? He was one of my favorites. The way he wakes Sleeping Beauty with a kiss . . . ," she finished dreamily.

"Only after slaying the fire-breathing dragon."

"Prince Charming was nothing in comparison."

"Prince Charming who? Didn't even warrant a perch in my memory, that idiot," Tilly announced.

They both sighed at the same time, then giggled. Verity's eyes had dried for the moment, but then they began to fill again.

"Have you ever met someone else so pathetic they couldn't bear to live?" she sniffled.

Tilly rearranged herself on the bed. "Yes," she admitted. "Me."

"You?" Verity's face registered shock. "But you're so strong."

Tilly smiled. "Thank you, though I'm not certain I agree. Sometimes I feel anything but strong."

"But did you ever attempt to take your own life—"

"No, but I came close," Tilly revealed. She hated thinking of that time in her life. Maybe, though, it could help Verity understand she wasn't alone. "I thought about leaving all the time. Mornings were the worst for me, too. I would wake up berating myself. Women are good at that, I've learned. Anyway, I favored a bullet in the brain over rat poisoning. The taste, you know."

"What happened?" Verity prompted.

Tilly shook her head. A smile crept onto her face at the memory. "For me there's always a point where things get so bad, they become funny. That time it came when I held the loaded gun in my hand. Like you, I thought how everyone I knew would be better off without me in their lives. Over and over in my head, this voice told me how I'd destroyed everything I held dear. It refused to stop, but somehow it changed. It went from accusing to . . ." She chose the word carefully. ". . . liberating. I mean, I couldn't have done a worse job of it. I had ruined everything. There was nothing left I hadn't already mucked up, which meant I couldn't mess up any further." Tilly shook her head. Why did she insist on telling other people what a complete lunatic she was? "I began laughing. I felt completely free. And I stopped taking it all so seriously. There was nothing left in my life worth that worry. It's only my life," she finished. She hadn't done a proper job of explaining, but hopefully, Verity would find some hope in her crazy confusion of words.

"Oh my," Verity breathed, her eyes huge.

Tilly shrugged, knowing there was little she could say. As always, she was at a loss when it mattered.

The two women lay side by side. Both stared out the open window. A warm summer breeze meandered in. The air on her face made Tilly wish . . . But wishes did no good.

CHAPTER THIRTY-EIGHT

After Tilly ran into the house, Jaiden and Ruth stared at each other awkwardly in the grass.

"I see your man is installing your carriage in the stable."

"Yes," Jaiden answered. "I hope that isn't a problem."

"Not at all."

Silence fell again. Jaiden didn't know what kept Ruth silent. He couldn't think of a single courteous thing to say. His mind stuck on one idea.

This woman could answer all his questions about Tilly.

But how to get her talking?

"So," she finally said. "Would you like to come into the house?"

"Yes, thank you," he said. They entered the large stone cottage together. "I'm sorry for intruding upon your household without notice like this," he said, hoping to ease some of the tension.

She paused as they entered the cozy living room and turned toward him.

Jaiden stopped, too.

"You brought Tilly home to me," she stated, her eyes boring into his. "For that I can spare a cup of tea."

Then she smiled, and it transformed her entire appearance.

"Come into the kitchen," she said, leading the way. "We don't stand on formalities around here, Lord Astor. Go on. Sit at the table. I'll just put the kettle on."

Jaiden obeyed as Ruth bustled about the kitchen. Once the filled kettle sat on the stove, she sat down across from him.

"This is quite a treat," she said. "It's a rare occurrence when I've an excuse to sit down and drink a cup of tea in the middle of the afternoon. And with a bloomin' lord no less."

Jaiden sat up straight, suddenly realizing why she looked familiar. "Olympia Chadberry, Duchess of Cadwell!"

Her mouth turned up. "Once upon at time. Now, I'm plain Ruth. Really, I'm surprised you recognized me. I was a bit before your time."

"You're legend," Jaiden told her. "Your portrait still hangs in the British Museum. I saw it last week."

Ruth smiled. "Then I'm doubly surprised you recognized me. My husband commissioned that painting over fifteen years ago."

"You look better, now," Jaiden told her. It was true. She had a few more lines around her eyes, but serenity surrounded her.

"I should," Ruth told him, rising to fetch the screeching kettle. "Not living in daily terror reflects on one's appearance."

"I've met your husband," Jaiden said.

"He's worse in private," Ruth said, demonstrating the impudence that had made her the toast of London fifteen years earlier. She set a cup of tea in front of him. "We don't have any sugar on hand, but if you'd like milk—"

"No, no, this is fine," Jaiden assured her, taking a sip from the cup.

She sat across from him, drinking from her own cup.

Jaiden couldn't stop himself. He had to ask. "How did you meet Tilly then?"

"Providence." Ruth's eyes sparkled. In her brown twill skirt and white blouse, she looked more like a farmer's wife than a duchess. "I needed a holiday from wedded bliss. The duke—yes, he insisted I call him the duke even in private. Obviously, the man needs a new hobby or a religious experience or something. Anyway, the duke had left for a hunting expedition in Ireland. I waited five minutes and went to visit a friend of mine from school. I met Tilly there. My friend had hired her to . . ." She clamped her lips together. Her eyes widened, then she recovered. ". . . well, as a companion of sorts. Tilly's parents had died only six months earlier. She was still pretty shaken, I think. It didn't take long for us to realize we could help each other."

"How did her parents die?"

She paused in the middle of sipping her tea. "You'll have to ask her."

He would. "And so you moved here?" Jaiden clarified.

"Yes."

"How long ago was that?"

Ruth sighed. "Six years now. Six wonderful, contented years."

Jaiden shook his head. *Tilly.* She went through life with such a carefree mien, refusing to let anything bother her, not kidnap attempts or threatening letters. And now he'd discovered this whole other half of her. A girl who stood up against dangerous men and rebuilt women's lives.

How did her many complexities manage to coexist in such a small body? A delightfully small, curvy, tantalizing body. And, how had he fallen in love with her when he knew nothing about her. Bloody hell, he didn't even know her age.

Well, that he could correct. "How old is she?" he asked.

Ruth chuckled. "She?"

Oh, hell. "Tilly," he clarified.

"I know. Don't ever play poker with her. Your face reveals your every thought."

Jaiden nodded. Seemed sensible advice.

"She's twenty-four."

Again, Jaiden nodded.

"You don't seem surprised."

He leaned back in his chair. "With Tilly, I've learned to expect nothing."

"Wise boy," Ruth muttered.

Jaiden stood. "More tea?"

Ruth raised her eyebrows.

"I was told they don't stand on formalities in these parts."

She waved her hand. "Well, in that case, by all means."

He carried both cups over to the stove where he set the kettle on once again. "You haven't been linked to the other wives," he commented, turning to lean against the counter.

Out of the corner of his eye, he saw Ruth straighten. Obviously, she had not thought Tilly would tell him. Of course, Tilly hadn't. A bit he had uncovered, and the rest he'd learned from Haversham.

"No," Ruth finally agreed. "I left my husband too early for that—though not early enough for me. Really, I'm surprised any of the others have been linked together. Seems like wives have gone missing since the beginning of time. That Sir Sheldon must be an intelligent one."

"He is."

"You know him?" Ruth asked, her voice gone soft.

"I trained him." Jaiden glanced over his shoulder at her, saw her swallow.

"And Tilly told you about us nonetheless?"

"Nonetheless," he agreed. No sense mentioning that little blackmail matter.

He thought Ruth might suffer a fit of apoplexy right there, but instead, she threw her head back and guffawed with mirth.

Jaiden hadn't expected that reaction. "Please know I would never betray your secret."

Ruth gave a dismissive wave of her hand. "Oh, pooh," she dismissed. "If Tilly trusts you, my life is safer in your hands than in God's."

"Quite right," Jaiden agreed. He fixed the tea. Behind him he heard occasional chuckles.

"And may I ask then, what has you chortling? I'm beginning to fear a gaping hole in my trousers reveals half my backside."

He carried the tea back to the table.

She accepted a cup and shook her head. The grin never left her face. "It's nothing, absolutely nothing, just a thought. Have no fear. Your trousers are in perfect condition."

Jaiden let the joke pass. The missing wives case had tied together five different women, all in the upper crust of society. It had not included Ruth. "So there are six of you living here now?"

"Seven women, counting Tilly, how did you know?"

"A guess. And has Tilly changed all the other five lives as radically as she has yours?"

"Five?" Ruth repeated. She started laughing again.

The oddest things sent this woman into hysterics. "Has the hole now moved to my head? My tea cup perhaps?" He made a pretense of studying the cup.

"No, it is . . ." Her laughter halted. "It's not funny, is what it is." She frowned.

Jaiden wished she'd invite him to the conversation. After all, he sat directly across from her. One would think—for courtesy's sake if nothing else.

"Lord Astor," Ruth spoke. She sounded grim, but a glimmer in her eye let him know she still found humor in his unwitting *faux pas*.

"Jaiden," he corrected.

Her mouth twitched upward in acknowledgement. "Jaiden, Tilly hasn't saved five lives."

"She hasn't?" Had he misunderstood everything?

"No," Ruth answered. "She's saved twenty-seven."

"Twenty—! What? How the bloody—" He stopped his stuttering and closed his eyes to clear his head. Twenty-seven, though! He looked at Ruth. "She hasn't brought twenty-seven different women here."

"She's only brought twenty-seven here. Those are the only ones I know about, but there are more. Mark my words. I met every one of the twenty-seven, mind you. Every single one of them. I saw with my own eyes the marks left on each of those twenty-seven bodies by another man who knew he could get away with it."

"My God, but twenty-seven! Damn, she's . . . How does one even . . ." He ran a hand through his hair. "How did she become so . . . ?"

"Everything you want in a wife?" Ruth supplied.

Jaiden sighed. "Exactly." But how to convince Tilly, after all the pain she'd witnessed perpetrated by husbands. No wonder she refused to consider the possibility of marriage. He shook his head. "Hearing about her past makes it seem . . . difficult."

"Whether she realizes it or not, you've won her trust. That's a lot harder than capturing a woman's heart, and if you can achieve both, she'll follow you anywhere."

That was the problem though. Jaiden didn't want Tilly to follow him. He wanted her to marry him.

And he was beginning to think that happy state would be a lot more difficult to achieve.

"Don't scowl so, my lord. You have other assets with which to convince Tilly."

"What are they?"

Ruth grinned. A mischievous glimmer lit her eyes. "Why, Parliament's ear, of course."

CHAPTER THIRTY-NINE

"Sometimes in winter, I'll get into bed with my stockings on, and then I'll get too warm—"

"And you take your stockings off," Tilly added.

"And run my bare feet between the crisp, cool sheets. That's one of my favorite things," Verity finished.

Tilly smiled at the ceiling. "Mine, too." The two girls had spent the last half hour lying on Verity's bed listing all their favorite pleasures.

Tilly hoped something might convince Verity to stay around for a while.

Verity shook her head. Tears still hovered. "But then, there are these other times—"

"No, there aren't," Tilly interrupted. She didn't want Verity focusing on the bad. Denial was an invaluable tool for recovery as far as Tilly could tell.

Verity, however, would have none of it. "There are, Tilly, and they are so painful. The whole world looks black." Her voice trembled. "And my soul hurts."

"Oh, Verity!" Tilly exclaimed. Her friend sounded quite the most pitiful thing in the world.

Verity sniffled. "It's horrible."

Tilly flipped over onto her stomach and propped herself on her forearms so she could see Verity's face. The poor girl was deathly pale. Her white lips shook with emotion.

"You know what I used to do when I felt like that?" Tilly asked.

"You don't feel like that anymore? Not ever?" Verity asked. Hope glimmered beneath her sea of depression.

"Not in years. I can't even remember the last time I felt remotely melancholy."

Verity nodded, her eyes wide. "So what is it you used to do?"

"Go for a long, brisk walk."

Verity looked doubtful. "That's it?"

"Yes, and the entire time I walked, in my head I'd rant about everything bothering me, including myself."

Wrinkling her nose, Verity asked, "Didn't that just depress your spirits more?"

"No, I wouldn't allow time for that. I would force the words too quickly through my mind. I didn't have time to think. And if you can't think—"

"You don't have time to feel," Verity finished. "And if you can't feel, you can't hurt."

"Exactly," Tilly said. "You grasp ideas quickly."

Verity sighed. "I think I've spent too much time deciphering your twisted logic."

Tilly laughed. "It's possible."

Verity managed a smile. "Enough of this. I need a distraction from all this sad stuff. Regale me with stories of your current unwitting pupil."

Tilly felt her cheeks warm. All the women at Muirfield loved to hear her ridicule the idiosyncrasies of the men she trained.

Unfortunately, for once she had nothing to ridicule.

"Well," Verity prompted. "What's he like?"

"He's . . ." Nice. Good. Beautiful. Bewitching. Tilly couldn't say any of those things. The inhabitants of Muirfield didn't have any rules, and certainly not any against praising a man.

And still, it wasn't done. "Well," Tilly tried. "He's tall."

"Tall?" Verity repeated.

Tilly tried again. "And he's . . . "

"In love with her!" Beth exclaimed from the door.

"Pardon?" Tilly said at the same time Verity exclaimed, "Of course."

Beth entered. She fixed an amused grin on Tilly. "That's what Ruth thinks. I was just eavesdropping," she said proudly, rocking on her boots.

Tilly sat up in the bed. She shook her head. "But, why would Ruth think that?" Even to her own ears, she sounded breathless.

Beth chuckled, "Because it's true. Besides, how could he not?" She plopped herself on the foot of the bed. "Do you love him?"

Verity giggled. "She does. You should hear her talk about him."

"I didn't say anything," Tilly said defensively.

"Exactly," Beth proclaimed. "Why, Verity that's the first time I've heard you laugh in a week. It sounds good."

Verity's levity vanished.

"Not so glum," Beth reprimanded. "We have a wedding to plan."

"Oh, stop," Tilly exclaimed, scooting off the bed and heading toward the door. "It's past time to leave, apparently."

"You better," Beth said to her retreating back. "Your love awaits," she added with a dramatic sigh.

Giggles broke out behind her. Tilly slammed the door to entomb them.

Why did everyone feel the need to accuse her of possessing tender feelings toward Jaiden? Were they really so bored they had nothing better to do than to speculate on nonexistent romances? Or was it merely because she counted Jaiden a friend?

Yes, a first, but certainly not worth this hullabaloo.

It couldn't possibly be because they were right. Jaiden was

not in love with her, and she had better not forget it.

For, if she allowed herself to believe he did care for her . . . well, she just might find herself in danger of falling the rest of the way in love with him.

CHAPTER FORTY

Tilly staggered into the kitchen, her usual bounce gone. Instead, she forced the merest hint of a smile underneath droopy eyes.

Immediately, Jaiden stood and moved to her side. He wrapped an arm around her waist to steady her and give her what support he could. Typically, she would have reprimanded him for manhandling her. Today, she leaned into him. She even gave a grateful sigh.

Poor girl. Didn't her friends see how much their pain cost her?

Ruth might have. "Tilly, you look miserable," she said. "Go show Jaiden his room, then have a rest. I'll wake you for dinner."

Tilly nodded, her eyelids nearly closed. She dragged herself from the room. Jaiden supported much of her weight.

"You've had a tiring day," he observed.

Another sigh escaped her. "It's exhausting work, trying to convince a woman to like herself."

"I can imagine." His heart went out to her. "Ruth's right. You need a rest. Beginning now."

Without warning he swooped her up into his strong arms. He expected a gasp of surprise from her, but she merely snuggled against his chest and closed her eyes as he carried her toward the stairs.

He enjoyed the feel of her female form relying solely on him, her soft bosom pushing into his chest. Her tiny hand curled between them as trusting as a sleeping child's.

Tenderness welled inside him. Every flicker of her face amazed him with the depth of its beauty. She took care of too many people. She needed someone to look after her.

"You've got the hang of this," Tilly whispered. "Much better than the first time."

Jaiden smiled, stepping up the staircase. He remembered spying her in his study that first night. She had propped one hand on her hip, tilted her head to the side, and stolen his heart.

God, he had wanted her. From the very beginning, before he knew the millions of things that made her unique, before he learned how wonderful life was when lived in her proximity. His body had grasped her essence before his mind had.

Jaiden pulled her tighter against him and replied, "I don't like to make thieves too comfortable."

She opened one green eye. "I didn't steal anything."

"So what were you doing then?"

Her eyes closed. "I am exhausted."

Jaiden threw his head back and laughed. The sound still surprised him. He'd rarely laughed before he met her. His duties had left no time for joy; or maybe he'd had no reason for happiness before her. Now, every second was a lesson in contentment, and the one thing he knew was that he would never let her go.

He didn't even want to set her down. He'd walk to the ends of the earth carrying her. She was not nearly so light as one would think to look at her, though. While slight of stature, she carried an abundance of beautiful curves.

"My room's the last bedroom on the right," she directed.

She trusted him. He knew it, although she didn't know it. Not yet. But she would. He would prove it to her.

Jaiden entered the small yellow room and laid her on the bed. The rose skirts of her dress fell over the blue covers. He pulled off her shoes. Her toes immediately curled into the covers.

"Thank you for the transport." She stifled a yawn. "I'll recommend you to all my friends."

He smiled. Then a thought turned his lips downward. "Would you like to talk about Verity? Perhaps I can help." He didn't want to leave her, even though he could see the exhaustion in her face. She was too small to carry her burdens alone. He could take them from her. He would make sure she never had to worry about anything ever again.

She stretched her arms and then curled them around her. "You can't help, and I don't want to talk." Her eyes closed. She rubbed her cheek against the pillow and made herself comfortable.

"Well," Jaiden said reluctantly. "I'll let you sleep."

Her eyes rose to half-mast. Her voice came out soft. "You don't have to."

He stilled. What did she want from him?

Not knowing what she wanted, he risked offending her in some way if he stayed. He couldn't take that chance.

Tilly scooted over on the bed. "Stay," she commanded, patting the cover next to her.

"Tilly. . . ." He began to refuse, but she shook her head.

"I don't feel so frightened when you're near," she admitted.

The whisper tore at his heart. How could he refuse that request? He lowered himself onto the bed built for one. It creaked under his weight. His feet reached six inches beyond the foot of the bed even while his head hit the headboard.

Tilly rolled against him, closed her eyes and let out a contented sigh.

He wrapped an arm around her and pushed the hair from her forehead. He thought of her last confession. "What are you afraid of?"

A tiny hand balled against his arm. "Failing," she murmured. Her eyelashes rested against her cheeks without stirring.

"Failing? Failing what?"

"Them," she whispered.

Jaiden felt as though she'd just given him the key to understanding her soul. He knew now—not how she'd come to care for those weaker than herself, or why she lacked the confidence to know she could do anything. Or even how she'd learned to make life enjoyable for everyone she met.

But now he knew what she lived for, what was important to her.

Why he terrified her.

"You won't fail them," he swore.

"I can't," she answered, her mouth barely moving.

"I'll help," he vowed.

Her lips curled into a smile, but she neither looked at him nor made a reply. Her arm, however, drifted across his chest as her breathing became even. She burrowed against his side.

Blood rushed his loins. Lovely. The girl was half dead with exhaustion, and he still wanted to ravish her.

Not seducing her might prove the most difficult task of his life. The next hour would be hell.

There was nowhere else he'd rather be.

Chapter Forty-One

In all her life, Tilly had never slept so peacefully. Indeed, she felt so comfortable, it woke her up.

She refused, however, to open her eyes. She wanted to savor her contentment. But no matter how hard she tried to stop them, little observations kept floating into her conscience.

Like the fact she lay atop something warm and large and . . .

Breathing!

Jaiden!

Her eyes squeezed more tightly shut. Heat rose to her face. How disgraceful! His hand even cupped her thigh just below her backside.

Oh, dear.

But his chest rose and fell in the slow rhythm of sleep.

Tilly's humiliation disseminated.

Mischievousness took its place.

No need to move just yet. Much better to enjoy the comfort while she could. Jaiden didn't seem to mind, after all.

She inhaled his scent and couldn't suppress her smile.

She'd never had a friend like him before—and a friend who had proven himself at every possible turn.

Not that she trusted him or anything foolish like that. He was still a man, after all. But he did take care of her when she needed it most. No one had ever done that for Tilly before. She helped others, not the other way around.

Until Jaiden.

And it was nice, having his help.

Tilly sighed. She just had to make certain she didn't grow accustomed to relying on him. Then, it wouldn't matter when they parted paths. As they would have to. Soon.

But not at the moment, she thought. They had today, and tonight he was all hers. His soft shirt warmed her cheek. He lay entirely at her disposal.

Any practical female would take advantage of that fact.

And Tilly prided herself on her pragmatism.

Her hand crept across the bed and traced his shoulder. The muscles bunched beneath her fingers. The maleness of him left her breathless. She turned her face to rest against his open collar and touched her sensitive nose to his silky skin. Who would have thought someone could be so hard and so soft at the same time?

She should investigate further.

She touched her lips to his throat.

A deep groan answered her.

Tilly pushed up onto her forearms, her eyes flying open, and she found herself staring right into Jaiden's gaze. His breath came in pants. His hands moved to grip the bed frame.

He was awake! That changed everything. She needed to get up—leave.

And, yet, she still didn't want to. Letting him see her desire was the biggest risk of all, but it was time she took it. Despite all her fears, she didn't look away from his eyes.

His body remained frozen except for the rapid movement of his chest, and she felt his every breath. He regarded her as if she were a skittish deer, as though a single movement might send her flying.

And she should go.

But she couldn't.

Tilly took a breath and then swallowed. His blue eyes seemed to read her spirit. They enchanted her with a silent, hypnotic song. Perhaps they stole her soul, for she could no longer tell where she ended and his eyes began.

Without shifting her gaze, Tilly leaned down slowly, imperceptibly.

Jaiden waited, clearly wanting something from her. His face remained nonchalantly relaxed. His arms shook with the force of his grip on the bed.

It was that grip that gave Tilly the courage she needed. He wouldn't touch her. He wouldn't pressure her. He wouldn't even ask. Only his eyes showed he cared, and even they didn't demand. They just revealed a destiny she couldn't resist.

Her lips touched his. His entire body tensed beneath her, but his eyes didn't move. Tilly lifted away an inch. Even that slight contact made her insides shake and demand retreat. Only for a second though. She couldn't retreat farther than that.

This time she pressed her mouth to his cheek, felt the stubble along his jaw line. Her trembling fingers spread from his throat to his temple. His beauty amazed her. She dropped another kiss on his face, this time above one eye.

Her heart raced.

They were only kisses. They didn't mean anything.

So why did she feel as if she'd just signed away her soul?

How did he make her feel this way? Why?

She wanted to ask, but she couldn't find the words. He made her need him, and she liked that desperation. And hated it. And feared it.

But she didn't fear him, not nearly so much as she feared herself.

"Tilly, I—Oh!"

Tilly rolled to the side and tumbled off the bed. Beth stood dumbstruck in the doorway.

"I—er—Pardon!" She dropped into a curtsey and then ran from the room.

Tilly stared at the abandoned space, then shook her head, trying to rid it of the fog filling it. She looked at Jaiden, who now sat on the edge of the bed. He still wore his shoes. His eyes watched her, but the corner of his mouth twitched.

Tilly burst out laughing. She laughed loudly, with complete abandonment. She fell to the bed. Her arms wrapped around her torso. Tears welled in her eyes.

The look on Beth's face! Her poor friend. Surely, she'd never expected to catch Tilly, of all people, in such an undignified state!

And what the hell had led Tilly to this juncture? How had she changed so much in the last . . . well, since meeting Jaiden?

Her laughter wavered at the thought. She had changed since meeting him. The knowledge bothered her, but not as much as she would have expected.

She glanced at the amused male next to her.

"Will you survive?" he asked.

Tilly grinned. She had the urge to ask for her soul back, but refrained. Maybe he wouldn't notice he possessed it.

She nodded. "Yes, I've had ample practice in losing my dignity. I barely notice the missing of it." Tilly clapped her hands against her skirts. "I do believe I'll go have a bath," she announced. "I find myself very much in need of a distraction." She stood. He followed suit.

Suddenly, unsure of how to take her leave, she stuck out her hand to shake his in gentleman-like fashion. "Well, thank you!"

He gripped her hand and turned it over to lay a kiss on its palm. A shiver ran up her spine. How this man did affect her!

He relinquished her hand, and it was only because every fiber of her being was focused on him that she noticed the tens of dots on his hands.

"Jaiden, what . . ." She pulled his hand closer to her face and peered at it. Tiny splinters poked his hands in dozens of places. "What the devil . . . ?" She trailed off, her eyes drifting to the bed as comprehension stunned her. The bed frame! It wasn't finished. Indeed, it was as rough as wood could be, and he'd gripped it.

All so he wouldn't frighten her.

He would rather suffer fifty cuts than hurt her.

She couldn't meet his gaze. Her eyes strayed back to the splintered palms, but water welled in her eyes, making the particles impossible to see. It mattered not. She'd never forget them.

Tilly swallowed. She tried to belittle his action in her mind, but she couldn't.

And her insides melted and streamed from her body, leaving scalding aches everywhere.

Jaiden would never hit her. He wouldn't.

It didn't matter.

And yet, it made all the difference in the world.

"It must hurt," she whispered, her voice thick with emotion.

"I can't feel anything but you," he whispered. "And that is an ache I refuse to forgo." He tugged gently at the end of a long strand of her hair. She refused to look up.

Tilly's mouth went dry. She gave herself a small shake. "I'll get a needle," she managed. She tore herself from him and made it to the dresser. Her hands shook as she lifted the lid off her sewing box. No matter how hard she tried, she couldn't stop herself from feeling that her life had just changed. That everything had changed.

She could try to keep her distance from him as much as she wanted, but no longer would she succeed.

Tilly took his strong hands in hers and went to work on them, digging out the splinters with infinite care. Then suddenly, she dropped a kiss into the middle of his palm. His fingers cupped her face. She took one deep breath, taking in the scent of his skin, and then straightened and went back to pulling at the splinters as though she hadn't just kissed him.

In her experience, as soon as a woman wanted to comfort a man, she was already half in love with him.

And that, Tilly knew, was a possibility she could not face.

CHAPTER FORTY-TWO

"I don't understand. Lord Astor was—"

"Jaiden," Jaiden corrected, his eyes glued to Tilly across the dining room table.

Beth blushed but continued. "Jaiden was doing so well in the beginning, and now look at him. He's floundering."

"Floundering?" Agnes repeated from the rocking chair. On her lap snoozed Kyla, the three-year-old daughter of Mary Katherine, another resident of Muirfield. "My dear Beth, you are too kind. He's clearly had the good sense the Lord gave him knocked clear out of his brain. Why does he continue to allow this torture to go on? Really, it's horrifying to watch, and yet I can't tear my eyes away. Who would have thought I could conjure such compassion for a man?"

"We did warn him, didn't we?" Ruth reminded. "I remember very specifically telling him not to take on the challenge of Tilly. All who do never recover. She's squashed greater men than he."

"Greater men than Jaiden do not exist," Tilly said, plucking a coin from her purse and setting it on the table.

Her words broke his concentration. Warm hope flooded over him. He met Tilly's eyes. They glowed proudly at him. A smile lit her face.

He opened his mouth to say thank you when she amended, "Indeed, great men don't exist at all."

Agnes let out a loud laugh, cut short so as not to wake Kyla. Even Verity, who had finally ventured out of her room to investigate all the noise, managed to turn a corner of her mouth up. Jaiden forced a frown at Tilly, but in truth her man-hating had begun to amuse him. She should dislike all men. All men but him.

Still, her cheek should not go unpunished. He tossed more coins onto the pile and announced, "I call." He dropped his cards face up on the table and arched an eyebrow. As they were the last two remaining in the game, he kept his gaze on her while the others leaned against the table.

Humor glowed in her eyes. He knew immediately she had beaten him again. "Four of a kind, and eights at that. Excellent, my lord. Truly. A very respectable hand."

Jaiden waited.

"You know, it matters not who wins or loses. The main thing is that you gave it your best. You saw certain defeat ahead of you but plunged right in anyway. It was no coward's act. Not a rational act, mind you, but no coward's act—"

"Tilly, put down your hand and leave the man a little dignity," Ruth commanded. "I don't want to see this one broken, and I've a hunch you don't either."

A small frown marred Tilly's face. She laid down her flush, but Jaiden saw her mind was elsewhere. Intermittently through-out the evening she had retreated to her worries. All the fun out of being trounced disappeared. Jaiden tried to come up with a way to get her to share her troubles, or at the very least, to distract her from them.

"When will you teach us how to win at poker as you do?" Beth complained.

Tilly stared at her blankly for an instant before smiling. "Just as soon as you have to make your living at the tables," Tilly promised.

Beth humphed. "I'll never have to so long as you're alive."

"Imagine that," Tilly replied.

Beth threw her head back. "But Tilly," she whined. "Why won't you teach me?"

"Because once I do, you'll abandon Muirfield to become a notorious high-roller, and I shall miss you too terribly."

"Are you mad? I'm never leaving Muirfield. Never. You shall have to bury my dead body under the rosebushes, because even death can't make me leave."

Tilly patted Beth's hand. "Then we shall share the ground beneath the rose bushes for eternity, for I mean to stay, too."

Beth stroked Tilly's hair. "No, you don't. You never stay."

"Beth! That's because Tilly must make money to support us!" Agnes cried.

Beth hugged Tilly. "You're wrong, Agnes. Tilly hates this house. She means to like it, but she just can't force herself to feel one way when she feels another. There are some things not even Tilly can control."

Agnes stood. Jaiden followed suit.

Kyla's eyes slitted open at Agnes's jerky pacing. Her mouth pursed, as she wavered between sleep and screaming bloody murder. "I don't want Tilly to have to spend time in a house she hates."

Tilly jumped from her chair and wrapped one arm around Agnes and the other around Beth. "I could never hate a place that housed my dearest friends." She dropped a kiss on Beth's head and one on Agnes's cheek. "It's true, I've had bad experiences here, but I've also had wonderful ones, and I have you dear girls to thank for the good times."

Jaiden watched as Tilly took Kyla from Agnes. She kissed the girl's forehead, then sat in the rocking chair Agnes had abandoned. He had never seen women carry on like this. He could not recall Adelaide and his great aunt exchange a single act of affection. It would have seemed silly and all too uncomfortably girlish, if not for the contentment on Tilly's face.

She loved these girls. She needed them, so he was glad they loved her, too. Besides, as long as she could learn to love them, she could love him, too.

"Well," Ruth drawled, gaining everyone's attention. "It is neither here nor there whether Tilly would stay given her druthers, since she is obliged to abandon us so long as we have no other means of paying the property taxes, and even if Lizzy sells her design, I fear it will be some time before we can afford to be women of leisure."

"I will pay the—"

"No," Tilly cut Jaiden off.

Agnes turned to Jaiden with a frown on her face, as though only now remembering his presence. Beth smiled at him, her eyes huge. Ruth grinned. Verity raised her eyebrows. Only Tilly remained unaffected.

"Tilly, it would be my—"

"Jaiden, stay out of this. I mean it. It is none of your affair." Her voice brooked no argument. Their gazes locked.

"Did Lord Astor just offer to pay the taxes on Muirfield?" Agnes whispered to Ruth.

"I believe he tried," Ruth answered.

"He did not try because he's not here," Tilly said. "He's never been here, never heard of Muirfield, never met any one of the residents here, and certainly he would never, never attempt to aid a woman in leaving her husband."

"What are you talking about, Tilly? He's standing right in front of you," Beth announced.

Jaiden laid his hands on either side of the table and leaned forward. "I want to pay the taxes. It is senseless for you to risk life and limb at the gaming tables just to maintain your property."

"She doesn't earn our living at the gaming tables," Agnes exclaimed. "She doesn't need to anymore. She makes perfectly good money training her—ow! What the . . ." Agnes saw Beth's glare. "Er . . . what I mean to say is, why don't you let Lord Astor help?"

"Because I will not rely on a man to keep you safe."

"Too late," Verity muttered as Agnes pointed out, "but it's not relying if you have a contingency plan, which you do. You can always go back to taming—ow! Stop that, Beth!"

Jaiden barely heard them over the blood pounding in his ears. "Do you really think I'm just another man not to be trusted?"

"Yes!" Tilly spat out. Her eyes narrowed. Her face hardened, warning him not to attempt to persuade her otherwise.

The fury left Jaiden as suddenly as it had come, shoved out by humor and certainty. He stood and propped one leg casually against the table. "You can't even convince me that you still don't trust me. How are you going to convince yourself?"

"I hate you," she mouthed.

Jaiden smiled. His long strides took him leisurely around the table toward her rocking chair. "No, you don't."

"I want to," she whispered, watching his approach warily.

"I know," he whispered and folded her and Kyla into his arms.

Both Verity and Ruth smiled at them. Beth scowled at their embrace. "This is hardly necessary," she muttered.

Agnes frowned. Then, suddenly, her eyes grew round. "She won't take the money because she's trying to protect him!" she proclaimed.

"Yes," Verity sighed, as Ruth answered, "Exactly."

"But, why would she try to protect a man? She wouldn't unless . . . Oh, my, she can't be in—ow!"

Jaiden felt Tilly's shoulders stiffen. He rubbed her back.

"I swear to God, Verity! If you pinch me one more time!"

"Think before you speak, and then I won't have to."

Their voices receded into the background. Tilly monopolized Jaiden's senses; her sweet face turned up to him. "I won't," she warned him under the girls' arguing.

She lied. She would love him. So certain was Jaiden of that fact that he figured he could grant Tilly time to get used to the idea. "No one is asking anything of you . . . tonight. Stop worrying. I'm here whenever you're ready. For you, I'll wait the rest of my life."

"Don't." Her brow furrowed. "I'll probably never come."

Jaiden brushed a curl from Tilly's forehead. "I'll take that chance."

She shook her head. "I don't want to hurt you."

"You won't. I won't let you."

Her eyes showed vulnerability. His heart ached. His hand clenched in desire to kill all the men who had taught her such distrust.

Tilly and Jaiden stared at each other until the sound of an exaggerated yawn drew their attention. All four women looked at them, revealing various stages of surprise.

"Well, I'm exhausted!" Beth exclaimed. "How about you, Agnes?"

"It is well past my bedtime," Agnes agreed. "Ruth?"

"You girls go along. I'd like a few words with Tilly, I think."

Jaiden felt Tilly stiffen again. He had already come to realize Ruth's opinion meant a great deal to her.

"I shall turn in also," he said. He gave Tilly's shoulders one last squeeze and then slipped Kyla out of her arms. The child's eyelids opened a crack, just enough to look up at him. Jaiden feared she would start screaming. Instead, she wiggled her flushed face against his shoulder. He could feel her hot breath on his throat.

"I'll show you to Kyla's room," Beth offered, walking to the doorway. "Goodnight, Ruth, Verity. Sweet—Ahh!" She stopped short. "Lizzy," she breathed. "You've returned!"

"So I have," a short, muscular redhead entered the room.

Jaiden's mouth went dry as he recognized the woman who had been eluding him for years. Mrs. Underplumb.

Lizzy Underplumb didn't see him as Beth hugged her. "I don't know what this talk of bed is. There is celebrating to be had!"

"You sold your design!" Beth exclaimed.

"We did. And the price Mary Katherine got! You should have seen her—" She froze, her eyes on Verity. "What's wrong? What's happened?" she demanded, disentangling herself from Beth.

"Nothing. I'm fine, truly." Verity's voice broke. Tears ran down her pale face.

Lizzy pulled her into her arms. "I shouldn't have left you."

Verity sobbed on her shoulder, her tall body curled against Lizzy's shorter one.

A blonde peeked into the room. She took in the crying woman. Her eyebrows lifted at Tilly and then jumped a mile upon spotting Jaiden carrying her daughter. She turned to Beth.

Beth shrugged. "You miss a lot in a fortnight."

Tilly moved over to the redhead and laid a hand on her arm.

Lizzy raised her face to her. "What has occur—" She started. Her arms tightened visibly around Verity. "Lord Astor," she exclaimed, catching sight of him for the first time.

"Mrs. Underplumb." Jaiden nodded. "The elusive," he added.

Tilly's face swung between the two of them. "You've met."

"Yes." Lizzy looked Tilly in the eye. She disengaged herself from Verity, only to loop an arm around Verity's waist. "But I don't know how he tracked me here, Tilly, I swear it. I'm so sorry."

"Hush," Tilly commanded. "I brought him here. It's not your fault."

"And your secret is safe," Jaiden said. "I'll not reveal it to anyone."

"Sir, I'm sorry for the way I abandoned you," Lizzy said.

Jaiden shook his head. If she were here, she had had her reasons for leaving. God, he should have known. He remembered her aches, her stories. He should have helped, but he had believed her tales of clumsiness, even teased her about them. He'd been wrapped up in his excitement over the camera. Jaiden took a deep breath. "Take care of your friend. We'll talk tomorrow."

"Yes, sir," she agreed, right before she and Verity left the room, arm in arm.

CHAPTER FORTY-THREE

"You know, Tilly, there are worse things in the world than falling in love."

Tilly groaned. Ruth didn't waste time. The talk came sooner than Tilly had expected. They sat in two chairs in front of a warm fire, and yet Tilly felt anything but comfortable.

"Tell Verity that," Tilly muttered.

Ruth's eyebrows dipped in disappointment. "You are not Verity, and Lord Astor is not Verity's ruffian of a husband. Don't punish him for others' sins."

"I'm not punishing him—" Tilly began.

"He loves you."

Tilly closed her eyes. Why did everyone keep saying this?

And why did she hope they were right?

Tilly's pulse raced. She looked at Ruth. "What am I going to do?"

Ruth smiled. "You could marry him."

The myriad of emotions at war within Tilly refused to be contained. "True. A husband. That is exactly what I need. Why didn't I think of the answer before? Someone who will steal my property, own my body, and have sole legal rights to my children, whom he'll just want to violate!"

Ruth opened her mouth to speak, closed it, smiled, and then laughed.

"It happens," Tilly maintained with a pout.

"You . . . er . . . could try trusting him."

"Trust a man?" Tilly raised her eyebrows in doubt.

Ruth laughed. "Some are trustworthy."

Tilly straightened. "Really? Name one."

"My father," Ruth answered. "If I'd but listened to him before marrying that scoundrel . . . but that is neither here nor there." She breathed deeply. "The point is, I have a feeling your Jaiden is a pretty steady fellow."

Tilly shook her head. "Then he deserves better than me, for I am not a steady woman."

Ruth frowned. "Don't belittle yourself, Tilly. It's ludicrous. You've taken care of more people than I know. Now, why don't you try being honest with your Lord Astor."

Tilly laughed. "I don't know what honesty is! I haven't gone an entire day my whole adult life without lying to someone, usually everyone. Jaiden's no exception. He can't love me. He doesn't even know me, and I certainly don't love him. I don't know the first thing about that kind of love, and frankly, it's always struck me as more bother than it's worth." Tilly folded her arms and stared at the fire, sulking.

Ruth turned to look at the fireplace, too. "Very well, you don't love him. I was wrong."

"Yes."

"I don't know what I was thinking. Clearly, you don't care for him. Certainly, you weren't trying to protect him earlier by refusing his help. No, you refuse money from men all the time. You've never been quoted as saying 'bleed 'em dry while you can.' And you don't glow every time Jaiden walks into the room either. It doesn't take you full minutes to tear your gaze from him after he speaks. My mistake. Obviously, he means nothing to you." She sighed. "Yes, you wouldn't care if he lived or died."

Tilly grumbled, "I didn't say that."

"Oh, you didn't? What exactly are your feelings toward the esteemed lord then?"

Tilly faced Ruth. "Look, I need your help. Can you stop teasing me for five minutes and help me figure out a plan?"

Ruth lifted her eyebrows. Tilly realized she was acting uncharacteristically serious, but she couldn't help it. Her feelings toward Jaiden were driving her mad.

"Go on," Ruth encouraged.

"I don't love him," Tilly began, "but I can't seem to stop thinking about him either. It's all become annoying and pathetic, Ruth, and I don't know how to stop."

"Why is it annoying and pathetic?"

Tilly squeezed her eyes shut. "Because I always want him near," she admitted for the first time. She opened her eyes. The words tumbled out. "I do. When I'm alone, I want to be with him, and when I'm with him, I don't want to leave. When he's there, everything is fun and exciting, but when he's gone, the whole world is . . ." She scrunched her nose and shook her head. "Lackluster," she admitted.

Ruth snorted. "Lackluster?"

Tilly scowled at her. "And pointless. I mean to say, things I do still have meaning, but I don't feel as if they do." She leaned back in the chair. "God, I find everything so dull compared to him, and that's not like me. Maybe I'm just suffering from *ennui*." She laughed. "How glamorous of me! Oh-la-la." She let out a long breath. She was not good for Jaiden, not that way. She would never be good for any man. Lord knows, she'd destroyed more than her fair share, and the others she'd come into contact with still didn't know what had hit them.

She never thought she'd regret all her skills in manipulating men, but for once, where Jaiden was concerned, she did. Adelaide's accusation rang in her mind. Tilly could control Jaiden too easily. It was second nature to her, and entirely unfair to him. It was impossible. She had too much power over men. Their romance was like a Greek myth—a human falling in love with a deity. The stories never ended well for the humans.

It didn't matter. She didn't love Jaiden. She couldn't love any man. And she didn't need to. She had Muirfield and Mary Katherine and Kyla and Ruth—though she would gladly trade Ruth for any number of men at the moment. She would be fine.

"I'll get over these doldrums," Tilly maintained, "and I'll do it without relying on Lord Astor." She stood, resolved.

"If you insist, Tilly, but keep your heart open just in case. Who knows? Maybe you'll find some excitement."

Tilly had had enough excitement for one lifetime. What she needed now was sleep. She stood to go to bed, but paused in the doorway. She had not wanted to start this conversation, but now that it had begun, she wanted to exorcise the emotions besieging her. Maybe Ruth could help.

Tilly sighed and leaned against the doorframe, resting her head against the support.

Ruth turned in the chair to watch her.

"It's just the things he says to me," Tilly couldn't stop herself from saying. "They're all lies, I know that, but I'd rather listen to his lies than . . ." She shook her head. Nothing compared to Jaiden. That was her problem. She was addicted to him, and the prospect of withdrawal terrified her.

She squeezed her eyes shut, and swiveled her entire body so she could rest her forehead against the doorframe. She contemplated giving it a few bangs with her head, but doubted even that would knock sense into her. The thought did make her smile though. She straightened, walked in front of Ruth and plopped on the floor between Ruth and the fire.

Tilly smiled. "I'd rather listen to his lies than eat your rum cake," she admitted.

Ruth laughed. "This is serious," she observed. "Sounds like you want him for your lover."

"Not my lover. I want him as a friend." The fire blazed

uncomfortably close to Tilly's back. She ignored it. "Is that madness?"

"Not madness," Ruth said, "but it *is* a bloomin' lie."

Tilly stood and paced. There had to be a way to make Ruth understand.

Ruth leaned back in her chair. "Picture him in the arms of his Miss Picky Skirts."

Tilly froze. "I told you. Too late for that."

Ruth crossed her legs. "And I know jealousy when I see it. Now listen to me for once. You might—" She stopped herself to try again more quietly. "You might know all there is about men's hearts, but you haven't a notion about your own. No, don't shake your head at me until you've heard me out." Ruth uncrossed her legs and leaned forward. "If some other woman snatches that man up, you're going to be miserable. You'll regret it as long as you live. I know you, Tilly. You don't give your heart in halves. The only way you're going to keep a man like that is if you trust him fully. Given your past, it won't be easy. I know it. But you can, Tilly, and you will. For the way I see it, love, you don't have a choice. Not if you want anything close to contentment in your life."

With that Ruth stood and exited to the room, leaving Tilly alone with the echoes of her speech.

CHAPTER FORTY-FOUR

Lizzy's eyes bulged as she stared at the bank draft. "Have you gone mad?" she breathed.

Jaiden laughed. "I promised you a share in the profits if your innovation panned out. It did. Consider this a first installment."

Lizzy's mouth opened and closed several times. Apparently, he had struck her speechless.

"You deserve it. I've only regretted that you haven't been there to see the project to fruition."

Lizzy smiled ruefully. "I wanted to be. I'm sorry for leaving without a word, for taking the prototype with me. It's worked though. Quite well," she told him. "We've improved it since."

"I'm surprised you took it."

"Yes, well, I . . . er. . . ." She took a deep breath, stared at the check for a moment. "I wanted a photograph," she admitted. "Of me," she continued awkwardly. "When I first came here, I wanted to make certain I never forgot . . . what he'd done . . . to me . . . in case, I wasn't brave enough to stay away." Suddenly her face lit up. "But it's been easy. It's been bliss!" she laughed, then her brow wrinkled, and she turned so as not to face him directly. "My leaving wasn't planned. The opportunity presented itself." She gave him a sidelong glance. "And by that I mean, I met Tilly, and . . . well, I ran." She looked back at the bank draft. "Are you sure this is all mine?"

Jaiden smiled. "Your innovation was crucial."

She looked at the numbers written on the bank draft. "Apparently," she said, folding the paper and slipping it into her pocket. "Looks like you might be paying the property taxes on Muirfield, after all."

"Not if Tilly finds out where that money came from," he predicted. She had been adamantly opposed to his interference.

Lizzy smiled. "Oh, I don't think she'll object to this. I—" Lizzy took a deep breath. "I didn't plan on stealing the camera. I didn't know I wouldn't be coming back. I—"

"Lizzy," he interrupted, using his implacable voice. "It's forgotten."

Her mouth closed. She nodded and shrugged. They continued their stroll, circling Ruth's vegetable garden. Walking made it easier to say what he needed to say. They could both gaze off into the hills instead of acknowledging the conversation. "I wanted to apologize," he began.

"Don't," Lizzy responded.

"I feel I must."

"You have nothing to apologize for."

Jaiden shook his head. "I should have realized."

Lizzy kicked at a shrub, staring at it. "I didn't want you to realize." She met his gaze. The corners of her mouth turned up. "I didn't want to think about it. At work, I didn't have to. Lord knows, you never gave me time to stew over my personal problems."

Lizzy was a brilliant woman. Jaiden could not imagine her taking abuse from anyone. "I wish I had done something to help."

She grasped his wrist. He paused, looked at her. "You did, Jaiden. I would never have left him had I not gone to work for you." She squeezed his hand. "You made me realize I was useful, and a worthwhile person, and that I could take care of myself, that I didn't need him. I don't think you'll ever understand what you did for me. You gave me the strength to be free." She smiled self-consciously. Her brow wrinkled and then she nodded. "I don't think you can understand, but I must thank you nonetheless. You're my savior," she admitted, then stood on her toes and hugged him quickly before pulling away.

Jaiden didn't know what to do or say. He felt heat surface in his face.

Lizzy looked at him, then laughed. "I will cease. It isn't good manners to embarrass one's knight in shining armor. Besides, if Tilly sees me fawning all over her favorite, she'll become Miss Jealousy and then God help you."

His ears perked up. "You think she would care."

Lizzy laughed and walked toward the house.

Jaiden distinctly heard her mutter, "Poor boy."

CHAPTER FORTY-FIVE

"So, it's the rose today, is it?" Beth said with an amused smirk.

"Rose?" Tilly asked preoccupied. She made certain Jaiden's footman placed her baggage into the carriage. She was not nearly so depressed by the prospect of leaving her friends as she usually was.

Her contentment should probably concern her.

Beth tugged at the lace at her collar and nodded at Tilly's chest.

Tilly looked down. Then, her eyes grew round and flashed back to Beth.

Beth kissed her cheek and in her ear whispered, "Let me know what happens." She turned to walk up the stairs to the cottage.

"I didn't intend to . . ." Tilly trailed off. Beth continued to ascend the stairs. The girl's hips began to undulate wildly, the way they always did when she mimicked Tilly.

Tilly chuckled at the sight. Her worry over the rose morning gown squashed the laugh prematurely. Tilly hadn't meant to pick it out that morning. She hadn't thought about it once as she put it on . . . which was unlike her.

And very dangerous.

For, Tilly only wore her rose gown on the direst of occasions—occasions when she needed a man to declare his love.

And she had no such need today.

CHAPTER FORTY-SIX

Three hours later, the green hills paraded outside her carriage window, and still Tilly stewed over her outfit.

That morning she had been preoccupied with worry . . . about Nora and Verity and exposure. She had picked out the gown out of pure carelessness.

Except she was never careless with her clothing. She could not afford to be. Her livelihood hung on her ability to dress perfectly for every possible goal.

But if she hadn't acted carelessly, then . . . at least some part of her had wanted to wear the rose today.

Wanted a declaration of love.

From Jaiden.

Oh, dear. She was in trouble.

"Tilly. . . ."

"It's not true!" She whirled guiltily toward him. Probably she hadn't needed to scream.

His mouth twitched. "What's not true?"

"I . . . er . . . nothing." She fidgeted with the skirt of the damned gown. "Only lost in thought. Pray forgive my outburst."

"Absolutely, if you'll trust me with what has you preoccupied." He laid a hand on top of hers. She jerked as though a bolt of lightning had struck her. Didn't he know the effect he had on her?

"I am not preoccupied," she croaked. "Whatever gave you that idea?"

His lips widened into a smile. "You've spent the entire first leg of the trip glaring at your lap. Surely, your lower limbs haven't affronted you." The smile widened into a grin. "They certainly don't offend me."

All thoughts of worry flew from her head. "Why, Jaiden," she exclaimed, patting his knee once with pride. "You just flirted again. And executed your flirtation with utter boldness, which I admire greatly." Though they would have to work on his subtlety. Couldn't have him complimenting the naive chits on the marriage mart on their legs. It would be the season's biggest scandal. Then again, it might scare off all those schoolgirls angling for a proposal . . . which was bad. Yes, bad. She needed to remember that. She sighed. "I have no doubt you'll be the most sought-after bachelor in all of London, especially if you blush this prettily at all the forward ladies." Damn it, he wouldn't intimidate the most sheltered of maids if he turned red like that.

Smiling, Jaiden shook his head.

Tilly grinned in response. These mood swings he inspired would drive her to Bedlam. It was a good thing their acquaintance was coming to an end. She needed to sever this attachment to him. If she delayed, she might find it hurt to cut the cord.

And Tilly made it a rule never to allow a man to hurt her.

Suddenly, the carriage careened. Tilly flew forward. Jaiden's arm caught her.

"What the . . . ," she breathed. The carriage bounced to a halt. An unnatural scream rent the air. One of the horses.

"Stand and deliver!" invaded the carriage. The standard highwayman's threat.

"Oh, dear," Tilly said with a sigh. She would have to talk the scoundrel out of skinning Jaiden. Couldn't very well have him losing baubles because of her when she'd already usurped so much of his time . . . and, well, his sister's money.

"Don't worry," Jaiden said, squeezing her arm. He pulled back the curtain and peeked outside the window.

"I'm not. I'll . . . ," but Tilly stopped as she realized she spoke to an empty cabin. Jaiden had hurled himself out the door.

"Oh, pooh." Men could not do anything without acquiring bruises. How they adored their badges of stupidity. War would probably end if doctors could discover how to erase scars.

Tilly scooted across the carriage seat, taking care not to get tangled in her skirts. She peered through the window.

She froze.

Jaiden—sweet, gentle Jaiden—slammed his fist into the highwayman's jaw. On the ground several paces away, a pistol gleamed in the setting sun.

Jaiden had already disarmed the ruffian. He would win the fight—but Tilly would not see it.

As Jaiden followed the highwayman to the ground, Tilly fell through a crack in time. No longer did she stand a competent woman, watching a friend defend her from manhandling. A different scene monopolized her mind, a memory more real than the present. Tilly again saw her father lunge at her mother. Once more, she heard the shattering cacophony of shrieks and curses. And, like the last time—like every time—she could do nothing.

But run.

Tilly twirled. She tripped and rolled out of the carriage. She fled into the darkness, into the muddy fields.

Into the nightmare she could never forget.

CHAPTER FORTY-SEVEN

"I surrender! I swear! I surrender!"

Jaiden checked his final blow. He'd already landed more than were necessary. It had felt too good to cease. The image of the ruffian holding a gun to Tilly was enough to make him go for a horsewhip.

He rose to his feet. He grabbed the cad by the collar and hauled him up. No more than skin and bones beneath the threadbare jacket. Probably six and ten. Maybe younger.

"I weren't gonna 'ert no one. 'onest. Me pistol tweren't even loaded," the boy claimed. His hands trembled, but his eyes showed determination.

The authorities would hang him if Jaiden handed him over.

"Please, Sir, I was 'ungry. Thought I might get enough coin to buy a pie. 'aven't eaten in two days."

Jaiden believed him. He reached into his pocket, pulled out a coin, and flipped it to the lad. "Go then, but the pistol stays. I won't have you robbing anyone else."

"No, Sir, I woul'n't. Truly."

Jaiden did not believe the boy's promise, but still it would take him a while to get his hands on another pistol . . . if he could at all.

Jaiden tossed the gun to the driver, Frederick.

"Thank you, Sir. Thank you. God bless!" The boy seemed incapable of deciding between bowing and fleeing. Finally, he backed into the trees and disappeared.

"Your heart is too soft, my lord," Frederick muttered.

It was easy to be kind when traveling with a goddess. Jaiden grinned. "I noticed you didn't shoot the cad either."

Frederick spat. "Don't shoot children, my lord. Meaner to let the boy live long enough for some woman to rip the heart out of his chest."

Jaiden arched a brow, feeling the bite of Frederick's words. "Excellent point." Speaking of women . . . "Tilly?" he called, turning to the cabin. "Are you all right?"

No answer.

Jaiden opened the carriage door.

The cabin was empty.

CHAPTER FORTY-EIGHT

"What the . . . ?" The opposite door banged in the wind.

Panic gripped him.

Had the boy merely acted as a distraction? Had it been a ploy to kidnap Tilly? Did some disgruntled husband have her in his clutches?

Had Jaiden failed her?

God!

Jaiden leaped around the carriage. A horse and rider could not have absconded with Tilly down the road without him noticing. They must have gone through the fields.

Jaiden raised a hand to block the setting sun. His eyes searched the horizon for a band of ruffians and a resisting woman.

Instead, his eyes caught sight of a solitary figure a few leagues into a turnip field. It was a woman, and she wore the same rose dress he had admired all morning.

But she sprinted in the opposite direction, so it couldn't be Tilly, for why would Tilly run from him?

Then again, why did Tilly do anything?

Perhaps she thought he could not defend her from that trifling boy. Amused, Jaiden shook his head. She should know better than to trespass on foot through turnip fields. Jaiden moved to unhook the lead horse from the carriage. Damned if he'd walk through that field after her.

Chapter Forty-Nine

Jaiden's amusement vanished abruptly as the horse galloped to within fifty feet of Tilly. For the first time, she looked over her shoulder at him. He waved, but to his amazement, she did not stop. Instead, she fled even faster before him.

Bloody hell! She ran from *him.*

"Tilly," he called. She only sprinted harder, out of the field and up a hill. She veered behind a patch of trees and disappeared from sight.

Jaiden gave the reins some slack, letting the horse run full out. He rode over the hill until he caught sight of Tilly. A stone wall blocked her way. It reached six feet into the air. She tried scrambling over it in vain.

Jaiden slowed the horse. It paced back and forth behind Tilly. Jaiden dropped to the ground. He walked toward her, his hands held out so she could see they were empty. "Tilly?" he tried.

She whirled at the sound of his voice. Her eyes rolled wildly.

What the hell had happened?

Suddenly, she burst past him. Jaiden had had enough. He lunged after her and grabbed her about the waist from behind. Her feet left the ground . . . and rammed into his shins.

"Bloody—" He stifled the curse.

She kicked her heels back again, but he swung her sideways at the last instant. Her feet missed him, but her elbow landed in his chest.

What the hell had got into her?

He turned her in his arms, pressed her against his torso. He tried brushing her hair back from her face, but she shook her head. Her fingers clawed at him. Her feet continued to kick.

Jaiden bent over her and trapped her hands with his arm. He could feel her tremble as she tried to jerk free.

"Calm down," he ordered. She had gone completely mad.

"Let! Me! Go!" she screamed, right into his ear.

"As you wish," he straightened his arms.

Tilly flew from his grasp . . . and hit the ground with a thud.

She rolled onto her back and glared at him. Her breath came out in pants. Mud covered her dress. He thought she would scream if he took one step toward her.

Instead, he nodded at her feet. "You've ruined your petticoats."

CHAPTER FIFTY

Tilly's brows drew together. She stared at the torn lace. The wildness drained from her mind. Her eyes focused on the torn and stained skirts.

"Oh, Lord," she breathed. She winced and looked up at him. Her breathing slowed to normal. "Jaiden. Oh, God." She shook her head and sat up. She buried her face in her hands.

He still did not approach her.

Tilly dropped her hands and looked at Jaiden. "I am so sorry. Oh, and look what I did to you!" She jumped to her feet. "You're bleeding!"

Tilly moved toward him, but he waved a hand.

"It's nothing," he said. "Doesn't signify."

"Let me just—"

"No. Really, I'm fine."

She stared at him, then let loose a shaky laugh. "Of course, you must be terrified to let me near you. After the way I behaved. God, Jaiden, I'm so sorry."

He snorted. "Tilly, I live to touch you," he said matter-of-factly. "I'll take you on this hill right now if it's what you want. I'll give you pleasure until you command me stop, but I think it might be better if we get out of this field and clean you off. Not to mention the fact that I would rather like to understand what just happened."

Tilly couldn't breathe. His words. God, did he have any idea what they did to her? He turned her into warm butter.

"You desire me, my lord?" Her voice sounded like an eight-year-old's even to her. Of course, he desired her. He was a man. They desired any woman. It meant nothing special. It did not imply that he respected her, or admired her, or had any sort of affection for her.

And yet, her knees threatened to give out.

He took a step closer. His hand brushed her cheek. She turned her face toward his palm, needing to feel his skin on her lips.

"Desire you?" he repeated with a laugh. He cradled her chin until she met his gaze. The laughter had vanished. "Desire you? Tilly, I love you."

CHAPTER FIFTY-ONE

There, he had said it. He had never spoken the words before, though no doubt she had heard them many times from many other men. The words had never meant anything to him until he met Tilly, and now they seemed his whole world. Her reaction might kill him.

Jaiden didn't exhale. He clung to the breath in his chest, fearing it might be his last. Even his heart stopped pumping as he prayed that she would tell him she loved him, too.

She did not answer. She did not say anything or move a muscle. She just stared at him.

He had said it aloud. He was fairly certain he had. He had not just imagined it. Nonetheless, he decided to try again. "Tilly," he whispered. "I love you."

"You don't!" she cried. She lifted her arms and slammed them against her sides just before her face crumbled, and she burst into tears.

Jaiden's mind reeled. Out of all the responses he had imagined, this one had never occurred to him. "I do," he maintained. He reached for her, but she evaded his grasp, shaking her head.

"You don't. It's not me!"

He chuckled in confusion and disbelief and, yes, even amusement. "Er . . . who then?"

"It's the dress," she wailed. More tears streamed down her face. Her mind must have rattled in her head from all her shaking. "You don't love me. You only think you do because of the dress." She plucked at what now was no more than mud-covered rags and sobbed.

Jaiden had never seen a more pathetic sight in his life. She truly was a candidate for Bedlam. Did she really think he felt the way he did because of a gown? A gown beyond all repair, at that?

All her responsibilities, all she'd accomplished, and this was what finally broke her. She was the most incomprehensibly ridiculous creature on the planet.

And he loved her for it.

CHAPTER FIFTY-TWO

Oh, God, why had she worn the rose again? To hear the words and know they were lies.

It was better this way. She didn't want him to love her. She didn't want any man to love her. Tilly had seen enough of love to last a lifetime. It wasn't a gift. It was a demand: bear my children, clean my house, obey me no matter how idiotic my notions.

And worst of all, love me back. Ahh, it could trap a woman till death did they part.

Tilly wanted none of that.

As always, though, Jaiden ruined her resolve. He once again read her mind. or perhaps just her face.

Jaiden took her hand. "I'm not asking anything of you except the chance to make you happy for the rest of your life."

Chapter Fifty-Three

Jaiden secured two separate hotel rooms, but he did not feel entirely comfortable with the arrangement. Trouble followed Tilly, and he wanted to be there to protect her from it.

But who was going to protect her from him?

A gentleman would never take advantage of a vulnerable woman, he reminded himself as he knocked once on her door. It swung open before he could knock again.

He looked down at her, but she had already crossed the room. Jaiden had intended to ask how she fared and then leave, but she clearly had plans of her own. Blithely, she rearranged her newly washed gown where it lay over a chair in front of the fire, bending over to give him a tempting shot of her perfect derriere. She did not realize the danger he presented.

His eyes traveled over the blue satin wrapper she wore. His blood gushed downward just thinking about what little lay beneath that robe.

Jaiden inhaled. He began to chant silently once more.

A gentleman would do everything in his power to rescue his lady fair, and then guard over her while she recovered.

A gentleman would certainly never accost a maiden just hours after a highwayman had set upon her. Instead, a gentleman would . . . he would . . .

Tilly looked at him over her shoulder. She smiled, the smile of Eve after eating of the tree of knowledge.

Damn being a gentleman.

Jaiden took two strides, pulled her close, and pushed his hands into her hair. He tilted her head back, ready to taste those luscious lips. Her eyes widened. They flashed vulnerability.

Jaiden froze. He wouldn't do this.

His eyes darted back to her lips. Her breath caught.

She wanted the kiss, too.

His hands shook. He gripped her head on either side. She couldn't have turned away from him if she wanted.

But he descended toward her slowly, taking a lifetime. She could tell him nay any minute. He half expected her to.

When his lips finally brushed against hers, he felt his soul groan. The gentle touch was both all he needed and the most unsatisfying thing in the world. It set his desires aflame and left him perfectly content. How did she do this to him? Why was it only she that burnt him with an onslaught of contradictions? How could he not perish in her fire?

"Oh, God, Tilly," he murmured against her hair.

"Tilly," he cried again into her mouth. She was perfection. She was everything he wanted. And she was his.

Her fingers gripped his shirt. He could feel her shudder even over the pounding of his blood.

He swooped down to claim her mouth. She whimpered. One hand circled his neck, clinging to him. Her eyes closed.

His concern was no longer for her, but for him. If he continued, he knew, he would never be able to claim his heart as his own again.

Madness rushed through his veins. She wanted him. He knew it, but he had to give her one last chance to protest. To save both of them from the flames.

"Tell me to stop," he ground out, kissing the corner of her mouth, gripping her hair in his hands, her head between his forearms, her legs between his thighs. He controlled the movement of her entire body. He'd be damned if he couldn't control her heart as well.

She cried out feebly.

God damn it, he couldn't act the part of the cad. He couldn't take her, wouldn't take her, unless she gave her assent. She, too, had to know they would burn. She had to agree to the heat, had to know that she chose him.

He pulled his face from her. She gulped in air. Jaiden gripped her hair until she opened her eyes, still panting. Their gazes locked. Her breath came in audible gasps. Desire clouded her eyes. She looked desperate, as desperate as he felt.

"If you do not want me to proceed, tell me to stop. Now," he demanded, while he still had the ability to walk away.

Her hand pushed at the back of his neck, trying to move his lips to hers. He wouldn't budge, not even when her teeth pulled at her bottom lip, not even as her breasts moved against him with every pant.

He tried again, slower, "If you want me to stop—"

Tilly's fingertips covered his lips. Her eyes lit, turning into their upside-down smiles. She let out a sound somewhere between a laugh and a groan, then grinned open-mouthed.

She stood on tiptoe. Her entire body trembled, but she kissed his cheek. "Thank you," she breathed, "for asking." She kissed his other cheek. "But don't ask again." She drew in a ragged breath. "And don't stop."

His tension vanished.

"Tilly," he whispered, prayed, exalted. His thumb slid down her cheek. His mouth covered hers. *Tilly.*

Never getting more than an inch away from her, Jaiden rotated her in a circle. Slowly, he guided her back toward the bed.

Suddenly, her hands shoved at his shoulders.

Concerned, he pulled away. He looked down at her furrowed

brow. Worry had inched its way into her passion-drenched gaze.

"Jaiden. . . ."

His hands tightened their hold on her. He forced them to relax. "Yes," he managed through the sudden ice in his chest.

"I . . ." She stopped. Disgust and reluctance warred on her face.

"Yes?" he said, forcing himself to calm.

Her lips tightened, like a petulant child's, and then she threw her arms in the air and stamped a foot. "I don't know what I'm doing!" she exclaimed.

She was letting him seduce her, was what she was doing. "I do," he spoke, then tried to kiss her.

"Yes, but I don't!" she complained.

"I'll teach you," he promised.

Her eyebrows jumped. She opened her mouth to speak, then closed it. A smile flicked at the corner of her lips. She grinned. "Then let's to it!"

He laughed—heartily and with his whole body. He leaned his head back and let it out, but his hands moved to her shoulders, refusing to let her go. She was too much.

And all his.

He laughed into her hair, and then against her cheek. The laughter turned into a kiss as she turned her lips toward him. He couldn't get enough of her. He swung one forearm beneath her bottom to lift her just so he had better access to her mouth, to her entire body.

Tilly was melting—into him, losing her very consciousness. She ceased being a separate entity—could no longer tell where she began and he ended.

He followed her onto the bed. Her robe loosened. She was lost.

He moved far enough away from her to pull off his shoes and his stockings and throw them to the floor. He pulled his shirt free of his trousers and began work on the buttons.

Cool air brushed against Tilly's bare, flushed neck. With it came reality.

She had to stop this. She had thought she was ready, had wanted him, but she hadn't expected this. She hadn't known she would lose herself, that her body would ache with need, though she knew not what for.

This wasn't like the time in his study. This was desperate and frightening, and somehow she knew she was gambling with more than her life.

It was wrong. She had to find herself. She had to remember that he was just another man. She did not need him, she told herself.

But she did need him. And *that* she could not allow. Tilly turned her face away from him as Jaiden pulled off his shirt. Her gaze searched, trying to find anything, to locate one object that wasn't him. One object to remind her of who she was and the strength she had always relied upon. One object to cling to in the storm that had taken control of her emotions and the hot ache that raged through her body.

She spotted the dresser. Panting, she tried to will her body to pull away from him, to move toward it. She could . . .

But then he grabbed her face. Her eyes met his.

"Don't shut me out," he commanded. His eyes flashed. "I won't let you. Not this time, Tilly. I've waited too long for you. Not your body. You."

The grip on her face turned into a caress, but it trapped her all the more.

"You will feel everything I do," he promised. "And when I fill you, you will know that it is I who does it. And you will know that I love you with everything in my mind, body, and soul. And I will have your mind, body, and soul in return."

New longing wracked Tilly. No longer could she remember

wanting anything other than this. Her eyes drifted down his bare chest. Skin flashed in the firelight. Muscle strained beneath his skin. Tilly traced his deltoid with her fingers.

Electricity surged from the contact.

"Look at me," Jaiden told her. He would not let her close her eyes. He would not allow her even that modicum of privacy.

Her eyes flew back to his. Her palm stroked his chest. It pressed lower to his stomach. He sucked in his breath in response.

She smiled as a tear rolled from her eye.

He didn't return the smile, nor would he relax his gaze. But then, it didn't matter, for the sensations overwhelmed all other thoughts. Jaiden took ownership of her, body and soul. His touch sent screams through her torso, legs, head, soul—howls of pleasure and need.

Tilly had always imagined the coupling between man and woman as an act of violence, of intrusion. She had never expected this . . . this sweetness. She felt worshipped and protected and desperate and . . . loved. Even when her eyelids drooped it didn't matter, for when they opened, Jaiden's eyes would still be there, holding her.

Afterward, she lay, exhausted, her head on his shoulder. "Is it always like this?" she asked, exhausted.

Not even close! "Like what?" His voice sounded miles away. He couldn't think past the feel of her around him.

"Like friendship?" she breathed. Another tear slid down her cheek. He caught it with his palm. She buried her face in his hand.

It had never been like friendship before. It had never been making love.

CHAPTER FIFTY-FOUR

Moonlight still glazed the room, as Tilly awoke to the feel of Jaiden's kisses on her back. That is, she did and didn't awaken. Part of her remained buried in the slumber world. Her worries, her doubts, her insecurities about him—they hadn't made the journey back to earth with her.

Tilly didn't miss them. She knew they would wait for her in the dream dimension. Tomorrow was soon enough to be saddled with them. Too soon. Tilly enjoyed this new light feeling—that and the tingles plucking at her skin.

God, it had been fun!

She laughed just thinking about it. The guffaw erupted low, the opposite of her usual giggle designed to put men on edge. This was unadulterated bliss with no room for self-consciousness.

Not that she could be self-conscious after what she'd done to him. Or what he'd done to her.

Tilly laughed louder, in ecstasy. She clapped her hands, twice. She could not contain her joy.

"The lady is pleased?"

Flipping onto her back, Tilly smiled into Jaiden's beautiful, brilliant, happy, lovely eyes.

The lady had never been better in her life.

Tilly sat up just far enough to ravish his mouth thoroughly, then fell back onto the pillows. She stretched, arms overhead, hand bumping the headboard, completely unconcerned about her nudity. She rather enjoyed the feel of her bare skin against the sheets. It was as if she'd been granted a whole new sense.

Jaiden, however, was not so unaffected by her nakedness. Tilly watched his expression turn from bemused smugness to admiration as she arched her back.

She went limp, and Jaiden exhaled. He threw himself next to her on his side and propped his head up with one hand to watch her.

Affection for him overwhelmed her. The pleasure he had given her! She felt like bringing him flowers, writing him sonnets, singing him love songs . . . that is, if she had possessed any musical talents, which she did not.

And his body. Maybe she was a tad biased, since it had just taken her for a frenzied romp through paradise, but truly, he must be the most beautiful male specimen on the planet.

Her eyes traveled over his long, strong legs, his thick wrists, his muscled arms. And his chest. Its size made her go all womanly inside. Not to mention those hands. They drove her crazy every time they came near her. She feared she would never be able to look at him again and not think of this night in his arms.

Tilly could no longer refrain from touching him. She sat up next to him and pressed a hand against his hard stomach and the other into the small of his back. She felt his stomach clench in response. Tilly next squeezed his thigh before moving on to press his calf.

"Are you attempting to wring me out?"

If she could.

I'm asking nothing of you . . . except to make you happy for the rest of your life.

He had said the words, and Tilly had known this night would come. In that instant, he had won her. With that promise, she had known. He could do what he wanted with her.

She hadn't expected it to bind her even more tightly to him.

Had she known, she still would have loved him this night. Who could resist such a statement? She certainly couldn't. His declaration had swum around in her head until she'd nearly flung him onto her bed and had her way with him right here.

Oh, wait. That's what she had done.

Tilly smiled and dropped a kiss on Jaiden's hip. It smelled like her perfume. She liked it, liked marking her territory.

Tilly couldn't fight against the promises he made. No matter how much she tried to convince herself that they were lies. Every time he looked at her, she wanted to believe.

In him. In fairy tales. In happily ever after.

In knights who rescued damsels in distress, who didn't beat them within inches of death's door.

None of those things existed, and yet, he made her believe they did.

The real irony was that she had been happy before she met him. Not when she was younger, but lately, for the last several years. Now she couldn't imagine how she hadn't been bored out of her mind, but she hadn't been. She had been content.

Until Jaiden came along and usurped her well-being.

The rake. Promising to grant her the happiness he had robbed her of in the first place. He really was a drug affecting her senses. Affecting her senses? Damn, he had commandeered them!

And yet, none of that could bother her this night. She laid a quick kiss on his shoulder. She traced little swirls on his arm with her fingertips.

Jaiden caught her hand and pulled it to his lips.

Tilly raised her eyebrows in surprise. She had been so busy thinking about him, she had nearly forgotten he was a conscious being as well.

"Are you trying to drive me mad?" he asked. "What are you doing to me?"

Tilly opened her mouth against his stubble. "I'm just saying thank you."

"Thank you? For what?"

Tilly sighed contentedly. "For giving me the most delectable sensations I have ever known." *For giving me tonight.*

Jaiden rolled onto his back. He grasped her hand and dragged her on top of him. She went limp as he began rubbing her shoulders. "My pleasure. Any time I can assist you similarly, just let me know."

"Mmm," was all Tilly could manage. Jaiden's caresses again granted her entry to paradise, just like they did every time he touched her.

Tilly would be erecting shrines in his honor soon.

"Any time I can assist you in any way, Tilly," he whispered against her hair.

Tilly didn't hear him. She had drifted into happy slumber.

Chapter Fifty-Five

Jaiden could hear the faint sound of Tilly's slow breathing—so different from her gasps of the previous hour. He felt her heart beat against his chest. Her chamomile taste lingered on his lips while the vanilla scent of her skin drifted around him. But it was her impish smile, even in sleep, that left him entranced.

He had satiated her. He considered that his greatest achievement. He had never felt this powerful in all his life, yet he couldn't stop touching her. He brushed back the damp hair, which had matted to her forehead. His hands then stroked her shoulders, down her back, to the curve of her buttocks and back up.

For the first time in his life, Jaiden lay in bed, not sleeping, not fornicating, doing nothing at all, and yet completely content. Happy, even.

Just touching her was activity enough. He would gladly massage her sleeping form every night for the rest of her life.

For once, he wasn't anxious to return to work. Indeed, he couldn't imagine what the allure had been. Why had he given up almost all human contact just to amass more money, when he already had accumulated enough to last ten lifetimes? Certainly, he enjoyed what he did, and he made a difference in his employees' lives—gave them all better working conditions and wages than they'd had previously. That gave meaning to his achievements, but it was not a reason to wake up happy every day.

Tilly was a reason for that.

Mayhap, he would hire an assistant at work and spend more time with Tilly. Yes, he knew just the woman he could promote. And then, he could lie with Tilly all day, stroking her hair and enjoying the heat of her skin.

Now, there was just the little matter of getting her to marry him.

Tilly snuggled closer, then rolled off his chest.

"Mmm," she let out, stretching next to him. She looked at him through half-closed eyes. "Hello there," she murmured. Her eyes drifted shut as she traced a finger down his arm.

Jaiden gave her forehead a quick kiss. "Did I wake you?"

Tilly flipped onto her side, throwing a curvy leg over his hip. She licked his shoulder experimentally for a moment before saying, "Yes, you woke me. You terrible scoundrel. You are entirely too comfortable to sleep on. I'm unaccustomed to such luxury."

A smug, possessive smile lit his face. He really didn't have even a speck of decency.

Tilly ran her foot up and down his calf. "I don't know why the very rich bother with purchasing beds," she said drowsily. "They should undoubtedly hire Jaidens instead. Then they would have wonderful nights of sleep and be so cheerful, they would start sharing their wealth, and all poverty and hunger would end. Wars would be averted. Heaven on earth would finally—Where are you going?" She propped herself up on her elbows to watch him. Her tousled hair made her look more adorable than usual.

"I thought you might have worked up a thirst," he returned to the bed with two glasses of water. He sat on the bed, handing one to her. The water felt magnificent sliding down his throat. All his senses remained heightened, it appeared.

"You manhandled me, Jaiden," Tilly pointed out. "Thoroughly."

"I did," he agreed.

A devilish grin broke onto her face. "But, oh, how I liked it!" She threw her hands in the air and let them fall to the bed.

Typical, mercurial creature. Jaiden caressed her hip.

"You do make an excellent instructor, Jaiden," she announced.

He chuckled. "You make a delicious pupil."

"Why, thank you." Her eyes gleamed. "Truly, you were wonderful. Let me know if you ever require a letter of recommendation. I promise to write you a sterling one."

"I don't believe I shall require any references for these particular skills, but your praise is well appreciated," he answered, taking another drink from the glass.

Tilly shook her head. "Nothing of it. I would be ungrateful if I didn't salute your skill. Indeed, I plan to recommend you to all my friends."

Jaiden stretched onto the bed and hauled Tilly against his side. "Somehow, I doubt this is what your friends need," he remarked.

"I wouldn't be certain of that. I think a night with you would be of benefit to any woman," Tilly announced. She closed her eyes and wrapped one arm over his chest. Apparently, it didn't feel right. She moved it to his abdomen, then sighed, satisfied.

Jaiden debated the comment for a full minute before speaking softly. "You can't hide them forever, you know."

"I know no such thing," she stated. Her eyes remained closed, but he felt her eyebrows jump. A plain sign he should stop while he was ahead.

He didn't heed the warning. "Don't you think it's time they built lives for themselves?"

Tilly jerked upright. "Let a man do unspeakable things to

you once, and get ordered around for the rest of your life," she commented. She placed her hands on her hips and glared at him. She looked like a Renaissance statue—all flashing, protective anger with the bosom of a man's most glorious fantasies. "They have built lives. They're just not lives that involve men. And how am I supposed to argue with you when the candlelight keeps teasing me with glimpses of your appealing chest? They're safe," she finished.

Jaiden repressed the urge to take her again. It would hurt her a second time. Only that thought allowed him to keep the thread of their conversation going. "There's more to life than safety."

"Really?" Tilly asked.

Jaiden sat up next to her but didn't allow himself to touch her. "Of course. Isn't that why you're here with me? I'm the biggest gamble you've ever taken."

Tilly took his hand. Her lips trembled. "I know." She looked him in the eyes. "Oh, how well I know. And I'm still here."

Her response surprised him. For once, she wasn't making light of their intimacy. She was offering her soul to him, at least conditionally, for the next few minutes. He couldn't stop himself from taking advantage of that fact.

"Tell me about your parents," he commanded.

Tilly closed her eyes, her long lashes brushing her cheeks. She took a deep breath, then gazed back at him. "All right. But I warn you. It isn't pleasant."

Jaiden swallowed. He might have lied about not hurting her. "I'll get your robe."

Chapter Fifty-Six

Minutes later, Tilly sat cross-legged on the bed, her robe tied securely around her. Her hands gripped a forgotten glass of water. For the first time in their acquaintance, her face revealed no emotion. She spoke clearly, but with no inflection. Her eyes fixed on the wall in front of her.

"My father drank," she continued. "A great deal. Everyday. And . . ." She paused. Jaiden knew she struggled to go on, but the effort was not visible. ". . . when in his cups, he was not kind."

"Damn," Jaiden breathed. He stood up from the bed. He couldn't hear this sitting down. He began to pace. "Is he alive?"

"No. Definitely not alive."

Jaiden gripped the bedpost, wishing it was the cur's neck. "Tilly, did he hurt you?"

"Once," she answered with less intonation than if they had been discussing the ingredients of scones. "Only once. I was young. Maybe four or five. My first memory. It wasn't so bad. Children survive worse every day. But I remember promising myself it would be the last time. And it was."

Her heart-shaped face tilted, but she still stared at the same crack in the wall. "I'm a quick learner. Most people are when the incentives are right. For my mother, the incentives were never right." Not a muscle moved in her face, and yet Jaiden could feel her sudden shame. "I used to think she liked it, at least a little bit. To let it go on. Day after day, year after year.

The attention meant he cared. It's what he would say—afterwards. He beat her because he cared. She believed him. I wanted no part of that kind of caring.

"I learned to handle him. I prided myself on how well I handled him, how I could keep his rage in check, make it go away." She paused. When she spoke again, her voice deepened, as if she had drifted back in time. "But then, I grew older. And lazy, or maybe just self-righteous. I let my emotions get the better of me until . . . It was the middle of the day—a bright, sunny summer day, so bright it hurts my eyes to remember. My father had finished half a bottle of whiskey, although it wasn't even noon. My parents began to fight as usual. He hit her, like he always did. But this time I heard it—not just the smack of fist hitting skin, but the other horrible, horrible crunch of bone shattering."

Tilly shook her head. Her nose scrunched as if a foul odor filled the room. "As long as I live I'll never stop hearing that sound. It was horrid. Usually, I'd cajole him or even make him cry from nostalgia. I'd done it a thousand times, but not that day."

She ground to a stop. Jaiden waited, but she didn't speak. He hated the story of her past, but he needed to hear the rest of it. He needed to know so he could help exorcise her ghosts. "What happened?" he prompted.

Tilly started at the sound of his voice. Her gaze saw only a past too painful to recount. She stiffened her shoulders and continued. "I stole a gun—his gun—a rifle. It was heavy, heavier than it looked. I'd never wielded a gun before, but I knew how. I'd seen him handle it a million times. I'd seen him load it."

Once again her mouth closed. Her eyes stared at the same crack in the wall.

Jaiden didn't blame her for killing her father. Saved him the trouble of tracking down and killing the beast. "Tilly, it's the past. It can't hurt you now."

Her eyes snapped to his. Her lips twisted into a sneer. "You lie. The past can kill. It can destroy everything you have and make the present so inconsequential you wonder why you bother getting out of bed. But then, you know, it's not really you—here and now. Not at all, because you are trapped in a time that should have gone. And you can never escape. Time might march forward, but you're not in it, only the shell remains of who you once were. And something evil and hateful and twisted, and only enough of you is left to realize how despicable you've become, but it's not enough to fight it."

She stared at him. Her hands rubbed her body hard as if trying to scrape away the memories from her skin, but they went too deep. Suddenly her fingers stilled, and she burst into a humorless laugh. Cackles shook her body—a desperate cry of someone who has nothing left to lose.

Amazing, such bitterness from a woman with a limitless capacity for joy. His brain couldn't make sense of the sight.

"What am I speaking of?" she squealed. "I don't have a bloody clue. You must be signing me up for Bedlam. Poor thing. I always was a babbling drunk."

Jaiden ran his fingers through his hair. "You haven't had anything to drink."

She smiled, shifting the glass in her hand. She shrugged. "Babbling sober person, then. But you must admit it doesn't have the same ring. I'm hungry," she announced, looking around the room.

He couldn't let her off the hook. She had to rid herself of the rest. "Tilly." He left the bedpost to kneel on the bed next to her. He clasped her shoulders. "What happened the day you acquired the rifle? Tell me."

Her eyes rested on his. "Why, I aimed the rifle at his chest and vowed to kill him should he ever raise his hand to his wife

again. I thought he might hit her then, but he saw me. He knew
I didn't bluff. Minutes passed, maybe a lifetime. Then I left.
Can't recall where I went or what I did. I just remember needing to get out, and then returning . . . hours later. The house
was silent. I couldn't feel her pain anymore. I could always
sense it before. Always. And it was gone. I thought she must be
dead. I knew she hadn't run away. She couldn't."

"Tilly . . ."

Tilly silenced him with a shake of her head. "I found her. She
was in my room, sitting on my bed. Her hands lay folded in her
lap. Blood crusted her chin. The gun pressed to the side of her
skull. I couldn't sense her agony because she didn't feel any.
She was resigned, even glad, I think. It was the only escape
she'd ever imagined for herself."

"She killed herself?" Jaiden asked.

"Oh, no! Such a decisive action? Not my mother. Where ever
did you get that idea—oh, I see. Wasn't very clear, was I? She
didn't hold the gun to her head. He did. I don't know how long
they'd waited, but wait for me he had. From the moment I
opened that door, he stared me straight in the eye, didn't say a
word. He didn't need to. He just pulled the trigger."

Jaiden took a breath and closed his eyes. He couldn't block
out the image of her standing there, watching her mother's
murder.

"He turned the gun on himself next."

"Oh, God," Jaiden breathed.

"God was occupied elsewhere that day. I promise you."

He studied her, saw the evil knowledge in her eyes. "You
must hate him."

Her eyebrows jumped. "God?"

"Your father," Jaiden clarified.

"My father?" she repeated in surprise. "Oh dear no. Never
even occurred to me. Why would I? He was just acting as he

was. Never expected him to behave differently. One doesn't hate a horse for kicking. Animals can't change their nature. No. It was me I hated. I mucked everything up. You see, it was the gun I'd brought into the room that killed her, probably gave him the idea. And I knew better than to threaten him, but I did it all the same. I'll never forget how good that felt, just that once to see the hatred in his eyes, to know that someone had stood up to him. Well, my mother died for my pleasure. Hope she thinks it was worth it."

"None of this was your fault."

"Jaiden, don't placate me. I know the excuses. I was young. I was the child, but the excuses don't justify what happened, because I knew better. And I ignored reality. So, my lord, I beg to differ. It was all my fault."

The weight she'd been caring all these years. Jaiden moved to hug her, but she eluded the embrace.

Tilly stood, walked across the room to stare out the window.

"Tilly, I understand you feel responsible—"

She whirled around. Her eyes flashed fire. "You don't understand, because I don't feel responsible. I don't feel anything. Ever. Not thinking about my parents. Not thinking about before they died. Not in the years after they died. I don't feel anything anymore! They killed my feelings, and all this time, I've been a pretense." Tears tumbled from her eyes. "I've pretended that I care, that I can be sad, that I am affected, all to disguise the fact that I don't, that I can't. I lost my soul that day! And now I'm nothing. I feel nothing!"

Her entire body trembled. She shook her head. "And I'm glad of it, Jaiden. Truly glad. It's safer to feel nothing, but other times . . ." Her lips quivered. She took a shuddering breath. Her voice dropped to the saddest whisper he'd ever heard fall from a pretty mouth. "Other times . . ." She looked him in the eyes. "I want to be part of the world, too. I'm sick of being the disinterested audience. I want a part. I want to feel. Please, Jaiden, please." She took two steps to him, and buried her face in his chest. "Make me feel. Make me feel something."

Jaiden thrust his fingers into her hair, made her meet his gaze. He waited until her tear-filled eyes focused on his. "You do care. I've never known anyone who cared so much, who felt so much. How could you doubt it?"

"You're wrong. I go into society—"

He let loose a laugh. "Society? Well, of course, you don't give a damn about that. It's ridiculous, and you're an intelligent girl. Yes, it's a game to you. How could it not be? You deal in life and death. Your actions shape people's destinies. You've gambled with the law, knowing your loved ones hang in the balance. What is the latest tidbit of gossip compared to that? What is the color of Miss Kensington's frock or the shape of Sir Reginald's cravat? Nothing. You're right to keep it nothing."

"But my parents . . . I never once cried when they died."

"Of course, you didn't." His hands moved to cup her chin, going from jailer to enchanter. "That's not because you don't care. It's because you care too much. Some things are too big to be reduced to tears. Some situations are too complex to feel the sadness without the anger and confusion. You go into emotional chaos. No single feeling wins. You just end up feeling ill."

"Jaiden, rid me of this numbness. Please. I think you may be the only person who can." Tilly bit his shoulder, kissed his neck, driving him mad. She knew she lied though. She already felt something, too much . . . of everything.

Especially desperation.

To have him, to hold him, to keep him for this night and never let it end.

"Jaiden, I beg you," she pleaded. "Do your ungodly things to be. Mold me into a real person. Make me who you want me to be. I can be it. I swear. For you, I can be anything." She wrapped her arm around his neck, clinging to him, praying he could keep her from drowning.

Jaiden groaned. "You're already exactly what I want. You're everything I want," he swore. He bent his knees so she could see more deeply into his eyes and read the truth. "Everything I need, and I'm not going to let you go."

"Don't let me go. Don't!" Tilly begged into his skin. She pressed her mouth to his shoulder, tasted the salt of her tears. "Have me. Here. Now. Again. As you did before."

Jaiden's jaw clenched. "I can't, Tilly."

The words sent terror through her. If he refused, she wouldn't survive the hour. She'd never told anyone about her parents, never relived that day. She had barely survived it the first time. A second time would kill her unless Jaiden gave her a reason to go on. "Jaiden, I need you. Please."

He pulled her hair, forcing her to look at him. "I can't love you as I did before. No, don't talk. It will hurt—"

"I don't mind the pain. I—I love you."

A shudder ran through him, and he actually winced.

"Tilly," he growled, his eyebrows lowering. "I swore I would never hurt you. I won't go back on my word already. Shhh. Hear me out. I will love you, just not like that. Trust me. For now at least, Tilly. For the rest of tonight as you have already."

When he linked his fingers through hers, Tilly could trust him with her life. "Tell me what to do," she said through the tears clogging her throat.

Jaiden swept her into his arms. "Just put yourself in my hands and enjoy."

CHAPTER FIFTY-SEVEN

"My lord, I don't believe it was your hands that wreaked havoc on me," Tilly commented later. She had no idea how much later. Time had ceased. She was exhausted. He had done all sorts of things to her. She had made the journey from heaven to earth so many times, she could barely keep her eyes open. Indeed, they kept drifting closed as she lay across Jaiden's chest, but she refused to fall asleep. She didn't want this night to end, ever. She didn't know what waited for her once the sun rose, but it couldn't be nearly as sweet. So, she kept talking, even if incoherently.

"My hands helped," Jaiden murmured. He brushed a tendril of hair from her forehead. His fingers worked at the tangles.

Good luck to him, trying to get through those curls.

He was so tender with her. And in their earlier conversation, he had been so understanding. He must have come by his understanding the hard way. "Your parents, too?" was all she had the energy to get out.

Jaiden's voice came out strong, just like the rest of him. "You once told me all parents fail with their first sons."

Tilly waited, but he didn't continue. Finally, she muttered, "Daughters, too, most of the time. Some escape, though. Some parents are so delighted in their daughters, they don't worry about spoiling them with too much love and affection. They cherish them. That's all children need." Tilly smiled at herself. Listen to her, talking about things she knew nothing about.

Ignorance had never stopped her before. "In my own, unin-formed opinion," she added. "First sons are a different matter altogether. The must *make something of themselves.* They are never shown love unconditionally by their parents. Too often, love comes in the way of violence. Make a man out of them, and what not."

"No wonder they beat their wives," Jaiden speculated. "What else do they know?"

Had any other male uttered such an excuse, Tilly would have scoffed. It was easy to be generous to the perpetrators when one had no chance of being a victim. With Jaiden, however, she tucked the comment away for later consideration. Maybe he had a slightly less biased opinion than her own. In fact, in the all the time she had spent mulling over her father's behavior, this idea had never occurred to her. Perhaps he had been a victim at some point himself. Maybe most of these abusive husbands had been.

Not that that made their behavior forgivable, but perhaps Tilly wouldn't have to consider all men various incarnations of the Antichrist.

Jaiden traced the inside of Tilly's wrist. "I didn't know God could create such softness until touching your skin. Truly, an all-powerful deity."

Tilly peered up at Jaiden. She smiled. "I usually feel dirty after revealing so much of myself. I don't with you." It was an awesome realization.

"Well, I should hope not." Jaiden touched the tip of her nose.

One corner of Tilly's mouth turned down for a moment, then the other followed. "I think I meant what I said earlier. I think I love you."

"Of course, you do. I've known it for quite some time. I only got impatient waiting for you to realize it."

Tilly propped her head on one hand. "I wonder if I still will tomorrow."

"Well then, I'll have to make sure you do," Jaiden said, pulling her close. He ravished her mouth yet again.

CHAPTER FIFTY-EIGHT

And she had thought his presence disturbed her before. Now she could think of nothing else. It was as if her skin had come alive for the first time. She had only to think he might brush against her arm, and gooseflesh spread across the limb in anticipation.

Frowning, Tilly stared out the window of the moving carriage. How was she to survive the journey to London? Every instant was an agony of wanting to feel even the slightest touch from him. And it only got worse the farther he moved from her. Oh bollocks! How was she to survive life? Would she have to chain him to her? Knock him out and assault his unconscious form?

Even that image could not restore her humor. She wanted him to touch her. Now. Forever. She would combust if he didn't. She would burn from desire. She would die, tortured. Every cell in her being seemed to split, spreading out in the hope of reaching him.

Touch me, Jaiden, she willed. For once, she had no plan to manipulate him, to mold him to her wishes. It did not occur to her to form one. No time. She needed his touch now.

Touch me, she begged silently. *Reach out. Now. Slide your arm behind my back. Take my hand. Press your leg against my thigh. Anything. Everything. Just touch me.*

Touch me. Touch me. Touch me. Touch me. Touch me.

CHAPTER FIFTY-NINE

Jaiden watched Tilly's eyebrows get lower and lower with an impending sense of doom. She sat as far away from him as possible, and with every passing minute, he wound up looking at more of her back.

So, perhaps he had behaved badly toward her the night before. Oh, whom was he trying to fool? He'd been a complete scoundrel. He'd taken her virginity in a second-rate hotel whose name he hadn't bothered to learn.

It was scandalous, insensitive, unromantic . . . and he'd be damned if he'd regret a second of it.

He'd be double damned if he would let her regret it.

"Oh no, you don't." Jaiden reached across the seat, pulled Tilly away from the window and onto his lap. She leaned her head against his chest. He felt her inhale deeply. He had feared more resistance. Her willingness pleased him, made him nod. "Much better. I know what you were attempting, and I won't allow it, Tilly. Not this time, not ever again."

Her face jerked up at him, a single delicate arch raised. A laugh escaped her, but not her normal chuckle at finding him merely amusing. This was pure joy, happiness in musical form. It resonated in his soul. "Of what are you speaking?" she asked.

Jaiden nodded again. He knew her too well for this. She could not make him doubt his insight, not even with the twinkle in her eyes. "You were over there, scowling out the window, cataloging my flaws, accusing me of a million future crimes, and all in all trying to distance yourself from what transpired between us, but I will not allow it. You are not going to talk yourself out of loving me, and every time you try, I'll just have to prove you wrong."

At the beginning of his speech, her mouth had opened wide in astonishment—most likely that he read her so easily. Then, her eyebrows rose saucily while he commanded her to love him. But now, as he prepared for her rebellion, she closed her eyes, rested her head on his shoulder, and snuggled closer.

"You are correct, as always, my lord," she murmured. "You know me too well."

Bloody hell! He'd been way off track all along! Would he never figure her out? And did it matter when her lips pressed against his throat like that?

CHAPTER SIXTY

They'd traveled only fifteen miles when Tilly made her announcement.

"I slept with another man—Why are you laughing?"

Jaiden shook his head. He'd gone a full ten minutes in peace. He'd begun to relax. He should have known better.

"Why are you laughing?" Tilly demanded, turning to face him.

"Because I don't believe you."

"I did," she maintained. "He was a very nice Scottish gentleman. Balding, but quite distinguished looking. Had an enticing way of calling me lass."

"Really?" Jaiden cocked his head. "When?" And how could he refrain from kissing her when she lied so prettily?

"This morning. While you were seeing to our things."

"Oh, so in less than fifteen minutes, you met another man, got him to your room, seduced him, got rid of him, bathed, changed, and met me downstairs for breakfast?"

Tilly raised her chin. "Yes, that's precisely what I'm saying." Her eyebrows lowered for a moment, and she looked down and to the right before nodding and raising her chin again.

"And you did this because . . . you were so enthralled by the experience last night, you couldn't wait to try again?"

Her brow wrinkled, then relaxed as she met his gaze. "Exactly."

"And you didn't want to try again with me because . . ." Her face lit up with the thought, and Jaiden knew she was more than ready to try again. He felt a moment of masculine pride. ". . . because you wanted to compare my skills with another man."

She nodded vehemently. "Yes, that's why. I wanted to know if it was you or the act. That's why I seduced a stranger this morning." She turned her back to him again.

Jaiden nodded. "Ah, I see." He leaned back in the seat and began rubbing her shoulder.

Tilly twisted again. "What? What do you see?"

"Well, as you have told me on multiple occasions, you are a prudent woman. Clearly, you would never dream of committing yourself to one man before you educated yourself about the alternatives, your opportunity costs, that is. Very good business maneuver. You do me credit. It's all settled then. I'll make arrangements as quickly as possible. How does Saturday three weeks hence sound?"

Tilly sat up straighter. "What arrangements? What's settled?"

"Why, our wedding day, of course. You now know the market, so I can only assume you are ready to settle on me. After all, you are here in my carriage and not trying to decipher the English language as butchered by some terrible, probably fake, Scottish burr." Apparently, he wasn't above feeling an ounce of jealousy even over an imaginary seducer. "Very well. I accept. With honor. I will see about a license today. Would you like a large ceremony or something small and intimate. Personally—"

Tilly covered his mouth with her hand. Jaiden flicked the tip of his tongue against her palm. Tilly giggled. She took her hand away, revealing his wicked grin.

"I didn't really, you know . . . with someone else," she announced.

"I know," he said, though his heart ached at the thought that she believed she had to test him.

Her eyebrows rose. "You do? How?"

"Because, my darling . . ." Jaiden kissed her temple. "My own sweet heart . . ." Another kiss. "You have . . ." A kiss on the opposite temple. "No prospects of being touched . . ." One on her cheek. "By another man." His voice continued slow, mesmerizing, interspersed with kisses. "No other man will ever feel your pulse race under his lips." He pressed his mouth to her throat. "And I am the only person who will ever know the curve of your ankle by touch." His hand slid slowly up her leg. He heard her inhale. "And only I will know the exquisite sound you make every time I nibble the outside of your ear." He gently tugged at her earlobe with his teeth. "And no other man will ever know the ambrosia of the gods, which can only be tasted by worshipping you." His thumb traced along her leg. Tilly's eyelids fell. She let loose a whimper. "And only I will understand complete knowledge of all that is good on this earth through the beauty of your face when I bring you to climax." A tremor flashed through the woman in his arms. He felt the gooseflesh rise on her skin. "And do you know why no other man will make your heart race and your cheeks flush and send flutters through your stomach?"

Tilly's voice came out breathless. "Because you won't let them?"

"No, because you won't."

"I won't?" she murmured.

"No. I am going to be everything you desire and leave you no time for other men."

"Oh," Tilly breathed, as all thoughts abandoned her head and Jaiden once again brought her to paradise.

CHAPTER SIXTY-ONE

It took a half hour for Tilly's mind to clear of its daze. She realized she was happy. Insanely happy. Happier than humanly possible, ensconced completely in his arms, breathing the smell of their recent escapade, gazing out the carriage window as they entered London.

Jaiden had not showed the slightest bit of temper when she'd announced her infidelity. Of course, he hadn't believed her either. But never mind that. Or maybe it was better that he knew her so well. Perhaps she wouldn't have the power to crush him after all if he could see through her ploys. He certainly had come a long way since that first night in his study when he had been overcome by her feigned faint.

Tilly congratulated herself on another male well trained. Oh, she was deliciously happy! Why couldn't everyone possess such joy?

An image of her last encounter with Adelaide filled her mind, and Tilly felt a tug of guilt intrude upon her happiness.

Adelaide wanted Daniel. She thought he would make her happy. For the first time, Tilly realized, that maybe Daniel had such power. If Jaiden could bring Tilly's life such joy, perhaps Daniel could do the same for Adelaide.

Well, clearly not to the same extent since Daniel was not half the man Jaiden was, but then, if he was the person Adelaide wanted, who was Tilly to judge?

And Daniel obviously wanted Adelaide, too.

Yes, perhaps it was time Tilly stopped dragging out the courtship and just let the lovers be together.

"Jaiden do you mind if we make a stop before . . ." Tilly trailed off unexpectedly. She flushed. She didn't know if he planned to take her back to her room in Cheapside, or to his townhouse. Good Lord, she couldn't finish the sentence! Either way it sounded presumptuous.

"Love?" he prompted.

Tilly stared at him blankly.

"You wanted to make a stop?" he tried.

"Pardon? Oh! oh, yes." Oh, dear. No wonder married women couldn't air their complaints to their husbands. Everything sounded like a sexual proposition.

After the intimacies Tilly had shared with Jaiden, how could she make polite conversation with him? She could comment on the weather, but the memory of his kisses played on her brain.

And the way he touched her.

And how he'd buried himself inside her.

"Tilly?"

The voice made her start. "Excuse me?" she spoke into double-lashed eyes.

"Stop blushing and tell me where you want to go," Jaiden commanded.

Her cheeks went from warm to fire. Good God, could he read her mind? Did he guess she'd been replaying the firelight flashing over his muscled back in her mind?

"Yes," he answered her unasked question.

Good Lord! Tilly's eyes widened.

"But only because I can't stop thinking about it either," he murmured. He pulled her close and kissed her hot forehead. "I doubt I'll ever stop. Now, name an address."

"Sir Sheldon's office," Tilly squeaked.

"Now, that wasn't so difficult." He squeezed her hand before relaying the directions to the driver.

Tilly sat frozen, mortified. It was ridiculous. The man had . . . he had . . . with his tongue . . . and she hadn't been embarrassed then. Jaiden arched an eyebrow.

"Please don't set the carriage aflame."

She moaned and buried her face in her hands. So much for mature dignity, or even the pretense of it.

Strong arms embraced her. His chest rumbled as he laughed. "Tilly, I was merely teasing. How can you be self-conscious with me after what transpired between us last night?"

"It's because of last night's events that I'm self-conscious."

More laughter. "Well, cease. Otherwise you'll just end up spending your remaining years flushed."

Tilly tilted her nose in the air. "You, sir, are presumptuous." Never mind the happy butterflies circling her belly.

"You didn't think that last night when I—"

"Enough! You win. Mercy. Mercy!" she cried.

"Are you certain? I wager I could turn your face the same shade as—"

Tilly buried her head in his shoulder. "Take pity on me!"

The vanilla scent of her hair wafted to him. Anything she wanted. "Why do you want to call on Daniel?"

Tilly withdrew her head but did not squirm away from his arm. She rather liked it cradling her. "Your aunt made a request of me. I only now realized how I could fulfill it."

CHAPTER SIXTY-TWO

Jaiden helped Tilly out of the carriage and gave Frederick instructions about where to wait for them. He glanced up and down the street. All sorts of low fellows visited the famous Scotland Yard—some had come willingly, some had not. Clearly, it was no place for a lady.

His hand sought Tilly's shoulder to steer her safely into Daniel's office, but it met only air. Jaiden glanced to where she had just stood, but the spot was empty.

His eyes crinkled at the corner. The little darling probably knew he was about to lecture her on safety and wanted no part of it.

Jaiden entered Daniel's offices, and immediately realized there was another reason for Tilly's hurry. She sat with one hip propped against Ben Pendergast's desk, less than two feet from the clerk's face.

Obviously she thought she could get farther without him.

"I really would *love* to see Sir Sheldon," she murmured in a low voice. Her hand moved to the clerk's arm. "It would be a *great* pleasure."

"I'm sorry, miss. I told you. No one sees Sir Sheldon without an appointment."

Jaiden leaned against the doorframe, enjoying the scene.

"Oh, but you silly! Sir Sheldon will certainly want to see me." She leaned closer, giving the clerk a glimpse of her ample bosom. "You do know who I am, don't you?"

Ben shook his head.

"I am Lady Ophelia of course!" Tilly announced.

Jaiden winced.

The clerk cocked his head. "The forty-four-year old Amazon who went missing years ago?" His voice reeked of doubt.

Tilly sat up straight on the desk and patted her coiffure. "I wear my age well."

Jaiden coughed to cover his laugh. Ben jumped from the chair. "Lord Astor," he stuttered. "I didn't hear you come . . . I mean, I didn't see you there."

"Understandably. I can see you have your hands full," he said to the clerk. His gaze met Tilly's. She slithered off the desk and stood unashamedly before him. She raised a challenging eyebrow.

"Oh, no, sir. It wasn't as it looked—"

"I'm certain you don't have to explain these things to Lord Astor," Tilly said, stalking the clerk, who backed into the desk. "He looks a virile sort. I'm sure he knows how it is between men and women. Sometimes there's just an instant connection. Something that can't be fought."

Ben whipped around. The blush traveled higher than his receding hairline. "It is not as she says. The lady . . . Miss . . . er . . . the lady wanted to see Sir Sheldon, but, of course, I wouldn't allow it. She didn't have an appointment, and she hardly looked like someone in dire straights or with pertinent information regarding a case or anyone other than another bored society lady who had come to meet our famous Sir Sheldon, and he specifically told me if I allowed another woman bent on seduction into his office, I'd find myself locked in the interrogation room along with all the rest of those dangerous to society."

Jaiden couldn't contain his grin. "Another bored society lady bent on seducing Daniel, eh? What think you of the description, my love?"

Tilly abandoned Ben. "How very glamorous of me," Tilly commented. "I do believe it is the height of fashion just now to appear both idle and bent on seduction. You must try to appreciate keeping such grand society a little more, my dear."

The clerk's face turned several shades deeper as he heard the endearment.

Jaiden took pity on the man. "Is Sir Sheldon in?"

The clerk swallowed. "Yes, and he's alone."

"We'll show ourselves to the room," Jaiden said, holding his hand out to Tilly who promptly joined him and let him lead her into a side hall.

"Well, my heart, how does it feel to have encountered possibly the one man in all of London whom you can't handle."

"I would have discovered a way. Besides, I thought him darling, especially while I was harassing him. I have just the friend I should like to introduce to him."

"Unless your friend sports a thin mustache like Daniel's, I doubt Ben will be too excited."

Tilly smiled over her shoulder at Jaiden. "Paul does not have a mustache, but he does have very nice golden hair. Do you think that will do?"

Jaiden laughed. God, he adored her. "I'm certain, if you set the match, they will fit smashingly."

Tilly dug her heels in just outside of Daniel's door. She looked up at Jaiden, biting her lip, considering something, then smiled. "Shall we?" she asked.

He held fast to her hand. "What were you debating?"

Looking casually away from his gaze, Tilly raised her other hand to knock. "I planned to tell you to allow me to do the talking, but then thought better of it."

Amused, Jaiden smiled. "You did?"

"Yes, I trust you know to remain silent."

Before Jaiden could react to the half-compliment, half-insult, the door swung open. A disheveled Daniel stood in the doorway. His eyebrows lifted when he spotted her.

"Good day, my lord," Tilly said, breezing past him. She seated herself and rearranged her skirts.

Daniel gave Jaiden a questioning look. Jaiden merely shrugged.

Daniel stalked behind his desk and plopped into his seat, all the while glaring at Tilly. "Mrs. Leighton, I do hope you are prepared to lay open the missing wives case for me. I can't imagine anything else that might warrant the interruption of my work day."

"Oh, I believe I have something to discuss of immeasurably more interest to you than some stuffy old case."

"Stuffy old case?" Daniel stuttered.

Tilly gave a trill of laughter and waved a gloved hand. "Well, you cannot claim to have solved this one posthaste, now can you—although certainly you're not to blame. Just look at the color scheme of this room. How could you possibly get any work done here?"

"I wasn't aware, Mrs. Leighton, that the room had a color scheme."

"Precisely. It doesn't. How can your poor little head be expected to fit together clues when your eyes are bombarded with violent juxtapositions of all the colors of the rainbow, and some unholy colors the rainbow wouldn't have. And I must say, the smell, isn't much better."

"The smell?"

"The stench is more like it. Stale cigarette smoke does not lead to productivity, only stagnation. You need some plants in here, something giving off oxygen. Maybe a potted—"

"Mrs. Leighton!" Daniel interrupted just as Jaiden began to wonder why Tilly bothered with him when she entertained herself so entirely. Daniel shook his head and pulled a cigarette from his gold encrusted cigarette box, maybe in defiance of Tilly or merely out of frustration with her. "What did you wish to discuss?"

Tilly straightened her already taut spine. "Oh, yes, that. Well, I thought it wise to speak to you about Miss Astor."

Daniel paused in the act of lighting his cigarette. "Miss Astor?"

"Adelaide," Tilly supplied helpfully. "Incidentally, the match is about to burn your finger."

Daniel lowered the match and closed his eyes. He shook his head, clearly praying for patience. "Yes, I know who Miss Astor is. What is it you wish to discuss about her?"

Tilly cocked her head. "I thought I should inform you that she's dying."

Daniel's face went ashen. "Dying?" he breathed.

Tilly pursed her lips. "Well, dead, really."

Daniel's eyes went to Jaiden for confirmation. Jaiden turned away. He didn't know what game Tilly played, but he hoped it was worth the pain on Daniel's face.

Daniel must have taken Jaiden's gesture for grief. He dragged his fingers through his hair. "But I saw her just . . . How could she be . . . ? How . . . how did she die?"

"Hmm. Oh, did I say she was dead? No, I meant she's alive and well. I always get those confused. Alive and well. Deceased. They sound remarkably similar. . . ." Her voice trailed off. "Sir Sheldon?"

When Jaiden looked back, he found Daniel hovering over Tilly. A vein in Daniel's forehead pounded. The muscles in his jaw flexed.

"Mrs. Leighton," he spoke in a low voice. "I consider myself a reasonable man, but if you *ever* confuse those two absolutely un-confusable phrases again as regards to Adelaide, I will personally see to it that every one of your precious gowns is burnt to a crisp."

Tilly stood, unfazed by how close she stood to Daniel's erupting temper. "That seems fair. Now, as to Adelaide, it is obvious by your burning face that you are in love with her, and by the fact that you are yet refraining from beating me senseless despite my recent display, I suppose you might make a tolerable husband. I, therefore, think it might behoove you to make your intentions clear to her as soon as possible."

Daniel sat back on his desk. "How does my connection to Adelaide concern you?"

"It shouldn't except that I've become embroiled in her affection for you rather more completely than I would have feared."

Jaiden could have sworn his friend stopped breathing.

"Adelaide has affection for me?" He shook his head. "But lately she's been avoiding me, and the last time I called on her, she refused to see me."

Tilly began to pace. "You see, Adelaide has these ideas." She held up her hand. "I know, I know, it's better for women to avoid such dangers as *thinking*, but sometimes it cannot be helped. So pray understand, Adelaide possesses these notions that it is dishonorable to flirt with you, and now she's taken it into her head that it is wrong to proposition you straight out—don't faint, Jaiden—which leaves her with only the option of being a complete dullard when you're near or avoiding you all together. Either way, she's miserable. I'm assuming this arrangement also leaves you wanting."

"So, you're saying Adelaide is not opposed to my courting her?"

Tilly rested her hands on her hips. "Well, since she desperately wants you for a husband, I'm certain she wouldn't mind if you popped around for tea some afternoon."

Daniel looked—well, stupid, was all Jaiden could think to describe it. Perhaps awestruck. "She wants to marry me?"

Finally, Tilly took pity on the man and smiled. "Yes."

Daniel's face broke into a grin. "What are we standing around here for? Let's go. Jaiden, I'm going to marry your sister."

"Apparently," Jaiden remarked, taken aback. He barely recognized this love-struck swain as the same friend who had captured some of London's most notorious criminals with him. Still, Jaiden could think of no one with whom he would rather entrust his sister's happiness.

"But, Sir Sheldon," Tilly continued. "There are some obstacles. Adelaide has taken it into her head that—"

Daniel grasped her arms and kissed her on the cheek. "Mrs. Leighton, no quantity of ideas is going to keep me from making Adelaide my wife. Let us off."

Jaiden heard Tilly murmur, "Spoken like a true gentleman," just before Daniel ordered them to make haste.

CHAPTER SIXTY-THREE

Daniel burst through the doors of the morning room. "You are going to marry me, and I don't care what you have to say about it!"

Adelaide whirled from the window, then froze at the sight of Daniel's belligerent pose.

Tilly winced. Why didn't men ever learn to entice? Why did they always start with demands? "Good day, Adelaide," she murmured, calmly peeling off her gloves as she entered the room.

Adelaide swung her huge eyes to Tilly. Tilly folded the gloves into her handbag. "I do believe, in his own unusual manner, Sir Sheldon just asked you to be his wife."

"I did not ask," Daniel maintained. He slung a possessive arm around Adelaide's shoulders.

"Yes, well, I was trying to gloss over your high-handed manner, Sir Sheldon. Not precisely the way things are done, is it? So, Adelaide, it is your move. You may accept, decline, or negotiate further. What is it to be?"

The poor girl looked bewildered. Her gaze traveled between Daniel and Tilly as though the English language had lost all meaning to her.

Tilly crept forward and took her hand. "Dear, whatever you want, it's yours for the taking," she whispered, nodding encouragingly.

Adelaide mimicked her nod, but then her head shook from

side to side. "No," she spoke through bloodless lips. "No." She backed out of Daniel's grasp. Her fingers abandoned Tilly's.

"Addie," Jaiden said from an appropriate distance.

Adelaide's eyes fixed on Daniel. "I can't marry you, Daniel. I'm sorry. So sorry."

He stepped forward. "Adelaide?"

"No!" She dodged his grasp, knocking over a lamp. It crashed to the floor, shattering. Glass flew everywhere.

"Oh, God, I'm so sorry," Adelaide cried, sinking to her knees. She attempted picking up the broken pieces, but her hand shook too badly. She lowered her head. Sobs shook her body.

Both Daniel and Tilly kneeled beside her.

"Adelaide." Daniel patted her awkwardly. "Marry me."

Not "what's the matter?" Not "why are you crying your eyes out?" But "marry me!" Why did men always need to make themselves the subject of everything?

Adelaide shook her head. "I can't . . . I . . . Oh, let me go!" She jumped up and ran toward the door.

"I love you," Daniel called after her retreating form.

Adelaide fled from the room.

Daniel moved to follow her. Tilly blocked his path. She dodged back and forth to prevent his following Adelaide until finally he halted. His hands lifted slightly, as though he were debating moving her bodily.

"I'm beginning to believe you're a bad influence on my sister," Jaiden spoke.

Tilly took a moment to glare at Jaiden around Daniel's chest before turning back to Daniel. "I'll go. Wait here."

Daniel glanced at the door.

Tilly spoke slowly as though dealing with a large, slow animal—in other words, a typical male. "Wait here. She'll be back."

Daniel met her gaze. His mouth tensed in resignation.

Tilly turned to the door. She saw the shadow move in front of her. She whirled around. Jaiden hovered behind her. His brows jumped.

Tilly propped her hands on her hips. "Where do you think you're going?"

The corners of his mouth twitched—as always. "I'm going to talk to my sister."

"I do not think that is wise, not at all. Adelaide's very upset. I don't think she'll talk if she has to worry about your reaction—"

"Tilly—"

"You know how you frighten her—"

"Tilly—"

"And what if she has some personal rea—"

Jaiden kissed her. She blinked in surprise, and then her thoughts melted. Her eyes drifted closed. *Oh, his lips were heaven.*

Then they were gone. Tilly's eyes opened.

He smiled down at her. His warm fingertips traced her hairline, turning her insides into warm butter.

She sighed.

His grin widened. "Let's go see my sister."

Jaiden led her from the room. Only as she walked up the stairs, did she recall their problem.

Oh, dear, where had Adelaide come up with all these problems?

Tilly knocked on Adelaide's door softly before pushing it open a crack. "Adelaide?"

"I'm here," came the trembling voice.

Tilly stepped into the large bedchamber. She spotted Adelaide on a chaise longue. Her eyes were fixed on the garden outside the window. "Care to talk about it?"

Adelaide shrugged. Her lips trembled. She looked down in her lap. "I don't think even you can help this time."

"I doubt that's true," Jaiden chimed in. Adelaide's face jerked in his direction. "I've learned there's nothing your friend can't do," he finished.

"Jaiden," Adelaide breathed. "I'm sorry. I . . ."

Jaiden squatted in front of her. "What have you to apologize for?"

Her brow furrowed. "I know this must be awkward for you."

"Never mind that. Tell me why you refused Daniel."

Again, she stared down at her lap and shrugged her delicate shoulders. Red blotches covered her skin—a sign she would burst into tears if she tried to talk.

Tilly sat on the chaise longue beside Adelaide and wrapped her arm around her. "Deep breath," she commanded.

Tremulously, Adelaide obeyed.

"Again."

Adelaide nodded, took in a deep gulp of air, then blew it away. "It's our mother," she blurted out, looking at Jaiden. "I don't want to become her, and I'm scared that I will if I marry, and I don't want to do that. I couldn't. Not to Daniel. Who's so good and daring and . . . and . . . and he deserves someone who will make him happy. And not just miserable." A tear escaped her lashes.

Jaiden blinked, shaking his head. "You think—How did our mother make anyone miserable?"

"Papa," Adelaide answered. "She made papa miserable. She manipulated him. She teased him. She made him buy her jewelry until he'd spent every dime, and then she stole his will to live."

"His will to live?" Jaiden repeated.

"Yes. You wouldn't know. You never paid attention, but I was there, all the time. She would tell me beforehand how she would wheedle a new bauble from him, how she would pretend whatever she had to in order to get it. And then she died on him. And he couldn't go on without her. He wouldn't even try.

She stole his very life. And I needed him." Adelaide crossed her arms. "Well, I won't follow her example. I won't make Daniel a puppet. I'll never see him again rather than change one drop of his perfection."

Perfection? God, love was blind.

Jaiden let out a loud guffaw.

Shock stilled Tilly's tongue for all of three seconds. "You rude beast! Don't you dare mock your sister's pain! Go! Go!" she commanded, standing over him. She nudged him with her shin. "I should have never let you come!"

Jaiden stood, rather than let her tip him over. "Tilly."

"Out!" She pointed at the door.

He grabbed her hands, pulled her to him, and embraced her. Tilly gave a disgruntled murmur, but it was impossible to maintain her wrath.

Still holding on to her, Jaiden turned his attention to his sister. "Adelaide, our mother didn't manipulate our father because she enjoyed it. She did it for him and for us. Did you never realize that?"

"What are you talking of? Don't you remember the way she was—"

"Yes. I remember it exactly. She did it for him. Because he needed the constant stimulation. Strange, I admit, but it worked for him. For both of them."

"What do you mean?" Adelaide shook her head.

"I mean, he needed her to keep their relationship interesting. And she did, and he knew why she did it. He worshipped her for it."

"But all those sapphires—"

"She wanted to keep him from losing that money at the gaming tables. Come now, I've never known a woman less interested in jewels than our mother. What she wanted was security for us. The jewels were her way of assuring it."

Adelaide shook her head, eyes closed. "But the riding accident—"

"Was just that. An accident," Jaiden interjected. His thumbs began making distracting circles on Tilly's forearms. She tried to shrug him off, but he wouldn't let her go. Hmm . . . maybe she didn't mind.

Adelaide's eyes narrowed. "Jaiden, our father was an excellent seat—"

"When he paid attention."

Exactly, Tilly. Pay attention. But she found it nearly impossible to do so in Jaiden's arms. Tingles had started creeping across her skin. Shivers ran down her spine. He really was turning her into an idiot.

Jaiden let go of Tilly with one arm so he could run his fingers through his hair. Tilly jumped on the opportunity to gain some distance from him and, hopefully, some sanity. She moved out of his grasp to stand near Adelaide's bookshelves.

"Addie, I had the same suspicions once, I admit it. But in the end, I cannot believe our father would consciously put Sir George in danger. Yes, maybe he was distracted by grief, but he did not take that fence with the thought that Sir George couldn't jump it. He loved that horse."

Tilly rubbed her head, hoping something inside of it would start working. Who the devil was Sir George?

Adelaide's lips tightened. "So distracted by grief that he brought down not just himself but also his beloved mount." She gave a horrible chuckle. "Don't you see? She killed him."

"It had been less than three days since her death, Addie. That he mourned her passing was a testament to what a good—not a bad—wife she was."

Adelaide looked out the window. A quiver passed over her lips. "I needed him."

Jaiden moved next to Adelaide and joined his sister in gazing out the window. Tilly reeled. No wonder the siblings had such dramatic coloring. Clearly, a tribute to their dramatic pasts.

"I know you did," Jaiden spoke. "And I didn't know how to be him for you. I thought if I supported you, then that would be enough, but it wasn't. You needed his presence, and that was something I didn't know how to give. I've been a terrible brother, Addie. I'm sorry."

Tilly rolled her eyes. She knew a man feeling guilty when she heard one. Apparently Adelaide didn't. She jumped from her chair, nearly knocking over another lamp, and threw her arms around Jaiden. "No, Jaiden, you've been the best brother. I love you. I know I don't say it, but I do. I couldn't ask for a better sibling."

Tilly smiled at the pair of them. Surely, Adelaide would feel more comfortable around Jaiden now. Yes, Tilly had done well. It was a brilliant idea bringing Jaiden along to help calm Adelaide's fears.

But really, that was all she could expect from him. As far as she could surmise, Adelaide was no closer to accepting Daniel's proposal.

Yes, it was time to take matters into her own hands. Hmm . . . perhaps she would do the trick with a little thing she liked to call reverse persuasion. Rather stupid, but it typically worked on both children and women in love.

Adelaide definitely fell in that latter category.

Tilly maneuvered herself to the window. It was a beautiful day; a little cloudy perhaps, but the flowers in the enclosed garden were in full glory. They glistened with overdone romance. Tilly nodded at the sight, then turned back to Adelaide, who stood a few feet from Jaiden now, wiping her eyes, looking sheepish.

"Thank goodness you refused Daniel!" she began.

"Excuse me?"

"Pardon?"

Tilly took a moment to savor their perplexed expressions.

"Yes, refusing him was clearly the right decision. So sorry to have steered you wrong. I mean, I thought for a time he might be a decent chap—but oh, my, did he dissuade me of that notion tonight."

Adelaide crossed her arms over her chest. "But . . . er . . . Daniel is a decent fellow. Better than decent—"

"Oh, please, Adelaide, you're too kind. And it does you credit, but really! You do not have to ruin your life for it. What was he thinking? Barging in here, ordering you about. You know, I've always believed that a man who had to order a woman like that was clearly compensating for some deficiency in his manhood. Daniel must suffer from an overly small—"

"Tilly!"

Tilly opened big, innocent eyes. "What?"

Adelaide flushed. She looked down at her hands. Her fingers fiddled with the seam at the side of the chair.

"Yes?" Tilly pressed.

"Well, I—er—" Adelaide straightened. She cleared her throat and met Tilly's gaze. "I rather like that he wants to marry me."

Tilly rolled her eyes. "Well, of course he wants to marry you. I admit it demonstrates his good taste, but that is no excuse for his lack of manners. Demanding that you marry him like that. I never!"

"Actually, I kind of like that he's so certain about the matter. If he wants to marry me even after all my outbursts, then . . . well, I suppose I shouldn't worry about his not knowing me."

"But Adelaide, you never have outbursts."

Jaiden swallowed what sounded like a chuckle.

And suddenly, Adelaide burst into laughter. "Apparently, I do!" She threw her arms in the air. Tears ran down her cheeks, but her teeth sparkled behind her grin. "Oh, Lord! I'm marrying Daniel! Oh, Lord! Daniel!"

In a flash of skirts, she ran from the room.

Tilly let out a breath and a smile.

Jaiden beamed at her. "Nice work."

Tilly shrugged. "I suppose you served a purpose."

"Tilly, I'm blushing."

He was doing no such thing.

"We make a good team," Jaiden continued.

Tilly turned back to the window. She felt Jaiden's warm hand on her back.

"You made another woman happy today," he noted.

Tilly didn't respond except to shuffle a couple of inches so that her skirts brushed Jaiden's leg. She couldn't help herself.

She felt his whisper against her neck. "But you did it by giving her the husband she wants. It bothers you, doesn't it?" he observed.

"He won't hurt her."

"No, he won't."

Tilly turned to face him. "Because I'd kill him if he did."

Jaiden wrapped his arms around her. "I think Adelaide might kill him first."

Adelaide was not the killing type. Tilly took a deep breath. "So, your sister is getting herself wed."

"Yes, seems marriage is in the air."

Tilly stiffened.

"Tilly, I have to ask—"

She closed her eyes. "Don't ask."

Jaiden stilled.

Guilt hit Tilly. For the first time, she deigned to give a male an explanation. "The answer is probably yes, and I don't want to admit it."

"To me?"

"To myself."

Jaiden exhaled. His hands traveled over Tilly's back. She felt his relief. She'd just agreed to marry him, and it felt good.

"So how do we occupy ourselves now?"

Tilly stepped back to look up at Jaiden. She furrowed her brow. "We go outside and peep in at the lovers through the window, of course." She grabbed his hand, moving toward the door. "Come. I want to see the look on Daniel's face."

CHAPTER SIXTY-FOUR

If Tilly grasped the branch of the willow just so and stood on tiptoes on the back of the garden bench, she could observe the affianced couple through the drawing room window without tumbling to her death—so long as she kept her precarious balance. She smiled despite her worries. Daniel and Adelaide prattled excitedly. They couldn't seem to keep their hands apart.

Tilly had oft wondered what couples did when she wasn't there to guide them. Apparently, they could get on rather well. Good to know, she supposed, not feeling in the least left out. Not at all. She didn't have to be the most important person in Adelaide's life. And besides, she would be again just as soon as Daniel made one wrong step.

"Are you quite finished with your spying?" Jaiden asked from beneath her. Tilly suspected he'd positioned himself in anticipation of her fall.

One corner of Tilly's mouth inched up. She didn't look down for fear of losing her balance. "Are you certain you don't want a peek? Your sister is glowing and Sir Sheldon looks like a performing monkey with his hair bobbing up and down every . . . Oh!"

Jaiden caught her, of course. It didn't look like an entirely natural fall, and she landed comfortably in his arms with her legs flung properly over one arm and her back supported by the other.

Jaiden raised an eyebrow, not fooled this time.

"To the bench," Tilly directed.

They plopped down comfortably. Her arm brushed Jaiden's side. His arm stretched across the back of the bench. She could feel his heat through the expensive satin of her dress.

Tilly let out a sigh. What more could she ask for than a beautiful day in a lovely garden with a darling man.

"I didn't like the trick you played on Daniel today."

So much for the darling part.

"It was insensitive to the point of cruelty," Jaiden said softly. "I hope you think the end justified the means."

His voice hadn't been harsh, or even reprimanding in tone, and yet, his words stung more deeply than Tilly would have thought possible. Well, she wasn't used to being criticized, she guessed. But really, it was *his* saying it that hurt. Curse it, his opinion mattered to her.

Tilly took a deep breath to rid herself of any defensiveness. "We learned that he loved your sister and that he's not quick to maul those weaker than himself. Considering that he's at this moment convincing Adelaide to make lifelong plans with him, I'd say they were both important lessons."

Jaiden tried to take her hand, but Tilly pulled away. She refused to need his touch while he believed her to be cruel and insensitive.

Jaiden shook his head. "Did you see the pain on his face when he believed Adelaide was dead?"

Tilly straightened away from him. "He's a male. How much pain can he suffer over a woman?"

Jaiden closed his eyes for a moment. "Men are just as capable of pain as women."

"Certainly when it comes to inflicting it," Tilly shot back, turning her face away. Heat rose in her cheeks. He, more than anyone else, knew what a sensitive puddle of mush she could be. How could he now think her heartless? If she was heartless, it was only because he'd stolen that particular organ from her! Damned if she wouldn't be getting it back!

Jaiden grasped her shoulder, forcing her to look at him. "You can't . . ." His hands dropped at Tilly's lethal glare. "My apologies."

"Don't. Manhandle me. Ever."

Jaiden pushed his palms on his thighs. He didn't apologize again, though. Instead, he used a voice underlined with forced patience. "Tilly, I know you've seen men act in despicable ways. I know you've seen the results of those acts. I know you've comforted their victims. But that does not give you the right to toy with an innocent man's emotions."

Tilly swallowed an uncomfortable wave of guilt. Not because of the way she'd treated Daniel, who could take a stroll to America for all she cared, but because she had played games with Jaiden from the very beginning. She hadn't been completely honest with him, or even mostly honest with him. Would he see her career as that of toying with men's emotions?

Tilly straightened her skirts. Manipulating her other clients had never bothered her. She had always figured men deserved whatever curses women cast. Rather like mosquitoes, really. Pesky, disease-ridden creatures who served absolutely no worthwhile purpose.

But Jaiden wasn't like that. He had provided employment for tens of people. He had supported his aunt and sister. He'd once upon a time brought wife-murderers to justice. He was as worthy of decent treatment as any woman. More than many women.

"I'd be desolate if I thought anything happened to you, Tilly. I can't imagine the misery it would cause me. How would you feel if you discovered you'd lost me?"

Tilly raised her chin. "I wouldn't miss you, Jaiden, not for long. I vow it," she swore with a final nod.

Not a muscle in Jaiden's face moved, and yet, he looked as if she'd struck him.

Tilly would not feel pity for him. She clenched her fists and crossed her arms over her chest. "You will not break me, Jaiden. I swear it. I will live perfectly comfortably without you. And if you ever, ever endanger anyone I love, I'll be the first to stab you in the back. Don't think I won't. I don't care how enamored I am with you or how much further you enchant me. I swear to—"

"You're enamored with me?" Jaiden broke in. A smile tugged at his lips.

Tilly blinked. Why was she threatening him again? Horror descended. "Oh, dear. I don't think you entirely deserved—"

"It's all right," Jaiden said. "You don't have to trust me yet. I've a lifetime to prove myself to you. And I'm never going to hurt you, Tilly."

"I know you won't. I . . . oh, I'll . . . ." She smiled, catching a train of thought. With a nod, she promised, "I'll ponder your suggestion."

A grin broke on his face. He dropped a kiss on her forehead. "I know you will."

Tilly planted her fists on her hips. "Now don't get into the habit of instructing me."

Jaiden brushed a tendril from her cheek. "Why not? You instruct me."

Tilly stiffened. "Yes, but I execute lessons in a much more charming and subtle manner than you."

Jaiden laughed. "I cannot argue with that. Very well. I'm done. No more lessons today."

Tilly looked at him beneath lowered lashes. "Not even tonight?" she asked in a husky voice.

Jaiden swallowed. His hand brushed the thin fabric of her skirts and burned her thigh.

Did he have this effect on all women? And speaking of that, where exactly had he learned his huge body of sensual knowledge that he was slowly bestowing upon her?

Curiosity quickly turned to jealousy.

"Jaiden," Tilly said, pushing a hand against his chest just as he was about to kiss her.

Jealousy turned to dread.

What if Jaiden had been initiated into manhood the same way so many young English men were?

In a brothel.

Tilly's stomach clenched. Could Jaiden really have done unspeakable things to some poor woman who was reduced to selling her body for survival? Or worse, to some child sold by her parents and drugged, kept locked away in some house of ill repute for months, maybe years, on end?

It was the way of things, but how could Tilly enjoy their love-making when some poor soul . . . She couldn't bear to think of it.

Jaiden leaned back on the bench and crossed his ankles in front of him. He gazed up into the overcast sky. "Go ahead and tell me," he said.

Tilly's brows dropped. "Tell you what, my lord?" *And don't think you can order me about, you scoundrel.*

"What it is that is bothering you now, of course. Out with it. The quicker you speak your mind, the sooner I can assuage your concerns, and we can get on with tonight's lessons."

Tilly shook her head. "It's mid-afternoon."

Jaiden waved that concern away. "Speak."

Tilly nodded. Made sense to her. "Have you ever coupled with a prostitute?"

Jaiden shot up from the bench. He glanced wildly around the deserted garden. "Jesus Christ, Tilly!"

"Well?" She would not be distracted by pretenses of pomp

and circumstance, especially after the things he'd done to her in the last twenty-four hours.

Jaiden threw his head back. Laughter erupted.

Tilly waited for the guffaws to subside.

Finally, he sat back down beside her. He slid an arm behind her once more. "You are incorrigible at the best of times, but today you've been positively mad."

Tilly folded her hands in her lap. "Yes, well, after the wonders of last night, I seem to find everything shamefully dull by comparison. So I'm reduced to lunatic measures in an attempt to entertain myself. In short, you drive me crazy. Now, pray answer the question, if you please."

"If I please?" His thumb traced the back of her neck. The tip of it slipped into her hair and sent shivers running around her skin. "No, I have never paid a woman for the use of her body," Jaiden said.

Tilly tried to concentrate on the conversation. "Not even a highly paid courtesan?"

Jaiden chuckled. "Not once. I do believe I mentioned this the first time we went for a walk."

Tilly frowned. Her hands came undone in her lap. "Where did you learn how to do the things you've learned how to do then?"

"Pray, be more specific."

Tilly lowered her brows at him.

"Ah, I see." Jaiden's lips twitched. "You are asking for a summary of my romantic history."

Tilly gave one nod.

"Er . . . well . . . um. Mostly widows, a few married women, one heiress fallen from grace. That's it."

"Married women? Really?" Tilly's face broke into a smile. She nudged Jaiden with her elbow. "You rutting dog!"

Jaiden shifted his weight uncomfortably, then shrugged.

"What can I say? There are many inattentive husbands in this world."

"Can't have women everywhere languishing for affection."

"No, we can't."

Tilly frowned with the sudden thought that Jaiden's bedroom activities might have led to an appointment at dawn. "Were you worried about their husbands' wrath?"

"No."

Tilly frowned. "I mean, what if you had married Miss Per—er—Haversham, and some man had attempted to seduce her? What would you have done?"

"Said good riddance."

Tilly's face went slack. "She would have been your wife."

"First, Tilly, Miss Clara would never have been my wife. Second, I did not seduce a single married lady. They seduced me, and third . . ." He caught her chin. ". . . if a man ever attempts to seduce you . . . well, I'd be a hypocrite if I didn't understand."

Tilly smiled. How mature for a male.

"Of course, that won't stop me from killing any man who dares try."

Tilly tried to frown. She really should. No good encouraging yet another male in his eternal thirst for violence.

But somehow her mouth refused to cooperate, and turned up instead. Maybe it was the flutters in her stomach or Jaiden's leaning his head down for a kiss. Either way, all she could do was stifle the giggle and close her eyes . . . for a kiss that never came.

Chapter Sixty-Five

"Well, well, well, Lord Astor. You are under arrest for the disappearance of your lover and for the death of her husband."

Jaiden looked over Tilly's curls to a much less inspired view. William Ramsey leaned against the frame of the backdoor. His golden hair gleamed in the sun. Must have rubbed on an entire tub of oil while combing it back. Through the door Jaiden saw Adelaide and Daniel attempt to pass him.

"Lover?" Tilly repeated. Her eyebrows jumped. She stood. Jaiden followed.

"Ramsey, there's no need for this song and dance. I'm certain there's an explanation. Just ask him about last Tuesday night," Daniel said, finally breaking into the garden as Ramsey sauntered forward.

"Lover?" Tilly repeated, this time not in surprise.

"Tilly. . . ." Jaiden grasped her shoulders

She looked up at him. "It's all right. Of course, you have one. You are an appealing man, and you certainly know how to pretend sincerity. It's not as if you've made any promises to me. Manipulative swine!" she suddenly burst out. Her knee bent to kick him in the shin, but Jaiden twisted her at the last moment.

"There is no lover," he growled. Ramsey could not have introduced his crazy story at a worse time. "Ramsey, what the hell is going on? Who the bloody hell is dead?"

Ramsey smirked, a smirk Jaiden very much wanted to send to the devil, along with the rest of the man. "Playing the innocent, are we? Why don't you just confess and save yourself further embarrassment?"

Jaiden could feel himself shaking. He didn't want Tilly to suffer through this, but it would only hurt her more if he sent her away now. Jaiden forced himself to lean against the tree, in a semblance of nonchalance. "If this is an example of how shoddy your investigations have become, it's no wonder Sheldon was promoted over you."

The smile disappeared from Ramsey's face, replaced by a sneer. "You always thought you knew everything, could get away with anything. Well, this time you're caught, Astor, and neither your friends nor your money nor your precious title can save you."

"Daniel?" Adelaide whispered.

"It's just a misunderstanding, love. We'll straighten it out in no time," Daniel comforted her, putting an arm around her and shooting Ramsey a glare. "Start talking, quickly, Ramsey."

Ramsey turned to Daniel. "He did it!" he said, pointing at Jaiden. "He killed the man, and we have a witness saying the wife came here."

Daniel's brow lowered. "Whom do you allege he killed?"

"Lord Jonathon Whenceworth. Bludgeoned him to death with a fireplace poker. Bludgeoned him to death and stole his wife. Probably killed her, too."

"Nora," Tilly gasped softly. She looked at Jaiden. His stomach dropped. He saw knowledge in her eyes, just before the eyelids crashed down and her body went limp.

He caught her about the waist. Nothing about this faint was feigned. Jaiden sat on the bench and laid her down. He cradled her head in his lap.

Her face spoke her innocence. It wouldn't be the first time it lied. The little imp. She'd had a hand in this.

Well, in that case, good riddance to Lord Jonathon Whenceworth. Hell and he deserved each other.

Time to separate Ramsey and Tilly. Well, after she woke up, but definitely before she started talking.

Adelaide came rushing back into the garden. Jaiden hadn't noticed her leave. She hovered over Tilly and waved a vial of smelling salts under her nose.

Tilly's eyes jumped open. She popped up and swung her head away. "Oh, God!" she cursed. "That stuff has an odor that would tear the tail off an octopus!"

"I beg your pardon," Ramsey said.

Tilly glared at him. Then her face fell. She bit her bottom lip and worried her hands. Tilly swung her feet on the lawn.

Jaiden stood up. "All right. Let's go." He headed for the door.

"Sir Sheldon," Tilly began. "I think I need to—"

Jaiden whirled on Tilly. He grasped her head. "Breathe deeply. Relax. Lie down." He forced her down on the bench. "You'll be all right."

"I—oh!"

She realized the import of his lowered eyebrows and narrowed eyes. He kissed her cheek. "Trust me to take care of this," he murmured into her ear. They both knew it wouldn't take two days of investigating her before Daniel—and worse, Ramsey—found out about Muirfield and all the women there illegally.

"But Jaiden, I—"

Jaiden kissed her, full on the mouth in front of everyone. He heard Adelaide's gasp and Daniel's soft curse, but he doubted Tilly did. As always when they touched, she went all soft and womanly in his arms.

He lifted his head, saw her bemused expression. He dropped a kiss on her forehead. "I will be back before you know I'm gone." And with that, he forced his hands to relax their grip on her shoulders. He turned around and strode out of the garden before she had a chance to protest.

All he could do now was keep Ramsey's suspicions centered on him. Shouldn't be too hard. Ramsey wouldn't be able to see the truth if it hit him in the face. Not where Jaiden was concerned, not with the possibility of vengeance.

The corner of Jaiden's mouth quirked up. He turned to Daniel and Ramsey and stretched out his hands in innocence. "Gentlemen, please allow me to obtain a few personal affects before we depart. I don't recall the holding cell having the best vintage of Madeira." Jaiden turned his face enough so that only Daniel could see him and let the smile drop meaningfully.

"Of all the—"

"Take your time," Daniel offered, cutting Ramsey off.

Jaiden executed a half-bow to Ramsey before turning on his heel and sauntering up the stairs two at a time. He forced himself to walk at a moderate pace—a pace much slower than his racing pulse dictated. Ramsey's vengeance could not have better suited Jaiden's purpose. To that end, Jaiden walked to his desk, pulled out an envelope and addressed it to Ruth O. of Muirfield Estates. After scrawling the quick note, he shoved it into the envelope, and placed both between the pages of an inconspicuous red leather book on his bookshelf.

CHAPTER SIXTY-SIX

Tilly sat up on the bench. Her ears rang in the sudden silence of the deserted garden.

What had she done?

What should she do now?

She winced. She'd botched everything. She buried her face in her hands. Adelaide's voice came out panicky and entirely too close to her ear.

"Where do we start?"

Tilly took a deep breath. A nap sounded good. She stifled a yawn. She always felt tired when overwhelmed. No time for rest now though. For Adelaide, she would find energy.

Tilly stood. "I have to talk to Mary." She strode through the back door and down the hallway.

"To whom?" Adelaide questioned breathlessly, hurrying to keep up.

"Mary. Mary. Your upstairs housemaid," she explained. Tilly passed through a door into the servants' corridor and then swung through another door into the kitchen. "Mary," she said, spying the girl in the sea of faces that swung toward them. Every servant in the house had gathered there to gossip about the arrest. Tilly's appearance silenced the cacophony of whispers.

Mary curtsied. "Yes, mum," she said. Her eyes bulged upon spying Tilly. Tilly could only imagine the fright she looked.

Adelaide studied the room as though she'd never seen her own kitchen, and she was the one who supposedly ran the house.

"Might I have a word with you in the morning room?" Tilly asked Mary.

"Of course, mum." Mary bobbed her head subserviently, but for a moment, she looked Tilly straight in the eyes. The girl had deduced the circumstances.

Tilly held the door open for the two women and then hurried through the hallways and past the foyer to the morning room. She turned outside of it and frowned at the other two women for not keeping pace, especially since both towered over her. She shooed them into the room and then closed the door behind her.

Tilly turned toward Mary before the girl had walked three steps into the room and grasped her hand. "I need your help," she said in a low voice, in case any of the servants eavesdropped.

Mary nodded resolutely. "Tell me what to do."

Tilly let out a sigh of relief. Adelaide followed suit, although she had no idea why she was doing so.

Dropping Mary's hand, Tilly ran her fingers through her unruly curls, which had escaped the simple ribbon she'd used in an attempt to tie back her hair that morning. Ridiculous to think that only that morning Jaiden had mussed it. And now, unless she did something, Jaiden wouldn't be mussing anything anymore, except maybe a hangman's noose.

Tilly forced herself to concentrate on the present. "I'll need you to tell Dan—er . . . Sir Sheldon everything you know about the night you woke me—how the woman came here, distraught and bleeding, and most importantly how she saw me and only me and not Lord Astor."

"My lady, are you certain?" Mary's face scrunched doubtfully. Jaiden might have paid her wages, but it was Tilly who had secured her loyalty.

Yes, Tilly was certain. Amazingly enough. She would protect Jaiden at the risk of hanging herself, but not until she had dealt with a prior obligation. She had to warn her friends first and make certain they were relocated to a safe location, one that, this time, Tilly couldn't know about. "It is the right thing to do, but not yet. Not until I return to London. Until then, you mustn't reveal anything to anyone."

Mary shook her head. "Oh, no, I wouldn't. I mean, I won't. Your secret's safe with me, mum. After all you've done for my cousin. I can't thank you enough."

Tilly drew a deep breath. "Do this for me, and I will be thanked a thousand times more than I deserve."

To Tilly's surprise, Mary hugged her. It took Tilly a moment to respond. She wrapped her arms around the tall woman, her face buried in her collarbone. Tilly reacted strangely to the tight hold. Maybe, it reminded her of her mother because suddenly she had the desire to cry and have her mother come to the rescue.

But her mother had never rescued her. No one had. Only Jaiden.

And this time it was her turn to rescue him.

Mary left the room just before Tilly started sniffling. Tilly turned to Adelaide. The woman still looked frightfully pale. "Adelaide, I must go for a day or two—"

"I'm going with you." Adelaide nodded once and tightened her lips to show her resolve.

Tilly shook her head. "You can't. Don't worry, though. I'll get your brother out of this pickle, but first I must go confer with a friend."

"At Muirfield?" Adelaide asked.

"Yes, and time is of the es—" She stopped. Her heart plummeted to her stomach. She watched Adelaide out the corner of her eye. The girl blushed. "How do you know about Muirfield?" Tilly asked in a careful voice.

Adelaide shrugged. "Everyone knows about Muirfield."

CHAPTER SIXTY-SEVEN

"Do you even know Mrs. Whenceworth?" Daniel demanded. Sweat jumped off his nose as he jerked his head. He must have lost a pint of water, and yet it was Jaiden who was being interrogated. Jaiden, who sat back in his chair with ankles crossed in front of him, keeping tolerably cool despite the heat in the holding cell.

Daniel's nervousness and Jaiden's calm weren't the only things peculiar to this interrogation. More odd was the fact that Daniel was trying his damnedest to prove Jaiden's innocence while Jaiden needed to appear guilty . . . at least for now.

"Yes, I *know* Nora," he said with a masculine gleam in his eye. No one could miss the implication of just how intimate his acquaintance with Nora was. Never mind that he was full of piss.

Daniel crossed his arms over his chest. "Really? What does she look like?"

Jaiden thought back to the night he'd seen her, the night Tilly had held her close and let her cry. It had been dark viewing, but luckily, Jaiden had an eye for details. "She's blonde, about so high." He lifted up a hand. "She favors the color yellow," he guessed.

Daniel narrowed his eyes. "Fine. You've laid eyes on her. Tell me something else. Something only a *lover* would know."

Jaiden quirked a brow. "If only her lover knows it, how will you confirm my tidbit?"

Daniel drummed the fingers of one hand against his arm impatiently.

"All right." Jaiden lifted his palms in surrender. "I'll tell you something, something both secret and verifiable. She broke her arm. More accurately, her husband broke it for her. She saw a doctor in Soho for it a few years ago. Of course, she made up a tale to protect her husband. The doctor knows nothing of that part. So you see, Ramsey, the man whose death you're so anxious to avenge was not a nice person."

Ramsey cocked his too-beautiful head. "Oh, is that what happened? You killed a man for correcting his wife? Or did you just murder him so you could have your lover, only then you realized it looked too suspicious so you killed her, too?" He rested both palms on the table, standing on the other side from Jaiden. "Either way you'll be hung up within the month."

"Ramsey!" Daniel growled.

Ramsey started. Daniel rarely lost his temper.

Warily, Daniel rubbed both palms against his face. "Leave us," he commanded.

"Gladly," Jaiden joked, swinging his feet off the table.

Daniel's gaze jerked toward him.

"Oh, you mean Ramsey," Jaiden said, earning a glare from his friend.

Ramsey sneered. He walked toward Jaiden, but Daniel blocked his path with an outstretched arm. "Go," he ordered.

Ramsey mimicked a noose being pulled around his neck before turning on his heel and walking up the steps out of the holding cell.

Daniel plopped into the chair across from Jaiden. "You want me to release you?" he asked in a monotone.

Jaiden leaned back in his chair, swung his feet onto the table, and crossed his ankles. "It would do your career no good."

Daniel followed Jaiden's example and stretched his legs above the old battered table. Finally, he looked the unshakable inspector Jaiden knew. "Some things are more important than work."

Jaiden lifted his chin. "Friendship?" he questioned.

"Adelaide's happiness," Daniel answered. "I can't imagine her being overjoyed at the prospect of marrying the man who hangs her brother."

"Perhaps I deserve it," Jaiden suggested.

Daniel cocked his head, considering, and then shook it. "You were telling the truth about Whenceworth being an ass," he announced. "And maybe about the affair, but that's it. The thing is, Jaiden, no matter how badly some man treated his wife, you would never interfere. You've got too much on your own plate to have any interest in managing someone else's personal affairs."

Jaiden would have once agreed, but then he'd met Tilly. Now, he would kill a man before allowing anyone to harm so much as the sweet expression on her face. "But then, you've never seen me in love." As soon as the words were out, Jaiden knew they were a mistake.

Daniel's feet thudded against the floor. A grin mushroomed across his face.

Jaiden grimaced.

"Until a little troublemaker by the name of Mrs. Mathilda Leighton entered your life." He leaned forward across the table. "This is all her doing, isn't it?"

"This has nothing to do with her," Jaiden stated. Even to him it sounded like an order.

"You're lying, and I know why." Daniel stood. "But I'm not going to let you die for that woman's shenanigans." He headed for the door.

"Daniel, stop," Jaiden said in a low voice.

Daniel turned and looked at him expectantly.

Jaiden lowered his feet to the floor and stood. He walked over to his friend, debating his next move. When he was only a few feet away, he finally decided to tell him the truth. "Daniel, if you want to do the right thing, both as a friend and as an enforcer of the peace . . ."

Daniel crossed his arms over his chest.

". . . forget everything you know, or think you know, about Mrs. Leighton," Jaiden took a breath, ". . . and prosecute me for the death of Lord Whenceworth."

Daniel muttered a curse before looking Jaiden in the eye. "Tell me not to prosecute you at all and close the investigation, and I'll do it. I won't feel right about it, but I'll do it. But I cannot let you take the fall for that woman."

A slow smile made its way across Jaiden's face. "Who said anything about taking the fall?"

CHAPTER SIXTY-EIGHT

Adelaide and Tilly propped themselves against the walls of the bumping carriage. Tilly had told the driver to get them to Muirfield posthaste. She had failed, however, to specify that she hoped to remain in one piece.

Tilly gave up waiting for the carriage to settle into a soothing rhythm and asked the question weighing on her mind. "What do you mean, 'everyone knows about Muirfield'?" she called over the sound of the wheels rattling over rocks.

Adelaide met her gaze without surprise. She attempted a shrug but a sudden lurch of the carriage cut it short. "Well, of course, not *everyone* knows about Muirfield. No men know, of course." She cocked her head, considering. "But it's hardly a secret amongst the women of society."

Tilly blanched. "What do you . . . How could that be?"

"Well, it's like this. Somewhere along the way, your reputation began to precede you. Whispers in ladies' lounges. Gossip traded over tea. A woman who could help. Little adjustments of one's husband? Certainly. A larger allowance, more freedom? Consider it done. And if the situation's dire? Well, this woman grants sanctuary—a sanctuary called Muirfield."

Tilly shivered with sudden chills. It didn't make sense. She furrowed her brow. "Then why don't more desperate women find me?"

Adelaide looked out the window. "Perhaps they're not ready, or maybe they feel they deserve to be punished," she speculated before looking back at Tilly. "No one ever says your name, you know. It's part of the unspoken code. Only those in dire need are granted an introduction to you."

If even Adelaide had heard of Muirfield, then truly the existence of the estate must be common knowledge. Tilly shook her head, no longer aware of the jerking carriage, although her teeth chattered with the violent movements. "I don't understand. If everyone knows, why haven't those fiends come to lay claim to their wives?"

Adelaide's eyebrows jumped. "Oh, no. I was serious when I said no men know about it. And none will ever know. We are . . ." Her brow wrinkled in seriousness. "We are so grateful to have a place of safety should we need it. I am . . ." She shook her head, but her eyes stayed locked on Tilly. "I am in awe at what you've accomplished. You are amazing Tilly," she continued. "You are living greatness."

Tilly shifted uncomfortably. She wished she could rub her forehead, but she'd go flying across the coach if she unwedged herself. "Adelaide, you exaggerate."

"No." The word rent the air like a gunshot.

Tilly stared at Adelaide, transfixed by her face. How had she never seen the strength in her jaw? In her eyes? Who was this woman?

Adelaide did not smile or give Tilly any other sign of comfort. "Someday, years from now, the daughters of England will celebrate you and what you have done to set them free."

Tilly tore her gaze away from Adelaide. What was going on? Daughters celebrating? Had Adelaide gone mad? Suddenly, the carriage seemed a thousand times too small. "Really, Adelaide, I've done naught to deserve such praise."

"Oh, I think you very much deserve it. Indeed, it's why I chose you for my brother."

Tilly frowned. Odder and odder. "You hired me to train your

brother because . . . Why are you shaking your head?"

"I didn't choose you to train my brother. I chose you to marry him."

Chapter Sixty-Nine

Daniel leaned back in the same chair that Jaiden had lounged in earlier and exhaled audibly. "And this is your plan."

It was a statement. Jaiden stopped his pacing and gave a single nod.

"You have balls of solid steel!" Daniel finally exclaimed. "But then, I guess I already knew that."

Jaiden's face remained passive. "So you're interested?"

Daniel beamed. "Sounds like a grand time." He extended his hand.

Jaiden felt relief rush through him. He needed Daniel's help, and now he would have it. He shook hands with his friend, not showing the immense gratitude he felt.

Daniel chuckled at Jaiden's insanity. "Well, do you want me to drop you off at your house?" he asked.

Jaiden shook his head. "We need to keep up appearances."

Daniel shrugged. "Suit yourself. I'll make sure Ramsey knows you're off limits. I'll also get Ben to bring you some food, wine, bedding, and whatever other necessities he can find. That is, if you're sure?" Daniel asked, pausing at the door.

Jaiden smiled. "I'll manage."

Daniel nodded, then left.

Jaiden heard the sound of the door closing but not being locked. His gaze traveled the small room. It would be a long night.

But a productive one.

Jaiden grinned. He was certain of one thing. Spending the night in the holding cell would be cake compared to Tilly's imaginings of the place.

Which would do more to secure her hand than any number of vows.

Yes, the holding cell was not so bad after all.

CHAPTER SEVENTY

"You see, Tilly, Jaiden and Clara were never planned as a match. Not beyond a glimmer of hope in old Haversham's head, at least. That glimmer was enough for me, though. It gave me the excuse to secure your services. Oh, I have no ambition for you to change my brother. I only wanted you to get into close enough contact with him to fall in love." Adelaide smiled, almost menacingly. "That didn't take long, did it?"

Tilly could not make sense of it. Fragile little Adelaide was actually the consummate manipulator? "But why?" Why would anyone go through that kind of bother just to make a brother end up betrothed? Unless . . . Had Adelaide planned that Jaiden would . . . No, she couldn't have known anything about Nora.

Adelaide's smile tightened into a sneer. "I know what Jaiden's opinion of our mother is. Maybe he's right. All I know is that he was waiting to fall as hard as our father. I've known it since he was a child. I couldn't change that about him no matter how hard I tried." She grimaced. "So I decided to do the next best thing. I determined that if he was going to make a fool of himself over some woman, at least it would be a woman worthy of him. It would be a woman of my choosing. Once I heard about Muirfield, you, Tilly Leighton, became my choice."

Disgust for herself and Adelaide swamped Tilly. How could she have played the fool in Adelaide's game? How could the most meaningful encounter of her life all be the result of some woman's scheme?

And how could she have let this one interfering girl ruin her entire life's work?

"Cheer up, kitten," Adelaide said in tones of condescension. "Things have worked out just as I wanted. You have found yourself a man who won't beat you to death's door, and my brother will marry a worthy bride."

"Your brother," Tilly enunciated through gritted teeth, "may be finding himself dangling from a rope, and it's all my fault. My fault because you thought to play God with both our lives. And more to the point, Muirfield will never provide a haven for another woman again. So excuse me if I fail to see exactly what you are so proud of."

CHAPTER SEVENTY-ONE

The world had gone mad. It had been years since rage like this had overtaken her. At least this time she had a living target. And what the devil was going on with Adelaide, anyway? Certainly, the girl could not have faked all that loneliness and need for approval. Now, however, Adelaide appeared only frustrated by Tilly's censure.

"Tilly, kitten, I believe you've overlooked one small but crucial part of my scheme. Daniel. Remember? My fiancé?" she reminded. "He's besotted with me. There's no way he'll let Jaiden go to trial."

Tilly shook her head. The girl had played with fire, and now they would all burn. "You couldn't have known Nora would . . ." Tilly stopped herself, uncertain how much Adelaide knew now, and not wanting to reveal anything to this stranger.

"No, but I knew there was a good chance trouble would follow you. I also knew Daniel was investigating the missing wives. It seemed best to have him in my control."

Tilly scowled. "You did know, that's right. You absolutely knew Daniel was investigating the crimes I had committed, and yet you led him to me repeatedly? How can you claim to respect the sanctuary Muirfield provides when you've gambled its future and lost?"

Adelaide shook her head. "Muirfield will continue. Don't you see, Tilly? Daniel won't prosecute Jaiden. There is no reason for you to testify. Muirfield can remain a secret." Adelaide tilted her head. "You have so much faith in your own powers of persuasion, why can't you extend me the same confidence?"

The statement rang true. After all, Adelaide had fooled her. Certainly, she could manage a stupid male like Daniel. "Daniel won't let Jaiden go to trial?"

"Daniel won't let my brother go to trial."

Tilly blew a piece of hair from her face. Did she order the carriage around and put Jaiden's life in Adelaide's hands, or did she continue to Muirfield and place her friends in danger but retain some control?

And would the driver even listen to her, or would Adelaide override her order?

Tilly took a deep breath. "I need to talk to Ruth," she announced finally.

CHAPTER SEVENTY-TWO

Tilly and Adelaide traveled the rest of the way to Muirfield with only the constant creaking of the carriage disturbing the silence. It was only after winding through Muirfield's long driveway and halting in front of the house that Adelaide finally spoke.

The footman opened the carriage door, and Adelaide scanned the house, hills, and trees. "So, this is Muirfield," she said in an awed voice.

"Yes." Tilly couldn't keep the emotion from her voice. Sadness, because this sanctity would, after six years of peace, be breached. Resentment toward Adelaide for her manipulation of Tilly. But Tilly also felt pride. At this moment, Muirfield still existed apart from the violence of the world, and as long as that was the case, there was still hope.

The women descended the coach steps. Tilly started up the path, but Adelaide grasped her arm to still her.

Eyes on the house, Adelaide smiled. "It's awe-inspiring."

"Did you ever want Daniel for yourself?" Tilly couldn't stop herself from asking. "Or was it an act to get his submission?" There was so much damage she had to repair, and yet this was the question that plagued her. Somehow both her friendship with Adelaide and her confidence in her own intuition hinged upon its answer.

Adelaide turned toward Tilly and watched a moment too long before answering, "Of course, I love Daniel. I love him with all my heart. I'm just lucky to love someone whom it's convenient to love." She glanced at the house. "Too bad the inhabitants here did not have the same fortune. What do you think they'll make of my presence?"

"I don't know if I believe you," Tilly whispered, too taken aback to try to get the girl's honesty by a circuitous route.

Adelaide did not move. "I don't know what I can do about that."

"I don't, either," Tilly said sadly. And yet she would be leading this untrustworthy person inside her beloved home.

Adelaide glanced to the ground, considering, and then met Tilly's gaze. "We're on the same side, you know."

"Really? What side is that?" Tilly demanded, crossing her arms.

Adelaide grinned. "Neither of us want my brother to be hanged, nor do we want to have the residents here disturbed."

Tilly nodded, and yet she could not find it within herself to trust the woman.

Adelaide started walking. "I'll gain your trust again. In the meantime, you have a conversation with Ruth to get on with."

"So I have." Tilly took a deep breath. How could she break the news of her failure to the one woman whose opinion meant something to her?

She was about to find out.

Tilly opened the front door, expecting Muirfield's usual calm. Instead, a cacophony of sounds assaulted her ears. The smell of baking bread was conspicuously absent. Unsettled dust caught her nose instead. She stifled the urge to sneeze, but her eyes still watered.

A door banged shut. Drawers were being yanked open and closed. Somewhere above, someone dragged furniture across the floor.

Beth's voice shouted from the second floor. "Should I bring my pink silk or the pale blue?"

No answer. Footsteps. A door squeaked open. "Pink or pale blue?" Beth demanded.

"Sorry?" came the muffled reply.

"Should I pack my pink gown or my pale blue one?" Beth repeated.

"Um . . . I don't know. Pack both. Who knows how long we'll be there."

"Ruth said to pack lightly."

Had they already got wind of the need for exodus? Then, why did suppressed excitement hang in the air instead of the sound of tears? Tilly would have guessed the women were planning their first coming out, not being driven from their home. "Hello?" Tilly called.

Two seconds passed and Beth's head poked over the balcony rail, seemingly atop a pile of clothing. "Oh, Tilly, hello!" Beth called. "Did you bring a carriage?"

"I . . . yes," Tilly stuttered.

"Excellent! I shall bring both!" Beth shot out of sight.

"Hello, Tilly! Be down in a flash," Mary Katherine called from upstairs.

What the devil was going on? "Where's Ruth?" Tilly yelled up the stairs in a most unladylike fashion.

"Um . . . try the storage shed. She might still be there."

The storage shed?

Tilly lifted her eyebrows at Adelaide, who shrugged. Right, how the devil would she know anything about it?

Except that she seemed to know an awful lot these days.

"I'm going to find Ruth," Tilly muttered. "You can sit in there." She nodded in the direction of the great room.

Adelaide bowed at Tilly's order before turning on her heel and obeying.

Tilly meanwhile cut through the kitchen through the back door and walked across the garden to the storage shed. The shed had once housed horses but now served only to store the women's personal effects that were too valuable to throw out but held too many painful memories to keep in the house where they might be stumbled upon.

Inside she found Ruth sitting on an old trunk and clutching the large photo album to her chest. She wiped a tear from her cheek.

So she did already know.

"I'm so sorry," Tilly whispered.

Ruth started, grasping the book all the tighter. "Oh, Tilly! You gave me a fright!" Her distinguished brow wrinkled. "What are you doing here? I assumed you'd meet us in London."

"London?" Tilly gasped. "Why would you be going to London?"

Ruth cocked her head. "For Jaiden's trial, of course."

Tilly's eyebrows shot up. "So you do know?"

"Yes, a man hand-delivered the message about an hour ago."

Tilly shook her head and took a step forward. "Then, you must know that London is the last place you can go. You'll be exposed there."

Ruth nodded. "Of course."

"Sorry?" Tilly must have misheard. Ruth couldn't want—

"I'm seeking exposure. Exposure of the most public, infamous kind," Ruth stated. The only thing that made less sense than the words was the excited anticipation in her voice.

"But . . ." Tilly closed her eyes. She hadn't understood anything in hours. Better start from the beginning. "What did the message say?"

Ruth dug in her pocket and handed Tilly an envelope as though she didn't have time to explain all the outrageous details. "Read it yourself."

The address slanted to the right in a distinctly Jaiden hand. Tilly pulled out the letter and read the four lines. Horror ambushed her. She jerked her head up to Ruth. "No."

Ruth touched her arm—her brows lowered in concern. "Tilly, sit down. You've gone pale as a ghost."

Tilly sat on the trunk. "It's too dangerous, Ruth. You can't do it. I forbid you to do it."

Ruth smiled, raising one of her high-arched eyebrows. "You forbid me?"

One did not forbid a duchess twenty years one's senior. Tilly turned away and crossed her arms over her chest. "I won't be part of this."

Ruth patted her hair. "Oh, I think you will be. Now, did you bring a carriage? We will need the extra vehicle for the ride to the station. . . ."

CHAPTER SEVENTY-THREE

No matter how vexed they became, the women of Muirfield did not raise their voices. It just wasn't done. Too many of them associated loud voices with the beatings they had once received. Some froze the moment a voice grew too strident. Others burst into tears. None of them could tolerate their bitter memories. Thus, for seven years the halls of the house had heard no more than a peep from its inhabitants.

Until the day Jaiden sent his note.

And then all hell broke loose.

Typical male, Tilly thought. "You cannot do this!" she yelled, grabbing the dress Ruth was trying to stuff in the overflowing carpetbag sitting atop the ransacked dresser. Drawers haphazardly revealed their contents. At least one gown had slipped to the floor of the wardrobe. In short, Ruth's room was the first casualty of the battle flaring inside the house.

Ruth yanked back the fabric. "Tilly, for the love of God! *Be reasonable!*" she screamed. "We both know you could not watch Jaiden go to the gallows—"

"Right now I'd happily tie the knot!"

They'd been fighting for a full twenty minutes. Both women were panting and red in the face.

Ruth's eyes narrowed. Her voice oozed sarcasm. "You can't tie the knot with a dead man."

The edge of Tilly's vision turned red. She tugged the dress out of Ruth's hands and threw it on the floor. Her hands trembled in rage. "You know what I meant!"

"I also know this is all your fault," Ruth taunted, taking a different tact. "If you hadn't got Jaiden arrested, we would not now have to leave Muirfield."

"Bollocks! You only have to leave Muirfield if I get involved in Jaiden's trial, and I have no such plans. The man can go to hell for all I care!" Tilly kicked the dress on the floor.

Ruth crossed her arms over her chest. "You know, I never realized what a temper you have. You quite remind me of my husband!"

The words kicked Tilly in the gut. She winced and sank onto the bed.

"I apologize," Ruth muttered, sitting on the bed next to Tilly. "Unfair shot."

Deflated, Tilly shook her head. "You're right. It'll kill me if anything happens to Jaiden. I just . . . How could he write this?" She picked up the horrid leaf of paper. "To you? Without so much as a by your leave from me?"

"From what you tell me, it doesn't sound as if he had much time for begging permission. And as for the note, he knew it was what I wanted. I'd told him while he was here."

Tilly read the first line of the note once more:

Ruth,

Still interested in the House's ear?

Tilly shook her head. "So you're going to what? Use Jaiden's trial as an arena to save all the women of England?" It sounded ludicrous.

"I'm going to try." Ruth patted Tilly's hand. "I know politics. Both my father and husband were active Whigs in their day. I paid attention. Most of the time, the law reflects prevailing societal opinions. It's true. But every once in a while, Tilly, the law can change those opinions. My father told me that." Ruth stood and picked the dress off the floor. "So the law is where we must begin."

Ruth gave the gown a good shake before laying it in a long trunk. "I think you tore a seam," she muttered. When Tilly didn't reply, she looked at her. Tilly scowled back.

"I would have thought the prospect of fighting for women's rights would appeal to you. You, Tilly Leighton, could single-handedly save thousands of women's lives. Not to mention all the good you would be doing for future generations."

"It's your life I care about," Tilly maintained. "Yours and Beth's and Verity's—"

"Tilly, I feel old."

Tilly blinked at the change of subject.

"When I came to Muirfield, I wanted nothing more than to live out my remaining years in peace, but somehow your vitality, your perseverance, has made me ashamed of my simple goals. I don't want to die knowing I accomplished nothing more than avoiding my cad of a husband in my last years. Finally, finally, I'm doing something that isn't about him." She smiled to herself. "When I lived in London with him, I used to daydream about him getting ill, just as he has done. I used to imagine going to his deathbed and spitting in his face for what he did to me. I know, I'm not exactly the proper person I appear to be. After six years here though . . ." She shrugged. "He's nothing to me. I don't care about revenge. Not a jot. And, if we can do this, if we can change the law to protect women, then my life will have been worth living—even my marriage to a monster."

Tilly exhaled. She couldn't argue with that. "And Verity?" she asked. Verity's husband sat in the House of Lords. It could do nothing for their cause to humiliate the reigning members of Parliament.

"She and Lizzy are going to Bath together. Lizzy has some

business she wants to conduct. And Tilly," she said as Tilly started walking dejectedly to the door, "we're doing the right thing."

Tilly prayed they weren't doing it in vain.

CHAPTER SEVENTY-FOUR

They would catch the first train to London in the morning. Tilly knew she should try to get some sleep. She'd had precious little rest in the last few days, but she could not stop worrying long enough to sleep. Her eyes stared fixedly at the ceiling of the dark room. Better there than at the stack of luggage in the corner. In the dark, it looked frightfully like a judge forcing all her friends to go back to lives of torture with their husbands.

And then there was the guilt eating her. She'd mucked up everything. Jaiden languished in some cell for criminals. Her friends, whom she'd sworn to protect, planned to storm London on some fool's mission. Adelaide had gone mad, if she hadn't been that way from the beginning.

Tilly didn't see how things could get worse. She hadn't felt so rotten in years.

"Go to sleep, Tilly," Beth whispered next to her.

Tilly had decided to sleep in Beth's bed and leave her room to Adelaide. Ruth had offered to let Tilly sleep with her, but Tilly had refused. She and Ruth had spent the entire evening arguing without Ruth backing down the slightest.

"This is all my fault," Tilly murmured.

Beth rolled onto her stomach and propped herself on her elbows. She watched Tilly's face.

"I don't know how things got so out of hand," Tilly complained. "I usually have everything planned and executed to the smallest detail, and this time . . . Oh, Lord, I can't believe what

I've done! I can't believe how many lives could be ruined because of me."

"Tilly," Beth said with a laugh. "You meddle in people's lives all the time."

"I've never sent anyone to the noose before," Tilly muttered.

"Gerry Hendricks would certainly disagree with you . . . were he still alive."

Tilly sat up and whacked Beth with a pillow. "That was not my fault! I merely pointed out to the authorities how he must have been responsible for that poor girl's murder. He deserved that end."

Beth pulled the pillow out of Tilly's hands and pushed it to the far side of the bed. "He did deserve it. The world is most definitely better off without him."

The words deflated Tilly. The world would not be better off without Jaiden. She curled onto her side. It certainly wouldn't be better for her friends with Muirfield exposed. "I'm so sorry, Beth. I promised you a home, and now I've gone and ruined it."

"I'll be all right, Tilly. I'm not worried about that, but . . ."

"Hmm?"

"Well . . ." Beth stalled. She flipped onto her side so that her face was less than a foot from Tilly's. "Please don't be offended by this. I don't blame you for anything, and I think things will turn out fine for all of us."

"But?"

"But I can't believe you rushed here, telling us all to move because of a man, when all you had to do was let him go to the gallows without saying a word and we would all be perfectly safe."

Tilly's face tightened. "I couldn't do that to him. He's in-nocent—"

"Yes, but that's what is surprising. You've never cared what happened to any man before—"

"I've never championed injustice—"

"Tilly! Your ideal of justice is to set all men aflame!"

Tilly humphed. That wasn't a bad notion, concerning most males.

"You've changed," Beth whispered. "I can't help but think he's changed you."

The words were too true. "You're right, Beth. I know it. Lord!" She dragged a hand through her hair. "I don't even recognize myself. I don't know what I'm doing. How could I choose to save some male over keeping my friends protected? How could I . . . ? I don't know why I'm behaving this way. Why I'm making everything worse. Why I feel this way."

"You love him!" Beth sat up. She grabbed Tilly's pillow and shoved it back at her. "I can't believe it. You've finally fallen." She laughed. "Oh, there, there. It's not so bad as all that!"

Tilly buried her face in the pillow. Beth pulled her out of it. "Really, it's happened to the best of us."

Tilly looked at her doubtfully.

"You never thought it could happen to you, did you?" Beth said, thoroughly entertained. "You thought yourself above something so impractical as infatuation."

Tilly forced a smile. "I have seen how imprudent an emotion love is." She closed her eyes. Jaiden's tanned face appeared in her mind, his vivid blue eyes twinkling, as always. "I was unprepared for Jaiden. I'm no match for the sensations he stirs in me, and Beth, when he touches me . . ." Tilly couldn't continue. There were no words. "I am helpless—with no morals, no principles, no rationality . . . only—"

"Joy," Beth supplied.

Tilly sighed. "Yes."

"Then think about that," Beth said, lying back in the bed. "Think about Jaiden, and you'll get through the night."

CHAPTER SEVENTY-FIVE

Tilly had spent the entire first leg of the ride to London trying to talk sense into Ruth, to no avail. Finally, she gave up trying. She still had one last hope to cling to, though. Maybe, maybe, if she prayed extra hard, she might be able to talk Jaiden into giving up this foolhardy scheme.

With that last prayer, Tilly stepped down into the holding cell. It was dark, except for a blinding light shooting through the western window. It sliced the room in half, across the floor, diagonally over the table, back to the floor, illuminating dust.

"You came."

Tilly looked up at the voice, her eyes adjusting to the dark. Jaiden stood on the other side of the bright divide.

She'd trusted him. He'd betrayed her, and yet even now, he stood there unapologetic, studying her as if she were one of his stupid inventions.

So why did she want to run to him—to have him make everything better?

Still, there was hope. Perhaps she could reach him, talk him out of this quixotic quest, stop him from ruining all their lives.

She closed her eyes, said a quick prayer, and then met his gaze. "I want you to stop this," she said. "I'll confess to the murder. I'll hang, but leave them out of it." *Get yourself out of it.*

He stalked forward, shining in the light for one moment, crossing the divide. Tilly stepped back, terrified of him, of his effect on her, that if he laid his hands on her she would bend to any desire he named. Jaiden slowed, seeing her fear, and still he cupped her shoulders. Tilly winced.

Jaiden shook his head. "You've been taking care of them for so long, you can't . . ." He trailed off with a frustrated wave of his arm, and then took her face in both his hands. He bent his knees so that their eyes were level. "Tilly," he beseeched, "trust them to make their own choices."

Exactly what Ruth had said. But this wasn't their choice. It was his.

Tilly closed her eyes, turned her cheek into his palm. Strength vibrated from him. Capability. Surely, if he staked his life on it. . . .

"Trust me to keep them safe," he whispered.

She couldn't. Her eyes popped open. She jerked away. "You told me never to trust you." Her voice grated, hoarse with desperation. She scooted around him and hurried to the other side of the room.

He turned toward her, his eyebrow cocked questioningly.

She remembered everything he'd said. She couldn't get a single utterance of his out of her head. "At the theater with Daniel and Adelaide," she reminded him.

Jaiden smiled, remembering—and remembering what had followed, too. He gave her a nod. "I was wrong."

Tilly's mouth opened. He was not going to inspire her confidence with confessions like that.

"I underestimated you," he replied nonchalantly, circling the table toward her. "I never dreamed you—anyone—could possess me. I won't underestimate you again," he vowed, his voice growing serious. "We—together—there's nothing we can't do."

She dodged out of his reach once more. "If you make this gamble, I will despise you for the rest of my life," she threatened. Even she didn't believe it.

Jaiden smiled—slow, knowing. "Only if I lose."

Her lips curled in disgust.

"I don't plan to lose."

"No one ever does."

He threw his head back and laughed.

Tilly hated him then, utterly loathed him—and wanted to bury her face in his throat, breathe in his scent, and let him convince her he could do it. Either that or deliver a swift kick to his shin. Why couldn't she make him understand the lives he risked?

"Stop your glaring, kitten." He dropped into a chair, propped his feet on the table. He linked his fingers behind his head. "I know you, gel. You thought you could trust me with your body and keep your heart and life locked safely away. You can't, though. You need me now, and the only way you'll have me is by giving me all of you, holding nothing back."

Arrogant pup. More so because he was right. Tilly turned to leave.

Suddenly, Jaiden was behind her, spinning her around. He thrust his fingers into her hair and pushed his hard, large body against hers. "I'll deserve your trust," he said. "Hell, I'll do a damned sight better than that. I'm going to give you your wildest dream. I'm going to free the women of England." With that, he dropped a kiss on her nose, of all things!

He was mad. His insanity swallowed her. She turned her face aside, trying to ignore the heat pulsating inside her. "I meant what I said. If you go through with this, I'll never know you again."

Jaiden captured her mouth. She responded. She couldn't stop herself. This was the last time she would ever be this close to him. She wanted to savor it, but already they weren't synchronized, not the way they had been. He'd created this distance, and it changed everything.

"Why?" she cried into his throat as he picked her up. She slid her fingers into his hair, tasted the salt of her tears on his skin.

Jaiden pushed her against the wall, his hand protecting her head. "Because we'll win," he growled, kissing her only to tear his mouth away. "Because it's right."

Closing her eyes, she tried to focus on the words as sensations confused her senses. "But—"

"Because you'll never marry me unless the law is changed."

It was exactly what Tilly feared, that his expectations were colored by some selfish motive, that he wasn't objectively weighing his costs and bloody benefits. She pushed her mouth against his, not wanting to hear anymore, only wanting to be with him as she'd once been.

She was drowning in him and wanted never to come up for air. Her body shook with the thumping of Jaiden's heart. All she wanted was this—not principles, not right and wrong—just this, and she hated herself for it. But then his mouth moved down her throat, and she could hear his vows.

"I will have you. Body. Heart. Trust. Soul. I. Will. Make. You. Happy. Even if it means ignoring your cowardice. You. Will. Have . . ."

Tilly lost his voice as she shoved him away and fell to one knee. She stayed there, staring at the floor—where her tear splattered it.

Jaiden offered no mercy. "Do you think this happens all the time?" he whispered, more to himself than to her, as she was now a thousand miles away. "Our night together—do you think that's the way it works for everyone? What we have happens once in a bloody eternity. Damned if I'll let you throw it away." He grasped her by the shoulder and pulled her up in front of him, then buried his face in her hair. "Tilly," he pleaded.

He was right. She would do what he wanted, and God help them all.

"Let me pass," she whispered.

Jaiden nodded against her head. He took a step back. Tilly tried to keep her face averted as she righted her clothing, but his hand stopped her. It gently wiped away her tears. More of them spilled out. Tilly's hands dropped. Why bother looking presentable? It didn't matter. None of it mattered.

She met his eyes, not bothering to hide her defeat. Her lips trembled. "I'm not so different from my mother after all," she murmured through the thickness in her throat.

As always, he seemed to read her mind. "She feared your father—"

"I'm afraid of you."

"You're not," he contradicted. "You're exhausted. You need sleep. Go home. Go to bed. Paint me as the villain, if you must, but don't lie to yourself, Tilly. You're not afraid of me, and you never will be. You know too well that I'd burn before I'd hurt you."

He believed it, she knew. Pretty intentions. They could destroy as easily as evil ones.

Tilly pursed her lips and gave a shrug. There were no words left. She walked to the steps without saying goodbye.

Without even saying a prayer.

He'd stolen that, too.

For in the end, it was her fault. She'd trusted him. She'd brought him into their lives and showed him Muirfield. Even later, she chose him over her friends. She went to Muirfield to tell them to go, so that she could stop him from hanging.

And he was ripping her world apart for it.

Because she'd given him the chance to do it. She, of all people, should have known better. You never let a man have power over you. Ever.

Well, she would be punished for her forgetfulness. So would her friends.

Chapter Seventy-Six

Tilly managed to breathe as she left Daniel's interrogation room. She forced the breaths in and out while riding in Jaiden's carriage. She continued breathing even as she entered Jaiden's townhouse, now overrun with women's advocates and defense strategists. She drew air in as she took her first step up the stairs, and she was fairly certain she would be able to exhale as well—so long as she focused on the breathing—the breathing and nothing else.

"Tilly. Excellent. I've been waiting for your arrival," Ruth called as she entered the foyer from the drawing room. "We were just going over—"

"Forgive me, Ruth," Tilly stated, "but not now. I can't now."

"Yes, now!" Ruth exclaimed, and before Tilly had time to adjust, the elegant, ever-proper duchess grasped her by the arm and whirled her around.

Tilly was so shocked, she momentarily forgot her misery. "Ruth, what has got into you?"

Ruth didn't slow down. She hauled Tilly into the morning room where, blessedly, they could be alone—though with the mad glean in Ruth's eye, Tilly didn't know if being alone with her was the wisest course of action.

Ruth violently released her hold and stalked toward the door to block Tilly's escape. Tilly scowled and rubbed her upper arm, where she could feel a bruise start to form.

Plopping her hands on her hips, Ruth glared at Tilly. "Damn

it, Tilly Leighton, I am heartily sick of both your nay-saying and the constant water in your eyes. We have a chance here, a real opportunity, of changing everything we hate, but damn it, I need you to stop thrashing yourself and start thinking."

Ruth was yelling at her. Again.

"I know this wasn't your choice, but, Tilly, think," Ruth demanded, waving her hand in exasperation. "As a member of the House of Lords, Jaiden can only be tried by that house, the same house that has blocked, or—" She began to pace, pausing in her speech to search for a word—"Annihilated every women's emancipation bill to come before it in fifty years. And why shouldn't they? They are men in power. They don't want to lose that power. It isn't in their best interest to acknowledge the rampant extent of wife abuse. In their minds, men need the right to physically correct their wives, to prevent insubordination, to keep everyone in their orderly place—God, country, husband, wife—"

Tilly shook her head, shifting from foot to foot. "I know all this," she whispered, though she hadn't really, not this clearly, at least. *God, why did Ruth have to attack her with this right now while she was still trying to come to terms with her visit with Jaiden? Ruth, of all people, should see how she just needed a nap—a chance to be alone for the first time in a week. A chance to say goodbye to Jaiden in her heart.*

"Then, you know the solution," Ruth announced. "You taught me the solution," she said, watching Tilly expectantly.

Tilly stared back, blank. Even the feeling of betrayal by Ruth's onslaught began to dim. Tilly had accepted the rules long ago. All-male legislatures did not grant women rights. The only power women had was that which nature bestowed and society denied—woman's superior intellect, the offset of her inferior physical strength. It served women well. At least, it served those who weren't fooled into denying its existence, as church, school, and men taught. But even that intellect could only be applied in individual situations. It was no match for the all-powerful, all-male Parliament. Men didn't understand logic. One could not reason with them.

And still, the way Ruth summed up the situation. . . . An idea flittered into Tilly's head, eluding her, but coming close.

"The government is not some malevolent deity out to destroy us," Ruth continued, her voice dropping. "It's just another collection of men. Not good. Not evil. Just men. Simple human beings. The same human beings you've been controlling your entire life." Ruth stopped her pacing. "Tilly, think."

The idea had flickered closer. No, not just an idea. The solution.

"How do you convince someone to do something he doesn't want to do?" Ruth pressed.

Tilly nodded, seeing it now, the thing Ruth, Jaiden, Adelaide, all the rest of them had understood from the beginning.

"You trick them into believing they do want it," Ruth answered.

Tilly stared at the solution in her mind. "Or that they're doing something else," Tilly finished.

"Exactly," Ruth answered, exhaling. "An entertainment, a lord, a peer, on trial for murder."

Tilly closed her eyes, shook her head. "They do not want to hear how husbands beat, maim, even kill their wives." Tilly met Ruth's gaze. "So you fool them into hearing about it. Just a man on trial."

"No talk of women's emancipation in that," Ruth continued. "But in the end, they will learn the facts, presented to them as to evoke their paternalistic tendencies, to remind them of their self-appointed duty to protect the weaker gender."

Tilly's eyebrows jumped as she envisioned the plan as carried out. It was anything but safe. The chance of its working without unacceptable sacrifices wasn't good.

"It will be tricky," Ruth allowed, seeing her doubt.

"Yes," Tilly agreed. *To say the least.*

"It will have to be choreographed just so."

With scientific precision. "Yes," Tilly agreed again.

"Don't worry, however. We have a secret weapon, an artist with perfect timing, perfect acting skills, the ability to persuade anyone of anything."

"He'll need more than that. He'll need a miracle," Tilly breathed.

"Oh, she is a miracle."

"What? Oh!" Tilly's eyes grew huge. "No, I don't know how. I couldn't possibly . . ." Not with Jaiden's life in the balance. Tilly lost every talent she possessed when it mattered, she knew that. And Jaiden—nothing mattered more.

"Sorry, love," Ruth patted her hand. "That's one of the duties of being our resident mistress of manipulations, our very own gentler of gentlemen, England's crowning man-tamer," Ruth teased.

And so she was, Tilly reminded herself. They were only men, after all. If she'd convinced Sir Gregory to limit his adulteries to his one disease-free permanent mistress, she could persuade Parliament to act with at least a modicum of common sense. She could at least fool them long enough to make them understand the vulnerability of married women.

She hoped she could, at least.

But, dash it, if she couldn't, no one could. Jaiden was already in custody. The Muirfield women had already put themselves in danger. These things would progress, with or without her.

It was imperative that Tilly made certain they progress in the proper direction.

Tilly gripped Ruth's hand and looked into her grey eyes. She smiled. "Man-instructor," Tilly corrected.

Ruth laughed.

Tilly was officially on board.

CHAPTER SEVENTY-SEVEN

The day before the trial began, Tilly stole out of the Astors' townhouse and into the garden in the hope of five minutes' peace. Every day for the last two weeks, more people had shown up to show their support. Someone must have rallied the London women's clubs. The house was packed with women. Certainly by now, all of London knew about their plan to turn Jaiden's trial into a women's rights exhibition. Though maybe not. If what Adelaide said was true, London women could keep secrets better than the Special Branch.

Nonetheless, she was grateful for their help, especially since many of them were very influential with certain members of the House of Lords.

Still, Tilly needed an escape. She had always thought her ideal household would be filled with women, all with a common goal and no petty arguments. At the moment, that sounded like a lesser circle of hell. Jaiden's townhouse was bursting at the seams with women, and even Tilly could only discuss the relative virtues of silk versus satin so many times.

Tilly ducked behind a group of trees at the back wall. She headed toward the one spot in the garden that was blocked from all views from the house, only to find that Adelaide already inhabited the bench.

Turning around, Tilly attempted to creep away unnoticed.

"Tilly," Adelaide said.

Bloody hell. Caught. Tilly turned back to the secluded corner.

"Hello, Adelaide," she answered, her voice uncharacteristically flat.

"Will you sit?" Adelaide asked, scooting toward one side of the bench.

"I'd better not," Tilly began. "I should prepare for tomorrow—"

"This will only take a few moments," Adelaide promised.

Tilly sighed, and then shrugged. She stepped nearer to Adelaide and perched on the iron bench. "Beautiful day," she commented, though really, the fog was as thick as pea soup, or Lord Haversham's study, even.

"I know you've been avoiding me," Adelaide began. "I don't blame you. I haven't been entirely honest with you. I'd apologize for it, but you'd know I wasn't sincere. I don't regret anything I've done," she finished, studying the ivy that grew over the back wall.

Tilly nodded. It hurt that Adelaide had lied to her. True, Tilly made a living by telling falsehoods, but she didn't lie to her friends. But that was the problem, wasn't it? Adelaide clearly didn't count Tilly as a friend. "So, your brother's on trial for murder, and you wouldn't change a thing?" Tilly countered, although she knew Jaiden's precarious position with the law was much more her fault than Adelaide's.

Adelaide gave a deep laugh. "You'll get him off. I've no doubt of it," she said, tucking her legs under her skirts so she could lounge against the bench's armrest and observe Tilly.

"Lord Trew said that even with the best of defenses, there's still a ten percent chance that anything can happen," Tilly informed her. How could Adelaide be so aloof about her brother's fate, and how had she failed to realize how unfeeling the woman was?

"Lord Trew made similar sentiments known to me. I'm not concerned."

"Very well," Tilly answered, flatly. She stood to go. She didn't know how to communicate with Adelaide anymore. She didn't even know who Adelaide was.

"I'd like you to stand in my wedding," Adelaide announced.

"Pardon?" Tilly could not believe her ears.

Adelaide looked down at her lap. She had a tulip resting there. Tilly hadn't noticed it earlier. Adelaide twirled the stem between her fingers. "Please stand in my wedding," she tried.

It was too much. "You're brother goes on trial tomorrow for *murder,* and you're planning your wedding ceremony?" Tilly winced at how high-pitched her voice was, but she couldn't seem to help it.

"Tilly." Adelaide sat up, putting her feet on the ground. She pushed the tulip into Tilly's hand so that it wouldn't distract her. Tilly had the urge to throw it to the ground but instead let it hang limply in her grasp. "I know Jaiden's going to be found innocent for two reasons."

Tilly crossed her arms, crushing the bloom against her chest. "Which are?"

"You," Adelaide announced, looking at her directly.

Already feeling slightly nauseated from the pressure, Tilly asked, "And the other reason?"

"My father's gambling," Adelaide stated without expression.

Tilly's eyebrows jumped.

The corner of Adelaide's mouth twitched. "You see, I've been pondering Jaiden's summation of my childhood, and I've come to believe he's correct. It makes sense with what I've observed of his interactions with my father's peers." She smiled. "They took our father's entire inheritance. Granted, he lost it to them, but still, they took it. Jaiden never held it against them, never reminded them of their greed. He even made their actions seem perfectly acceptable by going out and building his own fortune. They like Jaiden. They did not care for Whenceworth. No one did. Jaiden will be fine," she finished, standing from the chair and fluffing her skirts. "I'm not worried in the least," and with that pronouncement, Adelaide turned on her heel and left Tilly standing in the garden, staring at her retreating back.

CHAPTER SEVENTY-EIGHT

Finally, the third day of Jaiden's trial arrived, the day the defense presented its case. Tilly stood in a dark alcove in the House of Lords. All those lazy gentlemen reeked of riches and self-righteousness. Nerves assailed Tilly, making her back sweat. Her knees trembled with the desire to escape. Trying to distract herself from the knowledge that Jaiden's life depended on what she said, she peered up at the faces peeking through the spectator's slits. There, she saw the women who had thrown themselves into plotting to steal Jaiden's trial and use it to parade the House of Lords' failures in from of them.

Tilly caught sight of Ruth's profile. Surely, that was Sarah she was talking to. Every one of Tilly's previous clients had turned up to show their support, support doubly meaningful since they would have plenty of explanations to give their husbands after Tilly testified. In a matter of minutes, those husbands would hear how their wives had hired Tilly to dupe them.

Tilly would try to keep her man-instructing career out of the mess, although she could only do so much. Lying was one thing, perjury another. One was nothing but a convenience while the other landed you in prison. Oh, and then there was Beverly Rothswright. She had proved herself a formidable ally. She knew every member of Parliament, as far as Tilly could tell, and Parliament's secrets as well. Beverly could guarantee her twenty-five votes for Jaiden—or against him, if Tilly requested it.

Which, of course, Tilly would never do.

Jaiden. Tilly sighed.

Tilly hadn't talked to Jaiden since the day she tried to dissuade him in the holding cell. Over the last month, she'd had so many things to accomplish, she hadn't wanted Jaiden to distract her with his all-consuming passion. Besides, she still felt betrayed by him. What if this all went badly? What if he was hanged and her friends were revealed? How would she forgive herself?

She could only just see Jaiden from her hidden place in the alcove.

He was gorgeous, surely more beautiful than the last time she'd seen him. His dark hair had grown longer. It needed to be cut. His mouth kept twitching—a sure sign he had a trick up his sleeve. It had been his downfall in their poker match.

But then, no one else could read him as well as she could. No one else knew that mouth as intimately as she. She felt a wave of yearning hit her just thinking about it—or was it nausea?

And what if, during all this, her career was revealed? What if Jaiden learned that she had not only turned his world upside down, but that everything she'd ever said to him had been a lie?

Lord, she should be worried about Jaiden's neck, not her heart.

"Objection, your Honor!" broke in the prosecutor, a man Tilly was quickly learning to despise. Well, in all honesty, she had despised him since the first moment his arrogant, oily voice had oozed past the Lords' heads and into her hiding spot. Something about that slick voice had immediately repelled her. All his implications that Jaiden was a murderer didn't help, nor did his interrupting Dr. Gome's story. "I don't see how the victim's breaking her arm over two years ago bears any relevance to the night her husband was murdered."

"Your Honor, might I trespass a little longer on the court's good humor?" Jaiden's lawyer asked in his slow baritone. "I assure you, the good doctor's testimony goes directly to the ultimate issue of the case. I need it for foundation."

"I'm petrified," Mary whispered next to Tilly, drawing her attention from Dr. Gome. "What if I say the wrong thing and land the master in the hulks?"

Well, don't. "Tell the truth, Mary. That's all you need to do."

"But in front of all them men of quality . . ."

Tilly sighed. "I've met more than half of them, and I can tell you most of them don't have enough quality to fill a chamber pot."

A loud guffaw hit Tilly's ear, cut off instantly at Tilly's look. Mary dropped her head bashfully. Tilly looked around the room. Thank God all heads still faced the witness.

"Gore—Sorry, Mrs. Leighton. Didn't mean to . . . er . . . It's just that I'm fearful nervous."

Tilly could feel the girl shaking. Remarkably, her anxiety mitigated Tilly's nerves. Helping calm Mary could prove the best distraction from her own fears. Better get the girl to relax. "That man, third row back," she began with a nod toward the front of the hall. "Spectacles, mustache."

"I see 'im."

"He believes baths spread infection. He'll only take them twice a year. His wife won't share the same house with him, much less the same bed."

"Really?" Mary breathed.

"Absolutely, can't you see how the men on either side of him keep inching away?"

Right then, one of the men covered his nose with a handkerchief.

Mary giggled.

"And the man behind him. He thought he was being so clever, hiring a housemaid he had every intention of turning into his mistress."

"What happened?"

Tilly slid Mary a sideways glance. "His wife got to her first."

"No!" Mary gasped.

"Oh, indeed. And the gentleman three rows behind him with the wig that can only be described as blue . . ."

"Yes."

"See the way he has his back turned? He's so ashamed of a mole on his left cheek, he will only let the spectators see him from the right side."

"That's terrible."

"Yes, he crashed the family barouche trying to drive while covering his face."

Mary was giggling so hard she missed Lord Trew's assistant gesturing to her. Tilly had to tap her shoulder and nod to the man waving his arm.

"It's time," he whispered, fetching her.

Tilly gave Mary's hand one last squeeze. Sweat dripped into her palm. Poor girl. And then, Mary was gone.

Tilly's knees began to shake. How much easier all this would be if she could choose a character to play.

But it was never that simple when it mattered to her.

"How did I do?"

Tilly started. "Pardon?" she asked the doctor standing beside her.

His eyebrows lifted expectantly. "Do you think I provided the necessary background for your testimony?"

As if she had caught a word! With the blood pounding in her ears, she could barely hear him as he stood next to her. "You did a wonderful job," Tilly guessed. It felt good to lie. Safe.

"Well, that Lord Pumbermeyer doesn't let anything pass."

"Quite. . . . *Who?*"

"Tilly! Tilly! You're choking me!"

Tilly let loose her hold on Noah's cravat as she began to pant. "Lord Pumbermeyer! Lord Pumbermeyer is the prosecutor?"

"Have you failed to hear a single word of the trial?" he asked, incredulous.

"He's wearing a wig and a robe! How the devil was I supposed to recognize him?"

"The judge has said his name dozens of times."

Tilly no longer heard him. "I can't testify. I can't. He'll crush me and then send Jaiden to the gallows and probably figure out a way to resurrect Nora's husband—"

"Tilly, get a hold of yourself. You are going to faint."

"Oh, Noah, what have I done?"

Noah frowned. "Exactly my question. How do you know our esteemed prosecutor?"

Tilly tried to answer, but her voice came out a squeak.

Realization dawned on Noah. "Ahh . . . a former client of yours." He had learned a lot about her in the past month.

Tilly took a deep breath. She could handle this. She had to handle it. "Hmm. . . . Yes, I believe he took a particular aversion to me."

"And?"

"Not much. He thought his wife a henwit. I decided to show him a real henwit."

Noah rubbed his forehead. "We don't need this complication."

"No one ever needs a complication," Tilly answered. Immediately after saying it, she wondered if it was true. Were there people who suffered so terribly from *ennui* they needed complications?

"You've gone white," Noah announced.

Thank you, Doctor.

There was no way in hell Pumbermeyer would call an end to

the examination before he'd got to the bottom of her involvement with his wife, and thus, her career.

And this was how Jaiden would find out, not to mention all those noble husbands she'd tricked.

Serenity descended over Tilly, the calm of realizing she had nothing to lose.

"Sydney, Australia," she offered.

Noah looked at her blankly. Then, knowledge transformed his face. He grasped her hand.

"You want to go after her. I can see it." She sighed. "I suppose even the criminals need medical assistance."

She'd miss him, but devil take it, it was time to start letting go.

Something else she could blame on Jaiden.

"Humph," she grumbled.

Tilly debated leaving. She could never make Lord Pumbermeyer understand the desperation of the women who fled to Muirfield. Someone like him—pompous, patriarchal, unimaginative, but also decent and naive—could not comprehend the villainy that could exist in the wedded state.

But then something happened to Tilly that had never happened before. An answer popped into her head! An answer at the exact moment she needed it about something vitally important to her. She finally, finally knew how to make Pumbermeyer understand Nora's predicament. And it was all because she had already studied him, had already determined exactly how his stubborn mind worked. She already knew how to train him. She'd crafted the perfect character to inspire the reactions she needed. Today's trial would be no different from getting Charity her trip to visit her sister.

Tilly reached into her hair and began pulling out the hairpins she had so carefully arranged earlier.

"Tilly, what are you doing? You will be called any moment,"

Noah asked, his eyes bulging.

No time to explain. "Then help," Tilly ordered, shoving hairpins at him to hold. He took them as Tilly flung her head upside down so that she faced her own dark green skirts and her hair fell to the floor. Not for long though. Immediately, Tilly grasped the entire mass of it, and then straightened again, using her fingers to twist and comb. Damn, she wished she'd worn her plum instead.

"This is crazy," Noah sputtered.

Tilly gave him a smile. When she was crazy, she could manage anything. "Pins," she commanded.

He held them out to her. She took one and stuck it strategically in the taut bun at the back of her head. Then she stuck in another and another. By the time she finished, every curl was stretched and bound.

It was perfect. She could feel it. "How do I look?" she asked Noah.

"Terrible," he answered, his nose wrinkled.

Just as she'd hoped.

"So," Lord Pumbermeyer's voice boomed. "If, as you claim, Mrs. Whenceworth did not see Lord Astor the night of Lord Whenceworth's murder, what possible reason could there have been for her presence in his house?"

Mary's face flushed. She leaned forward. "To see Miss Mathilda Leighton, of course."

Murmurs rose in the house. Several lords began looking around, recognizing Tilly's name even with the *Missus* missing. It was showtime.

CHAPTER SEVENTY-NINE

Jaiden watched Lord Trew escort Tilly into his line of vision and couldn't contain his sigh. He'd missed her face terribly. Even from this distance, it made him ache to see her head held high, her shoulders back. Only the swish of her hips seemed subdued by the auspicious setting.

The bailiff swore her in, and Jaiden noted her steady hand. She could do this. She could change the country. She just had to believe in herself.

Lord Trew paced in front of the witness stand as he started with his first question. "Miss Leighton, Miss Mary Thomas just testified that you saw Lady Whenceworth the night Lord Whenceworth died. Is that true?"

"Yes, sir."

"And what did Lady Whenceworth tell you had transpired that night?"

"Only that she killed her husband," Tilly answered, all her usual spirit absent. Indeed, her tone fell strangely flat, as if she had no emotional investment in the proceedings at all.

Still, noise erupted on all sides. Jaiden refrained from watching the reactions of the men around her.

"Objection, your Honor. Hearsay," Lord Pumbermeyer said.

"Your Honor, we are not attempting to prove the truth of the words. We are merely offering an explanation of Lady Whenceworth's state of mind when she sought Miss Leighton's company."

"Overruled."

"Why?" Lord Trew turned on Tilly. "Why would any wife kill her husband?"

Jaiden saw Tilly's lips purse. He read her answer. *You've never been married to a man, I take it.*

"Objection, your honor. She's no expert in—"

"I withdraw the question. Miss Leighton, did Lady Whenceworth tell you why she murdered her husband?"

"Because she thought he was going to kill her."

"He'd come close to murdering her before, hadn't he?"

"Objection, your Honor. She can't possibly know the intimate, private life between a man and his wife."

"Sustained. Rephrase the question."

Lord Trew turned back to Tilly. "How did you meet Lady Whenceworth?"

"I was at Doctor Gome's office the day he set Lady Whenceworth's arm."

"Did she tell you how her arm came to be broken?"

"She said her husband broke it."

"Did you believe her?" Lord Trew questioned.

Tilly shrugged, her face pinched as though she found the entire subject distasteful. "Yes and no."

"Yes and no?" Lord Trew repeated. His surprise wasn't feigned. Even Jaiden could tell that Tilly had deviated from their script. "What do you mean by that?" Lord Trew asked cautiously.

"Her face was badly bruised, her limbs marked, her dress torn," Tilly iterated. "I believed her husband corrected her. I wasn't certain she didn't deserve it," Tilly said, offhandedly.

"Deserve to have her arm broken?" Lord Trew asked incredulously. Tilly's game became clear to him. Now, however, he would have to improvise, and that had never been his style. As always, Tilly had made it her own production, and everyone else was left trying to keep up. Jaiden couldn't have asked for a better turn of events. He had known all along that it would have to be Tilly's flair for drama that pulled them through if they were to succeed at all. Lord Trew might not have been comfortable with the results, but Jaiden felt damned pleased.

"A husband has the right to correct his wife, Lord Trew," Tilly reminded him.

"Yes, but in a reasonable manner. I would not think breaking someone's arm constituted reasonableness."

Tilly wrinkled her nose. "I am certain whatever Lord Whenceworth's reasons were, they were excellent ones. After all, we all know Lord Whenceworth to be a worthy sort of man, not one to fly off the handle, if you will."

It was so far from the truth, several lords coughed to hide their guffaws. A few didn't bother.

"What could she possibly have done to merit such a cruel punishment?" Lord Trew queried.

"Well," Tilly stage whispered, leaning forward with her hands on her knees. "Lady Whenceworth told me that she invited her mother-in-law to dinner. . . ." Tilly allowed the words to linger in the air before adding, "without consulting her husband." Tilly nodded her head, leaning back in the chair, a satisfied expression on her face. as if she'd just related the greatest evil imaginable.

Lord Trew plopped his hands on his hips and tilted his head. "She invited Lord Whenceworth's mother to dinner, you say?"

"Yes." Tilly nodded again. "Of course, it wasn't entirely Nora's fault. Nora's mother-in-law can be quite persuasive when she wants to visit." Everyone in the room knew this to be an understatement. It had never been a mystery where Lord Whenceworth had received his bad breeding. "Still," Tilly continued, her voice going back to its former indifference, "a gentleman shouldn't be forced to endure his mother's company when he didn't request it."

Lord Trew let his mouth go slack. Jaiden knew his dubious look to be an act, and yet, it was quite a good one. Jaiden suspected many of the members of the house were as amazed as Lord Trew pretended to be.

Lord Trew snapped his mouth shut and began pacing again. "And what of the night Lord Whenceworth died? What had Nora done to warrant her husband's rage that night?"

"Objection," Lord Pumbermeyer piped up. "Relevance."

The judge looked askance at Lord Pumbermeyer. "Seems very relevant to me. Keep going, Lord Trew."

"Miss Leighton, answer the question," Lord Trew instructed.

"Oh, yes, that night." Tilly arranged her skirts. "Nora—I mean, Lady Whenceworth—said she had interrupted her husband while he wrote a letter. She claimed she did not know he was in his study. She'd merely meant to take a stamp from his desk, but apparently, her husband was in the middle of a very serious piece of correspondence, and his wife's appearance ruined his concentration."

"And for that he tried to kill her," Lord Trew finished.

Tilly shrugged. "According to Lady Whenceworth."

Lord Trew walked farther from Tilly, and yet, Jaiden could nearly hear the crackle of the sparks igniting between the two of them. "Miss Leighton, why would Lady Whenceworth, knowing your attitude toward her husband, come to you, of all people, the night Lord Whenceworth died?"

Tilly let out a world-weary breath. "They all come to me."

Lord Trew swiveled on his heel, to freeze Tilly with his gaze. "*They* all come to you."

"Well, not all, naturally," Tilly allowed. "Not even most. But yes, they come to me."

"Who are *they*?" Lord Trew demanded.

"Wives who refuse to accept the consequences of their

behavior, of course. Wives who become convinced that their husbands will kill either them or their children."

"Wives?" Lord Trew repeated. "Wives who run away?"

"Wives who run to me," Tilly stated. "Just women. Insignificant women, to me, but to the press . . ."

"Yes?" Lord Trew prompted. "Who are they to the press?"

Tilly looked Lord Trew straight in the eye. She let the question hang before stating succinctly, "The missing wives."

A flurry of noise broke out around them. Jaiden saw Lord Trew and Tilly use the confusion to trade the barest twitch of a smile.

"Order!" the judge demanded, banging his gravel.

"Objection," Lord Pumbermeyer yelled, shooting out of his chair, his bulge bouncing up and down in his excitement. "Move to strike the last three witnesses' testimony! This is all preposterous! Women going to Miss Leighton to avoid abuse from their husbands? It's ludicrous. We are going to need more proof than just this woman's word—"

"I am so glad we can accommodate you, Pumbermeyer," Lord Trew stated. He held out his hand. The same assistant who had tapped Tilly earlier produced a large bound scrapbook and placed it in Lord Trew's outstretched hand. "As per Lord Pumbermeyer's request, the defense would like to enter as evidence this photo album. It contains photographs of various women who have resided at Miss Leighton's estate at one time or another over the last ten years."

"Objection, your Honor. Relevancy," Lord Pumbermeyer called, contradicting his earlier call for proof.

"Your Honor, the prosecution's case rests solely on the fact that Mrs. Whenceworth appeared at Lord Astor's home in London. It is our contention that Lady Whenceworth did go to Lord Astor's home, not because she had any connection to Lord Astor, but because Miss Leighton was in the habit of helping women in need."

"Your Honor—"

"I want to see the photographs before I make any decisions about their admissibility."

"These photographs speak volumes." Slowly, the judge looked at each one. "Miss Leighton, however, has not appeared in any of them thus far, and, therefore, I cannot see how these prove any connection between her and the distressed women whose pictures are captured here." He turned one more page. "Thus, I must—" He froze, transfixed by the picture.

It was only because Ruth had informed Jaiden of the childhood affection between herself and the judge that he recognized the movement of the judge's lips. They mouthed the syllables, "Alex," Ruth's nickname as a child, a shortened form of her previous Christian name Alexandria. Jaiden, Tilly, Lord Trew, they'd all counted on that affection. The picture showed no marks on Ruth. It was taken too recently to document her marital sufferings. Ruth had merely put the photograph in with the others to draw the Judge's attention—to show that people he cared about suffered from England's failure to protect its citizens.

"Your Honor," Lord Trew hurried to explain, "those pictures were in Miss Leighton's possession. They were taken at her home. Moreover, every woman pictured there is present today, prepared to testify that they went to Miss Leighton for help on the days of their respective so-called disappearances. Furthermore—"

"I'll allow them," the judge stated. At the word "present" his eyes had flickered to the women's gallery. Jaiden could tell the judge desperately wanted to speak to Ruth.

Jaiden watched as Lord Trew proceeded to question Tilly, expertly crafting a story, not of Jaiden's innocence, but of the horrors visited upon British wives everywhere, visited upon

Lady Whenceworth. After he finished with each woman's tale, her photograph would be passed around the chamber. Each Lord's face fell with compassion as he looked at the first photograph, the one of Agnes beaten nearly to death. All the while, Tilly's low voice mesmerized them and imbued them with the truth they'd never taken the time to notice, but which they could no longer ignore. Even Lord Pumbermeyer seemed unable to break the trance with an objection.

And Tilly.

She was magnificent—beautiful and brave, braver than any of the other men here could comprehend. Jaiden knew he had thrust this trial on her. He knew she took nothing so seriously as protecting her family of women, knew that it wounded her to lead them so close to the dangerous grasps of their husbands.

He also knew that if she had as much faith in herself as he did, she wouldn't stop with those twenty-odd women she had helped so far. She would reach for her true dream—to liberate women throughout the country, to give all of them more than merely the protection of Muirfield, but the protection of the law.

And so he'd forced her to try for more—even at the risk of gaining her antipathy forever—because she deserved to see her power in action. She deserved all her dreams coming true.

She would get his wish for her, too. He'd had doubts. Not many, but some. There were things that could have gone wrong. But not since she started speaking. Her sincerity, intelligence, and passion rang clear, inspiring all who heard her. She had fought Britain's fight for too long all by herself. It was time for the members of Parliament to remember that they sat as representatives of all Britain's citizens, not just the men. Tilly was a reminder that there was still good to be done.

Only one lord dared to break the spell.

Lord Durbishire, Verity's husband, banged the floor with his walking stick, "This is preposterous!" he said. "It's . . . It's . . ."

"Justice," Tilly supplied quietly but in a voice everyone heard. Her eyes locked with those of Verity's husband. No muscle moved on her face, but suddenly everyone in the chamber knew Durbishire had his own reasons for denouncing Tilly.

"I won't . . . Bah!" He stood and picked his way hurriedly out of his row and then rushed—walking stick and all—from the chamber.

Lord Trew turned to Lord Pumbermeyer. "Your witness."

Lord Pumbermeyer stood. With every other witness, he had shot questions at the first chance he was given. With Tilly, however, he walked in front of the witness's table and studied her.

Perhaps he'd lost his appetite for attack.

"So you're admitting to alienation of affection?" he assailed.

Perhaps not.

The atmosphere changed tangibly. Jaiden could feel the collective censure of Pumbermeyer's question. He shouldn't have gone for the jugular quite so soon after Tilly's canonization as Britain's newest saint.

Tilly lifted her chin. Her voice emanated cheekiness. "By the time they came to me, there was no affection left to alienate."

Pumbermeyer's face scrunched. He knew he'd misjudged her. He tried again, "Isn't it true you were residing at the Astor's townhouse because . . ."

Tilly stiffened. Her mouth lost its impish turn. Her eyes flickered toward Jaiden for the first time, then turned down.

Only then did Jaiden realize she'd hidden yet another secret from him, and this one had to do with their very reason for knowing each other.

Pumbermeyer stared at her, then slowly turned toward the judge. "Your Honor . . ." He frowned, and then lifted his eyes to the bench. He rocked back and forth on his feet before announcing, "The prosecution drops the charges."

The judge nodded. "Wise decision. Case dismissed."

Tilly blinked, several times. Confusion clouded her beautiful face. She looked at the judge, then at Pumbermeyer, her brows lowered as if she was unable to grasp the abruptness of the resolution of the case. Jaiden nodded, telling her silently they had just won.

Then, she closed her eyes. Jaiden watched her chest rise and fall as she sighed in relief. A tear escaped her eye. Jaiden watched her but did not share her emotions. He had never worried that he might be found guilty. As far as he was concerned, the not-guilty sentence was a foregone conclusion. He'd merely staged the trial to get the women's stories told in an arena where they were guaranteed the House's attention.

But now, with the trial over, he had to face the fact that he'd gambled with Tilly's trust, and therefore quite possibly lost it.

When Tilly opened her eyes, their gazes met and this time held. Jaiden no longer heard the other people in the room. Only she existed. He stared at her face, hoping it might reveal an inkling of what she felt. She didn't smile at him. He didn't smile either. Only her brow wrinkled, and then she looked away.

So, she hadn't forgiven him—perhaps couldn't forgive him.

It mattered not. He'd spend the rest of his life winning her back.

With luck, he'd succeed by the end of next week.

Even that might be longer than he could stand not having her in his arms.

CHAPTER EIGHTY

He hadn't smiled at her. Their gazes had met and he hadn't smiled—not even after hearing the not-guilty verdict.

He must have found out about her deception—that Adelaide had hired her to manipulate him . . . or, er, marry him. How could she make him understand?

In this case, it might be best if he didn't understand.

"Tilly! I still can't believe we did it," Beth murmured dreamily that night. She lay with her head in Tilly's lap as they bounced on the train to Muirfield. Her eyes sparkled with joy. "They have to change the laws now. They just have to."

"I think we have a good chance," Tilly said. She stroked Beth's hair. "Unfortunately, changing laws has to do with politics, and that's something I know nothing about, and even if I did, I wouldn't understand."

Beth yawned. The other women had opted to stay at the Astors' for a victory celebration. Beth, however, had been anxious to share the good news with Lizzy and Verity. And Tilly . . . Tilly couldn't face Jaiden.

He must think everything she'd told him was a lie. Oh, whom was she kidding? She had lied, even about the way she felt. Mostly about the way she felt. How could she never have said she would always love him, no matter how much she tried not to?

"Tilly, it was a good day," Beth whispered up at her.

"Yes, I suppose it was," Tilly said, placating her.

Beth turned onto her back to stare up at Tilly's face. "No, I'm not asking you. I'm telling you. It was a good day. They will change the laws, and all because of you, so cheer up. You've lost nothing and gained everything." Beth then rolled back onto her side and closed her eyes, leaving Tilly to ponder whether or not she had lost after all.

Two weeks. She would see him again in two weeks at Adelaide's wedding. Leave it to that girl to plan her own wedding while her brother was on trial for murder.

Tilly leaned her head against the window and closed her eyes. She was tired of enumerating all the ways she'd botched everything. She was sick of feeling the weight of the world on her shoulders.

Mostly, she was done with the horror of resigning herself to a life without Jaiden. All of life would be there for her tomorrow. Right now, she could escape it. Sleep would grant her peace . . . at least until they arrived home.

CHAPTER EIGHTY-ONE

Jaiden allowed himself to be toasted . . . again. He smiled and shook hands, accepted everyone's congratulations. Not being a murderer made a man popular, it seemed. His house was over-run with well-wishers, as well as every feminist in England. The Married Women's Property Committee, the Central Committee of the National Society for Women's Suffrage, the Committee to Amend the Law in Points wherein It is Injurious to Women all strategized and gossiped throughout his house. As far as he could tell, they were all one group of women who enjoyed collecting titles.

Adelaide, however, shone. He hadn't seen her this happy since she was a child, and Daniel was never far from her side. Jaiden did manage to nab her in a hallway outside the billiard room while Daniel held a wager.

"Jaiden," Adelaide exclaimed, eyes opening wide. Jaiden knew that innocent look too well to be deceived by it.

"Uh-huh. Outside," he said, causing Adelaide to grin. He nudged her toward the servants' doorway so they could avoid their guests.

They maneuvered around the cook staff in the kitchen and slipped through the side door.

Adelaide lifted her champagne glass. "Here's to keeping one's neck intact. Nooses are not at all the thing at the moment, you know. Cravats much more—"

"Right. So why was Tilly staying here?"

Adelaide looked at the ground and opened her mouth. She picked at the bark on the oak beside her. "Oh, that."

"Yes, that."

She peeked up at him through her eyelashes. "So no one's told you yet?"

"Told me what, exactly?"

Adelaide set the champagne glass on the step and then straightened. "Well, allow me to apprise you of the situation. Tilly is a professional man-tamer, or man-instructor, as she would put it. Ladies hire her to instruct their husbands, to get their husbands to give them things: nicer carriages, larger allowances, forgiveness for some transgression, that sort of thing. Her fees are exorbitant, and we gladly pay because we know the money goes to support Muirfield, a haven most of us also view as our shelter should we need it."

"*We* gladly pay?" Jaiden repeated. Whatever he had expected, it hadn't been this.

Adelaide nodded. He saw her gulp down air, but she met his gaze straight on. "I paid her fifty pounds a week."

"*What?*" His chief scientist didn't make that much!

Adelaide raised her eyebrows. "I'm certain you, of all people, should realize she's worth every farthing."

Jaiden closed his eyes and scratched his forehead. Tilly was a professional man-tamer. All this time, Adelaide had paid her to spend time with him to train him? "What did you want out of me?"

Adelaide chuckled. "Nothing. I didn't hire Tilly to train you. She thought I did, but that's not what I was after." Adelaide touched his jacket. "I hired her for you." She shrugged. "I knew. I just knew."

Jaiden nodded. Tilly was paid fifty pounds a week to train gentlemen? That was his woman, all right.

A smile lit his face. "Remind me to pay you back."

Adelaide's shoulders drooped in relief. She laughed again. "Well, I could use someone to give me away in two weeks."

Jaiden let out a bark of laughter and picked up her glass. "I would be honored. And delighted." He shook his head. "Let you make a mess of someone else's life for a change."

Adelaide smiled over her shoulder as she stepped toward the house. "It would be a sad life without me mucking around in it."

"So you have always claimed. I'm still waiting for the opportunity to make a comparison." He held the door open for her.

"Don't hold your breath," she said, entering the house. "Not coming?"

"No, I'm going to enjoy the air for a minute."

Adelaide nodded. "Don't worry. You'll win her trust again."

"Yes, I will," Jaiden agreed. He just had to figure out how.

CHAPTER EIGHTY-TWO

"Eight days of freedom."

Jaiden's head jerked up at the words. Daniel leaned against the doorframe of Jaiden's office.

"And you still haven't gone after her," Daniel finished.

Setting the contract he'd been trying to study on his desk, Jaiden leaned back in his chair and watched his friend saunter into the office, close the door, and sit in the chair across the stacks of documents.

"What are you waiting for?" Daniel prodded.

Inspiration. Jaiden took a deep breath. He didn't know how to make Tilly forgive him for going through with the trial despite her protests, and the prospect of seeing her and saying the wrong thing terrified him. He couldn't lose her. He needed her. He knew that now. But that only made the thought of losing her all the more devastating.

He'd had too much time to think about it these past eight days—ever since she had looked right at him at the trial and not smiled. Going into the trial, he had been completely confident that if he won, Tilly would forgive him anything. Now, he realized he didn't understand her, couldn't predict her reaction to anything.

Jaiden picked up his pen and rolled it over his knuckles. He didn't have an answer for Daniel. How could he explain that he hadn't gone after her because he needed her so badly, he couldn't live without her? It made no sense.

God, Tilly had rubbed off on him. This was what she would do—not going after what she wanted because she needed it too desperately—not he. He never hesitated to reach for his desires. Or maybe he had just never needed anything the way he needed her.

Daniel chuckled at Jaiden's brooding. "You know, I didn't like Mrs. Leighton before you explained her situation. At the theater, it became apparent that she was hiding information regarding at least one of the missing wives. I thought her motives dishonorable," Daniel admitted. He ran a hand through his wavy hair, uncomfortable, and then shrugged as he confessed, "I thought she was using you for her own nefarious ends. I didn't like to see you so taken in."

Jaiden arched a brow at his friend.

Daniel read the question in the gesture and explained, "I suppose I'm just trying to say that if you need any help or . . . or want to talk about her I'm here." And with that awkward statement breaching all former boundaries of their friendship, he stood. "Of course, you're probably just biding your time, letting her cool off," he said turning out of the room.

Daniel's hand reached the doorknob before Jaiden stopped him with the announcement, "I used to view the world as a clock."

Daniel turned around and waited for his friend to continue.

Jaiden stared at his fingers as they rolled the pen over and under each joint. His voice came out dispassionate. "I believed everything and everyone had its place and purpose, and that without any more conception than a spring possesses, we keep the world on time—so to speak." Abruptly, Jaiden plunked down the pen and looked at Daniel. "The nice thing about looking at the world as a clock is that everything is discoverable, and if some wheel of the timepiece goes awry, it can simply be fixed or replaced. The problem was that I never felt as though I quite fit my own groove inside this clock. I needed oiling or a slight adjustment or something, because I have always been just ever so slightly out of kilter." Jaiden's brow furrowed for a split second as he thought of Tilly. His Tilly. "In her presence, it was the first time I felt as though I was right where I was supposed to be, doing exactly what I was supposed to be doing. But then, she didn't fit inside my clock." He chuckled ruefully. "I can't explain her, and there is certainly no scientific explanation for what she does to me. It's the first thing in my life I can't make sense of, and I don't even want to. I . . ." *Need her. Am lost without her. Am terrified because I . . .* ". . . think I've lost her."

Daniel nodded and then cleared his throat. "Well, good luck with that," he said, turning to the door.

So much for this new intimate friendship.

Daniel stopped. He looked over his shoulder. "You know she's attending Adelaide at the ceremony?"

A drop of relief trickled into the knot that had been Jaiden's stomach for the last week. "Adelaide hadn't mentioned that."

Daniel nodded once more before ducking out the door.

For good or evil, Jaiden figured he'd better find some way to convince Tilly to marry him, and he'd better come up with the plan before he saw her at Adelaide's wedding.

CHAPTER EIGHTY-THREE

"With this ring I thee wed."

Of course, Adelaide had forced her to be an attendant in her wedding. A perfectly fine position usually, but this time Jaiden sat in the front row. An hour of service, of peeking glances at him, of hoping their eyes would meet, of dodging when they did. It was hell.

He'd gambled with her friends' lives despite her pleas that he desist. He'd gambled and won.

Of course, she'd gambled, too. She'd gambled with his trust before she had any idea how much it would mean to her, and by now, he would know what she'd done, that their relationship was a lie.

Curse Adelaide for all of it—hiring her under false pretenses, inviting her into the Astors' home, but mostly for insisting she stand here so close to the man she wanted so desperately.

And wasn't the not knowing better than finding out she'd already lost him? Or that she couldn't forgive him?

Or that he couldn't forgive her?

If only her rose dress hadn't been ruined.

Tilly didn't realize how loudly she'd sighed until the minister paused in his speech to lift an eyebrow at her.

Her gaze dropped to the bouquet in her hands. The minister began droning on again. Stupid, happy people. Why couldn't she be one of them?

After the wedding, Tilly allowed herself to be dragged to the

Astors' for the small reception. Tilly knew she had to attend, but she felt no obligation to refrain from hiding on the one secluded bench in the garden.

"Pouting, are we?" Agnes and Beth plopped down on either side of her, crowding the dainty wrought iron bench. "Or just hiding from the I-told-you-so's?"

"Brat." Tilly let the corners of her mouth twitch up. "Are you invading my cowardice for a reason?"

Beth laughed. She threw her arms around Tilly and kissed her cheek. "Wait until you hear!"

Tilly glanced at Agnes.

"We've a business proposition for you," Agnes began.

Oh, thank God. Anything to keep her mind off Jaiden.

"Jaiden wants to purchase Muirfield from you."

Tilly's heart leaped in her chest. Where would her friends go for sanctuary? Except that they couldn't go there anymore anyway, what with its secret having been revealed, but the judge had issued those few injunctions for the seven women currently residing there.

"Jaiden wants to deed it to Ruth," Beth explained. "Since her husband's dead, no one else can steal its management from her. That way you will know that you can always send as many women there as you like. Muirfield will always provide sanctuary."

Tilly's brow furrowed. "But it's already exposed. What's to keep men from driving out there and absconding with their wives?"

"You," Beth said.

"Excuse me?"

Beth giggled, but it was Agnes who spoke. "How else will you occupy your time? Muirfield wasn't the only thing exposed at the trial. You can't continue manipulating husbands when they all now know exactly what you're about."

All her former friends had come clean with their husbands about hiring Tilly. Since most of them had insisted they had hired her more to help her worthy cause than manipulate their husbands, forgiveness had been swift. Still, it did leave Tilly in search of a new career.

Agnes executed a decisive nod. "You can't," she said, answering her own question. "What you can do, however, more now than ever, is influence society. Already half the women in London are madly in love with you after hearing about Muirfield. All you need do is make it entirely taboo for men to trespass on Muirfield property."

"If anyone can do that, you can, Tilly," Beth said, squeezing her shoulders.

Tilly snorted. Although really, now that she considered it, it shouldn't be so difficult.

"And you only have to exert your influence until the laws are changed in order to protect wives."

Tilly shook her head at Beth's continued naivety. How a former prostitute could have such a high opinion of men, she'd never understand. "The law will never protect wives at the expense of their husbands, not while only men sit in Parliament."

"Well, then, you shall just have to change that, too, shan't you?" Agnes said.

Beth shook her head. "I think they'll vote for us anyway. You were pretty convincing at the House, and those photographs aren't easily forgotten."

Tilly smiled. "I adore that the two of you think that I, a girl with no family, no connections, no money, has that kind of following."

Ruth's voice came from behind them. Tilly turned around to see her friend walking next to the judge from Jaiden's trial. She heard Ruth say, "As Miss Leighton, you might not have connections, a name, or money, but as Lady Astor, you would have all three in excess."

Tilly's wrinkled her nose. "Ruth, are you trying to tempt me into a deplorable institution so I will have more influence in society?"

Ruth leaned over to rest her palm against Tilly's cheek while her male friend hovered near. "I'm attempting to give you an excuse to accept your heart's desire."

Beth laughed again. "Silly Ruth. Since when does Tilly need an excuse to take what she wants?"

Tilly turned her face to stare at Beth, astounded. Beth was correct. Tilly wasn't a martyr. She hated martyrs. Her mother had never believed she deserved anything, even a nonviolent existence. Tilly would never be that person.

She wanted Jaiden, and damned if she wasn't going to go take him.

CHAPTER EIGHTY-FOUR

Tilly spotted Jaiden talking to Mrs. Beesley and Aunt Hen in the morning room. Only Daniel and Ben occupied the room with them. Her quarry spotted, Tilly made her plan.

She scooted into the room, strode determinedly past Jaiden for three steps and . . .

"Ohhh," she murmured, slowing. Her hand rose to her brow, and she fell . . . right into Jaiden's arms.

"Oh, dear, is the poor thing all right?" Mrs. Beesley fluttered as Jaiden adjusted so that Tilly's head rested against his chest and his arms supported her back and the backs of her knees.

"She's fine," Aunt Hen remarked dryly. Tilly could hear Mrs. Beesley's hesitant steps as Aunt Hen dragged her from the room.

Daniel's voice came to Tilly. "Do you want me to get Doctor Shaunesey? Or Adelaide's smelling salts?" he asked Jaiden.

"Why don't you and Ben help Adelaide with the guests. I'll take care of Tilly." The sound of Jaiden's voice made Tilly ache. It seemed like forever since she'd heard it.

Tilly waited until she heard Ben and Daniel also exit the room.

"You frighten me when you do that," Jaiden whispered in her ear.

Tilly's eyes opened. "I'm sorry," she said, solemnly. "I won't do it again."

The corners of Jaiden's lips curled. "Not even for fifty pounds a week?"

373

Tilly winced. "It was bad of me to manipulate you."

Jaiden nodded. He walked to the sofa and laid her down. Tilly instantly sat up so that he could sit at the other end of the sofa, facing her. "It was bad of me to force the trial after you asked me to stop," he offered.

Tilly shrugged. "It was for the best."

Jaiden's voice dropped even lower. His eyes simmered. "As was your training of me."

The breath caught in Tilly's chest. "I'll forgive you if you forgive me."

Jaiden pushed the hair off her forehead. "Done," he whispered just before kissing her. Tears welled in Tilly's eyes. Words couldn't do this moment justice. She was overwhelmed.

"Stop that," Jaiden whispered, wiping a tear from her cheek.

Overcome with humility, Tilly swore, "I will never manipulate you again."

Jaiden smiled. "Yes, you will."

Tilly took in a deep breath. She cupped one of his large, work-roughened hands inside both of hers. He was strong and capable and good, and he knew her well.

And he made her world exciting.

More tears flowed. Her eyelashes grew heavy with them.

Jaiden chuckled, pulling out his handkerchief to wipe her face properly. "You must stop crying, Tilly. I have a business proposition for you, and we can't very well discuss it when you're weeping."

Tilly swallowed. "Giving Muirfield to Ruth. Beth told me. I'm amenable."

"I'm glad to hear it," Jaiden replied. He brushed a kiss against her temple. Tilly realized she was trembling. He had that effect on her. "But that's not the proposition I was referring to."

Tilly wrinkled her brow.

"I want to utilize your service. I would like to employ you," Jaiden stated.

Now that she was exposed, she wasn't good for much. "In what capacity my lord?"

"As my wife," he whispered, looking straight into her eyes.

Joy burst inside her. The tears immediately dried. There was no room for sorrow or yearning or even relief now, only for happiness.

"Would you do me the honor?" Jaiden asked.

Tilly grinned up at him. She knew this was not her best look, but cursed it if she could care. "We will, of course, have to negotiate the terms, but I'm confident an agreement can be reached."

With that, she tilted her head to kiss him, thoroughly and properly. He would be hers, all hers, and Tilly would even deign to marry if it meant having Jaiden for all time.

For Tilly Leighton knew men.

She knew this one was worth keeping.

ABOUT THE AUTHOR

One could charge **Molly Madigan** with a case of multiple personality disorder. By day, you'll find a sensible woman born in the Midwest who went to California to pursue a degree in economics at Pomona College. Madigan then leveraged that background to secure a law degree in Chicago and now practices in Northern California. When the sun sets, Madigan casts off these pragmatic shackles to pursue her goal of penning the ultimate romance novel. A social life enriched by a passion for dance and travel helps keep Madigan's love for romance burning.